NIGHT FLIGHT TO PARIS

DAVID GILMAN

HEAD
of ZEUS

First published in the UK in 2018 by Head of Zeus Ltd
This paperback edition published in the UK in 2018 by Head of Zeus Ltd

9 7 5 3 1 2 4 6 8

A catalogue record for this book is available from
the British Library.

ISBN (PB): 9781788544924
ISBN (E): 9781788544894

Typeset by Divaddict Publishing Solutions Ltd

Printed and bound in Great Britain by
CPI Group (UK) Ltd, Croydon CR0 4YY

Head of Zeus Ltd
First Floor East
5–8 Hardwick Street
London EC1R 4RG

WWW.HEADOFZEUS.COM

For Suzy

1

Paris
February 1943

The darkness moved. The night sky, black and heavy with menace and constant drizzle, curled in on itself as the massive swastika rippled in slow motion. Languid authority ruling over silent cobbled streets below. The gusting wind threw curtains of light rain, rushing over the echoing sound of running footfalls. A desperate clattering of fear in the curfew hours.

In the blacked-out room on the third floor of a five-storey walk-up, a curtain twitched. Through the sliver of glass, an old woman peered down at the dark street in the Eighteenth Arrondissement. Dim figures raced around the corner. Across the street others dared to ease back a curtain or a shutter, dousing their house lights, fearful of being seen, not wanting to be drawn into whatever was happening to the desperate fugitives below. The curtain twitcher saw two men and two women running for their lives. The older of the women snatched at a younger girl's arm as she almost stumbled on the wet cobbles. Ahead of them one of the men, perhaps in his forties, ran into doorway after doorway, desperate to gain access and escape from whoever was pursuing them. As he beat his fist on one door, the second man did the same to the next.

Every door was locked and no one who cowered in the dimly lit rooms was foolish enough to let the strangers in, despite their cries for help. The sound of fast-approaching studded boots told the old woman behind the curtain that the men and women were facing certain death. A dozen German soldiers turned the same corner, a couple skidding on the wet street. But then a command rang out: the soldiers stopped and raised their rifles. The old lady let the curtain fall back and retreated into her room. There was no need to witness what would happen next. She settled herself in the threadbare chair and pulled her shawl around her, bowing her head, gnarled hands covering her ears. Dreading the shattering crack of rifle fire.

Hail Mary, full of grace…

*

Despite the chilling rain, Alain Ory was sweating. Fear and desperation kept him banging on every door as they ran down the street. He begged; he cried out for help. There was no response. Soldiers appeared in the distance, spectres in the shifting rain. A voice called for those running to halt. Alain turned to the women, who had faltered. Suzanne Colbert had kicked her shoes off so she could run silently and with less risk of slipping. He had always desired her. She was similar in age to him, a courageous and beautiful woman. Now she huddled with her daughter in a doorway. In this desperate moment, he felt a surge of sadness that threatened to overwhelm him. He would have to abandon them.

He did not hear the German officer's command to shoot. Rifle fire rang out. Suzanne and her daughter clung to each other. Alain threw himself across them, smelling the musk of her daughter's hair and the acrid tang of urine as terror emptied her bladder. Bullets tore into the running body of their companion. The young man pirouetted silently, arms akimbo, turning almost gracefully on his toes. The illusion was shattered by the ripping of flesh and the sickening crunch of bone as he fell face first on to the cobbles. Blood seeped from beneath his body.

Alain pulled the women out of the doorway. He heard the mechanical slide of rifles being cocked, then pressed the women against the wall as another volley rang out. Bullets ripped stone fragments above where they crouched. A ricochet hit Suzanne's leg. She stifled a cry of pain and limped behind the others as Ory turned into an alley, hurrying the younger woman with him. He pressed against the wall, dared to peer around and then stepped back into the street to drag Suzanne after them. The soldiers were running and would not fire again until one or more of them saw their targets and then stopped and aimed. One leg was twisted under Suzanne; blood flooded her hand, which squeezed the wound. Her agonized look told him everything. She wasn't going to make it.

'Go!' she gasped.

He could not help her. She was pushing her identity card down the street drain. He turned and ran back into the alley.

'Save her!' cried the terrified girl.

He gripped her arms and tried to push her further into the darkness. 'No. We leave her!'

The girl wept, 'I can't. She's my mother,' and pulled back from him.

'Christ, you fool. Danielle, come on!'

She shook her head and tried to run past him back into the street. He pressed her shoulders against the wall, but she threw him off, her terror more powerful than his strength. For the briefest instant he cupped her distraught face in his hands. 'I can't help you. Good luck.' He turned and ran into the void as she spun around and stumbled to her mother.

'Danielle. No. For God's sake!' Suzanne begged, raising a hand to stop her.

No sooner had Danielle knelt next to her wounded mother than headlights flooded the street and the soldiers dragged her away, screaming. Tyres skidded to a halt, doors opened, and she was bundled into the back of one of the cars. It quickly reversed and turned. The headlamps of the second car, parked off to one side, threw long fingers of light across the wounded woman and the soldiers, standing with rifles now slung, smoking cigarettes as their officer spoke to one of the men in the car. Soldiers toed the man's dead body as others stood over Suzanne. She raised a hand to shield her eyes from the light and saw her daughter's face pressed against the back window as the car sped away. A German officer barked something and two of his men leant down and grabbed her arms; then they dragged her across the cobbles to the waiting car. Suzanne cried out as her wounded leg scraped on the uneven surface. The pain made her vomit. They cursed and one of them hit her on the back of the head with his fist. Stunned, she smelt the warm comfort of the car's leather seats and was flooded with fleeting images, memories of better days. A lover who became her husband; a leather sofa and the excitement of their first sexual encounter. Love and warmth. All that had long since fled. Now only cold dread remained.

2

SS-Standartenführer Heinrich Stolz of the Sicherheitsdienst pulled up in his car outside the Préfecture de Police, opposite the Hôtel-Dieu, Paris's first hospital, built in the Middle Ages. Stolz's destination offered no such succour. His tailored uniform was decorated with the Knight's Cross, Iron Cross and Infantry Assault medals among his campaign ribbons. He had served in the SS Infantry and earned a reputation for single-minded determination and courage on the battlefield. He was no stranger to fighting a vicious enemy, whether they wore a uniform or struck covertly as terrorists.

Oberst Ulrich Bauer, the Abwehr colonel in charge of military counterintelligence in Paris, waited for him on the steps of the Préfecture. The two men were of equivalent rank. They greeted each other and turned into the drab building. Bauer had twenty years on Stolz, who was thirty-six years old and one of the tall, fair-haired Aryan gods Bauer quietly despised. Stolz had been chosen by Himmler himself, and SS-Brigadeführer Karl Oberg, to control Paris with the SS, the security service and Gestapo under his command. All of which gave the Sicherheitsdienst officer a direct line to Berlin. He was the most feared man in Paris.

'Two weeks ago four Luftwaffe officers were killed by a grenade attack in a local café. You have made no progress in determining who was responsible,' said Stolz.

'It was not an organized attack by the Resistance.'

'Terrorists... call them what they are, colonel,' Stolz corrected him as they strode through the colourless corridors.

'It was a lone assassin. We're certain of it.'

'And I'm certain it's because the English sent agents here to train the killers,' said Stolz. 'The fifth floor?'

Bauer nodded, suppressing a groan, and fell in step beside Stolz. The SD officer always used the stairs and took them briskly. He was fitter than Bauer and the army colonel knew it was a simple ploy by Stolz to put him at a disadvantage.

Stolz glanced at the older professional soldier. Bauer's breath had quickened yet he seemed determined to keep up with the pace, even if it killed him. At least that showed a level of determination, Stolz decided generously. Bauer's face was flushed by the time they reached the commissaire's office. Stolz placed a reassuring hand on his shoulder before they entered.

'You should get yourself in shape, Bauer. A couple of sets of tennis aren't enough and you never know when we might have to run for our lives.'

Bauer felt a sudden stab of uncertainty, a pain that was not from his exertions on the stairs. Was that a veiled threat? German Army officers had been executed on the Führer's orders for failing in their duty.

Stolz smiled. 'It's a joke, Bauer. A joke. We mustn't lose our sense of humour.'

The army colonel nodded grimly. Humour was not an attribute the Sicherheitsdienst, the state intelligence service for the SS and Nazi Party and its sister agency the Gestapo, was known for. They stepped into Commissaire Fernand David's office and the man walked briskly around his desk to greet them.

David was head of the Brigades Spéciales, a specialist police unit used for tracking down internal enemies and escaped prisoners. Knowing Stolz was enthusiastic about breaking Resistance cells, David had dedicated a number of officers to tracking suspected *résistants*; all of his men worked in pairs, using a variety of undercover disguises: they would even wear the Star of David to lessen any suspicion from a suspect they were following. Many of the Resistance cells were communist-led and -inspired, and frequently in disagreement with nationalist cells; their infighting often made one betray the other. Fernand David had a particular hatred for communists and a reputation for torturing male prisoners by crushing their testicles with pliers, even though their resulting confessions were usually worthless. The commissaire tortured for the pleasure of it.

After the usual formalities, David ushered Stolz and Bauer to a wall where photographs of suspected Resistance fighters were pinned in an intricate pattern of names, addresses and known associates. Flowcharts linked Paris districts with suspects, their relatives and friends. 'We have been following this one group for some weeks, colonel. We arrested fifty-seven young Jews two weeks ago. They will be deported on charges of murder and terrorist activity.' Many of the commissaire's men were anti-Semitic and played a key role in rooting out Jews hidden by sympathizers in the city, which served the Germans well. 'After some persuasion at the hands of my men, we learnt that a résistant cell had been aiding them to smuggle out other Jews. We tracked four of the Resistance to an apartment above a bakery in Rue Stanislas Meunier in Quartier Saint-Fargeau, in the Twentieth Arrondissement. We alerted your local area commander and he caught them...' he tapped the wall map. '... here. Eighteenth Arrondissement. One man dead, one escaped and two women captured. There were more arrests in other areas. Twelve more suspects in addition to the two women. The Gestapo have them now.'

Stolz glanced at Bauer, sensing the Abwehr colonel's discomfort. The commissaire's department had tracked down the cell that had been rounded up by the Germans the previous night. It was a feather in the Special Brigades' cap, but it also stung that they were enjoying more success than the occupying force. Yet, if they could be offered even more support and resources their success would also reflect well on Stolz's security service. 'Is there any information on the man who escaped?'

'Very little, colonel.' David picked up a sheet of paper. 'We suspect his name is Alain Ory, 1.6 metres tall, medium build, fair complexion. He has brown hair and, when he escaped, he was wearing a light brown wide-brimmed hat, slightly raised at the back, a grey overcoat with brown longitudinal stripes, grey trousers, black shoes. My men have circulated his description to the Feldgendarmerie and your agents.'

'Thank you, commissaire. Please commend your men on my behalf.'

Commissaire David nodded his thanks. Stolz tapped some of the photographs. 'These men are still at large. When I took command here they were known to military intelligence. In one way or another, they are linked to the terrorists.' He did not turn to look at the perspiring Bauer, but there was no doubt to whom his comments were directed. 'Your task was to find them. You have not.'

'We have reports that some are dead, and others have escaped,' said Bauer.

Commissaire David remained silent and brushed an invisible fleck of fluff from his double-breasted suit. The German Army's military intelligence command in Paris and the Occupied Zone vied with Stolz's Sicherheitsdienst to be the most successful in the intelligence war, and with the Gestapo reporting directly to Stolz, there was little doubt who was winning that particular contest. The SS had long held the belief that Admiral Canaris, the head of Abwehr, was not as loyal to the Führer as they were.

'Then you've done your best,' said Stolz.

'Of course,' Bauer replied.

'In which case, the Gestapo and the state intelligence service are assuming overall responsibility from the Abwehr for this area.'

Bauer stepped back as if he had been struck. To be relieved of intelligence responsibility in front of the Frenchman was an insult. 'But I'm a professional soldier! Counterintelligence is my department.'

'We have a more... robust way of dealing with these people,' said Stolz. 'Now, let's see what the latest round-up of suspects has brought us.'

3

In La Santé prison the stench of stale urine and the chill of the dank cellars used to torture prisoners frightened Hauptmann Martin Koenig. The young captain rarely descended into the hell of these cells: his skills were put to better use analysing reports and compiling data. More than a thousand prisoners were crammed into cells no larger than 3.5 metres by 1.75 metres, six prisoners to a cell and two straw mattresses between them. He walked purposefully along the dimly lit corridor determined not to be thought timid by the guards. He passed closed rooms, the heavy door of one barely muffling groans, heading towards an open door, when a sudden cry, the voice of a woman in agony, made him falter. The silence that followed prompted him to pick up his pace again; the sooner his errand was over the better. He stopped in the doorway of the open interrogation cell. What he saw made him grimace, but he managed to suppress visible shock. A woman was bound to a metal chair, dressed only in her petticoat. An ugly bullet wound festered in her leg, one eye was closed from a beating and blood had run from her bruised nose down her neck and bosom. Her interrogators had slashed the soles of her feet with razor blades and the young officer knew they would have forced her to walk in a trough of salt. Her head was slumped and he could see it was the pain that had made her pass out. The brief absolution of oblivion.

A Gestapo agent looked up at him. Koenig knew him: Rudi Leitmann was a fresh-faced young man of similar age, dressed less formally than one would expect, in a loose jacket and slacks, a man who could be mistaken for a postgraduate student. He got up from the chair facing the tortured woman and stepped into the corridor.

'What are you doing away from your desk, Koenig? Slumming it?' he said in a pleasant tone.

Koenig looked past him into the darkened cell where two Gestapo interrogators in plainclothes were taking a rest from their exertions. The men's jackets were on the backs of chairs at the small metal table where cigarettes burned. Their sleeves were rolled, their shirts sweat-soaked and splashed with droplets of blood.

'Standartenführer Stolz wants to know if she's told you anything.' He hesitated, unable to take his eyes off the battered woman. 'My God,' he whispered, his mouth suddenly dry. 'Is she dead?'

Leitmann nodded to one of the thugs, who emptied a bucket of water over Suzanne. The shock of the cold water made her gasp back into consciousness. 'Tell him we're making progress. Another dozen were rounded up last night. We have our hands full here.' He returned to the small metal table and raised a stack of identity books. 'These are what they had on them.'

Hauptmann Koenig looked uncertainly back at the injured woman. If they kept up the brutality of this interrogation she would surely die before she gave them any useful information. Leitmann took a crumpled cigarette from his pocket and tugged out one of the stained identity papers. 'She had an English cigarette on her. These are her papers. She tried to shove them down a drain but the snatch squad got them. The man who was killed was French, a British-trained saboteur. She told us that much. His papers are in here as well.'

Koenig took the documents offered by Leitmann. Hiding his feelings of disgust he nodded his thanks and turned away, watched by an unperturbed Leitmann who straightened and lit his cigarette.

*

Around the corner from the Palais de l'Élysée, 11 Rue des Saussaies housed the Gestapo offices but Standartenführer Stolz had brought some of the most efficient of the secret police into his own Sicherheitsdienst headquarters at 84 Avenue Foch. Stolz's office was a few steps down from the fifth floor where prisoners were often brought in from the various city prisons for ongoing interrogation.

Stolz's office was uncluttered except for a few paintings he had looted from one of the galleries. He liked the Impressionists. Their work reminded him of his family's holiday home in Bavaria. The dabs of sunlight speckling across lakes, and the russet shadows of the forests. A vast Persian rug spread across the polished herringbone wooden floor offered warmth underfoot, and his desk, a nineteenth-century ormolu-mounted rosewood bureau seized from a wealthy Jewish family, was reputed to have been used by one of the presidents of France. Legends, as Stolz well understood, were often more powerful than reality. He shuffled the documents he held; there were others on his desk, a collection of papers seized from suspects. He studied each one closely, absent-mindedly correcting the position of the Knight's Cross on his tunic. Hauptmann Koenig stood at the door waiting for his orders but Oberst Bauer waited uneasily at the side of Stolz's desk. As Stolz finished looking at each document he passed it to the Abwehr officer.

'Himmler wants fifty executed for each dead Luftwaffe officer,' said Stolz.

'There will be reprisals?' the veteran soldier asked, surprised. He understood that the few rogue acts of violence in the city were nothing more than the scattered acts of malcontents.

'We prefer the term "retaliatory measures".' Stolz picked up and compared the captured identity and ration cards.

'Arresting and executing so many will seriously compromise whatever collaboration we enjoy,' Bauer argued. He had worked with the police these past two years, building a small network of informers, people prepared to betray others if they were protected from being rounded up themselves.

Stolz raised his eyes to meet Bauer's. 'I agree two hundred executions would be... time consuming... so I've persuaded the Reichsführer that twenty should be shot for each dead officer.' He smiled. 'We cannot be more reasonable than that, can we?' He looked over to where Koenig still waited. 'See to it, captain.'

'Yes, sir. Should I give orders to make random arrests on the streets?'

'No. Go through the prisons. Black marketeers, pimps, murderers, politicals – it makes no difference.'

Koenig hesitated. 'They would be under civil control, sir.'

Stolz looked at him and dropped the documents on to his desk. He lit a cigarette. 'Captain, what did you do before the war?

'I was an accountant, sir.'

'Which is why I asked for you on my staff. You're very precise. It's a quota; let's fulfil it. On reflection, Koenig, we must be seen to be actively pursuing our edicts. Random street arrests, for twenty or thirty, but use the gendarmes to do it, not our men.'

'Yes, sir,' said Koenig, and closed the door gently behind him.

Stolz returned to studying the identity documents on his desk. He fingered one badly soiled and damp document. 'Suzanne Colbert. I know that name.' He tapped his finger on the desktop, then opened a drawer and took out a sheaf of brown folders, quickly sorting through them until he found the one he wanted. He stabbed at a bearded man's photograph attached to the file. There were few signs of grey in the hair at his temples; it was dark and longer than the usual short back and sides, but his beard had flecks of silver and forewarned of greying in the not-too-distant future. Stolz flipped through the dossier. 'Henry Mitchell. Forty-five-year-old Englishman, lived here for years. A mathematics lecturer, yet he helped smuggle out some top people. He had a great deal of information that we were desperate to secure. He was a high priority at the time. He escaped to England. He was married to a Frenchwoman... a...' He turned a couple more pages and raised his head, smiling at Bauer. 'Suzanne Colbert.'

*

Stolz and Bauer stood with the young Gestapo officer Leitmann, at Suzanne's cell door.

'This is appalling,' said Bauer. 'Give us enough time and we will find the assassins that you are after. The Resistance

14

in this area is weak – there's no organization to speak of. And my men are better suited to extracting information than yours. Standartenführer Stolz, you torture suspects and their information is dubious at the very best.'

Leitmann, however, ignored the army intelligence officer and addressed his remarks to Stolz, who stood passively watching the wounded woman. 'She's not going to give us anything more than she has already.'

'And the other woman who was caught with her?'

'Danielle Marmon. We're checking on her, but she's so terrified she'd have told us if she knew anything. I think she just got caught up in the sweep.'

Stolz did not take his eyes from Suzanne. 'Get her,' he said softly.

Leitmann nodded to the two Gestapo interrogators as Stolz stepped into the cell and lifted the metal chair slowly – no sudden movements, no scrape of metal on the concrete floor sluiced with water and blood. Stolz placed his cap on the nearby table and ran a smoothing hand across his hair. He lit a cigarette. The pungent tobacco would ease the stench in the room.

'Your leg must be painful. The bone is shattered. Infection has set in already,' he said gently and then reached out as if to touch her leg.

Suzanne flinched. Stolz sat back and blew out smoke.

'It's all right. I can have the doctors look at it for you. I can take the pain away.' His voice offered comfort and the promise of relief from her agony.

Suzanne stared at the man who tormented her. One of her eyes was still closed; her petticoat was stained with vomit. Her lips moved but no words came. She knew they were going to inflict even more pain on her.

Stolz studied her. 'You are very brave, Suzanne. I know that because I have seen wounded men cry out for their mothers. And I have seen other terrorists beg for their lives after only a few brief hours of the pain.' He reached forward, and she flinched again, but he slowly and carefully eased a lock of hair away from her face. 'Shhh. It's all right,' he whispered. 'I know. I know. It hurts.'

Suzanne's eyes welled up and the tears tracked through the grime on her face. No matter who he was, his were the first tender words she had heard since the pain began and like a wounded animal a part of her responded.

'I also know you won't give us anything further.' He sat back and drew on the cigarette. 'I'm sorry you won't let me help you. I know who you are. Your husband is one of the men I would like to question. Very much. He has information that would be of great benefit to my work here.'

He glanced up at the doorway as two soldiers dragged a gaunt, terrified young woman into the cell. Danielle too had been stripped to her slip – but she was dirty only from the crude conditions of her cell. There were no signs of torture yet.

Stolz watched the girl, whose wide-eyed horror at seeing her mother rendered her speechless. She gulped air, desperately trying to stay on her feet, and Suzanne shook her head in warning. Say nothing. Deny everything.

Danielle bit her lip and turned her face away.

'You and the Englishman have a daughter,' said Stolz.

'I don't know where she is,' Suzanne croaked through her parched throat and swollen jaw.

Stolz turned his eyes on Danielle. He smiled, his voice carefully modulated, offering no threat. 'Your papers were not as convincing as the others. Enough perhaps for a casual inspection, but not for any detailed examination. Beneath your identity card photograph, we found the faint impression of another name. Your family name. Danielle Mitchell.' He raised his eyebrows. 'No? I think, yes.' He reached out a hand and lifted Suzanne's face from her chest where she tried to hide any hint of recognition. 'So. Do I execute you or your child? Where is the agent you were helping last night? And where is your husband? Did he come back here or is he still in England? What kind of a man abandons his wife and child?'

Suzanne stared back at him defiantly.

'No?' He pushed back the chair and took out his service pistol. The Gestapo thugs pushed Danielle against the wall. Stolz calmly put his pistol against her head.

'Mother!'

'I don't know! I don't! He's in England. We were supposed to escape together but we got delayed. We were separated.'

Bauer shouted at Stolz: 'This is inhuman. It's a disgrace!'

'Your duties here are over. You have been reassigned to something less demanding. Koenig, see the colonel out.'

What threat could Bauer offer to dissuade Stolz? None. Defeated, he turned away, followed by Hauptmann Koenig.

Stolz stepped back and indicated the chair. 'Put her in the chair, so her mother can see her face.'

The two interrogators held Danielle firmly on the chair; Suzanne couldn't take her eyes off her.

'Tell them, please... Mother... please...' she begged.

Suzanne shook her head. 'I can't. I don't know anything more.' She looked up at Stolz, who finally dropped the stub of his cigarette beneath the toe of his boot. 'Please don't hurt her... I don't know. I swear.'

Stolz pressed the muzzle of his pistol into the top of Danielle's head. His eyes stayed on Suzanne, watching every moment of her despair. The click as the gun's hammer was thumbed back seemed impossibly loud. Danielle's rasping sobs filled the room.

Suzanne's tears spilt salt on to her cut lip. 'I love you, my baby,' she whispered. 'I love you.'

No mother would sacrifice her child. Stolz knew she had no more information to give and he eased the hammer down and holstered the pistol. Both women nearly collapsed with relief. Stolz picked up his cap. He looked as though he had lost interest in the proceedings.

He turned from Suzanne to Leitmann. 'Execute her.'

*

In the doorway that led to the high-walled yard, a shivering, terrified Danielle was held by soldiers as Suzanne was dragged outside. Her injured leg meant she could not stand and had to be strapped to a post. A soldier was ready with a Schmeisser machine pistol. A junior SS officer stood to one side, pistol in hand, ready to deliver the final shot.

Stolz and Leitmann waited as Suzanne's manacles were fastened. Leitmann showed Danielle the picture of Mitchell.

'One last chance. Tell me what your mother could not. The agent who escaped, and your father. Where are they?'

Danielle looked from the picture of her father to her mother chained to the post, and then back at Stolz. Her eyes implored him. 'I would tell you; I swear I would. I don't know. Father is in England. That's all I know. He's not in France.'

'In times such as these it is a tragedy to be innocent,' Stolz said.

Hauptmann Koenig stepped forward. 'Sir. There is an explicit agreement between us and the French that we do not execute women by firing squad. Colonel, with respect, we have always upheld that agreement. Should we not send her to the camps?'

Stolz looked at the young officer. 'Thank you for reminding me, captain. You can return to your duties.'

Koenig wanted to say more, to push his senior officer into compliance with the long-established agreement. Women terrorists were usually sent to one of the camps or to Stuttgart where they were beheaded. His thoughts faltered as he saluted and walked away. She was his enemy, her fate was not his to decide, but if Stolz had her shot, when the names of those executed were entered into the records it would be proof of a breach of the agreement. Uncertainty clouded his mind. He was an accountant and now it seemed he was being asked to keep a double ledger. The records wouldn't balance otherwise.

Leitmann gestured to his interrogators to take Danielle away. Leitmann's thugs dragged her into the darkened tunnel which led back to the cells that awaited her and all the others who were swept up by the French police and Gestapo. She cried out, begging for mercy, her pleas echoing around the squalid airless passage and its dank walls dripping with condensation and the tears of the lost. As they hauled her away, a sudden burst of sub-machine gunfire thundered through the confined space, its heavy staccato beating down on her, hammering her into submission. She fell silent, her legs giving way as she collapsed into a deep faint.

Stolz and Leitmann watched as the executed woman's torn body was given the finishing shot to the head.

'What now, sir?' said Leitmann.

Stolz took Mitchell's photograph from his Gestapo officer. 'We bait the trap and snare him.'

'Sir, if the English have any suspicion that we have an informer in the Resistance, is it likely they will risk sending him?'

'Perhaps not. But if they do it will be soon. And once he is captured we will control any future British-led operations here – and break the Resistance.'

4

Buckinghamshire, England
February 1943

Harry Mitchell gazed up at the evening sky. The low cloud and impending rain offered the promise that no German bomber would tear open the earth tonight. Cloud or not, it would soon be time for the blackout. There were eleven scattered houses in the hamlet and soon, one by one, thick curtains would be drawn, extinguishing their presence, leaving darkness where once there had been warmth and light.

He checked his wristwatch. Time to cycle the six miles for his night shift. He dragged the curtains across the small windowpanes and rolled his waterproof cape under his arm. The room was modest. A single bed, a small desk and a moth-eaten rug on the draughty floorboards, but there was a coal fire and he needed little more. A place to sleep. And remember. He propped the small photograph of the two women he cherished on the desk. He always put it where he could see them, even when he lay in bed, and touching the picture kept their memory alive. Separated by two years and the English Channel, his wife and child were still missing.

Mitchell switched off the dim light bulb and, before he left for work, embraced them into a prayer.

*

Early the following morning a black government car drew level with the Midland and Scottish railway station directly opposite a drab-looking mansion. It was an ugly Victorian building surrounded by fifty-five acres of meadow and trees. Fifty miles from London, it was safe from German bombs. The car was stopped by a Royal Military Policeman to allow the passengers who had alighted from the train to cross the road. The two men in the car watched the stream of men and women as they headed towards the mansion and the clusters of low temporary buildings that surrounded it.

'More arriving every day,' said the older of the two. Like the man sitting next to him, Colonel Alistair Beaumont was in civilian dress, but looked more formal, like a businessman or the senior civil servant he was; he dressed as befitted his age. The younger man who shared the car was Major Michael Knight: he was thirty-seven years old and, although Beaumont outranked him, his demeanour was one of calm self-assurance in the presence of his superior.

'Literature dons and women who are brilliant at crossword puzzles. Publishing executives and even rare-bookshop owners. They're a motley lot. Thank God,' said Knight.

'Eccentric, some of them,' said Beaumont.

'Some of them. Not too off the wall, I hope. Pyjamas, slippers and trout flies in their hats is as far as I'd like to see on that score.'

Beaumont craned his neck to look past Knight. Another steam train sat on a separate track, its boilers hissing. 'Is that it?'

22

Knight looked. 'Yes. Always ready to go.'

Beaumont sighed. 'No stone left unturned, then.'

'Hope not.'

A few years back a lone German bomber had dropped a stick of bombs, aiming for the railway lines. The bombs landed harmlessly in trees, but the blast nudged Hut Four three feet sideways off its footings. It was then decided that if ever the Germans discovered Bletchley's vital importance and attempted to bomb it, the waiting train, its engine under constant steam, would transfer the vital code-breaking equipment to Liverpool for onward passage to America.

The military policeman waved them through. The car drove past troops manning anti-aircraft batteries and was then brought to a halt once again at the security checkpoint. The two men showed their identification, the sergeant at the gate saluted and the barrier was raised.

'Sir?' said the driver.

'Hut Six,' said Colonel Beaumont.

*

Hunched over a trestle table, Mitchell sat gazing at the elastic band cat's cradle spread across his fingers. He twisted it this way and that, his thoughts exploring labyrinthine possibilities of ciphers that had not yet been decoded. Then he released the cat's cradle, letting the intricate structure collapse, and picked up a code sheet. He was one of a dozen or more codebreakers in the hut; most were younger men, but not all. At the large desk at the head of the building, the hut controller, an RAF squadron leader, one arm missing, the sleeve pinned, worked his way through the sheaf of papers on his desk.

The lives of the codebreakers were rigidly organized: essential for the task at hand. The men were locked inside the poorly lit hut for their eight-hour shift, like the occupants of all the other huts. Shutters were closed and locked from the outside, denying those within any link with the outside world. The air was thick with pipe and cigarette smoke, hanging in a haze above the ceiling's yellowed light bulbs like London smog.

Mitchell was now toying with a five-by-seven-inch index card. He glanced at the earnest younger man who shared his table, eyes peering through round-rimmed spectacles, lips parted as he muttered code sequences to himself. The young man, an untidy public schoolboy called Ronald Bellamy, licked a forefinger and riffled through a shoebox of similar handwritten cards. With admirable thoroughness, he collated various cards with his code sheet, all the while feigning disinterest in Mitchell's silence and the card he held. Eventually, however, unable to resist, he darted a quick look in the older man's direction. Mitchell smiled. He was on to something. Bellamy sighed. The codebreakers worked as a team but it was a competitive world, and it looked as if Mitchell had won – again.

'What?' Bellamy asked.

'Remember the Luftwaffe deployment from January to mid-February?' said Mitchell. Just mentioning that was enough to secure Bellamy's undivided attention. Extracting the information about the deployment hidden in the codes had been a real coup.

'Have you got something?' Bellamy whispered.

Mitchell turned to face the younger man so that no one else could hear him. It was best always to be cautious. He tapped the edge of the index card on the table. 'This month's ciphers. Same recurring prefixes, same numerical response.'

'The same Luftwaffe groups?' said Bellamy.

'Stuka, Heinkel and fighter support. I reckon they're redeploying,' Mitchell said quietly.

'Bloody hell. Top of the class for that, Harry,' Bellamy said in little more than a breathless exhalation. He reached forward to look at the information, but Mitchell held back the card. Bellamy's eyebrows arched. 'What?'

'Fame and fortune here, Ronnie. The powers that be will fight to sprinkle talcum powder on your upper-class backside for this.'

Bellamy sighed. It was not the first time Mitchell had traded information. 'All right. What is it you want? My marmalade hasn't arrived from home yet.'

'Your petrol ration. You don't need it this weekend, do you?'

Bellamy groaned. 'How do I know you're not having me on... again?'

Mitchell slid the card across the table, face down like a card dealer. 'Ronald James Horatio Bellamy, saviour of this green and pleasant land. Pay to see, Ronnie.'

Bellamy winced, already worried about being spotted in a huddle with Mitchell. Mitchell didn't move, waiting for him to take the plunge. He relented and took out his petrol ration card. Both men eased their card forward at the same time and exchanged. Bellamy quickly scanned the information. It was special. He grinned at Mitchell, who scratched his beard, yawned and stretched.

'Pop it down the tunnel once you've shown it to the one-armed bandit.'

There was no note of cruelty in Mitchell's voice. The officer in the blue uniform had been an ace Spitfire pilot and 'the Bandit' had been his nickname because of his incredible skill in sneaking up on enemy aircraft. It was considered impolite not to continue the tradition of respect cloaked by gentle mockery. Hut Three next door housed the analysts who interpreted the material that those in Hut Six deciphered. As there was a constant stream of paperwork passing between the two huts which risked getting wet in the inclement weather, they had built a wooden tunnel and pushed trays of paperwork through it with broomsticks.

A sudden clatter shook the wooden hut as sentries outside slammed open the wooden shutters. Mitchell pulled on his coat.

'Shift's over! Right, breakfast and bed for me. Go on, Ronnie, show 'em your prize and make sure they only use the best talc.'

Light shafted into the smoky room, someone reached up and opened a window and the door was pushed open by another sentry. Two men in suits stood alongside Bletchley Park's Deputy Director, Commander Edward Travis. The codebreakers stopped in their tracks: no one got into any of the huts unless they were top brass. And even that wasn't a guarantee. Then the Deputy Director pointed out Mitchell to the two men.

*

The barest of halls, little more than a corrugated addition to the old pub, was unheated except for the small two-bar electric heater, and empty except for the two men who sat facing Mitchell. The village of Drayton Parslow offered accommodation, like many other surrounding villages, to those who worked at Bletchley Park and the six-mile bicycle ride each way kept Mitchell reasonably fit. His return every day after the long shift to his room at the public house offered the comfort only a pub, with its smell of spilt beer and rough-cut tobacco in the air, could. It was a comfort lost to memory and regret as the pub was now only licensed to sell beer to be taken away.

Mitchell sat opposite Knight and Beaumont. Despite the cold air and his fatigue Mitchell resisted showing any discomfort and had placed the small, inefficient heater closer to the older of the two visitors, neither of whom removed their overcoats. A small table in front of them showed two War Department folders.

'It's called the Ewe and Lamb but locals call it the Jug and Bottle because they can't sell beer except to take home in a jug, or, as is patently obvious, in a bottle. What miserable bureaucrat thought that one up? Imagine depriving a village of its pub,' said Mitchell in an obvious dig at the two suited men, who looked as though they could have been from the Ministry of Works, but, as Mitchell rightly suspected, were not.

Beaumont placed a pair of spectacles on his nose, tucking the curved ends carefully around his ears. 'I'm Colonel Beaumont, Military Intelligence. Three years ago, almost to the month, the prime minister, inspired it seems by the tactics of Sinn Fein, ordered the creation of an organization to sabotage, harass and kill the enemy and establish escape lines. It's called SOE, Special Operations Executive.'

Mitchell folded his arms across his chest in feigned indifference and to keep himself from shivering in the cold. He suspected these men bore bad news. 'I don't know anything about that.'

'Very few do,' said Beaumont. 'It's thought by some to be waging an ungentlemanly war.'

Mitchell shifted his gaze to the younger man, who had so far remained silent. 'And who are you?'

'Major Knight. From that organization.'

Beaumont opened one of the folders and read from the notes clipped inside. 'When you lived in Paris you and your wife put your lives at risk to help others escape. That was very courageous of you both.'

'You're confusing courage with panic.'

Beaumont ignored his remark. 'During your planned escape from Paris, you became separated from your wife and daughter. You've written twenty-odd letters to the Foreign Office –'

'Twenty-three,' Mitchell interrupted.

'– asking for any information on their whereabouts.'

'And had no reply,' he said.

'Before you left Paris you helped establish an escape route for downed airmen and vital French personnel.'

Mitchell remained silent. Whatever these men were here for they clearly wanted to impress him first with their knowledge of his past.

Beaumont's eyes followed the typewritten notes in his folder. 'More recently you advised that the Americans were sending through weather reports to their shipping in plain language and that this seriously compromised our own security.'

'Fairly bloody obvious if anyone had given it a second thought. We send our reports in code; it would hardly take much for the Germans to compare plain text with our encryption and break our codes.'

'But you gave this information to one of your American co-workers here at Bletchley.'

'Sam Henderson, yes. So what?'

'You might have claimed credit for it yourself.'

'Who cares who solves a problem?'

'You have a soft spot for Americans?'

'I'm happy that we have such fine minds as Henderson's working with us. This is all very tedious.'

'Our work often is,' said Beaumont with a self-deprecating smile. 'So you were known to the Americans in Paris? Those who stayed, I mean, not their airmen.'

'Yes. My wife and I knew Americans there. Both socially and professionally.'

'And those who helped establish the escape routes?'

'You don't seriously expect me to answer that.'

'There's a surgeon at the American Hospital in Paris and someone in the American Library who help downed airmen. Those who have not been incarcerated are still active in helping the Allies.'

'I wouldn't know,' Mitchell replied.

'Fortunately, we have information that some of those involved are not yet under suspicion,' said Beaumont.

'And how would you know that?' said Mitchell.

'Because last year a few French telephone linesmen spent a year tapping into the main underground telephone cable at Noisy-le-Grand in Paris that carried all German telephonic communication between Paris and Metz. They recorded every word and sent it by wireless to us. There was no mention of these Americans being under suspicion.' Beaumont sighed. 'Brave men, those linesmen. They were caught and shot.'

Mitchell glanced at the younger man. Major Knight had been studying him since he had first sat down.

'You're talking, but he's making decisions about me,' said Mitchell. 'What do you want, major?'

There was a subtle shift in authority. Major Knight opened the second folder and slid a photograph across the table in front of Mitchell, who didn't move. He could see clearly enough. The SOE man placed another photograph from the folder. He placed his finger on the first.

'This man was one of my agents. His name is Peter Thompson. Do you know him?'

'From Paris?'

'Oxford.'

'No.'

'I see. Understandable, he's quite a few years younger than you. But that's unimportant. Some months ago he was attempting to exfiltrate this man.' Knight eased the other photograph in front of Mitchell. It showed an identity card picture of a man who looked to be in his sixties. 'His name is Alfred Korte. A German. He's a scientist and a fervent anti-Nazi. He was arrested in Germany in 1941, was released to work with other scientists but he fled to France last year. He was hunted by Vichy and German forces, but he vanished from the face of the earth. He has vital information that we need.'

'Then they must have got him,' said Mitchell. 'Him and your agent.'

'We think not. We would have heard. No, he got as far as Paris, but we don't know where he is. Peter Thompson – Guy Neuville was his cover name – was close to getting him out.'

'And your agent?'

'Also gone to ground. Perhaps even been obliged to change his nom de guerre.'

'Or dead.'

'Yes.'

'And why are you sharing this information with me?'

'We need someone to go to Paris and find Alfred Korte and bring him to us.'

Mitchell failed to stop the derisive laugh that escaped. He looked from Knight to Beaumont. Neither man was smiling.

'I'm too old to go running around the back streets. The place is crawling with informers, gangsters, collaborators and a hotchpotch of French Resistance groups who at any given time are at each other's throats. No thank you. I'll stay in Hut Six and put up with the bickering and frayed nerves there.'

Knight and Beaumont lowered their eyes, seemingly disappointed.

'We had hoped we might have relied on your goodwill in this matter,' said Beaumont.'

'"Hope deceives more men than cunning does,"' Mitchell told them.

Beaumont sighed and removed his spectacles. After a moment's thought, he said quietly: 'Who said that?'

Mitchell shrugged. 'I forget,' he said uncaringly.

'I doubt that,' said Beaumont. 'Vauvenargues, wasn't it? Quoting a minor eighteenth-century French writer might impress those who take their beer ration at this inn but not us. You're not the only one who went to university, for pity's sake. We are not interested in people who are too clever for their own good.'

'Which can get you killed,' added Knight. 'Arrogance is the last thing we want. So keep your pretensions to yourself.'

Mitchell pushed back his chair. 'I'm cold and I'm tired. And I've had enough of your games.'

'Sit down,' said Knight firmly. 'We're not finished with you yet.' The command was spoken with quiet authority. Despite his wounded pride Mitchell did as he was told.

Knight took another photograph from the folder. 'The safe houses we had established in the city have all been closed down by the Germans. This man's name is Alain Ory. He was the second man we sent into Paris. His wireless traffic was intermittent before it fell silent. Then picked up again sporadically.' He gathered the photographs and retrieved the file. 'We believe someone is betraying our agents,' he continued.

'Or he has fallen ill, tripped and fallen, broken his arm: there could be any number of reasons,' said Mitchell. 'Perhaps the Germans were too close to his location and he couldn't use his wireless. There are a dozen scenarios why he hasn't been in touch regularly. And losing safe houses is down to nosey neighbours.'

'Perhaps. We have good people in the Resistance getting our people into Paris; it's once they are in the city that they are being betrayed. You know people over there. You can move more freely, you have contacts.' He paused. 'And I can't risk sending in another agent blind.'

'You want me to act as bait.'

'I want you to do whatever the situation demands. Make contact with Ory and find Alfred Korte and get him out. And then find the traitor and deal with him.'

'I'm an academic, not a killer.'

'We can teach you,' Knight said evenly.

'That's not something I want to learn.'

'Then find him and have the Resistance kill him. How the end result is achieved is immaterial.'

The two men stared each other down. Colonel Beaumont leant forward slightly. 'If you found your daughter and her life was threatened, you'd kill to save her, wouldn't you?' he said gently.

There it was, Mitchell realized. They had a card of their own to play, just as he had tempted young Bellamy. He tried to keep the nervousness from his voice. 'Only my daughter?'

'Your wife was with Alan Ory and another man who was shot at that time. They were running from a patrol. She used her maiden name as cover – she helped our people. I'm sorry, Mitchell. She was also betrayed to the Gestapo,' Knight said in a flat, unemotional manner.

Mitchell blinked. Knight was simply stating facts. He wasn't there to offer condolences. Mitchell's stomach squirmed and knotted as he struggled to hide the emotion.

'Where are they?' he asked, unable to stop his throat constricting, his voice barely audible.

'As far as we know your daughter is being held in La Santé Prison in Paris.'

Mitchell grimaced. La Santé was notorious. The thought of her being held there froze his heart. He calmed. 'And my wife?'

Major Knight, slowly, almost reluctantly, eased the closed folder towards Mitchell. 'These photographs were taken moments before she was executed. They were smuggled out by a member of the Resistance who works in the German photo laboratory. I'm sorry.' He let the moment settle. 'I truly am sorry, Mitchell. But I need to find Alfred Korte and the traitor.'

For a moment longer Knight and Beaumont watched Mitchell whose eyes dropped to the folder that held his worst fears. The two men stood without another word and walked away. At first, Mitchell did not reach for the file. Then, unable to resist, he opened it. A picture of Suzanne: like Korte's an identity card photograph. And behind it a blurred picture of movement, a woman being dragged by two guards. Other photographs captured her head slumped, body bloodstained, hair down over her face. And, finally, an SS officer aiming his pistol at her head.

Mitchell sucked in air. Stoically not yielding to the grief that clawed at him. They had known the risks. Suzanne knew. He knew. They had felt death looking over their shoulders the moment the Germans marched into Paris. Now the scourge had taken her from him. A pulse beat in his neck: a sickening heartbeat of loss. It took little imagination to see the images of torture in his mind's eye. See the suffering. Her agony. Her bravery. He tasted salt on his tongue as he laid his palm over the blurred photograph. More blurred now than the soft focus image he had seen only moments before. A lifetime ago.

'My love,' he whispered.

5

They had sent him north to a place where no matter what time of the day or night the mountain air chilled everyone. The training camp in the Scottish Highlands was deemed perfect for its isolation and ruggedness. A place to quickly weed out those who were unsuitable for the dangers that lay ahead. Men and women, all dressed in brown boiler suits, ran from one training session to another until fatigue claimed them. They slept at every opportunity. It was a myth, Mitchell had once been told, that soldiers could sleep on the march because of exhaustion. After three weeks of intensive training, Mitchell was prepared to argue it was no myth.

Major Knight stood with Sergeant Major Laughlin in a wooden hut, warmed by a potbellied stove. Laughlin was a family man with a soft heart for all things Scottish and a cold one for the bastard heathens who had claimed his son at Dunkirk. He knew his skills could help train others to kill the enemy, which is why he dedicated himself to these courageous men and women who were prepared to go behind enemy lines. He was in charge of the training teams and his no-nonsense approach demanded high standards. Through the window, the two of them watched as small groups of men and women ran past, shepherded by an army instructor. Further, in the distance, four more candidates were being taught unarmed combat. Somewhere in the background was the muted sound of gunfire.

'He's a fit man for his age. It's the killing he's no good at, sir,' said Laughlin.

A concerned Major Knight flipped through a file. None of the instructors was told anything about their charges: neither where they were from nor what they would be expected to do if they passed the test of the rigours placed upon them. Knight decided to share some of Mitchell's background. 'He served in the Great War as a junior officer. He was eighteen years old, rear echelon, a non-combatant. There was an... incident.' He handed the file to Laughlin open at the relevant page and let the hard man read the report. The dour Scotsman scowled, and then sighed.

'Is there anything else I need to know about him?'

Knight shook his head. 'He's your responsibility, sergeant major.' Knight took back the file. He checked his watch. 'I have to get back to London. Do whatever it takes. He's no good to me if he can't pull the trigger when he has to.'

*

Mitchell stood hunched in the cold at the firing range as Laughlin showed him the black metal pistol.

'It's .45 calibre. Single shot, semi-automatic, which means it fires one bullet at every squeeze of the trigger. It uses the force of the fired round to chamber another and reset the hammer. That prevents the striker from re-engaging the firing pin. Pull the trigger. And so on. Child's play, Mr Mitchell, sir.

It's the standard sidearm for Americans. Effective range is fifty yards. Seven rounds in the magazine and one in the chamber. Whatever you hit will stay hit. Now, that's just a drum of water,' he said, pointing to a forty-four-gallon drum twenty yards away. 'It doesn't talk, it doesn't goose-step.' He handed the loaded weapon to Mitchell. 'So, in your own time.'

Mitchell fired. The recoil kicked the weapon down and blew a hole in the ground five feet in front of him.

'Need to get used to the recoil, Mr Mitchell. Just a matter of knowing about it so you can compensate,' said Laughlin, standing patiently behind him. Almost tenderly, he corrected Mitchell's body position. 'Feel the butt of the pistol, bring your arms up, point and shoot. Both eyes open – can't shoot the buggers if you can't see them. Now... point and shoot.'

Another shot, another miss. Another slight adjustment from Laughlin. Another shot, a near miss. Laughlin positioned himself right behind Mitchell's shoulder. 'All right Mr Mitchell, sir, we've a bit of a problem now. I'm out of ammunition and I'm wounded and if you can't stop that SS man – he's going to kill me and you and then he's going to rape and murder your wife and daughter.'

Mitchell froze; then he turned and faced Laughlin, forcing himself not to react. He pressed back the fury he felt rise up in his throat, tossed the .45 down and walked away. This confirmed Laughlin's doubts. He muttered to himself: 'Christ Almighty, if he hasn't got the imagination to see what could happen, then he's no brain at all and as much use as a Catholic at a Rangers' game. Fucking bait.' Sectarianism was alive and well between the two Scottish football teams, Celtic and Rangers. That was history for you, he thought. And much good fucking history had done anyone with this mess they were in. He picked up the pistol and wiped a caring hand over the black metal, cleaning away a smear of dirt. Laughlin fired the .45 with rapid accuracy, punching holes in the water-filled drum. Mitchell's shoulders hunched, flinching from the gunshots, but he refused to look back.

*

Mitchell had washed and changed as darkness settled. He sat on his bed in the spartan hut that served as accommodation. Those who shared the room with him were already in the mess tent for the evening meal. He opened his footlocker, took out a large envelope and spilt its contents on to the bed. There were training sheets and schematic drawings of weapons and demolition charges. Pages of information on saboteur work skidded across the rough blanket. He sifted through the papers, ready to do his homework, till his hand brushed over a smaller government-issue envelope. He hesitated and then took out the photographs of his wife's execution. Knight had given them to him, no doubt in the hope that the reminder would spur him on. Mitchell needed no such inducement. He picked up the fuzzy pictures showing the bruised and bloody woman being dragged by two SS soldiers to the execution post. Nothing he could do would ever erase these images. He turned to the next grainy picture where she was tied to the post in the courtyard. Then the German soldier aiming a Schmeisser. Another picture taken from the same fixed angle. Suzanne slumped. Head on chest, knees sagging. The final glossy was of the German officer giving her the *coup de grâce*.

Mitchell raised his head, other earlier memories intruding on the images in front of him, visions he had long tried to suppress. His head snapped upright as he heard a gunshot. He listened. Was the shot real or imagined? He carefully shuffled the photos together and put them back into the envelope.

One additional photograph had been given to him when he had agreed to do what Beaumont and Knight wanted of him. A photograph of a German officer. Standartenführer Heinrich Stolz. Mitchell slid across a picture of Danielle to rest next to that of Stolz. The two photos lay side by side as he gazed at them. The sudden chatter of distant machine-gun fire broke his concentration and, outside the window, a flare curved up and illuminated the night sky. He saw his reflection in the dark glass and as another flare burst the red glow lit up his face, distorting his features. It was a face he did not recognize.

*

A week later, in the south of England, Mitchell sat in the warmth of the sun reading his briefing documents in the well-kept gardens of Beaulieu House in the New Forest. Major Knight, his suit jacket draped over a deckchair and his tie loosened, sat opposite him. Mitchell had gone through the documents while Knight waited patiently. As the last page was turned Knight could see that the man had absorbed the information easily. Mitchell had a quick mind. He offered Mitchell a cigarette, but the teacher raised a hand to decline.

'You've done rather well in the appallingly short time we've had available for you. So, just a final chat really, see how you feel about things.'

'More confident than when I started, and a lot more scared.'

'Well, that should help keep you alive,' Knight answered and studied him for a moment longer. 'You have to remember what problems an agent faces and has to solve. How to defeat the enemy; whom to recognize as having political influence or power; how to avoid local police and security people and finally how you are supposed to function in a practical manner on a day-to-day basis.'

'Yes, I understand.'

'What I'm asking myself,' said Knight, fixing his gaze on Mitchell, 'is what happened to that frightened junior officer in 1918 who found himself out of his cosy office and at a field headquarters close to the front.' He tossed a file on to Mitchell's lap. 'I know everything about you, Harry. You think I didn't?'

'Twenty-five years ago was another lifetime.'

'You were ordered to command a firing squad.'

'I was a junior transport officer.'

'You may have been in the wrong place at the wrong time but you were an officer and you couldn't give the man the finishing shot. He was already dead. And you couldn't do your duty.'

'He was alive. He looked right at me, for Christ's sake!'

'Putting the fear of God into your belly is what the enemy does, Harry, not some poor wretch who was shot for desertion.' He drew smoke into his lungs and exhaled. He studied the end of his cigarette as he turned it in his fingers. 'Question is, do I scratch you off my list or do I let you go?'

'I won't let anyone die because I have doubts about killing.'

Knight looked at him. It was decision time. An extremely important decision.

'Then I'll make the necessary arrangements to get you over there. Your training will finish here at Beaulieu.'

6

For eight hundred years Notre-Dame de Paris, Our Lady of
Paris, the cathedral dedicated to Mary, Mother of God, had
been a symbol of devotion. A place where kings and paupers
had knelt and prayed. In the streets not far from the revered
place of worship, a dozen or more French civilians lined up
against a wall, hands on their heads, while their identity papers
were checked. A German military police officer, distinctive in
full leather coat, helmet and the iron plate across his throat,
stood ready with his machine pistol, as did other members of
the Feldgendarmerie who had blocked off the street. A French
gendarme checked the identity document of one man and
passed it to a German officer, who looked at the document
and nodded that the papers were in order.

Leitmann stood further back, casually smoking, watching
the inspection. Down the line, a boy of about nine years
old stood like the others with hands on head. Leitmann
noticed that he kept looking nervously over his shoulder.
Leitmann took the few steps down the line towards him. The
boy's terror was plain to see. A plainclothes German could

only mean a Gestapo officer. The child turned his gaze to the wall.

'Turn around,' said Leitmann quietly, almost politely.

The boy did as he was told.

'You can put your hands down,' said Leitmann, but the boy was too frightened to obey. Leitmann slowly eased the boy's hands down to his side and as he did saw something tucked under the child's oversize jacket in what looked like a specially stitched poacher's pocket. Leitmann reached in and eased out a quarter of a loaf. The boy stared wide-eyed at him, and Leitmann smiled and then pushed the stale loaf back into the pocket. As he pushed the bread down he saw something glint in another inside pocket. He pulled the boy's coat aside and took out a gold fountain pen. He looked down at the boy's feet where a pool of urine seeped from under the boy's shoes.

Leitmann gave the lad a friendly smile. 'It's all right. There's nothing to be afraid of. Where did you get this?'

*

A dozen streets away in another arrondissement, in a curtained-off area of a working-class apartment, Alain Ory sat in shirtsleeves in front of a wireless transmitter in a suitcase, a string aerial hooked up from it. He sat smoking, headphones on, tapping out his coded message from the small pad in front of him. The Morse key clicked rhythmically.

Madame Tatier stood at her stove stirring a meagre stew, grateful that her son, Marcel, had found some bread, no matter that it was a few days old. Once dipped in the broth it would help fill their shrinking stomachs. Rationing was hurting everyone. She glanced over at the boy and her eye caught something out of the window down in the street below her first-floor apartment. Gendarmes and, behind them, Gestapo were moving towards the building. Her hand flew to her throat and then she turned quickly and pulled aside a curtain.

'Alain!'

He was writing down a message he had just received. Without a word, he switched off and ripped down the aerial as she pulled out a false bottom of a small dresser, and in one quick, well-rehearsed movement the radio was hidden. He pulled on his overcoat, slid open a window and was gone as the sounds of stamping feet were heard outside the passage. A sudden pounding on her door. She pulled her son to her.

'Marie Tatier! Police! Open up!'

Her stomach lurched but she tried to keep her voice normal and buy Ory time. 'A moment! I'm coming.'

But the door gave way as two gendarmes broke it down and rushed into the small room. With barely a glance at her, they pushed her aside and pulled open drawers, quickly finding the radio. Two shots rang out from the back street. She peered out and saw Alain Ory's body sprawled on the ground. A young, fresh-faced Gestapo officer stood over the fallen man, still aiming his pistol as another Gestapo agent searched the body.

*

At the security service headquarters, Koenig approached Stolz at his desk.

'Sir, one of the men we were searching for has been located. He was a wireless operator. This message was on him.' He stepped forward and placed some folded papers in front of Stolz. 'He had just decoded it. He was shot while trying to escape.'

'Is he dead?'

'Badly wounded. He won't stand up to torture.'

'I don't want him tortured. I want him to have the best medical attention possible. Understand?'

'Yes, colonel.'

Koenig was halfway out the room when Stolz called him back.

'Find me that signals officer who used to be with the field security police, the clever one who cracked that wireless group in Bordeaux earlier this year.'

'Leutnant Hesler?'

'Yes! That's him. Get him here.'

Hauptmann Koenig turned to leave as Stolz read the message. He lifted his head and smiled at Koenig. 'They're sending in another agent.'

★

Mitchell tossed and turned in a fitful sleep. The bare attic room was stuffy, with no window to open. He lay in a vest but had kept his trousers on. Never strip right down, they had taught him, you never know when you might have to make a run for it. The sudden gut-wrenching banging on the door snatched him from his sleep.

'Gestapo! Open the door! Open the door immediately.'

Before Mitchell reached the door it was kicked in by two heavy-set Gestapo officers. He backed away but they grabbed him and punched him in the stomach. As his knees buckled one of them pulled a black sack over his head and hauled him from the room. A wave of nausea threatened to swamp him but he fought it and tried to sense where they were taking him. He was thrown roughly into the back of a car and the Germans laughed and congratulated each other at how easy it had been to capture him. As far as he could tell they drove for about half an hour and then, when they pulled up, he heard an iron gate being opened nearby as one dragged him from the vehicle. He was hustled down a corridor and into a room. The door slammed and he was thrust on to a chair, his wrists handcuffed behind him. As they took the hood from his face he got a clearer picture of the two men, who were already pulling off suit jackets and rolling up shirtsleeves. There was an array of what looked like surgical instruments and a small table to one side, in the semidarkness of what seemed to be a cellar. One of the men turned a bright lamp on to his face.

He had no idea how long they questioned him. It was relentless and harsh. One liked to put his face close to Mitchell's and his guttural demands sprayed spit on to him. Hour in, hour out they asked him questions, trying to get him to contradict himself. The room was airless and the men perspired. At one point he thought he had fallen asleep; his chin rested on his chest, and blurred images confused his mind. It was a long night, and the lamp continually blinded him. The Gestapo interrogators smoked, and it was obvious they were getting tired, but not as exhausted as Mitchell, whose head sank again.

One of the Gestapo men snatched his hair and yanked his head back. The other threw down his documents on the small table in front of him.

'These documents are false,' said the one.

'You say you lived in Lyon?' the other asked.

'That's right,' said Mitchell.

'Where?'

'Near Perrache Station.'

One of the officers moved around him and gave him a quick sharp punch into his kidneys. 'You're English!'

Mitchell gritted his teeth through his pain. He shook his head. 'No. French. Born and bred.'

The man in front drew the chair closer to him. 'You say you're a teacher? You're lying. Your school was destroyed during the invasion.'

'That's why I teach privately now. It's the only way I can earn a living. I've done nothing wrong.'

'You said you came south by car?'

'Back then, yes. It took us days. The refugees clogged every road.'

'You're a smuggler. You're not a teacher. We have proof that you helped smuggle Jews out of the city.'

'I'm a teacher.'

The violent Gestapo officer behind him put his arm around Mitchell's neck in a choking armlock; at the same time, the other man leant his weight on Mitchell's legs so he couldn't buck free from the chair and on to the floor in any attempt to save himself.

'Smugglers are worse than black marketeers. That's why you'll be executed. For helping Jews escape,' said the armlock thug, and then released his grip, allowing Mitchell to suck in air. They gave him a moment to recover.

'I helped some of my pupils to safety during the fighting. That's all. I didn't have any Jewish kids in my class. I swear I didn't.'

'But we have information about you.'

'People lie. They get frightened. They lie to save themselves. They lie because they want to make themselves look important,' said Mitchell, being careful to avoid eye contact. They had taught him not to look directly at his accusers if he was interrogated, in case it seemed an act of defiance.

One waved Mitchell's ration card at him. 'You haven't drawn your tobacco allowance for three weeks. Why is that? Where have you been?'

'I had a really bad cold... I've still got a bad chest.'

The two Gestapo officers looked at each other. 'All right. Let's start again. Where do you live?

*

After hours of interrogation the two Gestapo, themselves near exhaustion, stepped out into the corridor. They left the door open where Mitchell, soaked in sweat, sat slumped in the chair. Major Knight was waiting.

'Even if he uses his own background, we think he'll manage,' said one man.

'We couldn't shake him. But we're not the Gestapo,' said the other.

Major Knight nodded his acceptance and the two men walked away. Mitchell raised his head and looked to the open door.

'Am I going on this damned trip or not, because either way, I need some bloody sleep.'

7

By the next afternoon, Mitchell had slept and bathed and joined Major Knight in the large bright room overlooking the gardens. It was a more relaxed SOE officer who handed Mitchell an envelope as they drank coffee.

'Do I open this now?'

Knight nodded. 'Your orders. As much as we can give you about our wireless operator in Paris, Alain Ory. Wherever he is he's running scared.'

'And he was definitely part of what my wife was doing?'

'Yes. The Germans are breathing down his neck. In order to draw out the traitor, we need to set up another circuit. Whoever's betraying our people will want to get close to you. We're calling your circuit Gideon, and your code name is Pascal.'

'The Old Testament sword of God and a French philosopher and mathematician,' said Mitchell and smiled.

'Well, we thought it appropriate. Your official identity is Pascal Garon. Mention Gideon only to those who are essential to the circuit. The fewer people know this the better; then if any of them get caught the name Pascal is all they know – unless the traitor gets to you first. Remember one thing over there – three people can keep a secret if two of them are dead.' Knight got up and poured himself a fresh cup of coffee. He gestured with the jug and Mitchell nodded. They sipped the hot sweet liquid and looked out of the floor-to-ceiling window to the gardens, whose beauty seemed so out of keeping with the violence being created by the men inside the house. 'And remember, we are there to fight the Nazis. Don't get drawn into French politics. God knows it's complicated enough. You'll discover that there are factions fighting each other. The PCF, the communists, loathe their own armed wing, the partisans of the FTP. You have to be aware of the danger that these partisans will take matters into their own hands and strike at the Germans wherever and whenever, despite reprisals. They pose a threat to the control and stability of their area.' The major paused and raised the cup to his lips. Then he placed his cup and saucer down. 'Now, over here, Harry.'

Mitchell followed him across the room to a long trestle table against the rear wall. On the table were a suit, shoes, tie, shirt, overcoat, and a soft narrow-brimmed felt fedora. Documents, small leather suitcase, money belt, a sheathed sleeve knife, a .45 automatic and four clips of ammunition. A folded silk map. Two small pillboxes. A cigarette case. Mitchell touched the items which represented his new identity.

'By the way,' said Knight, 'we've given you the rank of Lieutenant Colonel.'

'Colonel? Why?'

'The French respond better to someone of rank. Use it when and if you have to.'

Major Knight picked up a fountain pen case. 'We like to give our people something of a going-away present,' he said, handing it to Mitchell, who opened it. He took out a gold pen.

'None of us can imagine the fear and the loneliness of living behind enemy lines,' Knight explained and somewhat proudly added, 'it's gold, no incriminating marks. It's a very small gesture of our esteem.'

'No excuse not to send a postcard then.'

'And it might be helpful should you have to trade or sell it.'

'Thank you.'

Major Knight took a separate envelope from the table and gave it to Mitchell. 'Your various passes and identification documents. Only the photographs are missing; we need to do those today. Having lived there you might be recognized so you'll need to lose the beard.'

'When do I go?'

'Tonight.'

*

Later that day Knight's staff car took them north towards Cambridgeshire. RAF sentries checked Knight's credentials even though they knew him and his car by sight from the numerous occasions he had visited the airfield. They waved them through the gates of the unmarked airfield.

'RAF Tempsford,' Knight said. 'Home to our Special Duties Squadrons.'

Mitchell didn't reply. He sat, muscles bunched, holding his small suitcase to his chest. His mouth had dried and his face was cold, his shaven cheeks making him feel even more vulnerable. Hair trimmed shorter than usual, he felt shorn and exposed.

The car skirted the buildings and drove to a hangar's apron where a short take-off and landing Lysander was being equipped. Its high, slightly reversed gull wings made the aircraft look cumbersome as it squatted on its fixed landing gear, but its reputation was long established, its ability to take off and land in difficult places delivering field agents. Next to it on the apron, a Halifax bomber was being checked as ground crew loaded parachute containers into its bomb-bay doors.

Mitchell followed Knight out of the car and buttoned his overcoat. In one hand he held the shabby hat and in the other his small leather suitcase. Knight strode into the vast floodlit hangar.

'There's very little organized over there. Rag-tag resistance groups made up of communists, French interior forces, smugglers, murderers and thieves.'

'And some ordinary people risking their lives.'

'Of course. If you're stopped by the Germans and they check your background tell them you were born in Péronne. That's what your identity card will reflect.'

'Why Péronne?'

'The register office was destroyed during the battle of the Somme in the first war. They can't check.'

They stopped near a workbench and the major gestured for Mitchell to put the suitcase on it. A plainclothed SOE man approached and put a small case of his own on the workbench.

'Last-minute checks, Harry,' said Knight.

'Good evening, sir. Won't keep you a moment,' said the amiable man with a regional accent.

The SOE man began a very professional, gentle search on Mitchell, his fingers all the time feeling for any tell-tale labels.

'I'm ex-CID,' said the man. 'So I'll find any contraband.'

'That depends how far you're prepared to go,' said Mitchell, trying to relieve his own tension.

The probing fingers suddenly stopped and the amiable ex-police officer frowned.

'Just a failed attempt at humour… officer,' said Mitchell.

'Ah. Understandable, sir,' he said and continued with his careful examination of Mitchell's clothing.

'What do I do when the plane lands?' he asked Knight.

'Local resistance members will meet the aircraft. There'll be a *chef de terrain*. He'll get you clear. Then they'll unload the weapons and explosives,' Knight told him. He smiled. 'You'll be in good hands.'

Mitchell nodded. For all he knew Knight might have ignored his failures during training and put aside any doubts about sending him by ensuring he was chaperoned on the ground.

An RAF co-ordinating officer standing near the Lysander beckoned Knight to him.

'Excuse me a moment,' the major said and stepped away from the table area.

'They named the Lysander after a Spartan general, you know,' said Mitchell as the painstaking search continued. The man's stubby fingers had reached his collars.

'I didn't know that, sir.'

'Nor me,' said Mitchell. 'Think I read it on a cigarette card somewhere. Either that or some clever sod I worked with told me.' He forced a nervous grin. His stomach was in knots.

'And who was that Spartan gentleman? What did he do?'

'I've no idea,' said Mitchell.

The SOE man stood back as if to admire his work. 'We had problems in the beginning. French stitching was different, the cloth they used and all that. We lost a couple of people because of it. Now we get just about everything from refugees.'

'One careful owner then.'

'Oh yes. At least one.' He handed Mitchell a small pill container. 'One's Benzedrine, it'll keep you going for an extra forty-eight hours. The other is cyanide.'

'I'll try not to mix them up,' said Mitchell.

'Very wise,' said the officer seriously. 'Now, a final look at your wallet and then I think we're done.'

Mitchell handed over his wallet.

'Anything at all you shouldn't have on you? Matches, small change, anything you've picked up without thinking? Underground or bus tickets?'

'No, nothing.'

'Married in England, were you?'

'Yes.'

'Your wedding ring. It'll be hallmarked or stamped. I'm sorry.'

Mitchell nodded and managed to get the ring from his finger. The Special Operations man placed it in a small brown envelope, tied the red holding string to secure the flap and put it into his briefcase.

'It will be here when you get back,' he said. He laid out a jeweller's black cloth which had half a dozen rings tucked in small pockets. 'One of these should fit. Got them off French soldiers after Dunkirk. I mean, blokes who didn't make it.'

Mitchell chose one, tried it, and found another that fitted. The SOE officer finished checking the wallet but pulled out a picture of Danielle.

'My daughter.'

'Pretty girl. Taken here?'

'No. Lyon in '39.'

The man hesitated and then seemed to relent and handed it back to Mitchell. 'There we are then. All done. Nothing left now but to wish you the very best of luck, sir.' He shook Mitchell's hand and turned away to report to the major.

'Wait a minute,' Mitchell said and extended the photograph towards him when he stopped. 'If I'm caught and they find this it could put her in danger. Best keep it for me.'

The man nodded his understanding and took the photograph.

As he walked away Mitchell could not suppress the overwhelming sense of loss that swept over him.

8

Exhaust fumes billowed from the Halifax as two of its engines roared into life. The other two propellers fired and began to turn as Knight walked briskly back to Mitchell.

'We've only got the moon for tonight. Our people in France will be leaving for the landing zone any time now.' He paused and turned his face away from the Halifax. 'I'm sorry, Harry, but the Lysander has a magneto problem. It'd be suicide to even try and fly in tonight.

'It's scrubbed?' said Mitchell, uncertain whether the relief was more from disappointment now that he had mentally prepared to go.

The powerful engines of the Halifax roared, the vibration almost getting beneath Mitchell's skin, shaking his insides.

Major Knight looked from the bomber to Mitchell. 'They're doing an arms drop to help establish a group further south. We're sending in a wireless operator for them. The aircraft will make its run, then... it could return to your landing zone. It would give us time to alert the Maquis on the ground who'll set up the signal beacons.

Mitchell was already shaking his head. 'I'm too old for parachuting. You told me that yourself. Get me across in a boat.'

'The RAF needs moonlight for a run, the Navy insists on complete darkness – and we've got to get you in. I know you didn't sign up for this…' Knight left the sentence hanging.

'I didn't want to sign up for any of it, for Christ's sake!'

'If you don't think the death of your wife and the lives of countless others are worth the risk then I misjudged you. Your daughter might still be alive.'

Mitchell threw the suitcase down at his feet. His anger spilt over into venom he had long suppressed. 'You bastard!'

Major Knight was unconcerned by the outburst. 'When you get blood on your hands you'll know what's needed to get the job done. It's by parachute or not at all.' He waited a moment longer but Mitchell was shaking his head again. 'All right. We'll scrub it,' he said, and turned away towards the flight co-ordinating officer. Knight gestured with a cutting motion at waist height, indicating that Mitchell had said 'no go'.

Fear clawed its way up from Mitchell's groin into the pit of his stomach. He felt as though he was going to vomit. Bile stung his throat. He leant for support on the table as Major Knight shouted in the RAF man's ear. He was listening and nodding and then looked past Knight and pointed. Mitchell clutched his small case and hat to his chest as he took a deep breath, and strode into the back blast from the Halifax propellers and the waiting crewman. He turned for one last look at Major Knight, who gave Mitchell a brief nod of acknowledgement. Then, turning to the officer, Knight gave instructions for a message to be sent to the Maquis.

'Tell them the Lysander is cancelled, that we're sending in our man by parachute, but it'll be just before dawn.'

Within the steel ribs of the Halifax, the bare metal vibrated with the roar of the engines. Mitchell was surprised at how cramped the interior of the aircraft was; from outside the bulk of the bomber was deceptive. It was like a narrow alley; crew members bent and twisted their bodies to squeeze into their cramped positions. In the chill, dull glow of the aircraft Mitchell was helped to strap on a parachute on top of his overcoat. The crewman who would act as dispatcher pulled the final bit of webbing tight. Mitchell folded his fedora and stuffed it down the front of his coat as the crewman gave him the protective headgear. He shouted above the engines. 'Put it on before you jump.'

Mitchell nodded. The other man who shared the narrow ribbed fuselage wore overalls and parachute. He held his head protector as he squatted on the floor. The parachutist made a small gesture with the headgear and smiled. A shared journey into danger. Any friendly gesture was welcome. The man gave Mitchell the thumbs-up and then went back to reading a book.

The crewman gestured to where a hole in the floor would open at the rear of the aircraft. 'When the time comes, sit with your legs in the hole.' With his free hand, the crewman held the parachute's long static line. 'We hook this clip on the end, *this* clip,' he said emphasizing the sliding hook, 'on that wire. It opens the parachute for you. All right? Pulls the chute from the bag when you get to the end. Yeah?' Another thumbs-up.

'I might need a helping hand to jump.'

The dispatcher smiled. 'You wouldn't be the first. I'll put my boot in your back. Night jumps are easy, you can't see how far you are from the ground.' He grinned again.

Mitchell was uncertain whether the man was taking pleasure in his discomfort or was simply being blasé, as if jumping out of a perfectly serviceable aircraft was a natural thing to do. He gave another thumbs-up.

The dispatcher bent close to his ear. 'And when you're coming in to land keep your knees together and legs bent. That way you don't break a leg. Piece of cake,' he added cheerfully.

A sudden burst of machine-gun fire made Mitchell flinch. The crewman placed an assuring hand on his shoulder.

'It's all right. Testing the guns. Get some sleep. It'll be a while before we get to his drop zone,' he said, pointing to the wireless operator, destined to be dropped to the Resistance. He turned away and busied himself checking strapping on a number of large packages.

Mitchell tried to shout above the roar that the furthest thing from his mind was sleep, but the man did not hear him. There was nothing else Mitchell could do but to try and make himself as comfortable as possible on the cold floor. His body shook with the vibration and he fought not to let it get on his nerves. The aircraft droned on. Despite himself, Mitchell succumbed to the tiredness that anxiety can create and dozed off. He snapped awake when a roar of air whistled into the aircraft. Panic seized him, but he regained his senses and realized he was no longer in his dream when he saw that the crewman had opened the hatch covering the jump hole. He steadied himself and smiled at Mitchell as the other man pulled on his protective headgear. Mitchell realized he must have been asleep for hours. His mouth tasted stale.

'Ten minutes to the first drop zone. Still a long way for you though,' the dispatcher shouted.

The man's words offered little comfort to Mitchell but he nodded and gave the requisite thumbs-up. And in that moment all hell broke loose.

Mitchell was thrown face down by a terrifying lurch of the aircraft, a lurch which saved his life. An ear-shattering pounding echoed through the metal as cannon fire punched holes along the fuselage. Mushrooming steel, showering splinters inside, added to the explosive power of the bullets and cannon fire. He saw the dispatcher blown apart, foam and blood where once a man had been standing. It splattered Mitchell. He cried out, terror-struck. The man who had been readying to jump was torn apart too. Smoke started to fill the aircraft; engines screamed, changed pitch, roared and died and were tortured into life again. The pilot was fighting the controls, throwing the heavy bomber around the sky, trying to evade their attacker. The aircraft's rear and upper gunners were returning fire despite the crazy lurching death throes of the aircraft. Somewhere, someone shouted. 'Night fighter! Bail out! BAIL –' The voice was cut short as another strafing run from the unseen night fighter finished off the plane and anyone left alive, except for Mitchell. The aircraft lurched upwards, everything slid downwards and Mitchell was pulled towards the gaping hole.

He scrambled for his life. His clothes were smouldering. The acrid taste of cordite, burning rubber and electrical wiring caught his throat. The aircraft yawed across the sky. The engines spluttered, only two of them still operating, as it tried to defy gravity. Another violent lurch and he was thrown across the plane, the motion cracking his head. He almost fell into space. He tried to fix the parachute's static line's hook on to the stanchion which was the nearest strong point in reach. But the aircraft rolled and threw his attempt wide.

He was sliding now with no means of stopping himself. The thirty-pound parachute on his back made it impossible for him to roll clear. Sweat stung his eyes and soaked his back. His hands shook as he desperately tried to attach the clasp on to anything that would secure the static line. His legs fell out of the aircraft. He cried out, forcing strength into his arms as he desperately clung to the floor of the dying plane. He *had* to reach something. He lunged at a stanchion. And missed. Wires snapped and whined as they whiplashed through the fuselage. The slipstream tugged at his legs. He cried out and with extraordinary effort reached for the stanchion again and snapped the static cord's clasp on to it. And then gravity and the slipstream took him. He was sucked out of the aircraft. As he fell into blackness the plane rose up defiantly, fire raging where moments before Mitchell had been.

*

Less than four hundred feet below a poacher with four dead rabbits laid on the ground next to him was about to clear another from a snare when he heard the aircraft. The blazing aeroplane appeared from the clouds more than a mile away, wallowed across the sky at five hundred feet and banked as it eased earthwards, a dying comet trailing fire until it disappeared from view to crash unseen miles away. The sudden noise intruding into the silence of the countryside left the poacher dumbstruck, but when it died away a hushed rustling reached him as air whispered across parachute silk. He stumbled a few steps backwards and stood, jaw gaping, as the parachute descended into view out of the night sky. A man dangled in the harness. Dead or unconscious, he could not tell.

The parachute webbing bit deep into Mitchell's flesh. The twisted risers behind his head spun his body as the parachute unfurled itself. Blood covered his face from a gash on his scalp. Pain from his wound dragged him briefly back to partial consciousness. A confused blur of ground rushed up at him and suddenly he hit solid ground, hard. More pain shot through him. And then the night claimed him.

With a fearful look around, the poacher ran towards where the parachute landed. The silk canopy billowed and then settled, tugging at the man who lay still beneath its shroud.

9

The poacher tapped at the back door of a dark house. It was the home of a man who had died for the glory of France leading his soldiers as a rearguard for Dunkirk. His sacrifice had split the village. There were those who saw his death as a futile act in the face of the juggernaut of German aggression, but others who had learnt to respect him over the years before his death were inspired by his example to join the few who were determined to harass their enemy by any means. The poacher was one such.

After a minute a woman peered through the curtain, checking who was demanding entry so early in the morning, then quickly opened the kitchen door.

'Chaval?'

'A parachutist. He's hurt.'

'Come, here, into the kitchen,' she instructed. 'Quietly. I don't want to wake Simone.'

She made sure the curtains were tightly closed, then raised the wick on an oil lamp, its warm glow suffusing the room.

The big man eased the burden down from his shoulders on to the kitchen table.

'I heard the plane, but I thought I was dreaming,' she said, lighting another lamp.

Mitchell tried to raise himself, barely conscious but fighting the rising tide of confusion that threatened to plunge him back into the darkness. He could hear muted voices but they made little sense and the glow in the room caused his vision to blur. He didn't have the strength to lift himself. His head turned and he saw a bearded man standing next to him, a calloused hand resting lightly on his shoulder. Beyond him, a woman, a shawl wrapped around her shoulders and nightdress, was closing shutters. She said something to the bearded giant who stepped away to a stove and poured steaming water from a simmering kettle into a bowl. And then the woman leant over Mitchell, brushing aside his matted hair. Her lips moved. She was asking him something. Fractured thoughts raced through his mind – of the terror of the burning plane, the descent into darkness and the pain – as he gazed at the woman. She was in her forties, attractive. Her brown hair was tied back, revealing her features. She pressed against him as she put her ear to his lips. He tried to say something, but his words were confused: a dazed mixture of enquiry as to where he was and an overwhelming desire to tell the woman that she was as beautiful as an angel. He shook his head. He wasn't making any sense. The bearded giant looked down at him again, said something to the woman, who nodded. The man lifted Mitchell's shoulders and stripped off his torn and singed overcoat. Mitchell's hand instinctively reached for the gun in his pocket.

Chaval eased free Mitchell's hand and tugged out the automatic. Mitchell gritted his teeth, determined not to lose consciousness again. 'You won't need that,' he heard the man say in French as he placed the .45 out of reach on the table.

'The plane came down out of the clouds. I don't know where it crashed. Somewhere towards Voville,' said Chaval.

The woman squeezed out a cloth from the hot water and began cleaning the wound on Mitchell's scalp. His arm raised feebly towards her as the water stung the cut. Chaval gently pressed the arm down.

'Are there any more survivors? Any more parachutes?' she asked.

'No. I hid his in a ditch but I have to go back and bury it. There'll be patrols out.' He looked at the automatic. 'Be careful of him – he might be dangerous.'

She nodded and turned Mitchell to find the wound that had soaked his shirt with blood. 'It will be light soon. Bury his parachute and then fetch Dr Bernard.'

Chaval hesitated. She nodded. 'Go. I'll be fine. He's barely conscious. He's no threat.'

Chaval stepped behind the curtain and made sure no light escaped into the night. She heard the door close with a gentle click of its latch. For a moment she looked at the wounded man who lay before her. His eyes fluttered and his lips moved again, but he was too weak for any words to reach her. She wrung out another cloth. At least when the village doctor arrived the wounds would be as clean as she could make them. She reached for the gun to move it away from the table. Mitchell's bloody hand lunged and seized the weapon, but his attempt to keep close the only protection he had was in vain. Juliet Bonnier did not flinch, covering his own hand with hers she eased the pistol free. Mitchell slipped helplessly into unconsciousness.

As the grey morning light spread across the sky, fifteen-year-old Lucien Tissard eased his bicycle down a lane, watching a plume of smoke in a field up ahead rising above the trees and hedgerows. The overgrown lane dog-legged ahead and as he dismounted to push the bike across the rutted track he saw the back of a German lorry tucked into the side of the lane. The village gendarme, Marin, stood watching the soldiers search the field. The middle-aged gendarme glanced back, saw Lucien and with a shake of his head and a small dismissive gesture sent the boy on his way. Lucien backtracked and then pushed through the hedgerow. He saw the remains of what could have been a bomber. It was just a chunk of charred metal, still smouldering, and a dozen ordinary Wehrmacht soldiers were trying to sift through it all while their comrades spread out across the field to search the area.

Lucien felt the tinge of excitement prickle his neck. To see a destroyed aircraft in this part of the world was an event. Such privilege conferred status. Especially with the girls. One in particular.

*

Juliet Bonnier's house was the most notable in the village. Her late husband had been a successful businessman before the war and, although her circumstances were diminished, she was determined never to abandon the family home he had provided. Heating, however, was always a problem, for the chill settled in the rooms with their high ceilings and bare floorboards despite the scattered rugs, even in the cooler summer months. So, after his death, she had closed off all the bedrooms except for two, her own and the other for her young teenage daughter, Simone. The kitchen stove gave that room sufficient warmth for comfort and during the harsh winter of 1943 when the east wind blew with talons as ferocious as the invaders she and Simone had dragged mattress and blankets on to the kitchen floor.

Spring had so far delivered little by way of real warmth, despite the blossom on the trees. Her breath plumed as she stood with the village doctor at Mitchell's bedside in the attic room. Chaval had returned and carried the unconscious man up the three flights of stairs once Jean Bernard had stitched and dressed his wounds. They had waited, whispering in the kitchen about the man who had fallen from the sky and who must, surely, have been on his way to one of the Resistance groups. There had been no notification sent from London for their local group. By the time Chaval beckoned them upstairs their curiosity had become concern. The Germans would soon be searching for survivors.

Mitchell's shirt had been removed and his side bandaged. A blanket and eiderdown smothered his torso but he pushed the coverings aside and painfully eased himself into a sitting position. Chaval draped the blanket across Mitchell's bare shoulders. He nodded his thanks.

'You're not wearing a uniform. You're not aircrew. You're English? Your identity card says you are French. Pascal Garon,' said the doctor.

Mitchell took in his surroundings. A woman hugged herself into a woollen cardigan as the big man who looked to be a farm labourer stepped to her side. The man who was questioning him had to be the village doctor, he reasoned. The small black bag was his badge of office and his corduroy trousers and woollen jacket constituted a uniform. Similar in age to Mitchell, he would have status and authority in a small community and, given Mitchell's last sight of the darkened countryside before he hit the ground, he presumed that that was exactly where he was. In a village or small commune. In the middle of where? He glanced at the bedside table. His automatic pistol had been placed there within easy reach. A gesture of trust?

'It's not loaded,' said the farm labourer, who was watching the injured man closely.

Mitchell smiled. These people were sensible enough not to take unnecessary risks. The woman stepped towards him and handed him a money belt.

'We had to remove it before the doctor could stitch the wound on your back.'

He nodded his thanks.

'It wasn't shrapnel, it was a clean cut,' said Bernard.

'I caught my back when I jumped... the plane was badly shot up by then. Did it crash near here?'

'We don't know where it went down exactly. Most likely it is several miles away. We will soon know,' said the doctor. 'But the Germans will be looking for survivors. And that places us all in danger.'

Mitchell reached for the carafe of water, but the movement pulled at the bandaged wound. He winced and Juliet poured the water for him.

'Were you coming to this area?' she asked.

Mitchell glanced from the woman to the men. These people might have helped him but Major Knight's words still rang true. Trust no one.

'Where am I?'

'You're in the village of Saint-Just in what was the Un-occupied Zone.' Mitchell kept the glass of water to his lips to hide his concern. The Germans had seized back control from the Vichy government the previous year.

By all accounts, he was still hundreds of miles south of Paris. The aircraft must have been at it furthest leg when it was attacked.

The doctor voiced his impatience. 'You seek proof of our intentions?' He glanced at the bearded man. 'That is Chaval, the man who brought you here. This house is owned by Madame Juliet Bonnier. She has a young daughter in a room below. If the Germans come we will all be shot. We share your risk.'

'I was supposed to parachute into Norvé and make my way into Paris,' said Mitchell.

'My God, that's nowhere near here. Norvé have a Resistance cell operating already. Were you going to help them?' said Juliet.

'I can't tell you anything else. I'm sorry. But the aircraft coming here was on another mission.'

'There are men in the hills a few kilometres from here, near Saint-Audière... they're fugitives from the forced labour camps. There are less than a dozen of them. Most are untrained. They like to think of themselves as Resistance fighters but they're just frightened men hiding out,' said Juliet. 'Still, they might help you.'

'You know a lot about them,' said Mitchell.

The doctor and Juliet hesitated warily. Juliet nodded to Bernard.

'I am the local co-ordinator for the men around here and Saint-Audière. The parachute drop was for us,' he said.

'They were sending you a radio operator,' Mitchell said, remembering the young man smiling in the aircraft.

'To help us organize,' said Juliet.

'If I give you a coded message can you get it transmitted to London?'

'Yes. Norvé has a transmitter. I drive there for my instructions,' said Bernard.

'Is that safe?' asked Mitchell. Any unusual movement by locals could be spotted by German patrols.

'He's the doctor, he's allowed out after curfew,' Chaval said from the far side of the room.

'All right. We'll organize another drop for you and get you another wireless operator. Do you trust me to do that?' Mitchell told them.

The doctor and Juliet nodded.

Mitchell extended his hand to Juliet.

The warmth of her firm grasp was a reassuring comfort.

10

Spring in Paris promised much when it eventually arrived in its full glory, but it could be as fickle as those women who had once professed fidelity to France. A seasonal change had swept the city when the Germans had marched through their streets three years ago. Some stayed true, but survival meant different things to different people.

To Dominique Lesaux it meant enjoying the comfort and charming company of the German who now faced her across the net, lithe and agile in his tennis whites. She knew the risks she took being with him, she thought to herself as she tossed her hair back over her shoulder, but what woman, high born or low, would not grasp the opportunity that had come her way? Her well-connected family had history on their side; through the ages they had known how to make the most of connections to powerful men, how to do much more than just survive.

She had arrived in Paris four years earlier and soon entered Parisian society once it became known that her ancestry could be traced back to the court of King Jean II, even though she admitted lightly in conversation that hers was an illegitimate line from a lowly courtier. A mixture of shock and amusement had trickled through society. People, realizing that she loved to tease, were unsure whether she was simply trying to shock them. Dominique was well aware that gossip and snobbery had burnished the legend but was quite happy to leave them uncertain: in reality, she had long ago buried the truth about her background and the reviled race she had been born into, and keeping such secrets had become second nature. She knew women who had converted to Catholicism to escape wearing the yellow star – surely no worse than those who bowed the knee before the altar of Nazi philosophy to keep their lives of privilege intact.

Whatever they believed about her, Parisian salons embraced her as one of their own and sympathy and understanding followed once it was known that her family were trapped in Switzerland, unable to return to France, and that her allowance had been stopped by the Swiss authorities because sending money into the Occupied Zone was deemed to be breaking their strict rule of neutrality – blatant hypocrisy given that Swiss banks did business with the German Reichsbank. It was a harsh lesson, learning to live without work or money.

She had experienced savage hunger during the severe winter of December 1939, a bleak and bitter time that only eased the following March. Food had become scarce even for her. It was a brief and frightening peek into the reality of war far from the front line. It had proved more than close enough. She vowed never to want for anything as basic as bread ever again. Thankfully, Occupation brought with it opportunity. She had long abandoned travelling on the Métro where even a common soldier had priority over her for a seat. Now she travelled in a chauffeured car. Her lipsticked mouth did not want for food, or fine wine for that matter: rationing was something for others to be concerned about.

Rain had spoilt her tennis match yesterday but today the sun shone with the temptation of an early spring on the small château a few miles south-east of the city, which was cool enough in summer to escape the oppressive heat, yet close enough to be only streets away from the very centre. It was once home to the royal hunting grounds and now reserved for her German officer. SS-Standartenführer Heinrich Stolz, it was rumoured, was destined for great things.

Dominique dashed back and forth across the court as they volleyed to and fro, but couldn't make the final ball that he slammed her way.

'Heinrich! Not fair,' she complained as the ball sped past her. He could turn on the power of his shots as surely as he could his charm. She knew both concealed a ruthless streak that could make a grown man tremble in fear and a city beg for his goodwill. What little there was. And what little there was, she took.

'But now you serve to win the match. It was out.'

'It was?'

'You didn't look. It went over the line.'

She laughed, retrieved a ball and steadied her nerves. She was as calculating as him. And she had learnt that he appreciated her cunning. She got what she wanted most of the time; sometimes he knew she had manipulated him and other times he did not. And when he did not, she kept her ear to the ground and learnt vital information that could help those less fortunate, but who one day might turn on her and call her a whore and collaborator. It was a trade-off whose threat she had not yet reconciled.

She abandoned her petulance. She was a better tennis player than she usually let on but there were times when she couldn't control her wilfulness. She served, he lunged, but his racket scraped the ground and barely connected with the ball. He stumbled and fell.

'I won! Heinrich! I won. For the first time ever.' The laughter was back and so too was the innocent young woman, the twenty-five-year-old in the springtime of her life.

He feigned despair and lay back, arms outstretched, then raised himself on to his elbows and grinned, his sun-burnished face making his fair hair appear even blonder than it really was. It was no hardship, sleeping with such a good-looking man. He was gentle and considerate with her and he knew what she liked.

'How could I lose to the worst tennis player I've ever come across?' he said, picking himself up. 'It must be this damned chill in the air – my muscles aren't working properly. I swear Paris is as damp as a sewer at this time of the year.'

She glowered at him. 'You're not saying you let me win?'

He met her at the net and kissed her lightly. 'No, you won fair and square. Your game's improved, my dear – I must have been a very good teacher.' He smiled and she nuzzled his neck.

There was no denying she felt happy in his company and it was easy to push aside the frisson of uncertainty that sometimes caught her unaware. He put his arm around her shoulders as they walked towards the door.

'Are we dining this evening?' she asked.

'Of course. But now I'm late and I have to go.' He kissed her cheek and strode away.

She called after him: 'That's why you let me win.'

He turned and smiled.

Tucking his cap beneath his arm, Stolz pulled on his gloves. Hauptmann Koenig accompanied him as they made their way downstairs.

'Colonel, an aircraft identified as a Halifax bomber was attacked last night by one of our night fighters in the southern zone. South of Vichy, near the village of Voville. Ground troops have recovered what look like the remains of weapons containers and a radio transmitter. Perhaps this was the agent we were waiting for.'

'Any survivors?'

'Not that we know, sir.'

They clattered their way down to the second floor. 'They must double-check,' Stolz told him. 'Order a sweep of all villages that were on that aircraft's flight path. And check that the local area commander questions the French locals and any strangers who might have shown up. Tell him to use the Milice. They fear them more than our own Gestapo.' The French paramilitary force created by the collaborationist Vichy government was tasked with tracking down and arresting Jews and members of the Resistance and their sympathisers. 'I am going to the hospital with Leitmann and then home. I have an appointment this evening.' Stolz pushed open a door whose sign proclaimed the room beyond to be *Section IV*: the SD's specialist wireless section where thirty grey-uniformed soldiers sat hunched in front of their cathode ray screens watching for enemy short-wave radio sets transmitting within their given frequency range.

'Is everything ready for Leutnant Hesler?'

'As far as I know, yes, sir.'

'Make sure it is.' Stolz left the young captain at the door. He turned on the half-landing. 'Oh, Koenig, find any dental or medical records that might still be on file. Have our people compare them to the bodies in the crashed plane. And if anyone suspicious is interrogated by the Milice I want the report brought here.'

'We also intercepted a message from London. We still have the partial code from the captured wireless operator. It was in code for a circuit known as Gideon.'

'Are we aware of it?'

'No, sir. The message was for someone called Pascal.'

'Any reply?'

'Not as far as we know, but it seemed to me that if the British were trying to raise their agent so soon then they must be panicking. Pascal could well be the Englishman, Mitchell.'

'Why would you make such a leap of faith, Koenig?'

'Pascal was a seventeenth-century philosopher.'

'So what? Mitchell's no philosopher.'

'No, sir. But Pascal was also a mathematician. I... I thought it a coincidence worthy of consideration.'

Stolz stopped and stared at the nervous-looking young officer. 'A worthy coincidence indeed. Well spotted, Koenig. Very well. There's an SS major down that way who leads a Hunter Group, Sturmbannführer Ahren Brünner. Contact his group. He'll know what to do.'

Stolz left the young captain on the second floor. Koenig was grateful not to be accompanying the colonel to the hospital. He sickened at the thought of what fate lay in store for the wounded wireless operator whom Leitmann had tracked down. Koenig still struggled to cope among these people who controlled the unremittingly harsh world he found himself in. The reality was that they frightened him – yet his life could have been far more unpleasant in another posting. He was well aware that Lyon, with the brutality and frequency of torture and executions, would make his skin crawl. Being posted to Paris was a blessing in comparison. He had attended mass and confession, and the penance assigned to him by the priest gave him succour. He felt more able to bear the violence being inflicted in the prisons and in this building once he had performed an act of contrition for his own part in it. As he pushed through into the signals room he felt a brief moment of lightness in his chest. Forgiveness was a state of grace and it gave him the strength to do his duty.

*

Standartenführer Stolz and Leitmann drove from Avenue Foch through the traffic-free streets past the Arc de Triomphe and on to the Champs-Élysées. With petrol reserved for the Germans and permits to drive motor vehicles scarce, Parisians were left to their own devices when it came to travel in their streets. Stolz's driver swept the Mercedes past the few bicycles and vélo-taxis on the broad boulevard. The small two-seater rickshaws shuttled Parisians across the city, and the sweating men doing the pedalling cursed with effort, startling the horses of the drawn cabs that trotted past.

After three years of occupation, Paris still held delights for the conquering army and Stolz admitted to himself that the city was a place of rare beauty. He had admired the broad boulevards and gardens when he first arrived and Paris continued to charm him.

'Are you going to the opera this evening, Leitmann?' Stolz asked.

'No, sir.'

'You would be foolish to miss it, though I dare say it's sold out already. Von Karajan is conducting. They've brought the whole production from Berlin. It was a most impressive feat of logistics. It shows, Leitmann, that even in war we Germans appreciate high culture and are able to overcome all obstacles in mounting such a production. Our Chief of Staff Speidel has pulled off a minor miracle in getting it here. I dare say that if we had let him handle the invasion of Britain we would be watching it in London by now.'

The Gestapo officer looked askance.

Stolz smiled. 'Leitmann, we are not completely humourless.' He sighed. 'The invasion was a missed opportunity and we must live with it. But it is past, and what we do here and now is vital for the success of the war.' He smiled again at the uncertain Leitmann. 'Even if it means we expose the French to *Tristan und Isolde*. And mark my words: the French will lap up Wagner. Especially with their own soprano singing in the title role.'

'Too expensive for me, sir.'

'Leitmann, you should have said. I could have got you tickets. A reward for your excellent work.'

'Thank you, colonel, but sitting on my arse for five hours would numb more than my backside. I'd have thought it more Hauptmann Koenig's taste.'

'I did offer. But he also declined.'

'Koenig would probably be offended watching an adulterous love affair even if it was in an opera.' Leitmann hesitated. How much did Stolz really prize the accountant in uniform? Was he speaking out of turn? Then he pressed on. 'He's a pious prick, colonel. He loathes the work we do. He spends half his off-duty hours on his knees in church and the other with a French whore.'

Stolz looked surprised. 'Koenig has a lover?'

Leitmann nodded. 'Her name's Béatrice Claudel.'

'Nothing untoward is there? Not a Jewess? My God, that would cause problems.'

Leitmann shook his head. 'We checked. She's fine. In fact, she's quite a catch, I'd say.'

Stolz smiled. 'The boy has gone up in my estimation.'

*

The Rue de Rivoli, bedecked with swastika flags, led towards the Île de la Cité and less than half an hour after leaving headquarters their car drew up outside the hospital. The Hôtel-Dieu had been founded in the middle of the seventh century, which made it the oldest hospital in Paris, and its formidable walls reminded Stolz of a fortress. For a brief moment, he imagined what would have happened if Paris had been defended and not declared an open city. It would have been an almost impossible task fighting street by street and there was no doubt in his mind that German artillery and air bombardment would have flattened the most beautiful city in France. The hospital sat on the Parvis de Notre-Dame alongside its more prestigious neighbour, the Cathédrale Notre-Dame de Paris, which by comparison was modern, founded as it was some four hundred years later. Stolz was no student of architecture but he appreciated the grandeur of it all. The French had a flair that the Germans lacked.

The hospital's main building was divided by a long formal courtyard garden and Leitmann gestured for the colonel to take the stairs that would lead them to the hospital wards on the eastern side of the building. They ascended and turned into the arched colonnade that ran above the courtyard. It was as natural as breathing for them to walk in step, their footfalls a dull rhythmic echo along the seemingly endless tiled corridor which stretched the full length of the building. Arched windows gave a fine view of the gardens, and long wooden benches ran along the walls, their uniformity broken only by the double-height doors that gave access to other rooms and side passages. At the approach of the strident footfalls, two Wehrmacht soldiers quickly stood at the far end of the corridor and resumed their sentry positions either side of a tall glass-paned door.

Leitmann halted. 'He's in this ward, colonel.'

Stolz followed Leitmann's lead and looked through the glass. Beyond them was a private ward with two beds, one of which was occupied by Alain Ory, the wireless operator. A white-coated German military doctor accompanied by a nurse was examining the men's charts.

'That's the man we found in the apartment with the radio equipment. We know his identity but the doctors say it will be another week before we can have him.'

'Torture him, Leitmann, and all you will get is a pack of lies.'

'Colonel –'

'No,' Stolz said, cutting off any protest. 'I made my plans for this man as soon as I knew he had been wounded.' He smiled. 'I suspect I already have what I need to know.'

Stolz pushed through the door. Ory's heart quickened at the sight of the SD colonel. The doctor placed the bed chart back on to the bedstead.

'Colonel. May I help you?'

Stolz hovered at the foot of the bed next to Ory.

'I'm here to see if there is anything I can do for this officer.'

'This man has little to be concerned about, colonel. All the tests we have run have proved negative. I fear that we might have a malingerer on our hands.'

'And the wounded man?'

'The surgery was a success and, with rest, he will make a good recovery.'

'You think I've been talking to your stool pigeon, colonel?' said Ory.

The frisson of tension that began to surface alerted the doctor, who told the nurse to leave the room.

'You think I wouldn't guess that you'd put one of your men in here with me?' Ory said dismissively.

Stolz placed his cap on Ory's bed. 'Strictly speaking, he is not one of my men. My men, like him' – he glanced at Leitmann, who stood unconcerned against the wall – 'wish to torture you.'

'I didn't tell him anything then and I won't now. Fuck you and the Gestapo,' Ory said with a confidence born of desperation.

'Very brave of you. What do you think, Hesler?' asked Stolz.

'I have what I need, sir,' the young officer in the next bed answered.

Stolz eased open his cigarette case with a thumbnail. 'There, you see. No need for torture. You have given us exactly what I want,' he said as he lit a cigarette.

Ory's look of confusion made Stolz utter a sigh of pity. 'You think we are all unintelligent monsters? Of course we are not.' Almost tenderly he lifted Alain Ory's hand. 'You're injured, you're bored, you're a wireless operator... you tap your finger.' He smiled at the confused-looking Ory. 'As if you were sending a message.'

The wounded man's fear was obvious to everyone in the room.

Stolz nodded to the next bed. 'Leutnant Hesler is a distin-guished signals communication officer.'

'I needed your own distinctive style of sending a message. I've been watching you,' said Hesler to the stricken man.

'So now we'll send messages to London, and although it won't be perfect they'll believe they're coming from you. And I can trap the next agent – and the next.'

The blood drained from Ory's gaunt features as he realized the truth of what Stolz had told him.

'So... we have no further need of you,' said Stolz, picking up his cap and glancing at Leitmann, who beckoned the two guards.

'He is my patient,' insisted the doctor.

'He is an enemy agent,' Stolz told him as Leitmann instructed the two soldiers to haul Ory from his bed. The wireless operator struggled but suddenly Stolz had his small Walther in his hand and calmly fired two bullets into the wounded man. The guards recoiled in shock, as did Hesler. Ory's chest flowered from the bullets' impact as the well-aimed shots tore into his heart. He was dead before he hit the floor. The doctor stumbled away in horror, hands clasped to his ears, still ringing from the echoing explosion in the confines of the room.

Stolz glared at him. 'Your report will show that the prisoner resisted arrest.' The killing clearly meant nothing to Stolz other than giving him a brief moment of satisfaction. He turned to Hesler. 'Report for duty.'

11

Juliet Bonnier hauled out an old suitcase and rummaged through the folded garments. She quickly made her decision and tossed workmanlike clothes on to the bed.

'These will do you for now. They should fit.'

Mitchell sat on the edge of the bed, pleased that his tightly bandaged wound was showing no sign of bleeding through.

'Thank you. What have you told your daughter about me?'

Juliet shrugged. 'When she went off to school this morning she didn't ask anything. She heard nothing. She's a teenager. She sleeps like a log. If she sees Chaval or Dr Bernard they won't tell her anything. When she's home from school I'll tell her then. Now, get dressed. You can't stay here for long and we must make plans to get you out of the village.'

Mitchell looked at a small cluster of framed family photos. He picked up one showing a smiling man holding his skis against a backdrop of a snow-capped mountain.

Juliet took it from him and replaced it. 'My husband was about your size. He was killed commanding a rearguard at

Lille, protecting those at Dunkirk. Do you object to wearing a dead man's clothes?'

'No, of course not.'

'Well, then,' she said without sympathy. 'Hurry up.'

Mitchell painfully eased his arm through the sleeve of the coarse woollen jersey. 'It sounds as though he was a brave man.'

'Yes. Stupid as well. He could have escaped.' She held up the trousers she had chosen, gauging them for size. 'Try them. I'll fix them if they don't fit.'

'Thank you. Madame Bonnier, stupid men don't stay and fight a rearguard. It takes a great deal of courage. I know my presence here places you all in danger.'

She ignored him and stooped to pick up his overcoat. 'I'll stitch the tear in this. You should sleep for a few hours. I don't know when we can get you out.'

'I think I'd better stay awake for a while longer. Just in case.'

'Suit yourself,' she said. 'There's a privy out the back. Use the bedpan for now. We can't risk you being seen.'

She hugged his torn coat to her and closed the door behind her. Mitchell reached for the bits and pieces that had been emptied from his pockets, wincing from the pinch of his wound and the tenderness of a wrenched shoulder. He thumbed open the pillbox.

'Christ,' he whispered. 'Which bloody one was which?'

He chose and examined a capsule and then swallowed it with the water from the bedside table. He stood and flexed his back and legs, trying to ease the stiffness, then slowly began to pull on the trousers.

★

83

Simone Bonnier stood hunched against the cold stiff breeze. The sky had cleared but on the northern side of the village rooftops, frost still clung stubbornly. She walked home on the sunny side of the pavement, hoping that her mother had had enough flour to bake. Their larder was near bare since the Germans had taken control back from the French Vichy government and their demands on flour and foodstuffs had put everyone she knew in the village on short rations.

Lucien's bike skidded to a halt next to her. 'Hey, Simone.'

Like all the children in the village, they had grown up together, but Simone Bonnier was always cool towards him. He had a rough-edged charm and, like her, he had lost his father; but, unlike Simone whose father had died fighting, his had fallen drunk into a slurry pit and drowned. That was four years after his mother had disappeared on the weekly bus to Vichy and was never seen again. The scandal had split the village. Some of the women praised her courage for fleeing a wife-beating drunkard; others hissed that she had abandoned her only child. The village priest and doctor had failed to reconcile the two factions, but the upshot was that young Lucien Tissard was forgiven many a misdemeanour, and truth be told he had not turned out as badly as everyone had expected. He was taken in by his grandparents, who set him to hard work but never beat him. The lad had earned their trust and the villagers' affection. Simone liked him. A good-looking boy, but of course not from the same social class.

'Lucien. Why aren't you cleaning out your grandfather's pigs?'

'You think that's all I do?'

'It smells like it.'

'I haven't been near the pigs today.'

'You could have fooled me.'

A brief shadow of hurt crossed the boy's face and she immediately regretted taunting him.

But then Lucien smiled. 'That's OK, Simone. I don't mind. You're stuck in school all day and I get to roam free like a fox. I know what I'd rather be doing. Will you read to me again?'

'If you came to class you could read yourself,' she said, not unkindly.

'But then I wouldn't be able to spend time with you. And you tell really good stories. I have my own, you know.'

'Own what?'

'Stories. You don't know about the crashed plane, do you?'

'What plane?'

He swung his leg over the bike's crossbar. 'It's a secret. I can't tell you.' He laughed and pedalled away, hard.

'Lucien!' she called but he was already halfway down the street.

★

Dr Jean Bernard stood at his kitchen sink as Lucien crammed the last piece of bread and cheese into his mouth. He chewed quickly, eager to drink the cup of hot chocolate, a rare treat reserved by Dr Bernard only for a sickly child in need of comfort. Or for a boy who kept his eyes and ears open and reported to the doctor anything out of the ordinary.

'All right, Lucien, well done. You must swear not to tell anyone else. You swear?'

Mouth full, the boy nodded, but with his eyes averted.

'Lucien. Who have you told?'

The lad swallowed. 'Simone Bonnier. But I didn't tell her where the plane was.'

'No one else?'

'No, honest.'

'All right, wait here. There's more hot chocolate on the stove. I'll send for you when I need you. And remember, keep quiet about this. I'm relying on you.'

*

Simone ran home and dashed into the house. The kitchen was empty. She spun around and ran for the stairs. 'Mama! There's a plane that's crashed. Did you know?'

She came to an abrupt halt as she saw Mitchell on the landing above her. The stranger in her home was just like any common working man. A crewneck jersey and an old black woollen three-quarter jacket over rough trousers and boots.

The girl cried out and nearly stumbled back down the half-flight of stairs. Her mother appeared, wiping her hands on her pinafore, shouldering past Mitchell.

'Simone! It's all right. He's a friend. He needs our help. Don't be frightened.' Her mother quickly put an arm around her shoulders and guided her down the stairs towards the kitchen.

'Is he from the plane?'

As they reached the front hall Jean Bernard stepped through the front door. He could see at once that the situation was becoming complicated.

Juliet turned her daughter into the kitchen as Bernard glanced upwards to Mitchell who stood at the head of the stairs.

'You'd better come down,' said the doctor.

Moments later Mitchell joined Jean Bernard at the kitchen window. Further down the street, Lucien waited outside the doctor's house.

Mitchell stepped back. Juliet sat next to Simone, her hands covering her daughter's in reassurance. The girl seemed calmer. Perhaps, Mitchell thought, she was used to seeing local Resistance men come and go.

'Who's the boy?'

'Lucien Tissard. He's a good lad; fetches and carries for everyone. The Germans have a few troops at the crash site, which is several miles west of here. They might not even come this way.'

'You can't take the risk that the Germans won't nose around. I'm putting you all in danger. I need to get out of here.' He turned and looked at Simone. 'I'm sorry if I scared you.'

'That's all right. I wasn't really scared.'

'I didn't think so.'

Juliet squeezed her daughter's shoulder. 'Go upstairs and find a case for our guest so he can take some food with him.'

'I have my old school satchel.'

'That's fine.'

Juliet waited until she heard her daughter's footfalls on the stairs. She stood and pushed the chair back under the kitchen table. 'I don't want her listening. We're frightened for our children, not for ourselves.'

'We'll hide you outside the village for a few days,' said Jean Bernard.

'I have to get into Paris as soon as I can. It's imperative. There's someone I have to find,' Mitchell told them.

'Pascal, we're four hundred kilometres from Paris. You won't be getting there in a hurry. We'll do our best for you. As soon as things calm down we'll get you north.'

★

Lucien idly kicked a stone while he waited for Dr Bernard's return. He knew he had promised to wait but what harm could there be in going a few doors down to Gustave's bar?

He pressed his face against the glass-panelled door. Cupping his eyes he peered into the darkened interior where two old men sat in the corner playing a slow hand of cards. That was good. It was only Didier and Edgard and they were there every day except Sunday. More importantly, there was no sign of Gendarme Marin. With a final glance over his shoulder to see whether Dr Bernard was returning home, Lucien stepped inside. The old men barely glanced his way. The boy leant his forearms on the scrubbed wooden counter and grinned at the bar owner, who peered at him over the edge of his newspaper.

'I bet that paper's at least a month old, Gustave,' said Lucien cheekily. 'If you want to know what's going on you'd better ask me.'

'Clear off.'

'Give us a lemonade, Gustave.'

'What are you doing in the village? Chasing the Bonnier girl?'

'No. Just running an errand for my grandfather.'

Mention of the boy's grandfather suggested some kind of contraband might be traded. 'What kind of errand?'

'You give me a lemonade I'll tell you.'

Despite the two old card players being deaf to anything less than the roof falling on their heads, Gustave cast a wary glance in their direction as he stood up from his stool and folded the out-of-date newspaper. You could never tell who heard what in a village.

Gustave poured cordial into a glass and topped it with water. He slid it across to the boy. 'What errand?' he asked quietly.

Lucien slurped. He wiped his mouth on his sleeve and leant even closer, matching Gustave's caution. 'You got any cognac for my grandfather?' he said.

'Not today. My quota's finished.'

'You want another suckling pig? Like the one I got for you last month?'

Gustave wiped a glass that didn't need cleaning as he half turned and glanced towards Edgard and Didier. The black market was a dangerous business even though everyone was prepared to buy and sell on it.

'When?'

'Tomorrow.'

Gustave frowned, apparently uncertain. Then he relented and nodded Lucien towards the end of the counter. He bent and brought up a hip-flask-sized bottle from under the counter. He slipped it to the boy, who shoved it inside his jacket.

'Don't let anyone see that or we're both in serious trouble. You bring the pig; you kill it out the back. I damned near cut my hand off doing it last time.'

Lucien smiled and nodded and went back out into the street. Gustave nervously looked over his shoulder. Fear conjured up ghosts that saw and heard everything.

12

Juliet Bonnier prepared and wrapped food in brown greaseproof paper as Jean Bernard kept a watchful eye out of the window. He saw Lucien push his bicycle back from Gustave's café. No doubt the boy was trading. But now the lad stayed where he had been told to wait.

The doctor turned to Mitchell. 'I'll get your message up to Norvé; Lucien will take you to Chaval's place in the forest for the night. Are you strong enough to ride a bicycle?'

Mitchell nodded. 'Can we trust Chaval?'

'Chaval hates the French collaborators more than anyone,' said Bernard.

'He was in one of their detention camps,' Juliet added. 'They treated him badly.'

'All right. I'll do as you say.'

Jean Bernard shook his hand and looked to Juliet. 'Half an hour. That will give me time to warn Chaval.'

★

Lucien stood with his bike next to Bernard's car; excitement gripped him after he heard what was asked of him.

'Can I rely on you, Lucien?'

'Oh yeah, honest you can.'

'You make sure you're back long before curfew.'

'Yes, doctor.'

Jean Bernard placed a fatherly hand on the boy's shoulder. The threadbare coat offered barely sufficient warmth for a cool summer's day, let alone a winter or a chilled spring day like today. The lad was as hardy as a feral cat and his survival instincts were as finely tuned. 'This is a man's work, Lucien. We keep this to ourselves.'

The boy's face beamed with pride when the doctor shook his hand. It was all very grown up.

'Wait till Madame Bonnier calls you.'

'Can I wait by her back door?'

'No, you'll be wanting to impress Simone. Remember what I said. Men don't gossip. You stay here. Turn your bike over as if you're checking the chain.' Jean Bernard glanced past the boy to where Juliet looked out of her window. He nodded to her and then climbed into his car and drove away.

*

Juliet turned back from the window. The twist of fear in her stomach brought a hollow feeling should anything go wrong. The soothing notes of a Chopin étude flooded the house from the entrance hallway where the old family upright was kept.

She stood for a moment in the kitchen doorway and watched the Englishman who had come so far to try and save others. Pascal was sitting next to Simone giving her a piano lesson. She prayed that his presence would not jeopardize their lives. She had done much for the local Resistance, but that did not lessen the anxiety of capture.

'The left hand plays its own tune, and then the right hand can do anything it likes.' Mitchell showed the girl. He played a few more bars. Juliet turned from the doorway. She heard Mitchell finish with a makeshift flourish that was more vaudeville than Chopin and then encourage Simone to carry on practising. He stepped into the kitchen as she was tying the straps on the old satchel.

'I've put another jersey in; it can get cold in the hills at night. There's not much food, but it'll keep you going until Chaval kills for the pot.' She offered him the satchel.

'You shouldn't give me anything. I know there's rationing.'

'I get extra for Simone. It's all right.'

He stepped forward and took it from her; their hands touched. For a moment neither withdrew and a brief uncertainty struck him. Those final desperate hours in Paris years before had been so hurried and fear-fuelled that he had barely had time to embrace his wife before they were separated. And since then? A barren wilderness bereft of comfort or touch from a woman. She gazed a moment at his jacket, then brushed a hand across it as a wife would fuss at her husband.

'It's strange seeing his clothes again.'

Her discomfort embarrassed him. 'I'm sorry if it upsets you.'

'No...' She faltered for a moment, touched his lapel, then brought her hand to her face. 'I can still smell his tobacco.' Her eyes moistened and the brief smile she gave Mitchell held him in what felt like a moment of intimacy. Confused emotions pricked at them both. She touched his chest again. 'Good luck.'

Few hours of daylight remained and at first Mitchell struggled to keep up with Lucien's speed. It was clear to Mitchell that the boy was showing off but he managed to keep pace thanks to the years of cycling to Bletchley Park. A few miles from the village Lucien slowed without Mitchell asking.

'It's better we don't go so quickly now,' said Lucien by way of excusing the older man's slowness, a gesture not lost on Mitchell. 'Can't tell where Milice or German patrols might be in the woods. No one cycles fast unless they are in trouble.'

'Or trying to beat the curfew,' said Mitchell.

'Yes, that's a good reason.'

'But you're right, Lucien, slower is better,' Mitchell added quickly, just in case the boy wanted to speed up again.

Mitchell was pleased the satchel on his back held little more than food and clothing; his undershirt was already sticking to his back. He comforted himself with the thought that travelling this way allowed him time to build up his strength.

'Dr Bernard said you were Madame Bonnier's cousin.'

'That's right.'

'I do things all the time for Dr Bernard... he trusts me. I was the one who told him about the plane.'

'What plane is that?' said Mitchell, feigning ignorance.

'Oh... nothing... I saw a plane go over... that's all.' He fell silent and then, unable to resist trying to impress the stranger: 'There are men in the hills, you know.'

Mitchell concentrated on the road ahead, hoping his silence would draw more from the boy.

'Resistance,' Lucien said. He glanced at the stocky man who rode at his side and added cautiously, 'Are you Vichy?'

'No. No, I'm not Vichy,' Mitchell reassured him. 'I'm against all enemies of France.'

The boy grinned. 'Me too.'

Within an hour they were skirting the low, forested hills and the road had become twistier, the blind bends ahead meaning that Mitchell could not anticipate danger. His fears were soon realized as they rounded a corner and saw soldiers ahead – perhaps the same men who had been examining the downed aircraft site and whose search for survivors had widened. The men were relaxed and spread out along the roadside. They smoked, their helmets off; some ate while others brewed their ersatz coffee. A couple were relieving themselves in the nearby bushes.

Lucien jammed his heel into the ground. Mitchell had glided on a few feet ahead before stopping. He assessed the danger. There was no reason to assume these soldiers would do anything more than check their identity cards.

One of the soldiers nearest their end of the road was cutting a piece of dark bread and as he put it in his mouth his gaze rested on the stationary cyclists a hundred metres away. Still chewing the hard bread he stood, picked up his rifle and beckoned them forward.

Mitchell's hand went to the .45 butt in his waistband. He half turned as if talking to the boy and, hoping his body shielded his actions, tossed the weapon on to the roadside.

'Don't move, Lucien,' he said gently, attempting to assure the stricken-looking boy.

Lucien licked his lips, eyes darting around him. He touched the breast pocket where he had put the illegal bottle of cognac.

Mitchell knew instinctively the boy was going to panic. 'Lucien!' he hissed.

But the boy was deaf to his appeal. He turned the bike around.

'No, Lucien! Stand still!' Mitchell's stomach knotted.

'*Halten Sie!*' the soldier called.

Soldiers were arming themselves and one already had his weapon at his shoulder in the aim position. The scene blurred into static tableaux: some soldiers not yet on their feet, others tugging on their helmets, some striding towards the cyclists. A blue-uniformed figure scurried forward from the rear of the soldiers' ranks.

'Don't shoot him!' the gendarme, Marin, shouted. 'Hold your fire!'

Mitchell looked from the soldiers to the escaping boy. He shifted the bicycle in the hope of blocking the soldier's aim. He raised his arms in surrender. '*Nicht schiessen! Nicht schiessen!*' he bellowed.

Lucien covered less than four metres before the frightening crash of the shot rang out. The bullet entered his back beneath his shoulder blade and tore upwards and out, ripping through his heart. The impact smashed him to the ground. He crumpled, as if he didn't have a bone in his body and landed with one leg half bent beneath him, dirt in his tousled hair. His eyes were open.

Mitchell threw aside his bicycle, arms still in the air, running to the fallen boy. He knelt, cradling Lucien, whose blood seeped into the dirt track along with the cognac from the shattered bottle, the scuff of the soldiers' studded boots approaching quickly behind him. He raised his eyes at the rifles pointing at him. Shock had weakened him, his body trembled and he made no attempt to resist the hands that roughly hauled him away from the dead boy.

13

Saint-Audière was a bigger town than Saint-Just and when the soldiers dragged Mitchell from their truck in the main square he saw a group of about twenty or more younger Wehrmacht soldiers. Their ill-fitting uniforms marked them as new conscripts, most likely reinforcements for those scouring the area. One of them was sharing guard duty with a local gendarme, standing beneath a swastika flag and a French tricolour that hung side by side. Across the square, a knot of men wearing blue uniform jackets and trousers, brown shirts and wide blue berets turned and watched as Lucien's body was dragged from the rear of the lorry in a groundsheet. A short man made some quip and the others laughed, one flicking a cigarette stub contemptuously at the boy's body. A soldier from the search party on the road remonstrated with him. The blue-uniformed men fell silent and turned their backs. Clearly, Mitchell thought, the German soldiers detested the Milice for the collaborators they were as much as their fellow countrymen did. The soldiers escorting Mitchell shoved him through the door of the Préfecture de Police.

Inside the police station, the soldiers handed over the contents of Mitchell's pockets and the satchel containing his food and clothing to the desk sergeant. With little ceremony, his name was recorded in a ledger and the gendarmes handcuffed him and conducted him to a shabby room, empty except for a table and two chairs, one each side of the table. A bare light bulb hung over the table with a sticky brown flystrip dangling beneath it. A cluster of flies blackened the trap.

He was handcuffed to a chain that ran through an iron ring bolted to the floor and his captors left with a slamming of the door. Shaken, aching with weariness, Mitchell tried to rid himself of the image of Lucien's body. The child had bravely tried to help him and now – because of him – the lad was dead, his life torn away in sudden violence.

Mitchell gauged the time he was left alone by counting in blocks of sixty, mentally placing each of those counted minutes against the mortar line in a row of bricks on the opposite wall. The light diminished outside the high barred window. He heard muted voices. An hour? Or was it longer? His vision had begun to blur through hunger and fatigue. The yellow glow from the bare bulb cast a shadow on the wall making him lose track of the lines he had mentally scored. Moments later a civilian entered, opened a brown folder, took out some ruled paper and began writing. Mitchell watched the rhythmic sloping script cover the page. The man was in his late forties, he guessed, hair thinning above a sallow face with uneven teeth behind thin lips. His lips were slightly open as he concentrated on whatever he was writing; a fleck of white spittle clung to the small crevices at the corners of his mouth. He sniffed, withdrew a handkerchief, blew his nose, and went back to his report without raising his eyes to Mitchell. A clerk in peacetime or a minor official in the local mayor's office, thought Mitchell, elevated now to be what rank as a collaborator?

Then, seemingly satisfied that he had completed his task, the man rested the pen, steepled his fingers and looked at Mitchell. 'I am Inspector Paul Berthold of the Milice.'

Mitchell knew he would be lucky to escape torture if this man did not believe the story he had given to the Germans. The Milice were more insidious than the Gestapo, enthusiastic collaborators who knew their own backyard as well as the locals they spied on and arrested. Their job was to break the Maquis in their area; they operated with impunity and spread terror among the French population. Petty criminals and thugs swelled their ranks because any Frenchman who volunteered to serve with them was guaranteed not to be sent to Germany as forced labour. If any of these militiamen were killed then they undertook their own reprisals as swiftly and brutally as the Germans.

'I have read what you told the Germans. I think you're lying. How did you get to Saint-Just?'

'Like I told them and the gendarme who questioned me. I travelled on the bus from Bordeaux as far as Arronnes.'

'And you walked from there?'

'Yes, my bicycle was stolen.'

'And you reported this?'

'No. I was on the road for four or five days. A farmer gave me a lift on his cart.'

Berthold studied him. 'Very well. How far down the coast did you travel before catching the bus?'

'I didn't. I don't have a permit for the coastal zone.'

'Your accent. It's not from anywhere around here.'

'I lived mostly in Lyon and Paris. Look, I'm law-abiding. I keep my nose clean. I was just going to the station.'

'You were carrying a satchel with Madame Bonnier's daughter's name inside. A school satchel. Did you steal this like you stole Dr Bernard's bicycle?'

Mitchell swallowed his fear and coughed into his one free hand as he desperately tried to think of an explanation. He had made a fundamental mistake in not checking the old school satchel. Every child in the world penned their names in their satchels. And the gendarme must have recognized Bernard's bicycle.

'I was at Madame Bonnier's as a guest.'

'Why were you a guest there?'

'I knew her late husband.'

'Where's your own suitcase?'

'It went missing when my bike was taken.'

'So you stole the doctor's bicycle?'

'No. The boy got it for me. I was trying to get to the train at La Basson. The boy was going to take it back to the village for me.'

'Why did the boy run?'

Mitchell shook his head. 'I don't know. He was just a child, for God's sake.' The stark image of Lucien lying sprawled on the ground refused to fade in his mind's eye. 'The lad was frightened. He obviously shouldn't have had that bottle of cognac. I don't know where he got it.'

Berthold remained non-committal and studied Mitchell's identity documents.

'Pascal Garon, insurance agent. Your company's office closed last year. I checked.'

'That's right. I told you I'm trying to find work. I lost my job soon after the Germans invaded the free zone. Agricultural insurance became a joke. What the Germans didn't take the black market did.'

'How do you know Madame Bonnier's husband? He was a soldier. Did you serve?'

'No. I'm too old. I met him skiing ten years ago.'

Berthold considered all that Mitchell had told him. His answers were effortless. The quiver of anxiety in the man's voice was understandable. 'This is a quiet area. A shooting causes problems. A lot of paperwork.'

'I'm sorry if the boy's death caused any inconvenience.'

Mitchell stared down Berthold in an open act of defiance. A moment's weakness and against all the rules of surviving interrogation. Berthold suddenly leant across the table and slapped him for the transgression. Mitchell's ears rang as blood trickled from his nose.

*

Mitchell was marched to a bare cell, rank with stale urine and excrement. A single bed frame and stained mattress, a lidded bucket in a corner. The bed was already taken by a thin, ferret-faced man, unshaven, hair tumbling over his face, his grimy shirt tucked into oversized trousers tied with a piece of string. He worried a cigarette between his fingers, sniffing its pungent tobacco. When they pushed Mitchell into the cell the man beamed. The back of Mitchell's hand was blood-smeared from where he had wiped his nose.

'That's nothing,' said the prisoner, looking him up and down. 'You're lucky these bastards didn't shove a broom handle up your arse.'

The man chewed a toothpick, moving it around one side of his mouth to the other, but even this did not slow him down from suddenly regaling his fellow prisoner: 'Was Paul Berthold the man who questioned you? I bet it was. He likes to get his hands dirty. He's a bastard all right. Thing is these Milice, they know everyone hates them so it makes no difference what they do to you. They question you and if you're not careful they brown nose the Gestapo and hand you over. Bastards. Look at me...' he sniffed the cigarette again, its scent seeming to give him pleasure, '... all I said to him was: "Look, we do business every month. I buy the petrol you expropriate from the German supply trucks." Jesus, that was a big mistake. "Expropriate?" he says to me. "You mean steal? Christ! Steal? You're accusing a member of the militia of stealing?"'

Mitchell pressed his back against the cell wall, determined not to sit on the dirty floor, wishing the man's incessant droning would stop.

'You see, that's where language can mean the difference between success and failure, life and death,' he insisted. 'I've been in here for weeks. Haven't spoken to anyone since my arrest and I like conversation; a man is starved of life if he doesn't converse with his fellow beings. Not that I class these bastards as human. But I'm a salesman. It's what I do. I like to talk. And let me tell you when they finally let me out of this stinking hole it will be because money or goods have changed hands. I have friends. Lots of friends, people of influence, and they will find me. They'll know when I don't deliver what they want. There's no one else who can...' He paused as Mitchell reached for the bars on the window and pulled himself up to look through to the outside. 'No chance of escape, mate. No, no. Place is crawling with militia, Germans, police. Every fucker who can carry a gun is out there. Dogs as well, from what I've heard. Hear about the plane crash, did you? Shitting themselves that there might be survivors. Not fucking likely, says I. No, no. Not when you crash and make a hole deep enough to meet the devil.'

The town square was in darkness. Mitchell lowered himself back down.

'Anyway, the next thing I know I'm in here and he gives me a good hiding. Bastard. We'll do business again. We always do. But they have to show you who's boss. Bastards. All of them. Crooked bastards. But I make money out of them.'

'Seems to be that the less you say the better it is for everyone,' Mitchell said.

The man screwed his eyes. 'You telling me I talk too much?'

'Yes. Smoke the damned cigarette and shut up for a while.'

'If I could I would. It's all part of their torture. They let me keep these,' he said, gesturing with the cigarette, 'but they took away my matches. See what I mean? Bastards.' He showed Mitchell the packet with a couple of cigarettes in it.

'You want to trade? I'll get you a light, you give me the packet and the bed for the night,' said Mitchell.

'You've got a light? Nonsense. They'd have searched you.'

'The cigarettes and the bed. How desperately do you want a smoke?' Mitchell challenged him.

The man worked saliva in his mouth and nodded. 'All right.'

Mitchell teased out the silver foil from the cigarette packet and rolled it into a thin tube. He made the man move off the bed while he found a worn part of the mattress cover; using a fingernail he tore it away and plucked out a small finger pinch of kapok filling. He dragged the bed beneath the light socket and, licking his fingers against the heat, of unscrewed the light bulb. He beckoned the man closer and reached down, plucked the toothpick from his lips then twisted the silver foil tube tightly around it. He pushed it into the live socket, which sparked on to the pinch of cotton filling that Mitchell held ready. He stepped down, blowing on the smouldering cotton.

His slack-jawed cellmate gaped in amazement and then quickly lit his cigarette, drawing in a lungful of smoke, eyes closed with pleasure.

Mitchell pushed back the bed and claimed it for himself. 'Now will you shut up?'

The man grinned and extended his hand. 'Gladly. Vincent, Gerard Vincent. You want? I get. At a price. You clever bastard. Ha! You ever get to Paris and need a favour you look me up: 29 Rue Bertier. Yeah?'

Mitchell shook his hand. 'I'll remember that. I'm Pascal Garon.'

Vincent sat happily on the floor, oblivious to its filth as he savoured the cigarette. Mitchell could do little else but settle down for the night and hope the Milice would believe his story and release him the next morning. He was well and truly adrift now. Falling through a burning sky again without sight of the ground below his feet.

14

The next morning Juliet Bonnier was at the Préfecture de Police in Saint-Audière. Gendarme Marin stood subserviently a few paces behind Berthold, who faced her.

'I wish to question you about the man who was with the boy. This Pascal Garon. He says he visited you in Saint-Just.'

'Yes, that's correct,' said Juliet. A pulse throbbed in her neck, exposing her fear at being summoned.

'You understand, madame, that the killing of the boy was unfortunate. No blame can be attached. He ran when he was challenged. What was he guilty of, do you think?'

'I don't know. Gendarme Marin said he had a bottle of contraband cognac on him; perhaps that was why. He was just a boy. He was taking my friend to the train station.'

'At La Guyon?'

'Yes.'

'Your friend said he was going to La Basson.'

'Yes! I'm sorry, I meant La Basson. This whole thing is terrible. I can't think straight.'

'You're sure it was La Basson? Positive?' Berthold's stare challenged her.

She took a deep breath and nodded. 'Positive. Yes.'

Berthold looked as though he was considering her answer. He looked at Marin. 'Go back to Saint-Just and check out Madame Bonnier's house. You find anything untoward, you come to me. Anything.'

Marin nodded and with a nervous glance at Juliet left the room. Berthold addressed Juliet. 'Sit down.'

She sat on a bench against the wall, holding her hands together in her lap, shoulders hunched. It served not only to make her look cowed in front of the *milicien* but also to stop her hands trembling. Her courage had not failed her but the thought of being arrested and sent with Simone to one of the camps sharpened her instinct for survival.

Berthold sat beside her. She could smell the oversweet cologne on him mingling with stale sweat. His breath reeked of tobacco and rotten teeth.

'Why would a man travel so far to see your husband? He was posted killed in action. Would Garon not have known that?'

Juliet agonized before answering, her acting skills honed by her fear of this repugnant man so close to her.

'What aren't you telling me?' he asked.

She appeared to be gathering her courage, but a tear was forming. She quickly wiped it away and regained her composure. At least that was what Berthold saw.

'I'm a widow with a young daughter. If this gets out... I'm ruined.'

Berthold sat back as realization dawned. 'He's your lover.'

Juliet nodded and lowered her head in shame.

'Since before the war?' said Berthold.

She nodded. 'When he heard my husband had died... he thought he could just move in... I couldn't allow that. That's why I had the boy take him to the station.'

Berthold paused as he considered her explanation. 'All right, though I may have to question you again. You understand?' he said and placed a sweaty palm on her knee. His meaning was abundantly clear.

Without meeting his eyes, she nodded once more.

*

Dr Bernard had driven Juliet to Saint-Audière the moment the Milice had summoned her. He wanted to speak to Berthold on her behalf but she had convinced him that the fewer people involved with the investigation the better. Nonetheless, he insisted on driving her and had waited behind the police station. She would either be escorted out under armed guard or released. When she walked free with the Englishman he said a quiet prayer of thanks.

They spoke little during the drive back to Saint-Just. Mitchell told them exactly what happened. 'I'm sorry about Lucien. More than I can say. I tried to stop them from shooting him. I failed.'

Jean Bernard looked at him in the rear-view mirror and saw the man's anguish. After a moment's consideration, he said, 'You are not responsible, Pascal. You were sent here to help others. We are all just a conduit to get you where you need to be. Lucien was a good lad, but it was his own panic that killed him.'

'And a German bullet,' added Juliet.

*

Jean Bernard dropped them outside Juliet's house.

'Get your things. I have to fetch Simone; she's with friends – she'll be worried,' said Juliet.

Mitchell reached for her arm. 'What did you say back there?'

'I told him you were my lover.'

'Then he can blackmail you to sleep with him. You've put yourself in danger.'

'I'll deal with that when I have to, but if he ever tried I would cut his throat.'

She turned on her heel, leaving Mitchell in no doubt that she was capable of doing exactly that. He climbed the stairs to his room and when he opened the bedroom door he saw Marin sitting on his bed. His cap was off and the top button of his tunic undone. His service revolver was in his hand.

'You're lucky to be alive, wouldn't you say?' said the village gendarme.

Mitchell glanced behind him. Were there any other officers in the house? He tried to gauge whether he could lunge quickly enough to disarm Marin. The man was bigger and heavier and stood a good chance of overpowering him, but if it came to it he could have to try. He could not risk being taken back to the Milice.

'I've already been interrogated,' said Mitchell.

'I know. The man who questioned you, his brother-in-law, Gustave, runs the bar here in the village. He'll be watching out for anything unusual from now on, despite the fact he gave Lucien the brandy.'

Mitchell gently closed the door behind him. If he had to fight for his life he did not wish to risk Juliet and Simone coming home and being drawn upstairs. Marin stood and reached for something out of sight and then tossed Mitchell's money belt on the bed.

'That's a lot of money for an unemployed insurance salesman. You left it here on purpose. Madame Bonnier is implicated; I can see that, I'm no fool. Was she going to bring it to you? Women are not searched as thoroughly as men. Or were you planning to return? What were you really doing on that road?'

'How much do you want?' said Mitchell.

'Don't drag me into your dirty business! You come here and a boy is dead!' Marin spat. He shook his head in despair and then muttered more calmly. 'A boy who tried to help you. You bastard.' He lifted his cap showing the .45. 'I found this at the spot where Lucien died. Where you threw it.' He tugged his cap on. 'If you have anything planned get it over and done with and get out of my jurisdiction.' He stepped towards the door and faced Mitchell, who was blocking his way. Mitchell stepped aside.

'Why aren't you reporting me?'

'Because Lucien Tissard, a fifteen-year-old boy from this village, died helping you. His death changes everything. So... I'll stay around for a while to try and keep things calm. And to keep an eye on the bar owner.'

'I'm grateful.'

'It's not for you. Tell Madame Bonnier to be careful – she gets sucked in any further, and I won't be able to help her. The SS is now involved. There's a company of them out there hunting for someone. They're hard, battle-seasoned men. The elite. Bad bastards.'

He pushed past Mitchell. Mitchell stood for a moment. He had had one lucky escape; now it felt as if the net was closing. How long would it be before Marin informed on him? It was time to get out.

15

As Juliet approached her house with Simone she saw Marin come out of her front door and turn up the street towards Gustave's bar. As she closed the front door behind her she leant against it for a moment, thoughts racing.

'Mama?' said Simone, sensing something was wrong.

'Go into the kitchen, Simone.'

'What's happened? What's going on?'

'Simone!' she hissed, still wary of who might be in the house.

The girl recoiled. Juliet reached for her and held her shoulders. 'Darling, there's been an... accident,' she said gently. 'Please. Go into the kitchen. I will explain everything, I promise. All right?'

The girl nodded and obeyed.

Mitchell appeared at the top of the stairs and came down to meet her.

'I saw Marin leave the house,' she said.

Mitchell glanced towards where Simone waited in the kitchen, then took Juliet's arm, guided her into the front room and closed the door. 'He knows something's going on. But I don't think he'll say anything.'

'While I was in Saint-Audière Chaval came looking for you. He left a message with Simone.'

'He dragged her into this?'

'There was no one else he could trust. Jean Bernard and I were with you. He says the men in the hills are going to attack the railway sheds near Saint-Audière.'

'To avenge Lucien?'

'Yes. Chaval wanted to take you to them. He said he'd wait at the crossroads. I don't know if we're too late or not.'

Mitchell peeked through the window on to the street. Nothing appeared to be out of the ordinary. 'I can't. I have to go north.'

'But Lucien...'

'The boy ran! I couldn't help him!'

'These men don't have enough experience or weapons. You've been trained. If you can't help them, stop them. You're their only chance. You want them lying dead as well? What in God's name is wrong with you?'

Mitchell looked at her. She was utterly determined. Ever since he had been brought injured into her home the events that had unfolded had been at her insistence. 'Jean Bernard isn't the local co-ordinator. You are. He's the courier. That's why Chaval brought me to your house and not his. Because you'd know what to do,' he said.

'Are you going to help those men or not?'

He ignored her. 'That's why you came and got me out of prison, to make sure I took command here.'

She opened the door and looked back at him. 'Men don't always like taking orders from a woman. Help them. You owe us that.'

As Jean Bernard drove him out of the village towards Chaval's rendezvous, Mitchell checked the .45. Then he asked, 'Have you heard anything about the SS patrol?'

'Nothing. They must suspect that there are other survivors. The soldiers might have found the radio and weapons at the crash site. If they are in our area then it is a frightening escalation.'

'And Chaval and his chums won't make matters any better,' said Mitchell. There was a debt that had to be paid to those who had risked everything to help him. To abandon them now, no matter how urgent his desire to reach Paris, would have been a betrayal. And he knew that if London ever sent another wireless operator to this circuit then whoever it was would have no authority, and at worse, might be abandoned to their fate.

When they reached the crossroads there was no sign of the poacher.

'We're too late,' said Bernard. 'He'll be heading up the railway line the other side of that hill. Go after him. Stop them. Now is not the time for action.'

⋆

The doctor left him to clamber up the steep three-hundred-metre track across the hillside. Mitchell's feet blistered quickly and the strain on untested muscles tired him. His lungs burnt from the effort as he paused for a breather and looked back to see Jean Bernard's car turn on the empty road towards Saint-Just.

A cool wind buffeted his face as he scrambled up the remaining slope and when he crested the ridge he paused again to catch his breath and scan the ground in front of him. In the distance, a figure was making his way around a scar on the hillside that skirted the forest. The hulking size of the poacher with a rifle slung across his back could not be mistaken.

'Chaval!' Mitchell's voice reverberated down the hill and a moment later the figure stopped and turned.

*

Chaval set a hard pace. His grunting acknowledgement that nothing could have been done to save Lucien showed he had no ill feeling towards Mitchell, and it was soon obvious that he valued the Englishman's involvement in his quest to avenge the boy. Mitchell made no effort to dissuade him; the time was not yet right. Only when Chaval had taken him to those who were going to be engaged in the attack would Mitchell use his rank to stop them.

An hour later Chaval and Mitchell slid down the steep embankment of a railway track. As they reached the bottom Chaval quickly pulled Mitchell into a bush-covered ditch; he pressed him face down against the bank and whispered: 'Patrol.'

Mitchell had heard nothing through his laboured breathing. Remembering his training, he steadied his breath and ignored the pounding in his ears from his thudding heartbeat, and then he heard the unmistakable sound of boots along the stone-laid track. The two men were hidden from sight but they could have reached out and touched the jackboots of the passing soldiers, who smoked and laughed among themselves. The half-dozen men passed by. They didn't look to Mitchell like front-line troops.

Chaval's look of warning kept Mitchell silent but as the sound of the men's footfalls diminished and the soldiers disappeared around a bend, the big man sighed and spat. 'We've never had any trouble from patrols this deep in the countryside.'

'They didn't look that alert,' said Mitchell.

'Run like a rabbit across their path and see how alert they are. All right, come on.'

*

Half a dozen Maquis – rag-tag men, one of them black – lay in dead ground a few hundred metres from cavernous railway sheds, near a holding area with large mounds of gravel beneath an overhead hopper. They were further hidden from view by rolling stock and piled-high railway sleepers. Mitchell crouched, following Chaval down to the men once the poacher had given a low warning whistle. The men stared at Mitchell as Chaval whispered who he was. It seemed to offer the Frenchmen little reassurance and their expressions showed no sign of welcome. One of them, whose oil-engrained hands and stubble suggested he was a mechanic of sorts, appeared to be the group's leader.

'Christ, what are you doing here?' he said.

'This is the man I told you about,' repeated Chaval, nodding towards Mitchell.

'We don't need his help; he's caused enough trouble,' said another. This one was wirier and wore stained overalls beneath his workman's jacket.

'If you stay here the Germans will box you in,' said Mitchell.

'Piss off, we know this place,' said the mechanic.

Mitchell could see only four soldiers, who lazed around the railway shed taking a meal break. Laughter and muted conversations reached the waiting Frenchmen. Two of the soldiers kicked a football back and forth, yelping like kids as they dribbled and tackled. Mitchell saw that unlike the two other men, who were older, these were little more than teenagers. Which of the two pairs would turn out to be the most aggressive? Mitchell wondered. Were the older men die-hard Nazis or draftees who would rather be home with their families? It could be the younger ones who were keen to earn their spurs in this backwater posting.

'You're outnumbered,' said Mitchell.

The skinny one sneered. 'Fuck, he can't even count.'

'He's right,' said Chaval. 'We came in through the woods. There's a patrol moving down the tracks. Six of them. That's ten against your four and me and him.' It was obvious the *maquisards* hadn't known about the other soldiers and suddenly their bravado evaporated.

The black *résistant* turned on the mechanic. 'I told you we should have a cut-off ambush in place.'

'Shut up!' his leader hissed, but Mitchell could see he had no idea what to do next.

Mitchell squatted closer to the men. The black *maquisard* had a half-filled sack tied to his belt and, by its shape, Mitchell guessed it held explosives and timers. Each man had a rifle, except for the mechanic, who carried a British Sten gun. They were hopelessly ill prepared. 'Lucien died trying to help me so I'll do what I can to help you, but I'm not hanging around for that patrol to shove a bayonet up my arse.'

He gave them a moment to consider what he'd said and then turned and scurried away, crouching low, finding cover. Chaval spat. 'Idiots,' he said and quickly followed Mitchell. It only took a moment for the others to shove past the mechanic, who then had no choice but to follow.

Mitchell limped on his blistered feet and sank gratefully to ground in a brush-covered area a few hundred metres away.

Chaval was quickly at his side and watched as the others followed. As they sheltered, Chaval pointed out the men to Mitchell.

'Maillé,' he said pointing to the mechanic. 'Laforge,' the skinny railwayman; 'Bucard,' the black man; 'Drossier,' the one who might have been a clerk and least suited to the task – a thought Mitchell quickly dismissed as he considered his own background.

'I am Pascal. What do you have?' he said, pointing at the sack.

Bucard tipped out the contents: a few clips of ammunition, some detonators, a piece of plastique, a grenade. Meagre stuff.

'What's in those sheds?' he asked.

'A crane. They use it for lifting damaged rail tracks and tanks. There's only two of them in this part of the country,' said Bucard. That was a good target and Mitchell saw the value of destroying it. He fished out the cigarettes he had taken from Vincent in the cell and passed them to the men, who seized the chance for tobacco with murmurs of delight.

Drossier grinned. 'It's been a couple of weeks since we could get a ration.' Mitchell's gesture had softened them up. The men lit them, each smoking a lungful.

Mitchell poked a finger in the sack's contents. 'You haven't got enough here to destroy it.'

'It's all we could scrounge. It's what we have,' said Bucard.

'Back there I heard you talk about a cut-off ambush. Were you a soldier?'

'Yeah. North African Colonial Regiment at Lille under Général Moliné. We were fighting a rearguard for Dunkirk.'

'Don't listen to him. Most of them ran! The Germans came, they danced in the streets,' sneered Maillé.

Bucard lunged towards Maillé, who appeared unconcerned. Chaval easily stopped the ex-soldier. 'Don't let him wind you up,' said the poacher.

'Madame Bonnier's husband was at Lille,' said Mitchell.

'He was my company commander. He was killed there,' Bucard said, allowing his temper to cool.

Mitchell looked towards the mechanic. 'From what I heard those men bought time for the evacuation with their lives. Where were you when the fighting was going on?'

Maillé grimaced and was obviously shamed by the question. 'I did my bit. See if I didn't.'

Chaval grunted. 'You did well out of servicing Vichy cars in your garage, Maillé.'

Mitchell's guess at the man's occupation had been correct. 'I sabotaged as many as I could!' Maillé insisted.

The looks of those around him said differently.

'And my grandmother poisoned their bread in her bakery!' laughed Laforge.

Maillé had no choice but to swallow their taunts as Mitchell picked up the plastique. 'You can use this to destroy some track, but that's about it,' he told them. 'You have to get inside the sheds. Damage the machinery beyond repair. Otherwise, they just replace the parts you destroy. It's that simple.'

He had their attention now.

'What do you want us to do?' said Laforge.

'Create a diversion. I'll get into the sheds with Chaval,' he said, grabbing a fistful of dirt, 'and get this into the moving parts. We'll plant some explosives outside on the tracks, enough to cause the minimum amount of damage and make it look like an amateur attempt to disrupt the line. They'll have it replaced in less than an hour. You men go another couple of hundred metres down the track. You need to be well up on the embankment so you can escape. Fire a few shots and the patrol will double back and those four soldiers will join them. You distract and confuse them, and then pull back. We will meet back on the road to Saint-Just. Don't do anything clever or ambitious, just keep them pinned down while we do our job in the shed. It's a delaying tactic and as much as you want to kill Germans today, don't, or you'll have the SS swarming over everyone. Who has a watch?'

Bucard and Drossier raised their hand.

'Ten minutes,' said Mitchell. He pointed at Bucard. 'He's the soldier; do as he tells you.' He looked at the men expectantly and when they remained silent he shoved the explosive and timers beneath his jacket. He tapped Chaval on the shoulder and started back for the railway shed.

*

Mitchell and Chaval hunched down less than a hundred metres from the shed, its interior heavy with shadow where the lifting crane lurked monster-like. Both remained silent. Mitchell's nerves fed him a hundred things that could go wrong and his chest pounded with fear. He forced himself to slow his breathing and concentrate. He *had* to stay calm, he told himself. Blind panic would not get the job done. Chaval glanced at him with a look of concern. Mitchell nodded. He was OK. He checked his watch. Then the distant sound of sporadic gunfire started up along the track. The soldiers guarding the railway siding were momentarily stunned; then, quickly shouting orders to each other, they grabbed helmets and weapons and ran towards the inter-mittent shots.

He and Chaval moved quickly, skirting the shed's opening, cautiously checking that there were no more soldiers. Chaval stepped quickly into the shadows, followed by Mitchell. The poacher searched for and found a spanner and began unscrewing a feeder plug as Mitchell grabbed an oil-filling can, spilt a handful of the dirt from his pocket into it and then drained oil into it from an oil drum. Unconcerned about the spillage he plunged his hand into the can and stirred the gritty mixture.

'Chaval?'

'Ready.'

Mitchell poured the oil quickly. 'More oil!' he called.

Chaval took another oil can and filled it from the drum, then he too plunged his hand into his pocket and poured a fistful of dirt into it. Mitchell threw aside his own empty can and took Chaval's.

'You think this will work?' said Chaval.

Mitchell concentrated on pouring the oil. The gunfire down the track had increased. 'They start up and the grit will destroy anything that needs lubrication. They'll have to remachine everything.'

'Not round here they won't.'

'That's the idea. Go. I'll finish here. Put the explosive on a single track. Let's make them think that's all we wanted to do. It'll take their mind off the crane. I'll be right behind you.'

Mitchell replaced the feeder plug screw and tightened it with the spanner, then carefully wiped away any excess oil that had spilt on to the crane's bodywork. He wiped his hands, stepped back and let his eyes see what the Germans would see when they returned to the shed. Nothing looked out of place. He picked up the empty oil cans and put them back on the workbench with the spanner. Down the track, the gunfire had increased in intensity and, as he ran towards Chaval, who was already on his feet having fixed the explosives, Mitchell felt an overwhelming sense of desperation. Something had gone wrong.

16

They were well clear when the track leading into the siding for the crane exploded. The sudden crump made no impression on Mitchell's nerves. He had passed through the fear barrier and now ran on adrenaline. It was the silence from down the track that forced him to pump his legs and keep up with Chaval, who had glanced back at him. Mitchell saw in his eyes that he too feared the worst. As they got closer they darted to one side so they could make a different approach. Clambering up the embankment they pushed through the trees, then slowed to study the ambush site. The *maquisards* stood surrounding unarmed Germans. Two soldiers looked to be wounded, their comrades held at gunpoint with hands raised as Maillé and his men levelled their weapons. The raised voices of a furious argument between Maillé and Bucard could have been heard in London. As the two men swore and threatened each other Drossier and Laforge gathered the Germans' weapons.

'You stay out of this!' Maillé bellowed.

Bucard was dangerously close to striking the mechanic. 'You kill them there'll be reprisals!'

Mitchell and Chaval stepped right into the fray. 'What the hell do you think you're doing?' Mitchell demanded as Chaval once again got himself between the two warring men.

'We don't take prisoners! How can we? Are you mad! What do we do with them?' demanded Maillé.

'I told you to retreat once you'd attacked them! We needed a diversion!'

'He wouldn't! He said we could take them!' said Bucard, turning away in disgust.

'And we did! It's time we taught them a lesson,' said Maillé, looking from one man to the next. Laforge shrugged, Drossier averted his eyes. 'Fuck you,' said Maillé to the men and cocked the Sten gun, turning towards the fearful Germans.

Mitchell snatched it from his hands as Chaval manhandled him away. Maillé cursed and put up a feeble resistance but the big man pointed his own weapon at him. 'I will settle this, Maillé. You want to kill in cold blood? I will be the first, eh?'

'How many Germans in this area?' said Mitchell. 'I saw some in Saint-Audière.'

'Maybe another twenty or so at La Basson. Wehrmacht conscripts mostly.'

'There are SS out there as well,' said Mitchell, looking at the German prisoners, seeing how much of a threat they might pose. The two wounded men were only slightly injured and were supported by a comrade either side. That left six able-bodied men who could rush them. Mitchell considered them – two might be foolhardy and dangerous enough: a young lieutenant; and a sergeant who looked to be the most professional of them all – an older man who had probably fought on the front line at some stage. They had been part of the patrol that had gone down the line.

'You know somewhere we can hide for a few days?' Mitchell asked Chaval.

'Yeah. Anyone comes looking they won't find us.' He nodded towards the nervous prisoners. 'And them?'

'How far for them to walk anywhere?'

'Fifteen kilometres one way to Saint-Audière, twenty-odd to La Basson the other.'

Mitchell looked at the *maquisards*. 'Anyone search them?'

It was obvious no one had yet got round to stripping the Germans of the yokes that held their bayonet scabbards and ammunition pouches and the lieutenant still wore his belt and holster.

'Laforge, Drossier do it,' said Mitchell. He turned to Chaval. 'All right. Get going. Check the way ahead is clear; we'll follow. Take Bucard.'

'You can manage this?' asked Chaval.

'I'll send them on their way without boots and trousers. That'll slow them down.'

'All right. We will go no further than a kilometre ahead, OK?'

Mitchell nodded and Chaval and Bucard turned away. Mitchell covered the surrendered Germans as Laforge and Drossier did a quick body search, instructing the Germans to drop their equipment yokes and for the lieutenant to unbuckle his sidearm.

'Take your boots off. Your boots,' said Mitchell to the uncomprehending prisoners. He pointed downward with the Sten gun and they quickly understood and began pulling off their boots. Mitchell glanced back to see the direction Chaval and Bucard had taken. In that moment the sergeant looked at his officer, who nodded. Laforge and Drossier were talking like two men out on a fishing trip, carelessly not watching their prisoners as they bent and gathered weapons. Arms full, their own weapons slung on their shoulder, they walked back towards Mitchell. No one saw where it came from but the sergeant suddenly had a knife in his hand and as Mitchell turned his attention back to the men, the sergeant ran at him, blocking the lieutenant from his view. It was a sudden and frightening silent attack. As the sergeant lunged at Mitchell the officer bent to retrieve his fallen sidearm.

Mitchell spun around. 'Look out!'

Blind panic and fear swept over the two *maquisards*, a stumbling confusion that flashed by in seconds. Drossier and Laforge fumbled for their weapons, throwing themselves aside as Mitchell raised the Sten gun. Sergeant Major Laughlin's training kicked in. Mitchell had field stripped the Sten a hundred times. Blindfolded. Found every push/pull spring. Had been warned time and again that the Sten could be an unreliable weapon, as unreliable as Mitchell's desire to kill. It could misfire. Time and again. Jam. Thirty-two bullets snuggled each other in the magazine, side by side. Dirt could clog it. The spring in the magazine could be damaged. But this weapon did not jam. Time and again he had been drilled. He pressed the selector button to automatic, and as his finger squeezed the trigger gunfire shattered the air. His hands vibrated with the staccato energy that tore through the barrel. Rate of fire: 550 rounds a minute. Time and again Germans fell. He fired – and kept firing. Something shut down inside of him as the blurred images pirouetted in front of him. Bullets tore into the sergeant's chest; another caught his face and his skull shattered. As he fell the lieutenant was suddenly exposed. He was levelling his pistol. In time-stopping moments the soldiers around him fell. Some were standing rooted in shock as Mitchell's fire caught them. Some were shot in the back as they turned to run, others where they stood. Mown down around the lieutenant who somehow was not hit. He fired twice, one of his shots wounding Drossier. No sooner had he done so than Mitchell's sustained fire tore into him. He arched, legs buckling, arms thrown wide as he crashed to the ground. A part of Mitchell's brain calculated the rate of fire and the time it took to kill the ten men. A fraction under four seconds.

Chaval and Bucard had turned and sprinted back at the first shots, stunned to see the last few men going down. The position of the bodies showed them what had happened.

'Christ. He executed them,' muttered Chaval.

Neither Maillé, Laforge or Drossier had responded quickly enough; they looked dazed and then Drossier sank to his knees gripping the top of his bloodied shoulder. Maillé, who had been disarmed by Mitchell, had cowered, hands over his head. Mitchell stood stock-still in shock, the Sten still smoking in his hands. The weapon had fallen silent, the thirty-two rounds in the magazine fully used.

For what seemed a long time no one moved, no one spoke. The Germans were all dead, sprawled across the clearing. It was eerily silent.

Chaval reached Mitchell as Bucard went forward and picked up the fallen knife. 'Pascal?' he said gently, and then again: 'Pascal?'

'I hear you,' said Mitchell, finally coming back to himself.

'You all right?' said the poacher.

Mitchell nodded as Bucard tucked the sergeant's knife into his belt.

'Drossier?' said Mitchell. His ears were still ringing, his voice barely a whisper.

'A flesh wound,' Laforge told him.

The men looked at Mitchell.

'What the fuck do we do now?' said Drossier.

Maillé picked up the officer's small Walther automatic and gave the wounded Drossier a gentle kick. 'Stupid bastard. You didn't search them properly.'

'Pascal?' said Bucard repeating Chaval's question. 'What do we do?'

Mitchell gazed at the slaughter and then something kicked in and whatever it was that had shut him down released him. He collected his thoughts.

'Bury them,' said Mitchell.

'Bury them? Bury them?' Maillé snorted. 'We don't have time for that! And with what? Our bare hands?'

'Down the track,' said Mitchell. 'We take them down to the sheds.'

'We can't carry all these men, Pascal,' said Bucard reasonably.

'I know. Down at the shed, there's a …' he struggled to find the word he wanted, 'A… handcar,' he said in English, then remembered. '*Voiture de chemin de fer.*'

'And then?' said Laforge.

'Just do as I say,' said Mitchell.

★

Hours later Waffen SS-Sturmbannführer Ahren Brünner pulled the goggles off his dirt-streaked face and stepped down from his open-top vehicle. He examined the area around the torn rail track – there was no other sign of damage. Behind him his motorized company stayed alert; some scanned the hills and trees in case of ambush. Men and vehicles were spread out tactically as his men searched the area. He took a good look around but the damage seemed minimal.

'Major?' one of his men called.

He turned towards the soldier, who pointed to a group of his men halfway down the embankment in the trees where they had pulled aside the cut branches that had camouflaged the overturned handcar.

'There's a lot of blood on the handcar, sir. Looks as though the men were killed and taken somewhere.'

'There's no sign of fighting here,' said the major. 'No bullet holes, no signs of explosions other than one section of track.' He walked further along the rail yard. 'No, it's the other way around. They were killed elsewhere and brought here.' His eyes scanned the area until they fell on the gravel hopper, its lid open, the hopper empty.

'Here!' the major commanded. 'Dig here.'

The men nearest to him began scraping away the piles of gravel with their rifle butts; others grabbed shovels from their vehicles. As the gravel in the mound tumbled a dirt-laden hand flopped out.

17

Mitchell and the others walked steadily behind Chaval, who led the way across the rough animal tracks that he knew so well. The stress of their action at the railway shed and the subsequent killing of the German patrol began to slowly sap their strength. Mitchell was hobbling but he was determined not to be the one to call a halt. It was the poacher who signalled them to rest in a sheltered enclave of ferns and boulders.

'We stay here. Move on tomorrow.'

Mitchell had no desire to talk to the men and found himself a comfortable patch a few metres away. He unlaced his boots and peeled away the blood-encrusted sock. The cool air bathing his sore feet was a welcome relief. The men sat drinking and muttering quietly among themselves. Drossier's wound was only superficial and Laforge passed around a few cuts of meat, cheese and stale bread. The warmth and comfort offered by a fire would have to be forgone. Mitchell ran through the events in his mind. How had he come to kill so many men? It was as if someone else had kept their finger on the trigger. The images of the men's bodies being struck and torn were still vivid; they still nauseated him. Bucard sidled up and offered him a half-bottle of some liquid obscured by its dark green glass.

'It helps,' said Bucard. When Mitchell didn't accept, he pushed it into his chest. 'When I first went into action I was too scared to even throw up but after my first killings... it got easier... with practice.'

Mitchell took a sip and felt the brandy burn his throat and then settle its warmth into his knotted stomach. Bucard nodded.

'Good. Don't let the others see what you're feeling. Maillé was right... Some of us did run at Lille... but not all of us.'

He tugged out a dry pair of socks from his knapsack and took the sweat rag from his neck. 'Rinse your feet, wipe them dry with this and wear clean socks. A soldier has to look after his feet. Didn't they teach you anything in basic training?'

Mitchell gratefully accepted the gifts and the advice. 'I never got that far,' he said.

Bucard smiled. 'You'll learn quickly enough. You're not doing too badly.' He made his way back to the other men as Mitchell attended to his feet. When he had done as much as he could and strapped his boots back on he stood and slung the Sten over a shoulder. The men looked up at him.

'I'm going back to Saint-Just. Jean Bernard has arranged for me to go north.' He stood a moment longer and, with a final nod in farewell, started walking.

'North? What about us?' said Laforge.

Mitchell stopped. He had been briefed never to ask favours of men he was to lead in the field. An invitation always worked better than a direct order. 'If you want to come with me then you're welcome. If not, they'll send someone else,' he said. As he turned his back the others clambered to their feet.

'Screw that, Pascal. We stick with you,' said Drossier.

There was a murmur of assent from the others. Bucard's grin had 'told you so' written all over his face.

'As long as you'll have us,' said Chaval.

Mitchell looked at the sorry-looking bunch. 'You're welcome,' he said and walked away.

*

At Saint-Just Gendarme Marin and Gustave stepped into the street from the bar at the sound of rumbling vehicles in the distance. They looked up the street where the trucks had spread out. Marin stared across the open countryside. The SS were experts at boxing in a village and securing every escape route. A line of soldiers was advancing.

'What the hell are the SS doing down here?' said Gustave.

Somewhere in the distance the shrill repeated blasts of a whistle brought the SS troopers down from their trucks and they quickly began taking over the street.

Marin swallowed nausea that stung the back of his throat as he looked up at Juliet peering out the window of her upstairs bedroom. Fear etched her face. She held Marin's gaze and saw the look of resignation cross his features. He shook his head. And when screams from the top of the village were followed by the sharp crack of rifle shots she turned and yelled for her daughter.

Terrified, Gustave ran back inside his bar. Marin stayed where he was and fatalistically reached for his sidearm.

18

Chaval led them across the hills. Drossier slowed their pace; his injury still hurt like hell and the uneven terrain jolted the wound. Mitchell let the soreness of his blistered feet chastise him like a flagellant monk's penance. The pain was there to be endured.

As they crested a rise Chaval and Mitchell stopped dead in their tracks. The others quickly caught up.

'Mother of Christ,' said Chaval as they gazed at the pall of smoke that hung in the distance.

They stumbled, lungs heaving, into the ruins. Laforge sank to his knees; Drossier retched. Bucard and Chaval took a few more steps into the carnage that had once been Saint-Just.

The village was destroyed. A blanket of death covered it like the thick black smoke still swirling into the sky. A dead horse lay in its traces. Personal possessions from the houses had been thrown out on to the street – including Simone's piano, smashed and on its side. Jean Bernard's car still smouldered, its paint stripped to bare metal. Bodies of men, women and children lay where they had fallen – shot at random as they tried to escape. Dogs too. Killed for sport. Or were they simply victims of the sport of shooting the villagers? Eight men hung from the village trees, among them Marin and the bar owner, Gustave.

'Juliet! Simone!' Mitchell called.

There was no response. He and Chaval walked among the dead looking for the brave woman and her daughter. After identifying several of the corpses they stopped, gripped by despair. Mitchell looked at the hanged men.

'Cut them down!' he said, his voice hoarse from smoke and grief. Turning his back on the *maquisards'* efforts to lower the men Mitchell stumbled into the remains of the burnt shell of what had been Juliet Bonnier's house. Charred timbers glowed and acrid smoke stung his eyes. Here and there items had partially escaped the blaze. A half-burnt child's doll. A dress hanging forlornly from the upstairs room whose floor had caved in and where the wardrobe now balanced crazily half in space half on the broken floor. Simone's bicycle, a twisted skeleton. Her school notebook with its singed pages turned by an invisible hand. The same breeze wafted the stench of death in from the street.

Something moved on the periphery of his vision. He shifted his weight quickly; broken masonry barked his shin. A brick-built coal bunker's door swung open and a smoke-blackened and exhausted Juliet, Simone and Jean Bernard emerged. At first they didn't see him, their gaze held by the horror of the scene. Mitchell stumbled towards them, relief forcing another cry from his parched throat. They turned and Simone ran the few paces and wrapped her arms around him. He embraced her, pushing his face into her blackened hair.

'Thank God,' he whispered.

The child kept her face buried in the rough comfort of his jacket. 'Pascal... Pascal... they didn't stop shooting.'

'All right, all right,' he murmured, stroking her hair. He raised his eyes to look at Juliet. She was holding it together – just – nodding that she was all right, but tears had already cut through the dirt on her face. Jean Bernard went among the corpses in the forlorn hope that someone might still be alive.

'They're all dead,' Maillé called. 'Don't waste your time.'

Jean Bernard ignored him.

'Doctor, you can't help them,' the mechanic called again.

Jean Bernard swung around, tears streaming down his face. 'Shut up! Leave me alone!'

Maillé looked aggrieved, then shrugged and turned his attention back to helping Chaval lower one of the hanged men.

'What do we do now?' Juliet asked Mitchell.

*

They salvaged what supplies they could find. The indifferent wind had picked up, already pushing at their backs, urging them to leave the desolation.

'This is your fault, Pascal. They won't stop hunting us now,' said Maillé, throwing down a blanket roll and a haversack. He pointed at Juliet. 'She said she saw the bodies of the men you shot. In the back of a truck, covered in dust. They dug them out, for Christ's sake, and then they came here to find you.'

Chaval finished packing food supplies. 'Shut up. He had a reason to kill; you'd have done it in cold blood. And he saved your life, you stupid bastard.'

Mitchell ignored the belligerent Maillé as he looked through the clothing that Juliet had salvaged for Simone. 'Take only what you can carry. These are fine. This, and this, leave here. Keep the warm jacket – you'll need it.'

'I don't want any more to do with this,' said Maillé. 'Let's hoard what we can. We bury the dead. The SS won't come back again. Why risk moving on?'

Mitchell checked his own knapsack and tucked the automatic into his waistband. 'You give up now and it means they died for nothing.'

'It means the SS won!' Maillé spat.

'You give up now it means they died for nothing!' he said again, punching the lesson home. 'You survive. You take the fight to them. You do it for whatever reason you want. You decide. You take responsibility for what you do! Like the rest of us.'

Maillé's arm swept across the village. 'They had no choice!'

Mitchell squared up to him. 'What? You thought fighting them was some kind of game? Well, take a good look around! This is what it's about! You thought the SS wouldn't come here? They were always going to come!'

'Sooner or later, this would have happened,' said Juliet. 'We knew the risks from the beginning.'

'Because they believe they're right,' said Mitchell. 'Whatever they do they believe they're right!' He threw one of the captured Schmeissers into Maillé's chest and glared at the uncertain survivors. 'You want to stay with the dead, that's up to you. All of you. I came here to do a job – with or without you.'

'Pascal, we will go with you as far as we can, as long as we can,' said Juliet.

'She's right,' said Jean Bernard, 'there's nothing for us here. We're your group now.'

Mitchell looked at the huddled survivors, all anxious in that moment for someone to take responsibility. 'We all have a score to settle,' he said. 'Chaval will take us across country away from the roads.'

Mitchell looked at the fearful child and extended his hand with a reassuring smile. She placed her hand in his. Mitchell turned away, the others following him towards the darkening sky; the billowing smoke curled behind them.

19

Chaval's knowledge of the countryside kept them away from roads where the enemy might be patrolling. On the second night, as drenching rain beat down, he brought them to a blanched stone hut; its terracotta patina-tiled roof glistening in the wet suggested it would be warm, but the stone walls held their chill more readily than the forest. At least it offered a sanctuary and would keep them dry, and despite the pungent odour of animals that had been kept there the group flopped down exhausted.

Once Simone and Juliet had fallen asleep Jean Bernard eased himself towards Mitchell as he attended to his bloodied feet. 'You must let me look,' he insisted and helped peel off one of Mitchell's socks. 'I have powder that will dry those burst blisters and stop them from becoming infected.' He scrabbled in his haversack.

'Bucard told me to keep them dry but I haven't managed that with the wet ground.'

'Of course.' The doctor began tending the wounds. 'Bucard is a good man. He is like Chaval. Strong men who do not complain.' He sprinkled powder on to Mitchell's foot. 'Like you.'

'Oh, I complain all the time but it's in my head,' said Mitchell, wincing as the doctor trimmed off a small piece of torn skin.

The doctor smiled and then lowered his head to the task at hand. 'You know, Pascal, what happened... you... you must not blame yourself. The SS either came to us by chance or they believed we were responsible. Either way... you understand? Like Juliet said, they were always going to come. Sooner or later.'

Mitchell fell silent. He glanced across to where Juliet and Simone slept entwined for warmth. 'She's a remarkable woman.'

Jean Bernard did not bother to raise his head. He knew whom Mitchell meant. 'And has great courage. I have enormous respect for her. We have known each other since childhood.'

'You're a lucky man,' said Mitchell quietly, the comment slipping out carelessly.

Jean Bernard smiled. It was him that Juliet and Simone snuggled close to for comfort during the cold nights. 'She turns to me for warmth at night because she feels safe. There's nothing more to it than that.'

Mitchell's face betrayed his embarrassment. 'I meant no offence, or to imply –'

The doctor raised a hand, cutting off any further apology. 'None taken, my friend. Believe me, her husband was a man above the rest of us. No one else could take his place.' He pushed the tin of foot powder and surgical scissors back into his haversack. 'There, your feet will feel a lot better. I wish I had something like it for your grief, Pascal. Get some rest. Now it is we who look to you to keep us safe.'

After three more days of hard going low cloud lifted on the sixth morning and they heard a spotter plane criss-crossing the sky in the direction of Saint-Just. Despite the distance, they were fearful that any movement might attract attention and, on Mitchell's insistence, stayed huddled in the forest's dank chill for the morning. Mitchell had kept himself apart from the group when darkness fell as he tried to plan how best to proceed once he had reached the group of *maquisards* at Norvé. Before the massacre, Jean Bernard had got word to them that an agent had survived the air crash; it followed then that they would have advised London. Fear of discovery was now very much in his mind. He had been lucky so far and much of that luck was due to the training he had been given. As rushed as it had been something must have sunk in, a second nature had developed, ingrained by the instructors' constant barrage. It was the killing that haunted him. The blurred images of the soldiers twisting and turning and the disembodied sense that it was someone else doing the shooting. His reason had deserted him, abandoning him to a visceral instinct for survival. No matter how analytical his life had been up to then, that had all changed. He was no longer the man he had been. And that made him fear for himself. He now bore the burden of his own massacre. Killing the sergeant and the officer might be justified but the unarmed men were victims of what, he did not know – perhaps a part of him that crawled back into the cave like a creature that lurked in shame but was ready to lash out again.

Despite the relentless pace of their march everyone was holding up well but it was obvious to Mitchell that the enforced rest was welcome. It had become a matter of pride to him to keep up his dogged pace in front of the younger men. Chaval was the closest in age to Mitchell but the poacher's lifelong labour in the fields and foraging across hills gave him a natural resilience and strength that the middle-aged mathematician envied. Despite his aching muscles, Mitchell knew that he had lost weight and was fitter than he had ever been. Chaval gathered wild berries and mushrooms to supplement the food they had salvaged from Saint-Just but never was the thought of roasted rabbit or the comfort of a fire so tempting. Neither were enjoyed.

On the seventh morning, shivering from the night's dampness, Mitchell hunched behind a ridge of trees with Chaval. The low cloud threatened drizzle which kept the spotter plane out of the sky.

'We're twenty kilometres from Norvé but we will have to take a big detour south of that place,' said Chaval as Mitchell peered through his field glasses. 'Saint-Hilaire is a field hospital and vehicle depot so it's regular army down there. We might not get to Norvé by nightfall. Another cold night out here and it will start to wear some of us down.'

'We're going too slowly. Six days and we've covered, what? Seventy, eighty kilometres?' said Mitchell.

'It can't be helped if we are to stay off the roads.'

There was no argument to be made. 'Then we have to push harder. I want us with the Norvé group by nightfall,' said Mitchell.

Chaval shrugged. 'We can risk cutting across open countryside. There's a small bridge across a river that I was going to use. Barely wide enough for a horse and cart so there would be no German vehicle patrols on it but if we get our feet wet downstream then we could cut off a couple of hours.'

Mitchell slapped him on the shoulder. 'Skin is waterproof.'

★

They clambered down the hillside, zigzagging as Chaval followed animal tracks. At times the steepness of their descent slowed them further. Mitchell urged them on, refusing time to stop and rest. Simone's youth served her well; it was the adults who felt the knee-jarring strain. Maillé complained but Drossier kept him in check. He of all people, he told Maillé, should be the one to bitch because he was wounded. The bickering went on for an hour until Mitchell called a halt and threatened to gag Maillé, tie him to a tree and leave him behind. Before the mechanic could complain at such treatment Simone asked, with the innocent smile of a child assassin, whether it would help if she carried Maillé's haversack for him.

They went on in silence until they reached the narrow river. It was thirty metres across from bank to bank.

'I'll go across first,' said Chaval. 'See how deep it is. Shouldn't be more than waist high.'

'And that'll come up to my chest,' said Laforge.

Simone grinned. 'Walk on tiptoe.'

'We're exposed here,' said Mitchell. 'Stay in the treeline and then once Chaval is across, Laforge and Bucard go next to help give covering fire if it's needed. Then Jean Bernard with Drossier. Maillé and I will cover this bank. Then Juliet and Simone together. Maillé, then me.' He nodded to Chaval. The men spread out to give themselves a clear view of the riverbank up- and downstream. Mitchell swore quietly to himself. It felt as though they were in the middle of nowhere but the German depot posed a risk even if it was now five kilometres or so away. He watched as Chaval gingerly stepped into the water and found his footing. The water flowed quickly and buffeted his legs. Once or twice it looked as though the big man might trip, which worried Mitchell: if someone that size was struggling then the others might be in danger. He crouched and ran to Juliet, slipping off his haversack; then he undid the length of coiled rope attached to its straps.

'The current might knock Simone off her feet. I'll carry her pack. Wrap a length of this around your wrists. If she stumbles you'll have to steady her.'

Juliet nodded her understanding, doubled the rope's length and fashioned a two-metre-long tie between them. At the centre of the river the water had reached Chaval's thighs. Mitchell was thankful it was not as deep as he feared. The poacher reached the other side and waved on Laforge and Bucard, who stepped tentatively into the water; Chaval crouched on the far treeline covering them. Jean Bernard followed, striding confidently into the water, following the line the others had taken as he gave a steadying hand to Drossier.

'All right,' Mitchell said to Juliet and Simone. 'Take your time. Find your footing and be careful you don't twist an ankle on any boulders. Slow and steady.'

Mother and daughter edged into the river and Mitchell saw at once that the girl was struggling. She was, as Mitchell suspected, too slender to fight the current. She almost went down but Juliet hauled the rope, pulling her upright. 'Get in there and help them,' Mitchell told Maillé.

The mechanic hesitated, then slung the Schmeisser and shifted his pack as he waded in. He seemed strong enough to push against the current but he had stepped wide of where the others had crossed. His foot must have found a dip in the riverbed making him slip; he floundered and went down. The current dragged him but he twisted, raising an arm to throw himself face up and then kicked and struggled his way to the riverbank twenty metres further downstream, his cry of alarm sounding too loud in the settled quiet. Even the swirling water was no louder than an urgent whisper. Jean Bernard broke cover and ran to Maillé to haul him ashore as Chaval began wading into the water to help Juliet. Mitchell was already moving forward, raising an arm to silently halt Chaval's advance. He needed the poacher to guard their crossing. The double pack and the Sten gun were cumbersome but he shifted their weight so they helped balance him. Simone was shivering, clinging to her mother, stopping both of them from moving. Juliet had turned their bodies to offer the least resistance to the flow. Mitchell reached them, braced himself against the insistent tug of water and stood between them and the rushing stream, easing their passage. Slowly they made progress until they were close enough for Chaval to take a couple of his big strides into the water and lift Simone clear. Juliet stumbled and instinctively reached out for Mitchell, who pulled her to him. Their faces were close; perspiration plastered strands of her hair to her cheek. He muttered encouragement and steadied her. As she pressed against him she smiled gratefully, whispered her thanks and then concentrated on reaching the bank and Chaval's outstretched hand. A tantalizing thought struck Mitchell, because it seemed in that instant that an improbable intimacy had passed between them.

20

The chained dogs' barking alerted those inside the small château. Lights appeared behind the opened carved doors as a man came to the entrance carrying a shotgun. Jean Bernard gently called his name and was beckoned forward. After a brief whispered conversation he turned and gestured the others to join him from where they were hiding behind the château's outbuildings. This was the first step, Mitchell thought, in testing the security of the Norvé cell. If the rot started here then anyone being pushed further up the line to Paris was in danger of betrayal.

Mitchell and Jean Bernard were ushered down a long corridor in near darkness, following the oil lamp carried by the same man who had greeted them in the courtyard. Olivier Gaétan stood waiting by the warmth of a roaring log fire nestled in a medieval fireplace with an ornate mantel, typical of the period when the house was built. The grandeur of the edifice belied the worn rugs and frayed furnishings that told the story of a minor aristocrat who had known better times. Gaétan too seemed typical of the kind of man who would live in such faded glory. He was in his sixties, trim white moustache, a tall angular body ramrod straight with pinched features, who appeared to look down his beak of a nose at the unkempt men who had been ushered into his private quarters.

'Monsieur Gaétan, this is the man I told you about when the aircraft crashed,' said Jean Bernard.

The old patrician glanced at the clock on the mantel. 'You were not expected, doctor,' he said testily. 'But by the look of you, it is a matter of some urgency.'

The man who had ushered them in looked to be more of a groundsman or gamekeeper than a house servant. His rough demeanour told Mitchell that he was a man capable of shooting other than a few game birds on the patrician's estate.

'There are five other men, a woman and a child with them. I have them in the scullery,' he said.

Gaétan nodded. 'Feed them and then hide them in the cellar beneath the workshop.'

'It is Juliet Bonnier and her daughter,' said Jean Bernard.

Her status as co-ordinator for the area around Saint-Just seemed to carry no weight with Gaétan. He acknowledged the information and dismissed the gamekeeper with a nod.

'Saint-Just is destroyed,' said Jean Bernard. 'Retaliation for German soldiers being shot.'

'And who did the shooting?'

'I did. I am Colonel Pascal Garon,' said Mitchell. 'It was self-defence,' he added. 'The men I was with, those who accompany us now, they would have been killed had I not done so.'

'Perhaps it would have been less costly to have let them die. I lost three good men ambushed by the Germans who were waiting at the drop zone when your plane did not arrive,' said Gaétan. He shrugged. 'The fortunes of war, colonel. Or perhaps the message was intercepted.'

'Or perhaps there is a leak,' said Mitchell.

The patrician seemed ready to accept such a possibility. 'No matter how they came across my men, we can ill afford to suffer such losses. There are few of us.'

'And your work here is much valued,' said Mitchell.

'Do not patronize me, colonel. We play a small part but it is for the glory of France and its future. It is not for the glory of Mr Churchill or the likes of Englishmen who think of themselves as pirates and regard this war is an adventure.'

'There are men and women of other nationalities, Monsieur Gaétan, fighting this war. Including Frenchmen who are willing to return to their homeland and risk sacrificing their lives. And Madame Bonnier should be accorded respect and some privacy with her daughter. She has already endured some indignity since we left Saint-Just. It is not easy for a woman and a child to have the seclusion they need when travelling.'

Olivier Gaétan looked as though he was about to argue but something changed his mind and he nodded. 'I will see that they are given a room to themselves. Now, colonel, how may I be of service?'

A sudden wave of tiredness swept over Mitchell and he barely resisted the urge to step closer to the fire and sink into one of the overstuffed settees. It might be only for a brief time, but the château offered safety. He shook his head. 'I have to get into Paris.'

Gaétan stretched an arm against the mantel and gazed into the flames. His tone softened. 'I am doing everything possible under difficult circumstances, Colonel Garon. I will have to get a courier into the city and pass you up the line to a safe house. Let us discuss it further in the morning.'

It was a dismissal.

*

The men sat around the kitchen table eating their first hot meal in days. A cauldron of broth sat on the cast-iron stove that warmed the room. Chaval told them that Juliet and Simone had been given food and taken to a room in the château. The poacher ladled out bowls of the soup for the doctor and Mitchell. The hungry men had already torn into two loaves of rough grain bread. Mitchell and the doctor followed suit. Between mouthfuls, Jean Bernard spoke quietly to Mitchell.

'Your plane might have been shot down through sheer bad luck, but if there is a leak in this circuit's security then we must be wary of him using men we do not know to get you into Paris.'

'I was thinking the same thing,' said Mitchell. 'There's one place in the city I might be able to use.'

Jean Bernard ate hungrily. 'We can play along with his suggestion. My sister has an apartment there. No one knows about it. Not even Gaétan. I've never warmed to him. He thinks France was lost back in the eighteenth century when the Bastille was stormed. We are all peasants as far as he is concerned. He hates the left and thinks communists hide behind every gun in the Resistance. Were it not for his wife he would be even more insufferable.'

So the old man wasn't brittle because he lacked feminine company. He was simply a miserable bastard.

The shotgun-carrying servant looked in. 'You finished?'

The men grabbed the last of the bread as Mitchell raised the bowl to his mouth and swallowed the remaining broth.

They were led back across the courtyard, their guide ignoring the barking dogs. He swung open one of a pair of wooden doors that led into a workshop. The space to one side was shared by three vehicles. One of the cars had cobwebs stretching between the wheel and the wheel arches.

'An old Delage,' said Drossier with undisguised envy. 'Christ, he must have had some money to buy that.'

The second car looked to be polished and kept in working order. It was the more practical of the two, a four-door Citroën Traction Avant favoured not only by the French police but since the Occupation, also by the Germans. Maillé grunted with some satisfaction and pointed to the third car on blocks, a dust-smothered black vehicle with a thin red bloodline that swept along the vehicle's curvaceous lines. 'He likes his cars,' he said.

'And those 402 Peugeots weren't bad either,' added Drossier. 'When this war's over I'm going to have myself one of those.'

'Once a thief always a thief,' said Laforge.

'I only stole from those who could afford it. Never from comrades or the poor.'

Maillé ran a finger along the car's bloodline and cupped his hand to look through the shadowed window. 'You'll be lucky to own a bike when this is over, Drossier. The Germans will take everything and what's left the rich will keep.'

The first car was clearly less practical to run than the other, but it occurred to Mitchell that the patrician had somehow managed to secure a petrol ration from the Germans. And if that was the case what was he giving them in return?

The servant bent down at the back of the workshop and moved some toolboxes to one side. Pressing his hands against the wooden floorboards he found a latch and then lifted a trapdoor.

'There are straw mattresses down there and a bucket for a toilet,' he said, handing Bucard the oil lamp. 'There will be food and drink in the morning. God willing, that is. I hope to God you haven't brought the SS down on us.' He waited until Mitchell and the men descended into the cellar and then he lowered the trapdoor.

The oil lamp revealed scattered straw mattresses, stained and lumpy, and a pile of hessian sacks instead of blankets. The air below ground was musty and chill, yet each man went to a mattress without fuss or complaint and prepared for a night's sleep. Even Maillé remained silent. A slow, creeping fear trickled like water in Mitchell's stomach. Was this the kind of place his daughter was being held at in Paris? Had the Gestapo cast her into darkness and left her to imagine what terror lurked there?

'Leave the lamp burning,' said Laforge as he pulled sacking over himself.

No one disagreed.

21

Madame Louise Gaétan had served on the front line in the Great War when she was a twenty-six-year-old, strong-minded – wilful, her father had said – young woman determined not to be seen standing in the wings of a nation's greatest conflict. Now the former volunteer Red Cross nurse refused to be cowed during this, the second conflict twenty-eight years later. She ladled porridge from the stove, wiped her hands on her apron and then broke a dozen eggs into the skillet. A younger woman poured milk from a flagon into tin cups that sat on the table before each of Mitchell's group. Juliet Bonnier had offered to help but was gently shushed by the matriarch and told to eat. The cooked oats were spooned with a dollop of strawberry jam from one of the jars hidden behind the false wall of the larder.

'Marie, fetch more plates for these eggs,' she instructed the young housemaid. 'We hide what we can from the Boche,' she explained, raising a hand as if in confession. 'Ah, I know they are Nazis now, but to me, they will always be the Boche. Marie, hurry with those plates. They take everything. We keep our chickens in a pen in the forest; there are a couple of pigs there as well. We won't starve. Not in the country. And they know, the Boche, of course they know. But they benefit so we will be seen as collaborators when this is over.' She shrugged. 'I tell you this so that when the communists come to take everything someone can speak up for us. Good girl,' she said as Marie laid out the plates and gave each uninvited guest a clean knife and fork.

'Why do you think you will be called a collaborator, madame?' said Simone. 'I saw the photograph on the hall table of you in a nurse's uniform.'

Madame Gaétan touched her warm hand on Simon's upturned face. 'Child, I take eggs to the wounded German soldiers. Most of them are still boys. God shows himself in wounded men. And our faces are reflected in His. I take them eggs and they give us some gasoline. Then I am allowed to take what food I can to the orphanage in town. I buy from the black market and give it to the children. Here and in Paris. In the city I try and convince the Germans to help us with the needy children and I attend parties where rich women who enjoy protection and favours feel guilty enough to contribute.' She shrugged. 'Your brave mother will explain the consequences of our actions. How we survive and what we do can easily be twisted.'

'Where is Monsieur Gaétan?' said Mitchell.

'My husband does not eat in the kitchen with lesser mortals.' She beamed. 'And that includes me. I'm just a woman.' She laughed, and threatened the group with her ladle. 'You men will appreciate us one day.'

'One day when the earth stops turning,' said Juliet.

'Yes,' said Madame Gaétan. 'We are kept in our place. We stand in kitchen doorways and listen to what you men plan to do. And then you turn to us to carry messages in our camiknickers. We feed you, hide you and nurse your wounds.' She smiled again. 'I know about you, Madame Bonnier, and your late husband. I thank God for men like him and more especially for women like you.'

'These are good men,' said Juliet.

Madame Gaétan looked them over. 'I can see that,' she said.

The man Mitchell mentally called the gamekeeper put his head inside the room. 'Colonel Garon, if you please.'

Mitchell saw the eggs being slid on to the plates. He stood reluctantly and followed the servant down the corridor and into the room he had visited the previous evening. Olivier Gaétan got up from one end of a long refectory-style table where his own breakfast had been served and beckoned Mitchell to the other end where a map was laid out. 'Colonel, I have marked out a route to get you to the outskirts of Paris. And I have had a message sent to London. Another wireless operator is going to be brought in by Lysander. That person will accompany you to Paris.' He handed Mitchell a communiqué. 'I have been given no further information other than that the aircraft will in all probability be here tomorrow night. The weather looks good but we must pray we can get in and out before the Germans find us at the landing zone.'

'Thank you.' The older man seemed more forthcoming this morning. Perhaps, Mitchell thought, it was enthusiasm brought about by being given responsibility to help achieve a successful mission. Sitting virtually alone in a rambling house in the middle of the countryside could easily dull the senses and drive a man's instinct into self-preservation.

'You know Paris?' said Gaétan.

'I lived there.'

'When was the last time you were in the city?'

'I left in '41.'

'Then things have changed. There are some you should know about.' The patrician traced a finger across a Paris street map. 'You know about Avenue Foch?'

'Yes.'

'Very well. SS-Brigadeführer Karl Oberg commands Paris. The man most feared on his staff is SS-Standartenführer Heinrich Stolz. He pursues the Resistance in Paris like a hunter after his prey.'

At the mention of Stolz's name, Mitchell felt his heart skip a beat but he remained silent, not wishing to draw attention to his own mission to find and rescue his daughter.

'Now,' said Gaétan. 'You know the police are complicit. You can trust not one of them. Some may profess to being able to help, and some, I admit, are genuine. But unless they are vouched for you do not ask anything of them. Commissaire Fernand David is in command of the Brigades Spéciales at the Préfecture de Police. Here, opposite the Hôtel-Dieu. And Rue Lauriston. Sixteenth Arrondissement, yes?'

'I know where these places are,' said Mitchell. He realized that the older man was exerting his authority by displaying his knowledge, but he wished the man would come more quickly to the point, whatever that might be.

Gaétan glanced at him. 'Colonel, you are stepping into the lion's den without the same protection that Daniel had. The good Lord does not necessarily protect the righteous. However, I believe a man, righteous or not, who is patient and studies his enemy carefully might find an angel here and there to guide him.'

Mitchell smiled. 'Point taken. What about Rue Lauriston?'

The patrician accepted what appeared to be a vague apology from the Englishman. He wondered what this man was really made of. If he was anything like the other agents who were simply keen for sport against the Nazis then he could soon became little more than prey when faced with the enemy's overwhelming strength. 'Number 93 is a base for ex-criminals,' he went on, 'Frenchmen who work for the SD. Stolz has men like them all across the city.' He moved his finger across the map. 'Here, though it is not yet confirmed, there is a rumour that the Milice are preparing to move into the old communist party HQ at 44 Rue Le Peletier and also at Rue Monceau. You see, colonel, there are eyes and ears everywhere. Neighbours betray each other with anonymous letters, trumped-up grievances to settle old scores. Hundreds have been carted off to prisons and camps.' He lit a cigarette and blew the smoke into the air, studying it for a moment as a man studies the clouds that nourish his imagination. 'So I ask myself, why do you people come to risk capture and death?'

'My mission is to get someone out of Paris.'

'You will need a lot of money, colonel. Bribery and the black market can devour money faster than the Germans devour our food and drink.'

'I have enough and there will be more arriving with the new wireless operator.'

'Very well. But be warned: do not have too many five-thousand-franc notes. The Germans are suspicious of large denominations. These are small details that can have you arrested and questioned.'

Mitchell nodded.

'Who is this person you wish to get out of the city?' said Gaétan.

'I can't tell you anything more.'

'Until you learn to trust me?'

'Yes,' said Mitchell, holding his gaze.

'And what more could my wife and I do to gain your trust other than by how we live? My man here is a widower and his daughter works in our home. That's four people who would die at the hands of the Germans if you are discovered here. More if they unearth my group.'

Mitchell had wanted to question Gaétan's honour and trust and it had happened without him trying to do so. It was an opportunity worth taking. 'Where is the Englishman who disappeared? Guy Neuville. It was your circuit that got him into Paris.'

Gaétan showed no surprise at the missing agent's name. 'I do not know.'

'If he had been taken then word would have got out. If the Germans didn't seize him then where is he?'

'As I said, colonel. I do not know.'

'I think you do. And when you decide to tell me then we can move ahead in mutual trust.' Mitchell turned for the door, deciding to end the meeting, taking back control. No longer a man on the run but an English agent declaring his intent to move forward with purpose and to challenge those who thought they had authority over him. His only regret about the meeting was missing the freshly cooked eggs.

22

'We tend to prefer sending those we know as first choice,' said Colonel Beaumont to the young woman who sat before him. 'And I knew your father terribly well. He was a wonderful surgeon and his untimely death saddened me when I heard.'

Virginia 'Ginny' Lindhurst was a plain-looking twenty-four-year-old. She would not stand out in a crowd. Her almost spinsterish demeanour hid her tenacity and intelligence. It was a mantle as effective as any cloak of darkness described in the mythical legends she had enjoyed reading as a child. And it was just such a cloak that she always imagined hiding herself in when faced with danger. It gave her strength, and meant she did not have to confess her fear of violence to anyone. 'Luftwaffe bombs do not distinguish the great and good from the rest of us, colonel. At least he died in the operating theatre trying to help others. There's some comfort to be had in that,' she lied. There was no comfort at all to think of her beloved father blown to pieces. But after the bombing raid, the grief had turned to... what was it? Almost relief, she decided. She was free. Her mother had died prematurely several years before and her committed surgeon of a father saw little of his only child once the war started except to discourage any thoughts she might have had of volunteering for anything that would take her into the rough company of the common soldier. It was a known fact that nurses were easily seduced by men returning from the battlefield, he had said unfairly. Well, now that he was gone it didn't matter what he said. She was free.

'When you go across town to those… Baker Street Irregulars, as I call them, Major Knight will give you a thorough briefing. I will be party to the operation, of course, but it's his show. On certain matters, we and SOE do not always see eye to eye, but I have agreed to allow them to send you. You did well on your training course, my girl, and you are a first-rate wireless operator. Just what's needed for our man there.'

'And you said I would be taken quite a way south of Paris.'

'Yes. We have a group there at Norvé. Rather, the French do. So far they have looked after our people. It was they who sent a message telling us that the man we thought dead was alive and making his way to Paris. Originally we sent a wireless operator to a different group south of Vichy. They were a small group but SOE believed they would have proven effective. Sadly, that town has been destroyed and the group scattered. But the good news is that the man we wanted to get into Paris survived.'

'I was told in my briefing that his French identity is Pascal Garon.'

'Yes, that's correct.' Colonel Beaumont fussed over some of the papers on his desk. It was a simple means of buying himself time to find the correct words without alarming the young woman too much. He had known her since she was a child, but was able to separate the sentiment that was engendered from the necessity of sending her. She had proved to be the best on her course. Her mother being French meant she was bilingual, her French that of a native. Still, the girl needed to know the worst-case scenario if she did not already.

'Ginny, we lost one agent in Paris some time back, and our wireless operator there has gone pretty quiet except for some probing messages about when we are sending a replacement. These were out of his designated transmission time. So we are worried. If he had been captured and made to transmit under duress he would have given the usual warning code. No such signal has been received. Pascal will try and find him and also complete his mission in the city. But because of our uncertainty, he needs his own wireless operator. I will confide this much to you. Pascal's wife was taken by the Gestapo and executed. We were sent photographs of her being shot. It was this that motivated Pascal into going back to Paris for us.' He tidied the papers and rested his hands on them. 'My dear, should anything go wrong –'

'Colonel, I know the risks. Please don't worry about me,' she said quickly.

A little too breathlessly, thought Beaumont. But, he convinced himself, nerves were the order of the day for someone so young being sent into harm's way.

'I am confident that I can do my duty to the best of my ability. I won't let you down,' she said with a confident smile that disguised her own trepidation.

Beaumont gave her an equally reassuring smile, thankful that he had not had to share potential horrors with her. The reality of what could befall those sent on a clandestine mission was always acknowledged, but seldom discussed further. Fear was a key that could open a terrifying world in the imagination.

'Tomorrow night, then.'
'Yes. Tomorrow night.'

★

Mitchell's men kept out of sight in the workshop cellar and were allowed outside briefly so they could smoke. Should a sudden raid take place they didn't want any tobacco fumes lingering in the enclosed cellar which could seep through the floorboards into the workshop above. Drossier had admired the classic Delage and then sat in the Citroën's driver's seat. Even after a lifetime of hard work and petty theft, he would never have enough money to buy such a car. His fingers traced the numbers on the beautifully designed black-faced Jaeger rectangular speedometer. He played his hands over the steering wheel. As he drew the rough tobacco into his lungs he wound down the window and rested his elbow on the sill. It was not hard to imagine driving down a country lane on a summer's day with a girl in her frock that would settle above her knees. He leant over to the passenger side and opened the glove compartment. He found driving gloves and a half-leather-bound silver cigarette case. He opened the case and saw it was almost full of cigarettes. He eagerly tugged half a dozen free and tucked them away.

'What are you doing?' said Chaval, who had come up for air from the cellar. 'Come on, get out of there. Pascal wants us to trap rats in the barns.' He saw the cigarette case. 'Where did you get that?'

'It was on the seat,' Drossier lied quickly.

'Put it back. Don't take anything. Not even a cigarette. We don't steal anything from our countrymen. Nothing. Understand?

'Yeah, yeah, of course. Like I said, it was just on the seat. I'll put it in here for safekeeping.' He opened the glove box and closed it, then slid out of the car, the cigarette case already palmed and in his pocket.

*

Mitchell sat at the kitchen table with Juliet and Jean Bernard and unfolded a railway timetable. 'I want you and Simone to take a train into Paris. Jean Bernard, you will accompany them and take them to your sister's. At least you will be safe there. There is nothing more either of you can do with me from here.'

'Your sister's?' said Juliet to Bernard. 'How do we know we will be welcome?'

'She's a widow with a young boy a few years younger than Simone. It is a good idea. Pascal is correct. You will be safe,' he said.

'I have a wireless operator coming in tomorrow night. Gaétan says he has already sent a man into Paris to arrange a safe house,' said Mitchell. 'I have other plans for the wireless operator. But if there's a leak and there's an ambush at the landing zone then I want Juliet and Simone far away from Norvé.'

'Very well,' said Jean Bernard.

Juliet looked from one to the other. 'You are making plans about me and Simone and you don't ask my opinion. We are safer in the countryside. There are fewer Germans and less chance of being stopped.'

'And if you arrive at another village? How long before someone learns you are from Saint-Just? How long before someone who's afraid of SS reprisals betrays you? No, Juliet, I'm sorry but I believe the city gives you a chance to be lost in the crowd,' said Mitchell.

'He's right,' said Jean Bernard.

'Very well,' Juliet said. 'But if we are stopped and questioned? We need a good story.'

'*Colis familiaux*,' said Mitchell.

Jean Bernard grinned and nodded. Juliet looked uncertain. The doctor quickly explained. 'You've never lived in the city, Juliet. Food is always short. Even a cat or a dog is not safe from going into the pot. The Germans allow anyone in the city with relatives in the countryside to receive food parcels.'

'I have money to buy food from Madame Gaétan,' said Mitchell. 'We might even get her to give us a couple of chickens in a cage. Jean Bernard's sister can legitimately receive food parcels.'

'But Simone and I, what part can we play in this? What would we be doing in Paris?'

'You and Jean Bernard are engaged to be married. You're a widow with a young daughter and here's a professional man who has asked you to marry him. Once you're there I want him to get in touch with a doctor I knew and who I hope still works at the American Hospital. I'll give you a note by way of introduction. The hospital is still open, still being manned by American doctors. Most of the Americans living in Paris after America declared war in '41 were rounded up and sent to Frontstalag 122 internment camp.'

A look of incomprehension creased their faces. Mitchell realized that living in the small, insular community of Saint-Just they knew little of life beyond their own area. 'Fifty miles north of Paris at Compiègne,' he explained. 'Many were then repatriated in exchange for Germans in America but there are still some working in Paris. But once you're with Jean Bernard's sister you and Simone will be safe and it will allow

Jean Bernard to find work quickly. There is to be no mention of me being here. Not yet.'

'All right. When do we go?' said Juliet.

'Tomorrow. There's a train from Vichy that gets into Norvé at eleven. You'll be in Paris before curfew.'

'And the men?' said Jean Bernard.

'We keep this to ourselves for now. I'll get the old man to use his car to take you to the station. He'll give us a driver who'll know a way to avoid patrols.' He looked at the woman and man who had risked everything for him. 'I have things to do before I get to Paris. Once I get there I will be in touch.'

'When should I tell Simone?' said Juliet.

'Leave it to the last minute. I'll see what food I can buy. It might not be much but it will help.' He covered her hand with his own to reassure her. For a moment she looked in silence at this man who had fallen from the burning sky, and then gripped his hand tightly.

23

Olivier Gaétan posted men as lookouts on the approach to the château. He had sent others to reconnoitre the proposed landing zone for the Lysander that night. Madame Gaétan decided it would be she who would drive Juliet and the others to the station. The local German patrols knew her and would be more likely to believe she had relatives travelling than one of the men. The patrician's wife understood Simone's insecurity at being taken away from the Englishman with whom she had obviously formed a bond. It must have felt as if she were losing her father all over again. It had taken Mitchell and Juliet a half-hour to comfort the girl. Thankfully Jean Bernard's presence finally helped assure her that where they were going would be safer and Mitchell promised her he would come to her in Paris. Once she had been mollified Madame stepped in and asked her to help choose what could be packed into the suitcase that they found in an attic room. Madame Gaétan had put together a selection of food she had been storing. Two jars of jam and a piece of smoked ham wrapped in cloth, along with a full wheel of cheese.

'Will you really come to us in Paris?' Juliet asked Mitchell. 'Or are we unlikely to see you again?'

He watched as she folded her few clothes salvaged from the ruins of Saint-Just. 'The moment it is safe I will come to you,' he told her.

She stopped what she was doing and turned to face him. 'I know nothing about you, but you have been kind to us. Simone and me.'

'I destroyed everything you knew,' said Mitchell.

She thought on it for a moment and nodded. 'Every action has a consequence, Pascal. We all took our chances.'

They both fell silent and Mitchell wished he could walk with her, away from the tenseness of her departure for Paris and the impending night flight. He found himself saying, 'My wife was shot by the SS in Paris. She was in the Resistance. The Gestapo are holding my daughter somewhere. I have a mission to complete but I also want to find her and get her home.' It sounded more like a confession than an explanation.

Juliet could not mask her shock. 'Pascal,' she whispered, distraught. 'I am so sorry.'

It served no purpose for him to explain any further but he did anyway. 'I escaped from Paris two years ago. We were separated. I don't know how that happened and sometimes I wonder whether she even wanted to go to England. The marriage had its problems; I can't deny that. There was something wild in her. I was a simple mathematics lecturer. What she saw in me I'll never know.'

'Then one day I will tell you,' said Juliet, and kissed his cheek.

★

Mitchell was thankful it was a clear day and that the sun offered some warmth. As the Citroën drove away Juliet and Simone waved their goodbyes through the rear window until the car turned out of sight down the country lane.

'Better that she has gone,' said Chaval as he stepped from the workshop to stand at Mitchell's shoulder. 'But she is a strong and brave woman. I hope Jean Bernard knows what he's doing by taking her to Paris.'

No one had been told exactly where Jean Bernard was taking them. Mitchell turned back towards the house. 'He knows what he's doing, don't worry.' There was time to kill before Gaétan's men left for the landing zone and Mitchell did not want Chaval and the others kicking their heels. 'How many rats did you catch?'

'Four. Nice slinky brown ones. I had Drossier gut them like you asked.'

'All right, get the men together and find some twine and a needle with a big enough eyelet. It's time to stitch them back up.'

Chaval raised an eyebrow and shrugged. Whatever the Englishman had in mind probably had something to do with teaching the men how to stitch wounds. Obviously, he was expecting trouble.

*

Drossier and Laforge gazed intently as Mitchell instructed Chaval to peel back a rat's skin from its gutted chest and stomach cavity.

'Maillé, give me that plastique,' said Mitchel.

The mechanic handed him the palm-sized slab of explosive. 'Now, we mould it,' Mitchell told them. 'Just like you do when you pack it on a rail track, only this time...' he eased the elongated shape into the rat's carcass, '… we shape it inside the rat. And then you can attach a short length of fuse with a number twenty-seven detonator crimped on one end and a copper tube igniter on the other. Then you place one of these in a locomotive's coal bunker and when the dead rat is shovelled into the furnace, the fuse ignites and the plastique explodes.'

'Killing the driver and the fireman,' said Maillé.

'Killing the German driver and fireman,' said Mitchell. 'We use these for the German freight trains going back to Germany. But we can also use the rats in factory boilers. And don't forget to use them for a diversion and controlled explosions. If you don't use a lit fuse' – he reached for one of the timers – 'use one of these. These give you time to plant the explosive and be far enough away when it goes off. Shove the time delay fuse up the rat's arse into the plastique and then stitch up the vermin so it kills its Nazi brothers.'

Bucard grinned. 'I like it. I knew some of the demolition men laid booby traps when we fought the rearguard but this is neat. No one picks up a dead rat but sooner or later the Germans will realize what they might be.'

'If they do then they'll spend a lot of time being cautious. We soak up their security. And then every time they find a dead rat it will slow them down. All right, stitch this one up and then, Bucard, you and Drossier pack another carcass, Chaval, you and Laforge and Maillé do one and then all of you have a go individually,' Mitchell instructed them. He gestured to Maillé. The mechanic sidled over to him. 'That Peugeot on the blocks,' said Mitchell. 'Have you had a look at it?'

Maillé shrugged. 'It looks all right. I reckon the old man didn't want to run more than one car.'

'When you're done here, put your eye over it. Don't let any of his men see you. See if it will go.'

'We going to nick it?' Maillé said with knowing grin.

'Just have a look and let me know.' Mitchell turned away. At least, he thought, he had given Maillé a sense of purpose. He hoped that that might soften his inherent belligerence.

★

Gaétan found Mitchell sitting outside the kitchen, the chair rocked back against the wall, his face turned to the sun.

'Everything is set for tonight. I have alerted my men,' said Gaétan.

Mitchell nodded. He was lucky to be getting a flight and the wireless operator it brought. Only on nights immediately before and after a full moon was visibility good enough for the pilots to navigate their way. And there were few nights each month when flights could operate.

'Where is your transmitter?' said Mitchell. 'In the château?'

'No. It is the same type your people give your operators. We strap it to a bicycle and move around. It makes it more difficult should they use radio detection vans in the area. But so far we have been fortunate. The vans are further north, nearer the bigger towns. Not so many here, but we do not take unnecessary chances. When you are in Paris with your operator, be vigilant. The Germans are very good at detecting signals. They use grey baker's vans with the direction-finding equipment inside. That much we know. And once they track a careless operator, then many people can be rounded up.' He gave an almost imperceptible shrug. 'Many have been.'

'I'll be careful.'

'Of course you will. But it is easy to make a mistake. And there are enough people who will notice.'

'As I said, I have lived in Paris, Monsieur Gaétan.'

'Oh, and what do you think has happened since you were last here? You think you know how to live in an occupied city? Trust me, it is the small things that can trap a foreigner. How do you like your coffee?'

Mitchell frowned.

'Come now. How do you like it? I will go and fetch it for you myself. Give me your order. Humour me.'

'*Noir*. I drink coffee black.'

'Then you would be immediately suspect, colonel. No one orders their coffee black. There's not enough milk. Not in Paris. There is only black coffee. Eh? Small things, my friend.'

It was a good tip and Mitchell filed the information away. 'Perhaps I shall stick with alcohol,' he said, trying to distract the old man.

'Then you know the clubs and bars. A perfect place to make contacts and a breeding ground of informers.'

'I believe I still have friends in the city.'

'Then forget them,' the old man said. 'Forget their names. Wipe them from your memory. If you're picked up the Gestapo will soon get them from you.' He sighed. 'And we too will be dead.' He patted Mitchell's arm. 'You don't need me to tell you any of that. One's nerves can be fraught at times like this. And I worry for my wife. She takes great risks. Forget I said those things.'

'I take them as fair warning.'

Gaétan nodded. 'The landing zone will be ready to be lit an hour before midnight. They think there will be some passing cloud but there will be enough moonlight for the pilot to find us.'

'Then I'll brief Chaval and the others.'

'You will go with my men?' said Gaétan.

'Of course. You don't?'

'If I am caught red-handed then the circuit is finished. If my men are taken and tortured then I can proclaim my innocence and say that they had a grudge against me. That they must be communists working for me without me knowing it all these years. You see. We need to lie like thieves to survive. We all take our chances and we all dread the knock on the door.'

'They knock?'

Gaétan smiled. 'Quite so, colonel.'

'Jean Bernard and Juliet?' said Mitchell.

'Safely aboard the train. They went through the security checks without any trouble. And I have sent one of my men into the city to secure you a safe house.'

'Thank you.' Mitchell still planned to make his own arrangements but Gaétan was the key Resistance controller in this area and it served no purpose to openly challenge his authority. 'How many men tonight?'

'If yours are to accompany you then only three more. One of my men will take our horse to carry the weapon boxes from the plane.'

'And the *chef de terrain*?'

'My most trusted man, Edmond.'

'The one with the shotgun? I call him the gamekeeper.'

'Which he is. And why he is in charge of meeting agents and supply drops. A gamekeeper is like a doctor: they have a permit to be out after curfew. He will go ahead and see the lie of the land. If stopped by a patrol then he will not be arrested and can warn the others. He has been with my family since he was a boy.'

'And you trust him implicitly?'

'Of course. With our lives.'

'So he has information about your operations?'

'Naturally.'

'Then, like you, he would know where the missing Guy Neuville is.'

'I told you. We do not have this information.'

Mitchell eased the chair down on to all four legs as a cloud passed before the sun. 'Monsieur Gaétan, you and your most trusted man would not allow a British agent to simply disappear. Your lives would be at risk. So you would track him down and kill him to protect yourselves or you would have hidden him somewhere with a means of checking on him. He's a man who might be worth selling to the Germans when the bad times come. And if you betray him you keep all your other men in play.' He stood and faced the patrician.

'I would betray him?' Gaétan said indignantly. 'You think me without honour?'

'Perhaps we would all betray each other if enough pain was brought to bear. Why do you think I sent Juliet, Simone and Jean Bernard ahead of the agent being flown in? I don't want them knowing of each other's existence. The less one knows the better. They are out of the way. But if the enemy puts a gun against your wife's head then you would tell them everything. We are all human, and we are all fearful. Courage will take us only so far. Once the drop is over tonight I need to know where he is and you will tell me.'

24

They waited in the chill night air, their eyes adjusting to the shapes of the land. The darkened track they had travelled down cut through the high hedgerow banks; it was too narrow for a lorry to pass along, so German infantry would have to advance on foot if the *résistants* were to be discovered. But Mitchell and the others had seen and heard nothing since they had been in place. They lay on the cold grass, cramped but uncomplaining. The L-shaped landing lights had been laid out but were not yet lit. No one spoke, every man listening for any unusual sound that might travel and which would indicate the presence of a German ambush.

Mitchell gazed into the night sky. It was nearly time. He felt the edge of tension claw at his stomach. He was nervous not only for those on the ground but for the aircraft. The pilot needed 150 yards for his landing and this field gave him that with another fifty to spare. He would turn the aircraft at the end of the beacons and keep his engine running because the Lysander's batteries were prone to fail if the engines were switched off for too long and could drain quickly when restarting. Mitchell's briefing before his ill-fated parachute drop had told him all he needed to know about the skill required and risks involved. Flying low, the pilots would navigate by torchlight with a map folded on their lap. There was room enough for one passenger behind them. Two at a push. He imagined the agent sitting silently with complete trust in the man up front. He would not have spoken to the pilot, who would not have been told anything about the person clutching a heavy suitcase containing their wireless. And no doubt, Mitchell thought, the passenger would know the slow-flying aircraft was a sitting duck. A matte-black-painted duck hard to detect in the night sky but with a large Perspex cockpit that could shine in the moonlight. Mitchell lay on the dew-laden grass remembering how anxious he had been when told how and where the plane he was supposed to have been on would cross the Normandy coast. How low it would come across German held-territory, searching for familiar landmarks, and how, south of Chartres, somewhere near Blois the Special Duties pilot would fly over the River Loire and turn east to find his landing zone in the pitch darkness of the French countryside with little more than a dozen flickering beacons to land by. How any pilot did that confounded Mitchell. His own mathematical skills might have lent some weight to the pilot's expertise, yet they were an abstract science: he could not imagine himself adrift in the night sky. No more, he corrected himself, than he could have imagined himself adrift in occupied France. His reverie was broken by the distant clattering sound of the Lysander's engine. Mitchell and the men readied themselves to light the beacons. As Mitchell stood clear of the hedgerow facing the approaching sound the men ran forward, each to a flare lantern. Mitchell tilted the torch and aimed its beam skyward, pressing out the Morse call sign to confirm the pilot's destination. The letter P for Pascal blinked up into the darkness, his finger pressing and releasing the switch. Dot dash dash dot. His inner ear heard the rhythmic sound as surely as his finger had been on a Morse key: *di dah dah dit, di dah dah dit*. The engine pitch altered.

'Now!' hissed the *chef de terrain*. The meadow flickered into light as the men ignited the oil lamps. The aircraft appeared far more quickly than Mitchell had expected. In what seemed no time at all a shadow descended, landed, growled and the gull-winged blackbird was upon them. The pilot wheeled the aircraft, the backdraught from the propeller blowing the headgear from some of the men. Exhaust fumes stung eyes and throat. The deafening engine silenced any further shouted commands as Mitchell ran to the port side where the passenger ladder clung to the fuselage. Someone was already climbing down, a belted raincoat flapping about slim ankles, a beret tugged over neck-length hair. It was a woman, Mitchell realized with surprise. He had not expected a female operator to be sent. He knew it made no difference – there had been women at Bletchley and on his training course – but it still gave him a mild sense of shock that a woman had been suddenly cast into the darkness of this inhospitable place. When she was halfway down the ladder he reached up and relieved her of the suitcase. Its thirty-pound weight at an awkward angle above his head nearly wrenched his shoulder. It almost slipped from his grasp.

'Careful!' the woman insisted. She jumped off the lower rungs on to the ground and faced him. She was young but her eyes challenged him as she reached for the case he was now holding securely.

'I've got it,' he said, raising his voice above the aircraft's roar.

One of the men clambered up the ladder, leant in and hauled out a wooden box. He passed it down to another, repeated the retrieval again until three wooden boxes were on the ground, then closed the passenger cockpit. Men grabbed the boxes' rope handles and ran for the edge of darkness behind the aircraft. There would be weapons, ammunition, money and cigarettes in them.

Mitchell held her elbow, moving her away as the pilot raised a hand and eased the throttle. It had taken less than three minutes to unload his cargo. As the silhouette lifted into the sky the flare path was extinguished and darkness reclaimed the landing zone.

The silence made their ears ring and as the men gathered in their lamps he stopped himself from shouting. 'I'm Pascal,' he told her, guiding her down on to the track where one of the men was already strapping the wooden crates on to Gaétan's horse.

'Ginny Lindhurst,' she answered with a welcome smile but then quickly corrected herself. 'Thérèse Fernay,' she said, using her cover name. 'I really can manage the suitcase.'

As the gamekeeper marshalled the men from the meadow Mitchell guided her to where bicycles leant against the bank. He secured her suitcase under the spring clasp on the luggage rack of one. 'I'm sure that's so, but can you ride a bike?'

She answered his teasing question with a frown. 'I think I might remember how.'

'Good. We have ten miles to go before dawn and the going is rough.'

'I didn't expect it to be anything else,' she said.

Mitchell felt an immediate warmth towards the slightly built girl. She was obviously not as frail as she looked.

25

Ginny awoke to the idyllic sound of a farmyard chorus. Sun streamed through her bedroom window. Chickens clucked in the courtyard below along with the muted voices of the men going about their chores. The flight had been uncomfortable, the evasive flying at times tiring. She had managed to keep her anxiety hidden but before they had taken off from Tangmere on the Channel coast near Chichester she had hoped an opportunity might arise to go into town: a final walk down an English street would have been a welcome distraction to subdue her mounting tension. Naturally, though, she had been confined to base for the preceding hours. She had flourished during training but the beckoning unknown had made her nervous. Now she was here though, she resolved to dismiss the fear, pushing it far from her mind, refusing to see her mission as anything other than a challenging extension of her training and her own determination. She smiled as the tantalizing smell of cooked eggs wafted up from below. She could have been at home.

She rinsed her face and stepped into a floral frock, pulling on a cardigan against the chill morning air. When she entered the kitchen she found a matronly woman wearing an apron dishing out eggs and homemade bread to a half-dozen scruffy-looking brigands around the table. Mitchell sat at the head of the table, his back to her as she entered, but one of the men, huge by comparison to the others, quickly wiped a hand across his matted beard and stood up.

'*Bonjour, mademoiselle,*' said Chaval.

She smiled as the others stood. Mitchell turned, egg dripping down his chin quickly wiped by a napkin.

'Please, don't stand. It's not necessary,' said Ginny.

'My dear,' said the matron, wiping her hands on her apron and quickly taking Ginny's hand in her own. 'Let these scoundrels at least behave like gentlemen. I kept you a place here, next to the stove. I am Madame Gaétan. This is my home and you are welcome for as long as you wish to stay with us.'

'Thank you, madame. You are most kind.'

The men sat back down, but they couldn't stop themselves glancing repeatedly at her: she was so slender, so young, hardly cut out for such dangerous work.

Only Mitchell knew her real name. Though introductions weren't strictly necessary, it was possible that knowing the man at her side might save her life if trouble suddenly struck; and so he would introduce her, but give as little information as possible. 'Thérèse,' he said cautiously, catching her eye and seeing that she understood. 'Let me present you to the men who were with me last night.' The same demand for security extended to Ginny as well as the men. If she were captured it served no purpose for her to have the men's full names spilling from her lips.

Mitchell pointed to each man in turn and used only their Christian names. Laforge half stood and bobbed as Mitchell named him: 'Reynard.' Chaval stood to his full height again and nodded, locking his dark eyes on the pale girl: 'Victor.'

Bucard understood what Mitchell was doing. He pushed back his chair. 'I am Henri.'

Mitchell pointed to Drossier. 'Camille.' Who nodded.

Finally, he indicated Maillé, who bent his head to his plate as he mopped up the yolk. 'Nicolas.'

'Mam'selle,' said the mechanic. He ran his tongue over his teeth. 'Better eat Madame's breakfast. You look as though you need feeding up.'

The men grinned. Ginny felt the blood creeping up her neck but spoke quickly to hide her embarrassment. 'Nicolas, it looks as though you have already eaten mine. I see your trouser belt is on its last hole.'

Bucard spluttered as Maillé's mouth fell open in shock. Drossier gave him a friendly slap across the back of his head. 'She's right. You were snorting like the horse last night. You need to lose some weight.'

The men murmured their pleasure at seeing the usually belligerent Maillé meet his match. Mitchell smiled and held out her chair. 'I think you will fit in very well, Thérèse.'

Madame Gaétan slid some eggs on to her plate. 'And for you, my dear, there are more if you want them.'

Laforge was about to protest but Madame shot a look at him. Defeated, he ran a finger around the plate and scooped up what little yolk was left.

★

After breakfast, Mitchell walked with Ginny past the château's barns to find a quiet corner in the run-down walled gardens. They settled on an old bench and for a moment he studied the young woman who was prepared to risk her life with him. Back in England, if he'd seen this plain but fresh-faced girl he would have thought her a kindergarten teacher. She appeared naïve and at times hesitant, but he knew that if she had passed through the rigorous training then both Colonel Beaumont and Major Knight must be confident in her ability. She fumbled for a cigarette and offered him one. He shook his head as she placed one between her lips. He wondered whether she would ever wear make-up to try and make herself look less plain because it was no secret that German soldiers were more likely to let an attractive woman through their checkpoints without too much fuss. He reached for a box of matches and lit her cigarette.

'You don't smoke?' she asked.

'I packed it in. Decided I didn't want to be dependent on them. Nothing worse than craving a cigarette.'

As he watched her exhale, a touch of a smile crinkled the corner of her mouth. 'It was the thing to do when I was an undergraduate. Almost an obligation.'

Mitchell stopped himself from asking her which university she had attended. The next question would be to query what degree she had taken, one thing would lead to another and pretty soon he would know where she was born, who her parents were, where she lived and whether she had ever fallen in love. He had no desire to know anything about the girl who might soon be dead, quite possibly because of his own actions. The life expectancy of a wireless operator was estimated to be six weeks.

She caught his stare and wondered whether he doubted her ability. 'I know I look a little on the frail side, obviously, but

I am quite strong, you know. And I'm a more than a decent shot. I came first in pistol shooting on my course.'

'Well, that's a long way better than me,' said Mitchell, giving her a reassuring smile.

'What I'm saying, Pascal, is that I don't have any qualms about using a gun if I have to. Just because I'm a girl.'

'I have always believed it is better to avoid trouble if at all possible, but I know how circumstances can inflict violence on us. It can happen quickly and when you least expect it.'

She shrugged and, raising her face to the sun's rays, blew more smoke towards the blue sky. 'I do hope the weather stays good,' she said. 'I could do with a spot of colour on my face. Make me look less like I've crawled out of a crypt.'

Mitchell studied her a moment longer. She had ignored his comment about potential violence. Was that deliberate? Despite her declaration that she was a crack shot, shooting at cardboard targets was not the same as facing down a man intent on killing. He realized he was analysing her and that wasn't his prerogative with someone trained and sent by SOE or MI6, but his life might depend on this slightly built young woman and perhaps she or one of her instructors had been careless. 'You could draw attention to yourself if you have a packet of cigarettes in public. Women aren't permitted to buy tobacco and they don't get a tobacco ration.'

'Not sure anyone mentioned that.' She looked embarrassed for a moment. 'Training course was a bit of a rush. Well, then.' She slipped a couple of cigarettes out of the packet. 'For later,' she said. And handed him the packet.

'London sent enough money to keep us going for a long time. There's a change of plan, Thérèse. I am going to send you ahead of me to Paris.'

'Oh,' she said. This was unexpected. Colonel Beaumont had instructed her to go to Paris with Pascal Garon as his wireless operator and secure a place to transmit on her schedule. But then, everything changed in the field. That had been drummed into her. Adaptability was the key to being selected. 'All right. You tell me what it is you want me to do and I'll do it.' She smiled and ground out the cigarette.

'Are you aware the powers that be believe there to be a leak over here?'

'I'm not sure that was spelt out. I was told the operator in Paris had not transmitted according to his schedule.'

'Well, there's a leak somewhere. As far as I'm concerned I don't trust anyone here until they prove themselves and even then I shall be looking over my shoulder. Monsieur Gaétan has sent a man ahead of us to Paris to find a safe house. Rather than go where they suggest I'm sending you to an apartment that I am familiar with.'

'And am I to meet someone there?'

'No, the apartment has been empty for a while. It's on the top floor of a four-storey building. There's a skylight in the roof and on the far side of the building is a fire escape should anything ever go wrong. It was a place I used before I escaped from Paris.' He waited for her reaction. She reached the obvious conclusion.

'And so there must be someone else living there now,' she said.

'No. It was owned by a great-aunt of mine. She died more than twenty-five years ago. I used to visit her during the last war when I got leave. She was a bit of a mad hatter but she took a shine to me in my English officer's uniform. She left it to me in her will. I lived there before I met my wife and I hid there before I got out. If anyone asks, you have rented the apartment from a salesman you met in Lyon.'

She took it all in and nodded. 'Give me the key and address and I will make my way into Paris and wait for you.'

'The key is pushed behind the front-door frame. You need a hair clip or a penknife to get it out.'

'All right. How will I get to Paris without you?'

'By train. It's the least problematic.'

'When?'

'Tomorrow. Top floor, apartment eight, Rue de Loret, Ninth Arrondissement.'

She nodded.

'There's a cheese shop on the ground floor and there used to be food shops up and down the street. I don't know what's left there now. Once you are in the apartment look across the street. There's a bar. The front window has a broken blind. If it is dropped down then go to the owner, he's a Corsican and sometime brothel owner in the rooms at the back. If the blind is down it will mean I have telephoned him because something important has cropped up or there's danger. He owes me a debt that he knows he can never repay and I trust him. I'm going to instruct Chaval to do the same. We will need a means of communication.'

'I understand.'

'Take a trolleybus or vélo taxi from the station. It will be a few days until I can join you. Familiarize yourself until I get there. On the third day and every day afterwards until I arrive, go to the Café La Pointe Saint-Eustache at eleven. Don't stay any longer than fifteen minutes. Twenty at the most. If trouble comes your way there's an exit through the kitchen that leads to an alley. That will take you to a main street and plenty of narrow passageways between the buildings. You would have a chance to run from there. If things go very badly wrong then I can't help you. You're on your own.'

Ginny smiled bravely. 'I know.'

26

The patrician looked over the edge of his reading spectacles and lowered the previous week's edition of the newspaper as Mitchell entered his library.

'When I am in Paris how do I contact you?' said Mitchell.

The old man permitted the intrusion without comment. After a moment's consideration, he gestured Mitchell to sit in the chair opposite. 'I will give you a telephone number for our house in Vincennes, several miles south-east of the city. We move there in spring and spend summer there. I will need you to telephone me every three days as a minimum. Otherwise, I cannot move my men in time to help you. Edmond will be able to use his gamekeeper's pass when we are at Vincennes and he will lead the men to support you, but I will not risk their lives needlessly.'

'Understood. And we speak plainly on the telephone? What if they are listening on your line?'

'Last winter was one of the worst we have had. You will say you are the plumber and you are checking on the state of our boiler. Tradesmen these days... God knows they can be a nuisance, those that haven't been sent to Germany that is; the rest need work but who has money to pay them? You can offer to come to the house and check it. That way we can meet. We do not think they listen, but we must exercise caution. Not so?' Gaétan poured them both some cognac. 'It allows us to stay in touch with what is happening in the city. My wife helps run a charity for orphans, and there are many of them. Too many, but her work is convenient in that she hears gossip. There are still the well-to-do in the city. Not everyone fled when Paris was occupied, and many of these people socialize with the Germans. It's how we piece together information.'

'She runs a risk getting too close to them,' said Mitchell, unable to erase the thought that if there was a weakness in the Gaétan circuit it might be staring him in the face.

'She is determined,' said the patrician. 'And it allows us the freedom to travel from here to Vincennes without raising suspicion. It is where all of this started for me.'

Mitchell sipped his cognac. Better to let the old man talk and give information without being prompted.

'The British Military Mission was based there and I was contacted by them before France fell. I served France in the first war and I agreed to work with London and pledged my allegiance to de Gaulle. Everything my wife and I have done since the jackboots echoed down the Champs-Élysées has been to see them driven out.' He paused, ran a finger around the edge of the glass. 'I hope I live to see it.'

Mitchell studied him. 'There's also the risk that your contact with the Germans casts suspicion on you. Your wife has already told us of her fear of reprisals once the Nazis are defeated.'

'And it is then that we turn to those we help,' said Gaétan. 'We would need protection from the likes of you, colonel, and the people we both serve in London.'

Mitchell swallowed the last of the cognac. 'I and my men have been here too long,' he said. 'Let's take Thérèse to the station and then we'll leave.'

'You're not going to Paris with her?'

'No. There's something else I have to do, as you well know.'

Gaétan frowned and sighed. 'I had hoped you were not going to press me on the matter of the other Englishman.'

'Then your hopes are dashed. But first, the girl.'

The Frenchman seemed resigned to Mitchell's insistence on being told about the missing agent, Guy Neuville. 'Colonel, I agree about Mademoiselle Fernay, but we must exercise caution. Yet another trip to the station might arouse the authorities' suspicion. How many guests can a man have staying with him all the way out here?'

'I thought of that as well. Is there a bus route anywhere nearby she could use?'

'Too dangerous. She would need to change three or four times to get into Paris. She is not familiar enough with the route.'

'No, I was thinking of a bus to the railway station.'

'Ah. Yes. We can do that. One of my men has a house a couple of kilometres from here. There is a weekly bus that would stop at the station. If she boarded there then we could have a decent enough cover story for her. He has relatives down near Vichy. But that bus won't come till tomorrow.'

Mitchell felt a quiver of anxiety. He wanted to be away from the château by then but leaving Ginny in the patrician's care worried him. If the leak in the circuit originated here than she could be betrayed and never even reach Paris. He quickly analysed his options. The risk to him and the men staying any longer was the greater. Were the SS still looking for them or had they satisfied their bloodlust back at Saint-Just?

Olivier Gaétan watched Mitchell as he considered what to do next. What kind of man had London sent? Problems and the often difficult decisions that needed to be taken to solve them could give the measure of a man.

'We'll go and you will ensure she gets on that bus.'

So, Gaétan realized, the Englishman had decided to trust and favour his own survival over the girl's. It was the correct decision. Colonel Pascal Garon was far more important. 'As you wish.'

'I would like to take the Peugeot.'

'If it runs. There is no fuel.'

'It runs. One of my men has checked it over. We can draw petrol from the Citroën.'

'You leave us with little fuel.' Gaétan sighed, but nodded his agreement.

'Good. Give us three days if you can. Take the horse and cart into the village and report the theft of the Peugeot to the gendarmes. You tell them that your petrol was drained from the Citroën. Now, where do I find Neuville?'

'Colonel, I would beg you to leave him in peace. In truth, he was a man who should not have been sent to do such dangerous work. His nerve broke. Had he been captured by the Gestapo he would have betrayed me and my circuit.'

'So you executed him,' said Mitchell, suddenly aware of how much a loss to his own mission the agent's death would be.

'That was my intention, yes.'

'Then you've failed in your duty.'

'He is an educated man. I believed that the day would come when he would have recovered sufficiently to go back to Paris. He had made contacts there that would have benefited everyone. It was a gamble that I took. And I do not wish to kill an innocent man.' He looked at Mitchell and said deliberately, 'I am not a murderer.' The implication was obvious.

Mitchell had no desire to explain the circumstances that led to him killing the German soldiers. Perhaps it even served a purpose if Gaétan thought him to be ruthless.

'You will understand, colonel, that I am extremely reluctant to discuss his whereabouts because I do not know what your intentions are. I will not allow you to kill him.'

'I respect your feelings, and I give you my word that that is not why I need to find him. He has information that I need.'

The patrician studied Mitchell. And then he nodded. 'He found refuge with a Frenchwoman with whom he had fallen in love when he first came here. They masquerade as man and wife. Madame Ferrand is a widow with two small children. There are many such widows in France, colonel, and for them to find a caring man is their good fortune. I had documents forged for him.' Gaétan hesitated again. 'Charles Ferrand.'

So, Mitchell realized, Major Knight's instinct was accurate. Peter Thompson had discarded his cover name and taken another.

'The village is a few hours from here. I would beg you to exercise extreme caution. If you are being hunted and they discover anyone there has helped you...' He let the sentence hang.

'I know exactly what that means,' said Mitchell. 'Where is the village?'

Gaétan hesitated. 'I will give you the information you need, colonel, but I want something in return.'

'I'm not here to bargain,' said Mitchell.

'You are here under my roof and protection and now you wish to deprive me and my men of valuable fuel. There's a

German fuel dump for local troops and, with your men, we could steal enough to keep us operational for several months.'

'Drums or jerrycans?'

'Cans mostly. They have bowsers and drums but the cans are used for quick resupply.'

'How much fuel are we talking about?'

'I would need at least fifty.'

'How heavily guarded is this place?'

'About fifteen men, mostly non-combatants. It is a motor pool so there will be ancillary staff, motor mechanics and the like. But I cannot risk raiding the place with so few men of my own.'

'But you speak of reprisals.'

'The fuel depot is twelve kilometres from here. There are very few villages in that area and when I report the theft of my vehicle to the gendarmes and my suspicion that a group of thieves or perhaps even the men being hunted have passed through, then the Germans will be looking for you. I have hiding places for the petrol.'

'All right, but we'll need fuel as well. I want as many jerrycans as can fit in the boot of the Peugeot.'

'Then we are in agreement?'

'When do you wish to do this?'

'Mademoiselle Thérèse will be safely on her way tomorrow morning.'

'Tonight then.'

27

Gaétan's gamekeeper, Edmond, led six men down a darkened track. There was barely enough moonlight to penetrate through the tree canopy, sparse though it was. Behind them, Mitchell led his own group. One of Gaétan's men had switched off the engine of an old open-back lorry and coasted downhill until the lorry pulled into the bushes less than a hundred metres from where they would go through the wire perimeter. Mitchell and Gaétan's men had been briefed by the gamekeeper. The German perimeter fence was at its most vulnerable when it ran along the edge of the forest. It was also the furthest point from where the German soldiers were billeted and their vehicles parked. The plan was to cut through the wire and to manhandle as many of the cans of fuel as possible back to the waiting lorry, and then escape without raising the alarm. The gamekeeper had gathered the men before darkness fell and made a model in the dirt, scratching a track through the bits of twig that represented the forest and using baling wire to show the extent of the fuel dump compound. Small stones represented the soldiers' sleeping huts. Once everyone was satisfied that they understood the plan of attack Mitchell acknowledged that this would be Gaétan's operation led by his *chef de terrain*, Edmond. Mitchell would designate two of his men to establish ambush positions which would catch any German attack in a crossfire. Mitchell emphasized to everyone that they were not there to kill Germans but to steal fuel. Laforge suggested it was the ideal time to destroy the fuel dump but Mitchell insisted the primary aim was to steal rather than destroy. No matter how remote the area, a conflagration would surely bring major forces to bear on the area. And that would jeopardize not only Gaétan but also Mitchell's mission in Paris.

The men stumbled along the track, each one gripping the length of rope held by Edmond at the front, guiding them until they reached the wire fence. Chaval and Edmond, poacher and gamekeeper, knelt side-by-side as Edmond's men cut through the wire.

'There are boars in the forest,' whispered Chaval. 'I can smell them.'

Edmond glanced at the big man who was obviously a hunter, perhaps a woodsman, most likely a poacher. It took skill and years of tracking to be able to pick up the scent of the boar. Men usually took dogs to root out wild pigs.

'They'll stay well clear of us,' Edmond whispered.

'Not if we're using their foraging trail,' Chaval answered. It sounded like an accusation and Edmond realized that Chaval knew that that was exactly the route he had used to bring them alongside the wire. The final snip of the wire cutters stopped him from answering. Without another word, the men slipped through the gap in the fence. Mitchell had ordered Bucard to use his experience to set two of their men in the cut-off positions. The soldier took Maillé and Laforge either side of the hole cut in the fence and gave each man a field of fire across the compound. If the Germans staged an attack their initial assault would be slowed by the two men, allowing the others to fall back. Fifty metres along the track where it widened sufficiently two of Edmond's men had positioned a four-wheel trolley used for carrying milk pails. As the cans of fuel were carried back they would load it and manhandle it to the lorry. Mitchell gauged the time needed would be at least an hour and no one knew the guard roster or the times when they changed over. It was a risk but if a basic standard operating procedure applied to the German army as it did with the British then he assumed each sentry would have two hours on and four off. Bucard suggested that if they worked on the twenty-four-hour routine of a soldier's day then they were about to see a changeover of sentries.

'Wait,' Mitchell urged Edmond. Men were already man-handling the jerrycans. Edmond was disciplined enough to take the warning seriously. He told the men in a whisper to remain still and silent. The men's eyes had adjusted to the darkness and, through the canyons of the stacked-high fuel cans and drums, they saw a figure moving in the distance. An orange glow spilt out into the darkness as the sentries' hut opened and four soldiers stepped out. They hunched and yawned but quickly became more alert when their guard commander joined them. He barked his orders, and in time-honoured tradition, the German soldiers braced to attention and then marched across the compound and out of sight to relieve the previous watch. The waiting *résistants* listened for any movement that might indicate a guard close by. Bucard gestured that he was going to sneak forward and establish where the sentries were stationed. Mitchell saw him move quickly through the shadows until he disappeared from view.

Mitchell looked around to where the men waited patiently, alert to any untoward sound. The night was silent except for the occasional screech of an owl. A movement in the shadows quickened Mitchell's pulse but it was Bucard moving back to them.

'A couple more minutes and the previous guards will be back in the warmth of their hut,' he whispered to Mitchell and the gamekeeper. 'The sentries looked to be fairly stationary; each man is moving no more than twenty paces. Ten left, ten right.' His teeth flashed in the darkness. 'I heard one of them counting to himself. Being on sentry duty can be boring and, besides, these are Germans and they don't do more than they are ordered.'

He stayed on his haunches, cupped a hand around the luminous dial of his wristwatch, and then nodded and pointed towards the hut. Sure enough, the returning sentries were standing down by what was most likely a corporal of the guard. The men's muttered relief at being off duty floated across the compound. The orange light came and went as the door opened and closed.

'I'll go back down and keep watch,' said Bucard.

Mitchell nodded and tapped him on the shoulder. As the African soldier slipped away into the darkness again, Edmond whispered for the men to continue. Grabbing a jerrycan in each hand, Mitchell joined the nine other men and laboured back through the fence, sweat already prickling his skin at the combined weight. Clouds shifted across the moon as the wind rustled the treetops. It brought more light to see the path and the creaking trees would help disguise any noise. As the moon was cast back into darkness the men stumbled, but they pressed on, their curses little more than vehement whispers. Mitchell was glad that his own misfortune had led him to these hardy men who laboured with him and that the Norvé circuit, as small as it was, was manned by brave *résistants* prepared to risk everything. A thought crossed Mitchell's mind. Gaétan had given authority and responsibility to his long-serving gamekeeper and the man knew everything: the landing and drop zones and the place in Vincennes outside Paris. If anyone was a risk to the Norvé circuit it was Edmond. He followed the stocky gamekeeper's figure towards the drop-off and knew that if anything went badly wrong that night, he could not allow Edmond to be captured alive.

Everything was running smoothly. The men worked tirelessly, lifting, carrying and then stacking the cans. The operation became a rhythmic line of men passing each other in the night. And then the unconscious beat of steady movement shattered. Somewhere along the track where Laforge and Maillé sat in the treeline, their weapons aimed across the compound, there was a sudden crash, an animal sound of grunting, squealing anger and the fearful shouts of alarm as one of the men broke the silence. A shot rang out from their position.

'Away!' shouted Mitchell immediately. Men dropped the cans they were carrying and unslung their weapons. Floodlights flared from the four corners of the compound. A klaxon howled. Mitchell saw the sentries running, uncertain where the shouting and gunshot had come from. The sound of staccato sub-machine guns rent the air as Bucard turned his aim on to the lights. Laforge and Maillé opened fire too, their bullets tearing up the dirt in the compound. He saw Bucard step into the light, shoot out another lamp and duck into the alleyway of stacked fuel drums. The Germans had spilt out of their hut at the first gunshot and taken up a defensive position. Gaétan had been correct in that they were not front-line troops, but they hadn't forgotten their basic skills and followed the guard commander's bellowed instructions where to direct the fire. Now the camp was alive. Other huts emptied out mechanics and cooks, all bearing weapons. Edmond directed fire from the trees as the men moved rapidly towards the lorry. Laforge and Maillé swept their aim across the open ground.

'Bucard!' Mitchell yelled. 'Come on!'

He saw the soldier appear briefly, raise an arm to acknowledge and turn back to give another burst.

Maillé stood and sprayed gunfire to cover Bucard's withdrawal. Laforge moved position and caught two soldiers trying to outflank the colonial soldier.

Mitchell shot at the guard commander's position, which, with the sustained fire from the *résistants*, gave time for Bucard to run towards the fence. He was almost at the wire when a single shot rang out and he pitched forward. One of the sentries had appeared behind him at the mouth of the alley. Mitchell's heart thudded wildly; his man was down. Chaval was suddenly at Mitchell's shoulder as the Englishman squeezed the trigger – but missed because he was already running towards the fallen man. Chaval fired rapidly, killing the sentry. Sporadic gunfire chased around the perimeter as men either tried to find targets or shot haphazardly to try and keep their enemy's head down.

Mitchell turned the fallen man. There was no pulse in his neck. His eyes stared, blood filled his mouth and the shattered chest showed where the bullet had torn through his body. Chaval slung his weapon and bent to pick him up and carry him.

Mitchell grabbed his arm. 'No. Leave him,' he insisted.

'We take him, Pascal. He's one of us.'

'He has his army papers on him. They'll trace him, perhaps even back to Saint-Just. The Germans might think it was a group of deserters who did this.'

Chaval immediately understood. He grabbed a handful of Mitchell's jacket and hauled him to his feet, then turned towards the hole in the fence. A line of flickering red tongues spouted from the *résistants'* weapons but they were already moving away quickly under Edmond's command. By the time Mitchell and Chaval joined them on the track the shooting had halted as the men began to clamber on to the lorry. The engine coughed; the gears grated. The driver revved hard, pushing away into the trees and the track towards home. Low branches whipped at them as they clung to the swaying lorry. Only when they were below the treeline did the driver switch on the headlights to see where the track led, and then quickly doused them again.

Intermittent firing continued in the distance as the lorry lumbered away with its cargo and survivors, the Germans shooting in panic, not realizing the men had escaped.

The men were silent. Bucard was gone. Mitchell gripped the rail, rolling with the bumpy ride. Death had struck so swiftly. The loss wounded him. The cold night air stung his eyes and brought tears to his cheeks.

28

It had been a bitter return to the Gaétan château. The flurry of excitement as Edmond reported to his master was quickly put aside as the fuel was carted off to be cached. Mitchell instructed his men to fill the Peugeot's tank and then put as many cans in the boot and footwell as they could. Recriminations began as soon as the night's work was finished. Maillé accused Laforge of panicking when the boar pushed its way through the undergrowth. Laforge had fallen and his weapon had fired inadvertently. The bickering between the two became heated until Chaval pointed an accusing finger at Edmond claiming that the stupid bastard had put them in danger from the very beginning and that he, Chaval, had warned him.

Emotions were running high and the two men quickly came to blows. They were dragged apart by the others. It was nobody's fault, Mitchell told them. The unexpected happened. Bucard's death would serve a purpose when his papers were discovered and the Germans began their investigation into him. Gaétan's men filtered away into the night to return to their homes. Edmond faced Mitchell's men.

'I am sorry your comrade died. He was a brave man. I took the only route I knew that would give us the best chance to seize the fuel.'

Mitchell thanked him for his words and the patrician dismissed his loyal servant for the night. Gaétan had brandy brought for Mitchell's men.

Mitchell gathered his men around him. 'You drink tonight and toast your friend. I will raise a glass with you; then I'll leave you to your grief. Bucard once gave me his wisdom: I honour him for it and am saddened by his death, but it's for you to share his memory between yourselves and not with an outsider. Chaval, the men must be ready to move at dawn. All right?'

Chaval nodded. 'Fuck the gamekeeper.' He raised the bottle to his lips and then passed it to Laforge who swigged and made the same toast, and then Maillé and Drossier followed.

Drossier passed the bottle to Mitchell. 'We're in this together, Pascal. Why should we be the only ones with a thick head in the morning? The others nodded and grunted their agreement. Mitchell took the bottle and took a pull of the burning liquid.

'Fuck the gamekeeper,' he spluttered.

*

Ginny Lindhurst had kept her distance from the weary men, letting them curse the war and the loss it had brought them. When the morning came she felt the same kind of nervousness she had experienced before climbing into the Lysander for her flight to France. The men said their goodbyes to Madame Gaétan and her husband and piled into the Peugeot. Once again she was to be alone and dependent upon her own resources. However, Mitchell's quiet reassurance steadied the doubts that she kept hidden from him, and the thought that she would see him again soon comforted her and helped steel her resolve. These were still early days, she told herself; when she began the work she had been sent to do, this constant trepidation would surely leave her. She would have other things to concentrate on. She stood with Madam Gaétan and watched the sleek car disappear from view.

The Peugeot's suspension sank under the weight of the men inside. Maillé was given pride of place behind the steering wheel with Mitchell at his side. The other three men squeezed uncomfortably in the back with the smallest of them, Drossier, lying almost across their knees, his back propped against the door. Mitchell had a folded map on his lap with the route to Thompson's village marked out by Gaétan.

Within four hours Mitchell and the men had been lost twice. The narrow country lanes were unmarked and were it not for the path of the sun and Chaval's countryman's eye for nature's signs they would have spent even longer traversing the labyrinthine back roads. As they came to yet another unmarked T-junction, Laforge suggested they turn right, Drossier left. Chaval insisted they needed to be going straight ahead, but the road did not give them that choice.

'Wait,' said Mitchell. He pushed open the door and clambered on to the car's bonnet and then the roof. He raised the field glasses and swept the horizon over the hedgerows and trees. As he traversed left to right he saw movement in the distance. Stationary vehicles were just about visible through a distant treeline. He held his breath. Whoever it was must also be lost. As far as he could make out there were a half-dozen vehicles with, like him, men standing on the top. His grip tightened on the binoculars. Their backs were to him but the pennant that fluttered from a whip aerial showed the SS skull and crossbones. He instinctively ducked and slid down on to the ground.

'SS,' he said as he slammed closed the door.

'Fuck,' said Maillé. 'Where?'

'Ahead. Right across the fields. Must be a mile or more.'

'Which way are they heading?' said Chaval.

'Right to left as far as I could tell. And they look as lost as we are.'

'If they're lost we could ambush them,' said Maillé.

'Don't be stupid,' said Laforge.

'Listen!' said Maillé, twisting around to face the men in the back. 'London sent us ammunition and explosives. If they're the bastards who did the slaughtering in Saint-Just –'

'No ambush,' said Mitchell. 'We wouldn't stand a chance.'

'We should try!' Maillé insisted. 'We could cut them down while they're stationary. Half of them will be taking a piss on the side of the road, cocks in their hands not guns, the others looking at maps. Christ, we could get them in a crossfire.'

'No,' said Mitchell. 'We run from them. As far and fast as we can.'

Laforge rubbed a nervous palm across his face. 'The old man never mentioned SS around here, did he?'

'How could he know?' said Drossier. 'We're miles away from his area. Pascal?'

'I don't know,' said Mitchell, but kept the thought to himself that the circuit might have sprung a leak again. Coincidence was a fine thing, but it being the SS rather than a normal German patrol raised the stakes. 'Chaval, Drossier, Laforge, out. Go left and right. No more than a few hundred metres. See if there any roadside marker stones. Maillé stays here. I'll keep watch. If I see or hear any movement I'll whistle.'

The men tumbled from the car. Chaval ran forward and instructed the others which way to go, then all of them disappeared from view.

'If a patrol comes either left or right down that road we're caught in the open,' Maillé moaned.

'Turn off the engine. Stay behind the wheel,' said Mitchell. He left the car door open and clambered back up on to the car's roof. He crouched, keeping his profile below the hedgerow, and then cautiously peered above it. The sun was behind his left shoulder so there was no chance of its rays glinting from the binoculars' lenses and if the SS were looking his way they would be looking into the glaring sun. They were still there. Their vehicles silent. Mitchell looked at the tops of the trees and saw them quiver slightly from the approaching breeze. He and his men were downwind of the Germans. He strained to pick up any shouted commands, but the voices were so indistinct as to be unintelligible. And then he heard the unmistakable sound of engines starting up. He dared to watch a moment longer and saw they were moving off to his left in the direction they faced. He slid down the car bonnet and opened the map, desperately searching for his own location in case the road in front of him met the road the Germans were taking.

Laforge ran quickly back into view. 'There's a marker stone a couple of hundred metres to the right. It's ancient, but from what I could see there's the village called Bussy. Seven kilometres away,' he said.

Mitchell scoured the map, his finger tracking back and forth. 'That's it. Bussy is ten kilometres from where we need to be and there's a forest there where we can lay up. Get the men back.'

Laforge ran to the junction and gave a low whistle as Mitchell studied the map.

29

Peter Thompson gazed at the stocky, unshaven stranger, his face burnished by the weather, who removed his cap and eased the garage workshop door closed behind him. Thompson's heart beat faster.

'Monsieur Ferrand?' said Mitchell. 'Charles Ferrand? I was at the house and your wife said I'd find you here.' Mitchell gave a reassuring smile, which seemed to ease the man's tension. He had been leaning over the raised bonnet of an old car when Mitchell had entered and in a reflex of fear his hand had gripped a large spanner. There was no mistaking the look of anxiety that crossed the man's features. He was younger than Mitchell by ten years and his slender build and hands belonged more to a concert pianist than a car mechanic and secret agent.

'How can I help you?' said Thompson.

'I have a car that's running rough. A Peugeot 402. People in the village said you were the man to see.'

Thompson stared at the visitor. He didn't look like a member of the plainclothes Milice and he wasn't German by any stretch of the imagination. But if he had a decent car and fuel to run it then he had influence with someone in authority. 'Where's your car?'

'A couple of kilometres from here.'

'It's broken down?'

Mitchell took a step closer. His voice lowered; the smile vanished. 'No, it's hidden in the forest along with five *maquisards*.'

Thompson was visibly shaken. 'What do you want?'

'Alfred Korte,' said Mitchell in English.

Stricken, Thompson stumbled back. He barged into a tool trolley, nearly fell and then helplessly pressed his back against a work bench. 'Christ, you're an agent. How did you find me? Are you going to kill me?'

Mitchell raised a hand in an attempt to calm him. 'Peter, it's all right. I won't harm you. That's not what I'm here for.'

'Who are you?'

'That doesn't matter.'

'How did you find me?'

'You know how. When you went missing you must have known they would send someone else and that person would have to go through Norvé.'

'The bastard betrayed me.'

'No, I convinced him.'

'London sent you to replace me?'

'To find Korte. And the wireless operator in Paris has not been transmitting on his schedule.'

'Ory. Alain Ory. He must have been taken. He may even be in hiding.'

'You abandoned him and Alfred Korte.'

He shuddered. 'I wish they had never asked me to come here.'

'You volunteered.'

Thompson nodded. He wiped his oily hands on a rag and spent too much time wringing the cloth. Eventually he spoke. 'I thought I could do some good. But... panic seized me. My nerve went. The Gestapo were everywhere. Some of the gendarmes were more brutal than the bloody Nazis. And they had informers everywhere.' Sweat had broken out on his face. His hands trembled.

Mitchell stepped closer and offered him a cigarette. 'Easy, Peter. I just need information.'

Thompson managed a smile. 'Haven't had a proper smoke for ages. Mostly roll-ups these days.' He bent his head to the flare of the match Mitchell cupped in his hands. 'People here haven't questioned me,' he said, the cigarette seeming to calm his nerves. 'We told them I had lived in another *département*. That I had a heart condition that stopped me being called up to fight. I have a knack for fixing things,' he said almost apologetically. 'They appreciate that. A university degree wasn't much use to me after all, was it?'

Mitchell remained unimpressed by Thompson's self-pity. 'You're a serving British army officer. And now you're a deserter. You ever go back home you'll spend a long time in jail but when the Allies land you could be shot.'

'God help me but I tried, you know. I didn't just cut and run. I reached Korte and was ready to get him out but it was a trap. Someone in the circuit betrayed us.'

'Any idea who?'

Thompson shook his head. 'I had half a dozen men working for me. It could have been any one of them. And my radio operator was a tough man. If anyone could survive he could. I barely made it out alive.'

'Did you know a woman called Suzanne Colbert?' said Mitchell, casting his hope and fears into Thompson's void. Had the man come across his wife?

The cigarette had quickly become a stub from Thompson's nervous smoking. He got what he could from it and then ground it underfoot. He shook his head. 'There were a lot of people operating in Paris. Different groups, different political persuasions. Mix that in with the criminal elements and you couldn't tell who was betraying whom.' He seemed less stressed than when Mitchell had walked into his workshop. No gun had been levelled at him. No threat made. 'What do I call you?'

'Pascal.'

Thompson nodded. He knew that there would be a cover name. 'You go to Paris, you put your head in the lion's jaws. You won't find the old man now.'

'Let me decide that.'

Thompson sighed. 'What is it you want from me?'

'If Alfred Korte is still alive then I want to find him and get him to England. You can help me finish the job you started.'

'You want me to go back to Paris?'

'Yes.'

Thompson shook his head.

'Listen to me,' said Mitchell evenly. 'You come with me into the city and help me find him. You will convince him that I am there to get him to England. Just like you were going to do. Do that and I will tell London that you are dead. They will have no further interest in you and you can stay here with your adopted family for the rest of your life. Peter Thompson will cease to exist. That's the deal.'

'And if I don't agree?'

'Then I will have no choice but to tell them where you are.' Mitchell watched the man's agony. 'Take the deal, Peter. Have the life you want rather than lose it.'

✱

Mitchell sat around a small scrubbed wooden kitchen table. Five soup plates were laid out. In the centre of the table a loaf of bread that looked as hard as a brick had two slices already cut from it. A square of salted lard rested on a plate waiting to be smeared on to the slices. The soup pan steamed on the wood-burning stove. Opposite Mitchell, a small child that he guessed to be about four years old sat patiently waiting for her evening meal. She gazed at Mitchell with a look that signalled fear at the effect this stranger at her table might have on her family, and resignation too. Her dark hair was tucked behind her ears but unusually, he thought, her eyes were blue. To Mitchell's left, a boy perhaps two years older than his sister rested his chin on the edge of the table and made small popping noises with his lips. Mitchell sat upright on the stiff-backed chair, forearms resting on the table, waiting patiently for the raised voices in another room to subside.

Minutes went by until the tearful argument quietened. And then Peter Thompson came into the kitchen, touched the boy's hair and bent and kissed the top of the girl's head. He pulled out a chair and sat, reached for the bread and spread a thin film of lard across each slice. It was obvious that food was scarce. Thompson gave each child a slice of bread and instructed them to wait for their mother before beginning to eat. Mitchell's stomach rumbled but he declined the offer of a slice.

'I'm not that hungry,' said Mitchell. 'Give it to the children.' Thompson nodded, understanding. 'Thank you.'

Madame Ferrand entered the kitchen, her eyes red-rimmed. She stuffed a crumpled handkerchief into her apron pocket and deflected her distress by ladling out the water-thin soup with traces of old vegetables. Once seated she clasped her hands in front of her face, followed by Thompson and the children. Mitchell followed suit as Madame Ferrand whispered grace and urged the good Lord to keep them all safe and to send his angels to protect the man she loved and who cared for her and her children.

She glanced at the guest at her table and Mitchell saw in her eyes an entreaty not to take Peter Thompson from her.

They ate in silence.

30

SS-Sturmbannführer Ahren Brünner had run a search pattern across the area north of Saint-Just. The slaughter of its inhabitants was a reprisal others would not forget. Putting the fear of God into these French partisans was essential. Over the days he had driven through half a dozen remote hamlets and villages and there had been no sign of strangers being given shelter. His arrival soon brought the fearful inhabitants out on to the street and their protestations of innocence were quickly confirmed. If the *maquisards* had sought refuge in any of these places he would have found them.

Brünner could not know as he led his column of vehicles along the forest track towards Furchette that Chaval and the men were crouched in the trees hidden behind their camouflaged car. Yet again Chaval had had to restrain Maillé from ambushing the SS as they passed, and the roar of the German vehicles and the stench of their exhaust lingered in the *maquisards'* ears and nostrils even when they were out of sight.

Chaval ordered his men to be ready to move quickly if they heard gunfire in the village. He dreaded another massacre if the Englishman were discovered. What to do then? Assist the villagers, or escape should the shooting start? It was too late to warn Pascal, and they were too few to challenge the ferocious SS. They would wait and pray that somehow the man who led them could escape.

*

Mitchell slept beneath the work counter in Thompson's garage workshop. His plan was to strike out for the forest once the nervous Thompson had spent the night comforting his wife and children. He was awake when the deserter brought him coffee and a piece of stale bread accompanied by a wrinkled apple from their winter storage.

'We're going to need another car. There are too many of us. What about that one?' said Mitchell, dipping the hard bread into the hot coffee.

Thompson nodded. 'It will get us there if we don't overload it. The suspension is close to collapse.'

Mitchell kicked the tyres. 'It'll be you and me and one other. We need an extra armed man in the back in case we run into a patrol.'

Thompson raised his own cup of coffee to his lips, but it took both hands to steady it.

'Peter, it is impossible for us to avoid contact with the Germans or French police. You have to brace yourself for that fact. You've told your wife you're going?

Thompson nodded again.

'She won't stop you?'

'She knows I have to do this. It's what's right. I should never have run. I'll hold it together for as long as I have to.'

Mitchell placed a hand on Thompson's arm. 'Peter, it'll be all right. A few days and you'll be home and everything else will be forgotten,' he said quietly. Before another word was spoken the sound of approaching vehicles made them move quickly to the workshop's open doors. The unmistakable sight of an SS Hunter Group came quickly into view.

Mitchell turned back and tugged free the .45, lifted the top tray from a toolbox and dropped in the pistol. He stripped off his jacket and rolled up his sleeves. Thompson was rooted to the spot as the SS vehicles slowed and stopped in the village street. Mitchell lifted the bonnet on one of the cars and rubbed oil and grease on to his hands and arms with a dab on his face for good luck. 'Peter, I'm an itinerant mechanic looking for work. I got here yesterday. You needed help with these cars and the old tractor.'

Something in Thompson's training made him quickly pull on his overalls and slide beneath the old tractor moments before a tough-looking SS major strode in. Behind him, NCOs were shouting orders to secure the village. 'You,' said Brünner, pointing at Mitchell. 'Is this your garage?'

Mitchell shook his head and pointed to where Thompson slid out from the beneath the tractor. 'Him. Monsieur Ferrand.' Mitchell buried his head in the car's engine again. Brünner looked at the tall man who stood and wiped his hands on his overalls.

'How can I help you, major?' said Thompson, shoving his hands into his pockets, an act that helped steady their trembling.

Brünner glanced from one man to the other but Mitchell did not look up. 'Your garage?' Brünner repeated.

'Yes.'

'I have a vehicle that requires attention.'

'Major, in case you didn't know there's a motor pool with army mechanics fifty or sixty kilometres from here.'

'I need this vehicle repaired. I do not have time to retrace my steps.'

'All right. Bring it in and we'll have a look.'

'Your papers?' said Brünner.

Thompson dug out his identity card. Brünner examined it, handed it back and called out to Mitchell. 'You. Your identity card.'

Mitchell took his time. He reached into his jacket that hung on a nail and then handed his card to the Nazi. Brünner studied his face but Mitchell held his gaze. 'Sergeant!' Brünner called. 'Bring the book.' He handed the identity card back to Mitchell, who turned back to continue his work. 'Wait,' said Brünner, beckoning him back. 'You don't live here. Your card says you're registered in Péronne. That's a long way from here.'

'That's right,' said Mitchell. 'Born and bred. But I need work and a place to sleep so I am trying to earn enough to get down south.'

'Where?'

'Somewhere warmer than up here. I nearly died this last winter. I thought Lyon was the place to go. No work in these parts. It's the arse end of the world. A crust and bowl of watery soup are what he gave me last night. I slept in here. Times are hard. I need decent paying work. So, I said to myself, go to Lyon. At least there they've got women who don't look like the back of a cow.'

Brünner showed no sign of amusement. A sergeant stepped into the workshop with what looked like a small photograph album. Brünner flipped through a few pages with practised ease. Thompson was tall enough to see past the SS officer's shoulder and his eyes flicked over two or three faces before settling on a photograph of a bearded Mitchell. He swallowed hard.

'You're an ungrateful bastard, Garon. I said you could stay a couple of days and help out but you can pack your bag and go now,' he said to distract the Nazi.

'You owe me money,' said Mitchell. The game was set. They had to play it out as best they could.

'You insult my wife's cooking and my hospitality,' Thompson spat, raising his voice.

'Shut up, both of you,' demanded Brünner. He lifted Mitchell's chin and turned his face left and right. Mitchell with a couple of days' worth of stubble bore no resemblance to the bearded man in the photograph. And his hair was shorter and his face more burnished. Brünner suddenly switched to English. 'You have come a long way from London,' said the German.

Mitchell looked blank and then glanced at Thompson.

'What did he say?' he asked.

Thompson shrugged. 'I don't speak the language.'

'I don't understand what you asked me,' Mitchell bluffed.

The SS officer handed back the album of wanted men and women to his sergeant. 'Show me your hands.'

Mitchell extended his bare hands and arms. 'Look, major. I'm a mechanic. I know I shouldn't have insulted Monsieur Ferrand here but the SS scare a man so I spoke out of turn. Where can I go looking for work except in the city?'

Brünner had checked Mitchell's calloused hands. 'I could send you to Germany and forced labour like many other of your countrymen. But that is not why I am here.' He nodded to his sergeant. 'Bring it in.'

The sergeant shouted an order and a spluttering Kübelwagen – the German equivalent of a jeep – was eased into the workshop. The driver killed the engine and stepped out of the mud-splattered vehicle.

Mitchell and Thompson stepped around to the back of the vehicle and lifted up the small engine cover.

'You,' said Brünner to Mitchell, 'you attend to this. Report back to me when the problem is identified.'

'All right,' said Mitchell without hesitation. He looked at the driver. 'You had a go at this? Tried to fix it?' The soldier looked dumb.

'Not all my men speak French,' said Brünner. He spoke rapidly in German to the driver, nodded him away and then turned back to Mitchell. 'We are equipped to be self-sufficient in the field but apparently this has proved irritatingly difficult to solve. Fix it as soon as possible.'

'It could take some time, major,' said Mitchell. 'We might need spares. Which way were you heading?'

Brünner frowned. 'You ask an innocent question and yet to my ears it does not sound innocent at all.'

'I mean no harm,' said Mitchell. 'It's just that there are bigger towns that might have the parts. It might be a fuel-line problem, it might be a dozen things.'

'Then strip out these vehicles and use whatever you can – but do it quickly,' said Brünner. He turned and joined the soldiers outside.

Once Brünner and his men were out of sight and earshot Mitchell sighed. 'Well done,' he whispered. Sweat was trickling down his back. This officer and his SS Hunter Group were most likely the butchers of Saint-Just. 'Go and warn your wife of my cover story.'

Thompson looked ashen. He stepped towards a waste bin and vomited.

*

The open-topped vehicle had been jacked up on to stands. It took a couple of hours for Thompson and Mitchell to work on the engine by which time Brünner had stationed the Kübelwagen's driver to watch them. The German knew his engine but Mitchell did not. The advantage the two Englishmen had was that the driver did not speak French, so as Thompson pointed out the engine's components he could guide Mitchell's hand to the fuel filters, screens, and lines. He instructed Mitchell to close the fuel valve then to remove the filter bowl and screen.

Mitchell grazed his knuckles more than once. The SS soldier grinned and grunted, showing the back of his own hand. The engine was a bitch.

'All right,' Thompson said quietly. 'Open the valve, drain the sediment from the tank until the fuel runs clear.'

Mitchell kept looking for guidance to Thompson, who would either nod or shake his head without the German seeing. Finally, when the soldier got tired of watching over them and stepped to the door to light a cigarette, Thompson whispered final instructions. 'Now, clean the bowl and screen and reassemble the filter. Unless you think we should sabotage the damned thing.'

'No, we have to get them on their way. They're canny enough to spot if we do anything stupid. I don't want these murdering bastards taking revenge on the village. But we could buy time. Make the repair look more complex than it is. Send them on their way. We could have it fixed by the time they return but by then we can be long gone.'

As Mitchell did as instructed Thompson took a closer look and tore away part of the filter bowl gasket.

'Hey,' he called to the German driver. 'Fetch the major.' The soldier looked uncertain. '*Sturmbannführer*,' he said, gesturing to the men outside. The man nodded, pinched his cigarette and tucked it away. 'Come here,' said Thompson to Mitchell. He handed him the filter bowl. 'It will look better if you explain. Blind the bastard with science. Tell him the gasket's gone and it will take time to try and make a new one. Then make him feel he can trust you. Tell him that once you've done that you have to get the fuel pump back on, check it for leaks and that the pressure has to be right. But tell him there's water in the fuel. We need to drain the tank and for him to give us a can of fuel to replace it. That way we get some free fuel from them.'

Mitchell smiled. A good trick. Peter Thompson's nerves seemed settled enough now.

Brünner came back into the workshop and Mitchell repeated everything, and as he did so Brünner translated the words into German so that the driver understood. And then he asked the driver if everything that had been related to him by the Frenchman was correct. The driver nodded.

'We will return tomorrow. It must be ready,' said Brünner.

'It will be,' said Mitchell.

Brünner was a man in a hurry with a group of murdering partisans to track down. No time to stand idle waiting for one vehicle to be repaired. The driver returned with a can of fuel and within minutes the convoy sped away from Furchette.

Thompson sat heavily, relief flooding through him. Mitchell gazed down the road in the direction the convoy had driven. He turned and took a long look at the Kübelwagen. 'They weren't all SS registered vehicles. This one's army. See? WH plates, not SS. Brünner will have cause for complaint when he gets back to the army vehicle pool.'

'So what?'

Mitchell gave his hands one last wipe with the rag and threw it across the workshop. 'It can help us.'

*

Madame Ferrand's recriminations turned into heartfelt despair as Thompson hugged the children and embraced her. His assurances washed over her, useless words that wounded rather than healed. Who would wish to step back into the turmoil that was Paris, where every other man or woman could be an informer, willing to insinuate themselves with the German or French authorities? she had begged. Watching the emotional intensity of their separation, Mitchell felt his own loss all over again. He wondered what he would have done had the tables been reversed. Mitchell and Thompson had briefed her on what to say when the SS returned. The German vehicle had been repaired so there would be no recrimination. And as a final act of defiance Thompson had prepared an invoice for the work done on the vehicle.

Reunited with the group that now called themselves Maquis de Pascal, Mitchell and Thompson led the way in the two cars towards the occupied city.

31

Jean Bernard's sister's modest apartment had sufficient rooms for Juliet and Simone to be made welcome. Jean Bernard would sleep on the couch, which would prove no hardship once he was working at the hospital for his time spent at the apartment would be minimal. The young widow was pleased to see her brother; it gave her confidence to have a man around again and his presence would have a positive influence on her son, Marcel, who missed his father. Juliet's daughter would be company for the boy and having Juliet living there would give Marie a chance to show off her knowledge of city life to the woman from the countryside. A woman alone sought any way to improve her status. And the extra ration cards would put more food on the table. They had already registered the new arrivals at the local food office, queueing for hours in the rain to have their cards stamped. Afterwards, they had endured more queues to register again at the local butcher and baker. It was exhausting trying to get enough food, and no Parisian ever managed to. It was an old and bitter joke that the meat ration was so small it could be wrapped in a

Métro ticket. The coarse root vegetables tore into people's guts and filled the hospitals with appendicitis cases. Simply staying alive was a challenge thrust upon everyone in the city.

The woman's anxiety was exacerbated by concern for her son and the danger of him stumbling into a round-up. The men who had taken Alain Ory had applied the threat that every mother feared and that threat compounded her silence. The Gestapo were watching but she could not admit to her brother why – that she had been persuaded to help a *résistant* in the city. Jean Bernard was a doctor from the countryside: what could he know of such things, nestled safely down there? She shuddered to think of his response if she had confided in him. A well-respected professional man such as he would most likely refuse to stay under the same roof. Explaining would have done no good: that someone from the Resistance had promised black-market food and protection in return for a favour; that a little extra food had arrived and the wireless operator had followed, but the protection had vanished the moment the wireless operator was seized. Her life and that of her son hung in the balance. She had promised to inform on anyone who asked her to help the Resistance or to accommodate another stranger who carried a heavy suitcase. Mercifully, she assured herself, having her brother stay with the woman he intended to marry meant that no danger would be inflicted on them. At long last she and Marcel were safe.

*

Rudi Leitmann sat on a bench writing notes in his pocket-book. The gold pen taken from Marcel Tatier and which had ultimately betrayed the wireless operator wrote well. It was well balanced and nestled neatly between his nicotine-stained fingers. He drew on a cigarette and blew the smoke towards a clearing sky. The tree-fringed square where he sat had a fountain, the water tumbling in a pleasing splatter on to its cobbled base. Spring flowers were in bloom and the city was regaining some warmth after its winter chill. When summer finally arrived the stifling heat in the city saw Parisians crowding the banks of the Seine, plunging in to gain some relief. It was always a pleasant time to associate with young Frenchwomen, who were so attuned to their passions. The German military women, those usually overweight and hideous 'Grey Mice' drafted in to work in all the clerical and administrative departments, were willing enough – not for nothing were they known as 'officers' mattresses' – but their drab uniforms did nothing to inspire romance or incite lust. No matter how poor the French girls were they always found a pretty summer frock to wear and, somehow, rouge and other make-do cosmetics. It was a matter of pride for them to always look feminine and, like every other man in the city, he was grateful for their efforts.

'How is that?' he asked the boy sitting next to him, a school satchel tucked by his side, his legs swinging on the bench.

'Good,' said Marcel. 'Would you like some?'

'No, I don't like ice cream that much.'

'You don't?'

'No.'

'Why not?'

'I don't know. I just don't. Of course, that means there's more for you.'

Marcel thought about it for a moment and then nodded, and returned to licking the ice cream.

'So,' said Leitmann, 'has your mama had any visitors?'

'No. Only Uncle Jean.'

'And is he staying long?'

'Don't know. He brought some food for us.'

'And where did he get the food from? Did he go and buy it for you?'

'No. He's visiting us from the country where he lives. He's a doctor. And he brought his wife with him, well, she's not really his wife but Mama says that they are going to get married.'

'And does this lady have a name?'

'Juliet. Madame Juliet, and her daughter is now my friend. She's older. But she doesn't try and boss me around.'

'And was either Uncle Jean or Madame Juliet carrying a heavy suitcase?'

Marcel shook his head and crammed what was left of the ice cream into his mouth. Leitmann looked at the boy's smeared mouth and cheek and gave him his handkerchief. 'Wipe your mouth. We can't leave any clues about eating ice cream, can we? Remember, if I am to keep you and your mother safe then our meetings must remain a secret. You understand? No one must know, not your mother or even your friends. Otherwise, it could cause a lot of trouble.'

Marcel nodded and tugged on his school satchel. 'Can I go now?'

'Of course. I'll see you next week. Maybe by then I would be able to find some more chocolate. That'd be good, wouldn't it?'

'Yes, thank you.'

'Right, off you go then,' said Leitmann. As he finished making his notes he glanced up to see his innocent informer disappear across the street.

*

Across Paris, on a busy intersection, Gilbert Riffaud's stooped shoulders meant his eyes never rose above the tray he had carried for forty-four of his sixty-three years. He had been a waiter at La Pointe Saint-Eustache for all those years. The world had passed him by every day and the regular faces that had once sat at his tables had also come and gone. Some returned. Some tried to engage him in conversation, pass the time of day. He might let a grunt of acknowledgement pass his lips but in this day and age it was better to refuse to be drawn in. Who did these people think they were? Family? They were just strangers wanting a coffee or a cognac, nothing more. And who had money for cognac, even the poor-quality stuff available these days? Black marketeers, traitors and Germans were who. And they never left a tip. None of them. Riffaud was a student of human nature: he had been studying it all his life and the longer he lived the less he liked the subject matter. The Wehrmacht officers who sat on the street tables never returned the salutes of the lower-ranked soldiers who were obliged to salute when they walked past. Arrogant Boche ruling class. Didn't kill enough of them the first time round. He sniffed the water from his nose. Spring. He hated spring. Damned flowers made his eyes raw and his nose drip. He didn't mind the droplets finding their way into the Germans' coffee. He spat in their soup whenever they ordered it. He gathered up the crockery and glasses from the Germans' table. The bastards thought him little more than a servant; thankfully he did not run the risk of being sent to Germany as forced labour. He knew for a fact that the sour-faced man in the corner table who was pretending to read his newspaper belonged to either the Brigades Spéciales or Milice. And he was watching the young woman sitting alone at the pavement-side table. What was he, Gilbert Riffaud who cared not a fig about others' stupidity, supposed to do? Let the woman be picked up? Mother of God, who was this stupid girl? Where was she from? She was no prostitute, that seemed obvious. He doubted she was even French.

He sighed. She had asked for a white coffee. He shielded her from the prying eyes of the man behind her and smothered his response, letting the words whisper through his bad teeth, bending his face to hers as if he had not heard her order. He was an old man; who would suspect there was nothing wrong with his hearing? Mademoiselle, he had muttered, telling her quickly that no one asked for white coffee. No one unless they did not belong there. Understand? She had nodded quickly, a flush creeping into her cheeks, but she had suppressed her panic. He had seen that look of alarm in a woman's eyes before when plainclothes men had pushed through the passers-by and arrested a woman who was a wanted *résistante*. He cursed himself as he went inside to fetch her black coffee. Why had he done that? Protected her? It was none of his business who the stranger was. He saw that the sour-faced man had returned to his newspaper. She was a slip of a girl and she had kept her nerve. She was waiting for someone. Nervous glances at her wristwatch. Watching the crowd. He delivered the coffee. She smiled at him gratefully. He ignored her. Customers. Holy Mother of God, life would be easier without them.

Ginny had waited fifteen minutes. Then another five. She quickly left the café and turned the corner up the main thoroughfare. She was a brisk twenty-minute walk from the apartment and by the time she reached it she was clammy from her efforts and the fear that had made her hands sweat when the old waiter had warned her. A simple mistake but one that might have proved fatal in the long term. Every moment was fraught. But then she chastised herself. She had to get her fear under control. She pushed through the door into the building's lobby and began the slow climb up to the top floor. There was no sound from any of the apartments. She thought she heard a muted radio in one but it went silent as her heels clattered past. Her anxiety peaked when she reached the penultimate floor. The door of the flat below Mitchell's opened a crack. A shifty-looking man, gaunt cheeks, his black hair greased back, smoking a soggy-ended cigarette. His frayed shirt collar exposed a grubby neck pockmarked with blackheads. His eyes followed her as she ascended the stairs and then the door clicked shut.

When she had closed the door of the apartment she dug out one of the cigarettes salvaged from the packet confiscated by Mitchell. Her hands shook. She needed to calm down because the time was looming for her transmission to London. And the Morse key needed a steady hand.

32

By the time Mitchell and his men reached the outskirts of Paris the SS had rolled back into Peter Thompson's village. Brünner checked the garage workshop, calling out for the two mechanics. He gestured for his sergeant to check the vehicle. The sergeant started it up and it gave a satisfactory rhythmic sound. Then he pressed the accelerator pedal a couple of times and the high revs made no difference to the engine pitch. The fault had been fixed.

Brünner turned towards Thompson's house across the street. Madame Ferrand had heard the SS Hunter Group arrive and stood back from the lace curtains on her window, watching as the SS officer o rdered h is m en t o c heck t he workshop and storerooms for the absent man she thought of as her husband. The repaired vehicle was driven out and put back in line with the others as the German strode towards her front door. She clasped her hands together and prayed desperately that she could do as she had been instructed. With an unconscious flick of her head, she raised her chin defiantly and answered the heavy knocking on her door.

'Yes?' she said to Brünner. 'What can I do for you?'

"Where are the two men who were in the garage? Your husband and the other one. Where are they?'

Madame Ferrand's fear gave impetus to her pretence. 'You think I know, major? If I did I would have the police on him, the bastard.'

'What are you talking about, madame?'

The concocted story spilt from her aided by her genuine distress. 'That man who was here, he was a mechanic all right, but he wasn't looking for work, he was here to entice my husband to go with him to Lyon. They are old friends, drunks both of them. By now they're probably halfway up the stairs of a brothel. If you find him, you can keep him. In fact, you can shoot the bastard. I've had enough. He won't ever set foot in this house again no matter how many times he crawls back begging like he has done in the past. No, major, I don't know where he is. You men, you are all bastards.'

Brünner turned to look at the gathered men and his grinning sergeant.

'Well, major, she is right about the brothels. The French are the best,' said the sergeant.

The men laughed and murmured their approval.

'All right, if we find him we'll tell him what you said.' Brünner smiled. He turned back the waiting troops.

'Wait,' said Madame Ferrand. She pulled a folded piece of paper out of her apron pocket. 'Who's going to pay'?

Brünner gave her a quizzical look and took it from her hand.

'How am I supposed to live if people don't pay their bills?' she said with as much courage as she could muster.

Brünner unfolded the paper and glanced at the invoice. She watched his expression; had anyone ever challenged the SS to pay for anything?

The major smiled and turned to his men. 'She wants us to pay for the work.' It caused a ripple of laughter among the battle-hardened SS troopers. Brünner looked back at the defiant and angry woman. He considered for a moment and then nodded. 'Very well, you shall be paid.' He took out his wallet from his tunic pocket and counted out the notes and then handed them to Madame Ferrand.

'Thank you, major,' she said.

Brünner carefully folded the invoice into his wallet and tucked it back into his tunic. 'We are not undisciplined soldiers. And we have wives and loved ones of our own at home. We understand the difficulties of a woman left to fend for herself and her children. Good day, madame.'

She watched as the troops formed up and Waffen SS-Sturmbannführer Ahren Brünner led his column out of the village.

She closed the door and pressed her back against it. The relief was enormous and despite the fear she had felt and the void left by Thompson's departure, there was the undeniable sense of having achieved a small victory over her enemy. What the Germans had failed to notice was that the repaired vehicle's WH designated number plates had been stolen and were now attached to the car that her husband was driving to Paris.

*

The car that Mitchell had taken from Thompson's garage finally gave up the ghost close to where the rest of the men were to stay hidden. The German plates were swapped on to the Peugeot. Peter Thompson was gaunt with tension as Mitchell directed him to drive through the back streets of Paris. Swastika banners loomed large, pronouncing the unbeatable strength of those who occupied the city. Thompson glanced nervously at him. 'Do you know where you are?'

'Yes,' said Mitchell. The familiarity of the city embraced him. It was everything he remembered and memory stirred his emotions. Behind the urgency of his mission, the desperate hope that his daughter might still be alive was what gave him the courage to risk everything. He had tortured himself by directing Thompson to drive down the Rue de la Santé, past the imposing walls of La Santé prison. If London's intelligence was correct then somewhere in that bleak labyrinth was his daughter. When they had driven slowly past the gates Mitchell suppressed the despair that closed around his chest and directed Thompson across the Seine.

'Christ,' Thompson whispered, 'this is crazy. You're going to get us caught.'

'Calm down. Pull over there.' Mitchell pointed towards a side street.

Thompson guided the car to where Mitchell had indicated. The side street gave them a clear view towards the colonnaded building which served as the German Army HQ. Parked vehicles belonging to the Germans lined the Rue de Rivoli outside the building.

'All right, ease the car forward and find a place to park.'

Thompson swallowed hard. His hands gripped the steering wheel until his knuckles whitened.

'Listen to me. We need to hide the car in plain sight. Understood? And this car is no different than many the Germans have commandeered.'

Thompson nodded nervously. Mitchell was clearly in no mood to be contradicted. He eased the car forward and as they reached the intersection he and Mitchell scanned the street. A mix of German and French marques belonging to the German HQ lined the street. 'There,' said Thompson, spotting an open space. He swung the car and parked it. No sooner had he switched off the ignition than he reached for the door, desperate to be far away from the coming and going of German soldiers.

Mitchell grabbed his arm, watching the street, scanning for any immediate threat. 'Wait.' Four soldiers had stepped out of the entrance and were walking towards them. Two uniformed German women accompanied them. The group seemed relaxed. The women were laughing, forage caps pinned into brushed-back hair, crisp white blouses beneath grey tunics. Young soldiers flung together in the most desired posting – far from home yet also far from the fighting. Eager to enjoy the pleasures of Paris and each other. They walked past the car without a second look, their voices light with the freedom of the end of a working day.

Thompson controlled his rapid breathing. Mitchell nodded and swung open the door. The two men walked away. It took them near enough an hour to walk north, criss-crossing the streets, avoiding any impromptu identity-card checks the Germans conducted on street corners. The light was fading and Mitchell wanted to be in the apartment before curfew. He hoped that Ginny had arrived safely and that no suspicion had been raised by her presence in his old flat. If she had done as he had instructed then she should be in the clear but their late arrival in the city meant going to the building instead of making the rendezvous at the café as planned. It was also more dangerous. If things had gone awry then the Gestapo might be waiting for them.

*

Mitchell led the way upstairs, the memory of when he had last been in the building tinged with self-recrimination. His wife and daughter had been separated from him as they tried to make their escape from Paris. This apartment was a long way from where they had lived and worked and wasn't on the German radar. He had abandoned the city and made for the coast where a fishing boat had been arranged to take them to England. That was where Suzanne and Danielle would have headed, he had told himself. But when he reached the boat there had been no sign of them. The tide was on the turn and the information he had gathered since the city had been occupied needed to be recounted to someone in authority in London. And that had made him step aboard and leave France, his wife and his daughter behind.

He knocked quietly on the door.

A floorboard creaked. Mitchell pressed his face close to the door and listened. A part of him sensed the presence of someone on the other side. If it was Ginny then she would not be expecting anyone.

'Thérèse,' he said softly. 'Pascal.'

The door was unlocked and the anxious face of the young Englishwoman peered through the crack as it opened. Seeing them, she opened the door wider and ushered the two men inside. Mitchell saw that she held a small automatic by her side. She quickly closed and locked the door. 'You scared me,' she said, brushing a wisp of hair from her face, looking from Mitchell to Thompson. 'Who's this?'

'I'm Charles Ferrand,' he said in English. ' I'm here to help Pascal.' He extended his hand; Ginny shook it.

'Hello,' she said. 'I didn't know we had another Englishman in the city.'

'It wasn't planned,' said Mitchell.

'I see. Well then, I've a small pot of soup on the go. I got my bread ration today. We'll have to make do with that. The electricity is on and off but I found candles for when it's dark. There's no heating.' She ushered Mitchell into his own apartment. The years the flat had been unoccupied had given rise to a permanent smell of damp. The air was chill and Ginny had layered herself with clothing for warmth. The steam from the pot on the electric cooking ring clung in droplets to the kitchen wall.

Mitchell looked around: nothing had changed. A curtain separated the sleeping area where he saw Ginny's clothing spread out on the bed and side chair. She would never be able to move in a hurry if the alarm was raised. But now was not the time to instruct her to keep out only essential clothing. The old overstuffed sofa was still good enough to sleep on; he would claim that for himself and let Thompson sleep on the floor. He went to the window and looked up and down the street. It would not be long before curfew and the city was already falling silent. Soon there would only be the sound of German hobnailed boots as the five-man units patrolled the streets. He had lived in the threatening silence before and knew what fears crept into the imagination when a rifle shot pierced the stillness, or a high-powered car roared through the streets as the Gestapo dragged away a suspect. It was not hard to picture his own wife and daughter falling victim to the night.

'Any problems?'

'No. No, not really,' she said, laying another two places at the small table. 'Man downstairs doesn't look very enticing. Comes across as a rat sniffing the air for bait.'

Mitchell couldn't suppress a smile. Her understatement couldn't be more damning.

'The neighbourhood's gone downhill since I was last here, then,' he said. 'Ignore him. I don't know who he is, but the less we have to do with these people the better. No one wants to get involved in anything. If he ever comes up here nosing around tell me and I'll pay him a visit. Sometimes a quiet threat is all you need. Once he knows that your "uncle" might be visiting then his curiosity might be satisfied.'

'Thank you,' she said, placing the meagre rations on the table. 'Where are the others?'

'I've left them a few miles away on the edge of the city. They're in an abandoned farmhouse. I put Chaval in charge. If we need them we can reach them in under an hour. We have a car.'

'Here?'

'We parked it opposite Hôtel Meurice,' said Thompson.

She looked at Mitchell in disbelief. She had been sufficiently briefed in London to know where the German Army headquarters was located.

'Anywhere else would have raised suspicion,' said Mitchell. 'If it's picked up then so be it. We'll be careful. I doubt we'll use it again unless we need to be somewhere in a hurry. What we need to do now is find a man called Alfred Korte. And that's where our friend here comes in.'

Ginny Lindhurst looked at the tall figure hunching his shoulders as he brought the spoon to his lips. There was a noticeable tremor to his hand, spilling the soup. She glanced at Mitchell, who gave a barely perceptible shake of his head, unnoticed by Thompson who was concentrating solely on getting the food to his mouth.

In that moment she realized that she was not the only one feeling apprehensive about being in the city, where informers could be at your shoulder as you walked down the street or pressed close in the Métro. Any slip could lead to betrayal. She decided she would not mention the incident at the café.

33

Mitchell felt a tangible excitement at being back in Paris. The light still blessed and shaded the beautiful buildings but the city was almost silent. So few cars and buses were on the street that it was mostly the muted shuffle of pedestrians' feet or the tinkle of bicycle bells that he heard as Parisians went about their business. Birdsong heralded the spring weather as they nested. How long had it taken them to return? he wondered. When the Germans had rolled into the city in June 1940, their columns of motorized troops came down from Saint-Denis and Montrouge. Leather-coated motorcyclists and sidecars arrived first, followed by their tanks. The French had burnt their oil and gas supplies as the jackbooted Nazis approached. The suffocating black smoke had smothered the city, poisoning all the birds. But now, like him, they were back and their trilling helped lift his spirits.

He had gone to where Thompson said he had hidden Alfred Korte, but what had once been a bookshop was now boarded up. Had the Germans shut it down? His heart raced. If they had then odds were the German scientist had been taken. He asked one of the street sellers what had happened. No one knew. One day there was the usual rack of books outside, the tattered old canopy pulled down against the sun – not that there had been much of that – to protect the books in the window from fading. And then? Gone. Boarded up just like it was now. One of the women heard the conversation. No, no, he was told, the old lady was sick of the Germans visiting her. She didn't want their custom so she had closed up shop. She was admired for putting her principles above money. Mitchell left the street sellers debating among themselves whether such a moral stance made sense in a time of occupation when there was no food or fuel and what there was had to be bought on the black market. Money was money.

He walked briskly towards the Métro station. The Métro was a favourite place for the German and French authorities to conduct spot checks but it was a risk he had to take: Mitchell did not know how many of his old friends still survived or were still living in the city; the surest way to find out was to ask his contact at the American Hospital, who had known Mitchell and his wife when they lived in Paris, and the hospital was in the western suburbs of the city at Neuilly-sur-Seine.

The previous evening, after the evening meal had been cleared away, the three of them had settled down for the night. Blankets and pillows served Thompson on the floor as Mitchell made up a bed on the sofa. Ginny's transmission was due the next day and Mitchell instructed her to keep it brief, to inform them Pascal was in place and that he had met up with an old friend from university days. That would tell London Thompson had been found. Then he had changed into clothes from a suitcase that he had left in the apartment years ago and set off, insisting that Thompson and Ginny stay inside until he returned.

Mitchell joined the crush of travellers at the Métro and kept his eyes lowered as the crowd shuffled on to the platform past the searching gaze of a gendarme making a random examination of identity cards. He was jostled as people tried to edge towards the platform's edge to give themselves a chance to board the next train. At one end of the platform a different group of people waited as patiently as the other tired-looking citizens, but they wore the yellow star that meant they were obliged to travel in the rear coach. Mitchell hunched his shoulders, making himself smaller, wishing to be less obvious than he felt. The Wehrmacht officers stood at the far end of the platform, relaxed, smoking, some reading a newspaper as they waited for their separate carriage. Everyone was boxed and confined according to who they were. Sour breath from garlic, cheap wine and tobacco wafted over Mitchell as he listened to the grumbling that went on around him. The Occupation was a strange mixture: the city was suppressed by German soldiers, yet they showed every courtesy to those they controlled. The soldiers were well behaved: if they were not they were court-martialled. The German troops did not force Parisians to make way for them on the pavements; they gave up their seats on public transport for the elderly, though many Parisians declined the offer, their refusal a small act of defiance. The soldiers showed kindness towards children. Yet they ate well, and to be so well fed indicated their power. These same courteous men used rifle butts to beat unarmed civilians in the round-ups, shot anyone breaking curfew and executed the innocent in reprisals.

Mitchell escaped the crush of the train and walked unhurriedly towards the American Hospital. He suppressed the

'Are those bastards going to catch up with us, Pascal?' said Maillé.

Mitchell shook his head and folded the map. 'Not today. They're going the wrong way and there's no road that tracks back on to this one.'

The men returned and Mitchell told them what Laforge had discovered. 'Bussy is ten kilometres from Furchette, which is where we need to be.'

The car doors slammed. Maillé gunned the car.

sense of urgency which demanded he quicken his pace but could draw attention. After fifteen minutes he stood opposite the main building. He lingered briefly, watching the coming and going of people into and out of the hospital. The street was quiet as he strode across to the side entrance where they used to smuggle downed aircrews into the hospital and from there south to Spain on the escape route.

He pushed through the swing doors and found himself suddenly facing an old concierge. He wore a faded jacket, and a scarf and mittens against the cold. A veteran's medal from the previous war was pinned to his lapel. Another act of French pride in the face of an occupying enemy. He recognized the man from years before but hoped that the elderly man would not remember him now that he was clean-shaven. Anyone who was not a close acquaintance could no longer be trusted. Henry Mitchell must not be known to have returned to Paris.

'Eh? M'sieu?' grunted the elderly man, peering over the top of his spectacles and putting down the folded newspaper rather too quickly, which made Mitchell think he might be reading one of the news sheets put out by an underground press. Mitchell's sudden appearance had flustered him. Perhaps, Mitchell thought, wearing an overcoat and fedora made him look like a French policeman. He glanced down at the newspaper and then back to the worried-looking concierge.

'What news?' he said gravely. 'Have the Germans stopped eating sausages?'

The old man's jaw dropped but Mitchell quickly followed his question with a smile. The concierge guffawed with relief. 'Be careful, m'sieu, there are those in the hospital who would report such words.'

'But not someone who fought them last time.'

'No. Not someone who did.' He coughed and cleared his chest and then studied Mitchell again.

'Do I know you? There's something about you that seems familiar.'

'No, I am new in Paris.'

'Uh-huh. Well, this is not the main entrance.'

'I know. I am looking for a friend. One of the surgeons.'

'I see,' said the veteran. 'His name?'

Mitchell hesitated.

'M'sieu, the Germans leave us alone here at the hospital. I have been here since I left my regiment back in '18. These Americans have stayed throughout. We are a family within these walls. I cannot let strangers in who might be intent on causing harm. For all I know you are a jealous husband looking for the man who screws your wife when you are at work and wish to inflict violence on her lover.'

'Or I could be someone who has bandages and medicines to sell to friends who are desperately short of supplies.'

'Ah, in which case it's best I don't know who it is you wish to see. Such knowledge can be dangerous.' He lowered his head to his newspaper letting Mitchell walk past through the service area. The ducting and water pipes on the ceiling led Mitchell towards a labyrinth of underground corridors but he knew where he was and turned up a set of stairs that brought him to the medical staff offices. He stepped cautiously into the corridor. The wards where nurses attended patients were at one end. Mitchell crossed the corridor and opened the door with a plaque that told him that F. Burton MD was its occupant. He stepped inside and a grey-haired man of fifty wearing a doctor's coat looked up from his desk, pen in hand as he studied a report. Burton was caught unawares but before he could challenge the intruder Mitchell grinned.

'Hello, Frank. It's been too long.'

'I'll be damned,' said Burton and quickly rose extending his hand. 'Harry.' He waved a finger across his own clean-shaven face. 'The beard. You shaved it. Nearly didn't recognize you. Come along, sit down. How wonderful to see you.' He lifted the telephone receiver. 'I'm not to be disturbed. I'm in a consultation.' He opened a drawer and took out a bottle of cognac and two glasses. 'When Jean Bernard came to me and said an Englishman had sent him I felt sure you were back in town.'

'He's here? You managed to help him?'

'Yes, he told me everything. What a dreadful situation. He's fine. I have him here for three days a week. We kept a number of our beds for the French railway workers who are caught up in air strikes and injured. He's ideal. And then I send him across to colleagues at the Hôtel-Dieu. Lot of French patients there and they are short of doctors. Now, come on, I want to hear everything.'

Mitchell took a sip of cognac. 'I was supposed to be flown here but my plane was shot down. There's too much to tell, Frank, but as Jean Bernard has told you, it was hell for an awful lot of people. Though I don't imagine Paris has been immune to terror.'

Burton nodded. 'Last year was particularly bad. Near enough fifteen thousand Jews rounded up. They held them in the Vélodrome d'Hiver stadium until they were put on the trains. The stench from the stadium was appalling. No food. No water. They even arrested patients at the Rothschild, no matter how sick. They separated children from their mothers. Dear God in heaven, Harry, it was inhuman. The Germans use the gendarmes a lot of the time, but the end result is the same. They were shipped off to the concentration camps. You've heard the rumours? How many are being murdered?'

'Yes.' Mitchell sipped the cognac. 'It doesn't make sense. The Germans are sending thousands of Frenchmen as forced labour to Germany. Why would they be killing so many Jews? You would think they would rather use them as labour here in the city.'

Burton shook his head. 'Racial laws. God only knows, Harry. But they're shipping all our food out of the city and that's damned near starving everyone here. Parisians are struggling. Health issues alone have increased the mortality rate – forty per cent higher, it's been, over a decade. Tuberculosis cases have doubled. There's so little food available. You look around and you see people who've thrown off weight as if they were dying. Infections are rife. And the psychological effects of malnutrition undercut any desire to strike back at the enemy. Thanks to the Red Cross we manage to keep a meagre flow of medicines coming in.' He sipped the cognac. 'It could be worse, I guess.'

'And the Germans leave you alone?'

Burton nodded. 'Any Americans allowed in the city have to report to a local police station every week. The Germans check on us; they usually send high-ranking medical types who would be keen to make this a military hospital for their troops, but we manage to fool them. Every bed is occupied, all two hundred and fifty, and that stops the Germans from sending any of their men here. When we get internees sent to us we keep them as long as we can. You've seen the army *Kommandantur* across the road? Well, they're keen not to interfere with us. We've a damned great red cross on our roof and that keeps the Allied bombing away.' He grinned. 'We're helping protect the goddamn German army. As I said, we're desperately short of supplies of course, but we manage. We've hundreds of patients and staff to feed so we dug up the gardens and planted vegetables and of course we buy on the black market.' He shook his head. 'Enough of that. My word, Harry, it's good to see you.' They clinked glasses. 'You know, back when you made your escape and we didn't hear, we thought you'd bought it. Suzanne and Danielle went to ground but Suzanne worked with us until, oh, nearly a year ago now. She moved to another part of the city.' Burton handed Mitchell a generous tipple. 'So, you're back to find them?'

'Frank, Suzanne was executed by the Gestapo.'

Burton's glass was arrested halfway to his lips. 'Harry, I am so sorry. I didn't know. And Danielle?'

'She's in La Santé as far as I know.'

Burton's face fell.

'I know,' said Mitchell. 'The Gestapo might have killed her already or sent her to one of the camps.' His stomach tightened as he spoke the words. It was impossible to erase the images that plagued him.

'Harry, I don't have any contacts in the prison. This past couple of years since you've been gone…' He shook his head. 'We lost a lot of people.'

Mitchell saw in his mind's eye those who had defied the Germans. 'Marguerite? Luc? Professor Albert? Madame Masson?'

Burton shook his head. 'Dead or scattered. Mauriac is alive. He runs the escape route down near Lyon. Things got too hot for him here.'

'He's a good man. You still have my old feeder lines open?'

'Yes, and we have added more. But, as I said, getting more difficult by the day. The Germans are offering a fifty-thousand-franc reward for any downed airman; we know of only one betrayal and the Resistance shot him, so punishment like that exerts some sense of retribution. But the Nazis are offering ten times that amount for a captured British agent.'

'Money has a way of blurring patriotism,' said Mitchell. He thought for a moment. 'What about Louis Crillon? He was a genius at getting people out.'

'Crillon is in Spain for when we take the airmen across the Pyrenees. But the others, well, some have scattered, some are missing. We work in very small cells now, Harry. A handful only at any one time. Trust is something in short supply.'

'Do you know of a wireless operator by the name of Ory, Alain Ory?'

'No.'

'He's in hiding somewhere. Seems he escaped when Suzanne and Danielle were taken.'

'When you left a lot of the organization crumbled. People were scared. You know too much, Harry. If they catch you they can still root out a lot of people who helped us.' Burton poured them both another drink. 'You were a big fish, my friend. Still are. So, can you tell me why you're back in Paris – other than to try and find Danielle? I'm assuming there's more to it.'

'I've a handful of armed *résistants* with me and an English wireless operator.'

'A new circuit? You're going to harass the Germans here?'

'Yes, it's called Gideon. It would help if I could find at least a few from the old cell.'

Burton shrugged. 'There are those who will help hide you and the girl if things get rough. Not the men; it's too dangerous. The Germans penetrated some of the groups. We can only trust those we know and even that... well, we never know. It's a huge risk. I'll do what I can.'

'Thank you. And, Frank, my cover name is Pascal Garon and I'm beginning to think there are too many people who know that. I could do with another identity card. I can get my photo taken at a department store's Photomaton, but if Mauriac is in the south then who do you have as a forger?'

'There's a young photographer here in the city. His father was a railway worker we treated. He's the best source we have. He tried using solvents to erase the Juif stamp for many of the Jews when his people were trying to get out of the city. He couldn't make it work so he started forging a complete document from scratch. He's making fifty or more a week and we get a handful. He has a way of getting cardboard and paper that looks original and then watermarks it and treats it with some kind of dust that ages the document. And then he makes a police stamp. It's how we get the downed airmen out.'

'Can he make me new papers?'

'Harry, we are all on edge these days, and that slows things down a helluva lot. It would take time. There are so many plainclothes men on the street. The Special Brigades, the detectives, the Gestapo, informers. They pick up one suspect and the next thing you know twenty people are up against the wall or dozens put on to the transport trains. I can ask.'

'No, he has enough forging cards for those who really need them. I'll come back to you when I have to, if that's all right?'

'Of course, and if it becomes urgent we can press him.'

'Frank, I'm looking for someone on the run. Alfred Korte. You know about him?'

'The name, yes. But if he's in the city I don't know where.'

'There was an English agent here trying to get him out. Korte's important. I need to find him. The agent said he had found him a hiding place in one of the bookshops but it's since closed.'

'You're certain?'

'I checked on my way here. The place is boarded up. I had hoped Korte would have been safely tucked away. Who would know what happened to the people in the bookstore?'

'I'll give you the name of someone in the American Library. She would know the booksellers in the city. The Germans continually visit the library so be careful.' Burton scribbled on a desk pad, tore free the page and handed it to Mitchell, who glanced at it and tore it into tiny pieces.

'Burn it. If I keep it and get stopped then she would be implicated.'

Burton sighed and lit the pieces in the ashtray. 'Stupid of me, Harry. I've been cooped up in here too long. Not thinking of the risks of being on the streets.'

'If I find him I have to get him out in a hurry. Can you help me?'

'South?'

'No, I'll bring in a Lysander. But I'll need people to look after him until I can arrange it.'

'Find him and bring him here. Then we'll plan what's best.'

There was a tap on the door. Burton hid the glass, Mitchell did likewise as the doctor opened the door. A French nurse stood there with an armful of folders. 'The medical reports you wanted, doctor,' she said, glancing past Burton to the man in the overcoat.

'I told my secretary I wasn't to be disturbed,' said Burton brusquely.

'I apologize, doctor. I came straight from the ward.'

'All right. Thank you,' said Burton, taking the folders. The woman left and he dumped the casework on his desk and swallowed the remains in his glass. 'Come on, let's go up on the roof. I need a smoke and I'll tell you more about the woman at the library. It's information that'll help. You never know who's listening at the door these days.'

34

Peter Thompson had been fine for the first hour of Mitchell's absence, but then became increasingly tense as he paced the apartment, looking repeatedly out of the window on to the street below. When Ginny had set up her wireless for transmission he had helped her raise the aerial. 'You won't say anything more than what Pascal told you?' he had asked, his voice laced with concern. Ginny had reassured him but saw him concentrating on what she was sending as she tapped out her coded message. He could not know her codes but it was obvious he understood Morse. She had done exactly as Mitchell instructed and sent the message without any embellishment and then quickly closed down her wireless set. The German radio direction finder vans continually patrolled the streets and she knew that if she lingered too long on the key then they could locate her.

'We're safe here,' she told him. 'Safe as can be anyway.' She smiled encouragingly.

'You've no idea how bad it can get,' said Thompson, trying to roll a cigarette, the tobacco spilling from his trembling fingers.

Ginny tried to calm him and quickly made a cigarette for him, licked the paper and handed it to him. Thompson sucked gratefully on the lit cigarette and nodded his thanks. But then the confines of the room began to close in on him.

'I have to phone my wife,' he said.

'Charles!'

He turned. The small automatic in her hand was levelled at him. 'You must do as Pascal instructed.'

'There's a phone box down the street. I'll return as soon as I've spoken to her.'

'No!'

In that moment Thompson seemed to relax. 'And what are you going to do? Shoot me? You would bring every gendarme and German patrol in the area down on us. And that's the end of everything.' He turned quickly and closed the door behind him. For a moment she was flustered and then pulled on her coat and shoved the pistol into her pocket. On the landing outside she saw him disappearing down the stairs and followed him.

As she reached the street she looked left and right and saw the tall Englishman making his way to the next intersection. She walked briskly after him, not knowing what she could do to restrain the frightened man or to coerce him back to the relative safety of the apartment. As she hurried she gripped the gun tightly in her pocket. She suddenly realized that she had left her identity card at the apartment in her haste to follow Thompson. No identity card and a weapon in her pocket. It was incredibly stupid to have taken the gun on to the street and the quickening fear of what would happen if she were stopped suddenly became a reality. Two German lorries appeared at the intersection, the soldiers quickly blocking the street. Thompson was already beyond them. She turned but there was no escape. Three police cars had driven up behind her and gendarmes spilled from them, cordoning off the street. The Parisians were used to spot checks and those that had been caught between the two roadblocks resigned themselves to their journey being interrupted. The gendarmes herded them towards the soldiers who, three or four at a time, checked identity cards in an organized and efficient manner, moving people through so the Germans could go on to their next impromptu checkpoint. One of the men argued with a soldier, who gestured to his comrades to escort him to the back of the lorry. He resisted and was quickly subdued. Fear murmured through the waiting crowd. Ginny's mouth dried as she looked around desperately for any escape route. She made a quick decision. If they arrested her then she would shoot her way clear and run for it. Several people ahead of her were checked and passed through and then she was next. She was beckoned forward. There was no demand for her identity card, only the outstretched hand of the German soldier. She smiled apologetically.

'My child ran out of the house and I left without my card. He's just over there, around that corner. I only wanted to get him back inside. You know how kids are.'

'Hey,' the German called to one of the gendarmes. 'No identity card here. Says she has a kid on the loose.' He raised one hand to summon the policeman while the other gripped her arm.

Ginny's heart threatened to burst and her legs began to tremble. She shifted the automatic slightly, testing to see that she could withdraw it quickly. She smiled at the young German. 'Is there a problem? Really? I live just down the street. Please, I don't want my son running free, he'll get into all kinds of mischief.'

'You wait here,' said the soldier as one of the gendarmes pushed his way through the crowd.

'What is it?' the Frenchman asked.

'Woman says she lives on this street and that her kid's run off.'

'Officer,' said Ginny plaintively, 'I just want to get my son. I ran out of the house without my identity card and –' The grim-faced gendarme seemed unimpressed but as he was about to question her the low wailing of a siren soared across the rooftops, its evolving pitch warning of an air raid. In that moment the soldiers reacted, shouting orders as the lorries' engines coughed into life. 'The Métro!' shouted the gendarme. 'Take cover!'

Everyone scattered. The nearest Métro station was two hundred metres away. Trenches had been dug across Paris since the beginning of the war to offer shelter and there were some of these across the intersection by a small square, but they were useless against heavy bombing and would only protect against flying shrapnel. Paris had so far escaped being bombed by the Allies except for industrial areas but now the sullen roar of heavy bombers approached. Ginny ran in the direction Peter Thompson had headed. Streets were emptying as people ran for the trenches and Métro. She saw a public telephone booth. A long-haired youth swung open the door and made an urgent attempt to rip away the sticker on the window banning Jews from using the telephone. The sirens became more insistent and the crump of falling bombs sounded from across the city. The youth's defiant gesture gave way to self-preservation and he ran for cover. Ginny scoured the area and saw Thompson hunched in a doorway. She scanned the clear sky: there was no sign of the bombers; they were delivering their ordnance further away towards the river. She squeezed in next to the cowering man and put her mouth close to his ear.

'You run from me again and I *will* shoot you and damn the consequences. When the all-clear sounds you're coming back to the apartment or I'll kill you here.'

She was surprised at how threatening her words were. But she meant them.

*

Mitchell and Burton had no sooner reached the vantage of the hospital roof than the sky darkened with the approaching bombers. Sirens wailed as anti-aircraft guns boomed, their shell bursts puff-balling the air around the approaching aircraft flying west of the hospital as they delivered their payloads over an island in the River Seine. The droning thunder of the American Fortresses' engines beat down from the crowded sky. Mitchell felt rather than imagined the tension within each of the B17s whose ten-man crews were flying in a hail of bursting shrapnel. The chattering gunfire from the aircrafts' gunners was already lacing the sky with intermittent tracer.

'It's the Renault car factory, Harry. They make tanks and armoured vehicles for the Germans. My God, it's a big one. There must be a hundred planes. The factory will take a pasting.'

The two men were transfixed by the erupting bombardment and the aerial attack as German fighter planes soared up into the sky to shoot the B17s down. The heart-racing drama roared on as specks of men tumbled into the sky from their stricken aircraft. Most were arrested by a billowing parachute canopy. One parachute barely opened as flames shredded the canopy and the unfortunate airman plunged to his death. Two aircraft screamed earthward; three more soon followed, smoke and flames searing the torn fuselages. The sound of the tortured engines thrust Mitchell back to his own terrifying experience in the aircraft that had brought him to France. He realized he was gripping the edge of the wall with such force that the rough masonry had torn away some of the skin from his fingers.

'Poor bastards,' said Mitchell.

'I'd better get back,' said Burton. 'There'll be casualties coming across the river into the other hospitals but we do what we can to help. And I have people who bring in the airmen on the run so we we can get them out.'

Mitchell turned for the stairs with Burton and clattered down the steps to the corridors below where staff and patients lined the windows looking up at the aerial attack. The hospital was far enough away not to be in danger and Mitchell knew that the Allies' flight charts would indicate the hospital's position. It wasn't Paris that was being bombed; it was the industrial plants that fed material to Germany. The scale of the bombing raids gave hope that the Allies were getting ever closer to invading mainland Europe, but the cost in lives was increasing.

Burton ushered Mitchell into his office. 'Harry, I'm sorry, I need to speak to my staff now,' he said as the anti-aircraft guns boomed in the distance, but placed a hand on his friend's shoulder. 'There's still time for you to catch up with your friend.'

⋆

Jean Bernard stepped from behind the drawn curtains around a hospital bed and caught Burton's beckoning gesture. The surgeon opened the door of his office and let the refugee doctor step inside.

'Pascal!' he said when he saw Mitchell at the window, watching the first wave of shadows in the sky wheeling for home. The two men shook hands.

'I can't stay long, not with this air raid going on. Are Juliet and Simone all right?'

'Yes, yes, we are fine, thank you. Simone is already in school and once Juliet gets her papers in order at the Préfecture my sister says she can help her find work.'

'No trouble getting here?'

'None. And you?'

'Well, it got interesting for a time. I'd like to come and see you all at your sister's apartment. Would that be all right?'

'Of course. There's a phone in the entrance outside the concierge's room. Why don't I give you the number?'

'Do you trust the concierge?'

Jean Bernard shrugged. 'Who knows?'

'Then that's too dangerous.' He turned to Burton. 'Can I phone the hospital to speak to him?'

'Of course. Ask for me and I'll bring him to my office.'

The sound of the air raid faded and the all clear sounded.

Mitchell pulled on his hat. 'I'll leave the same way I came in.'

35

Once the all clear had sounded the administrative staff at Avenue Foch headquarters poured back up the stairs from the basement shelter. The huddled mass, mostly of men in their drab green-grey uniforms, wriggled like a giant caterpillar. They were laughing, fancying themselves veterans of war for having survived an air raid that had been miles from the city. Someone below barked out an order for silence and for them to get back to their desks. Koenig could not help feeling a slight sense of superiority over them. When the air-raid sirens started he had been with Leutnant Hesler in the signals room on the floor below. As others ran for the shelter he and the dedicated signals man had stayed put. Even Koenig knew how to gauge the distance of exploding bombs and Hesler had said that enemy agents often used air raids as a cover to send their signals. It was usually the one time the radio detection vans were not in operation, but Hesler had given strict orders that his men continue their sweep. As Koenig and Hesler waited patiently in the radio room the muted bombardment had continued but no further signal had been noticed other than the one that had been sent that morning.

There were men, Hauptmann Martin Koenig decided, like himself and the clever young signals officer, who served their country loyally but who did not agree with many of the methods used to defeat their enemy. Hesler was as much a part of those who hunted the Reich's enemy as was the SS major who scoured the countryside with his Hunter Group. And he, Koenig, was efficient in bringing statistics and numerical accuracy to those captured, tortured and slain so that records were in good order and the facts could not be distorted. Both men were an essential part of the German war machine but neither were required to see the end result of the skills they brought to bear.

Koenig waited patiently until Hesler pulled off his headphones and shook his head. It was doubtful that the wireless operator in the city would transmit any more today, he told Koenig as he handed him the report he had made on the earlier wireless activity.

'She's good, captain,' Hesler acknowledged.

'And you're certain it's a woman?'

'As sure as I can be. There's a lightness to her key transmission. A certain… feel. We'll catch her eventually. They all make a mistake sooner or later and that's when we'll get her.'

*

Hauptmann Koenig waited while Stolz looked at the report.

'Leutnant Hesler couldn't locate where this transmission came from?'

'No, sir, but it's a new wireless operator. Hesler is almost completely certain it's a woman. And he tells me that the British are very poor in their security. We know that they instruct their wireless operators to routinely place a deliberate mistake in their transmission – usually a transposition of a letter by a few places – to make sure that their wireless operator is not in our hands. This is something we can do nothing about so we run the risk of the British questioning any of our false transmissions. Yet they often miss or ignore the mistake. It will be their downfall, colonel.'

Stolz smiled. 'Not everyone is as fastidious as you, captain, but I agree, British arrogance makes them careless. Has Leutnant Hesler kept requesting London for a meeting with their agent?'

'Yes, sir. Every afternoon at Café Claire.'

'Very well, we must play this out as long as we are able. This message that Hesler picked up specifically mentioned Gideon again and Pascal, which means Pascal – or, as we hope him to be – Mitchell and this other man, Gideon, are here together.'

'Gideon is not a French name, sir. If it's associated with Pascal it might be a cover name or a group he's establishing.'

'Are you certain, captain?'

'Well, no, not certain, colonel. But the name denotes destruction. Gideon slew the Midianites.'

'Koenig, I don't know who the Midianites are or where you get this kind of information from' – he raised a hand quickly to stop Koenig from explaining – 'and I don't want to know. But it is a fair assumption. So, let us think of it as being this Pascal's group. It's a start at least. The SS Hunter Group hasn't found anything, so what I want you to do, Koenig, is bring that Milice inspector who sent us his reports, what was his name? The one from Saint-Audière.'

Koenig took a moment to recall the man's name. 'Inspector Paul Berthold.'

'Yes, that's him. Get him to Paris. We need a description of the man he interrogated and then we set him to work here with the Milice and Brigades Spéciales. Let's flush this Pascal out. Tell Hesler that he must keep transmitting and asking for London to arrange a meeting. Finding this agent might be easier than we thought. If our ruse to bring the Englishman Mitchell back into the city has worked then London has given him this new wireless operator for a specific reason.' He opened his desk drawer and took out the sheaf of brown folders. Choosing one he opened it and fingered aside some of the clipped documents. Finally, he settled on the information he had searched for. 'Koenig, the woman Suzanne Colbert was not part of any known terrorist cell. The wireless operator Alain Ory was working with an English agent who has disappeared. Perhaps dead. Perhaps fled.' He raised his eyes and smiled. 'Better the former rather than the latter, but either way we are missing vital pieces of information by not having him in our custody. The traitor Alfred Korte is somewhere in this city. One lonely old man who has information that Reichsführer Himmler is desperate to secure. Given the number of disparate French Resistance units in and around the city would it not be reasonable to think that they would send an agent and wireless operator here to co-ordinate the groups? No – because they are at each other's throats most of the time. They turn on each other like dogs after a bone. London has sent these people to find our German traitor. And if they are prepared to risk more agents' lives then they must have information as to his whereabouts. We capture this Pascal and fortune – with help from Leitmann – may smile upon us and give us the man the Reichsführer wants.'

As Koenig walked back to his office two Gestapo men dragged a man up the stairs. He had already been beaten;

blood matted his hair and stained the side of his neck. His legs gave way on the final flight up to the fifth floor and the interrogation rooms. One of the Gestapo men cuffed him hard against the side of his head to urge him on. How stupidly brutal these men were, Koenig thought, pressing himself back against the wall to allow the terrified man to be dragged past. The poor wretch was barely able to walk and so the thugs beat him harder. Moments later Leitmann skipped up the stairs two at a time. He grinned at Koenig.

'Is the colonel in?'

'Yes.'

'Who's this?' Koenig asked, indicating the stricken victim being hauled upstairs.

'We got a tip-off that a *résistant* from a terrorist cell in the south was securing a safe house for an agent.'

'Who warned you? The colonel's informer?'

Leitmann shrugged. 'Who knows? Anyway, we got him.'

'Wouldn't it make more sense to have him followed and then when the agent was in place you could have hauled in the fish rather than the bait? Or don't you and your strong-arm men have the brains to figure that out?'

Leitmann scowled at the insult. 'Koenig, go back to your ledgers and leave the real work to those of us who aren't afraid to get our hands dirty. By tonight he'll talk. And by tomorrow we'll scoop up the agent.'

The Gestapo man pushed past him. Koenig calculated the odds whether this résistant had anything to do with Pascal being in the city. Coincidence could play a vital part in capturing an enemy agent. And the coincidence in this instance was lessened by the man being betrayed by an informant in the pay of the SD and Gestapo. Koenig looked back down the corridor to where Leitmann had stepped into the ambitious colonel's office. The Nazi had vowed to sweep up resistance in Paris and as far as Koenig could see the fear that Stolz and the Gestapo had created was working. Stolz would rise ever higher in the ranks and the likes of Leitmann would follow in his wake. A sudden cry of pain echoed down the stairwell from the top floor. He crossed himself and muttered thanks to God that he was nothing more than an accountant in the service of these monsters. And tonight the fear he felt at being so close to the ruthlessness would melt away even further when he lay with Béatrice Claudel. He was quickly falling in love with the young Frenchwoman. She made no demands on him and asked for nothing. Her affections towards him, he had determined, were genuine and when they made love she wept with pleasure. How beautiful it all was and how far removed from this violence.

36

Peter Thompson sucked nervously on a cigarette, hunched over, his foot incessantly tapping. Ginny leant against the galley kitchen's counter watching as Mitchell spoke to him, his voice lowered, like a doctor with a patient. When Mitchell had returned from the hospital she had told him what had happened. Mitchell had restrained his anger. He realized that if he was to get this deserter to help him he would have to help the man control his fear, and venting his own frustrated impatience would cause more harm than good. Mitchell tossed Thompson one of the packs of cigarettes that had come in on Ginny's Lysander.

'Thank you,' Thompson said, sniffing the packet for the rich tobacco aroma.

'The reason I asked you to stay here in the apartment with Thérèse was that you are very important to the success of this mission,' Mitchell told him.

'I had to see if my wife was safe.'

'And did you speak to her?'

'Yes.'

'And you did not speak to anyone else?'

'Like who?'

'Is your phone a party line?'

'No. I had it for the business. For the garage.'

'And she's all right?'

Thompson shrugged. 'As well as she can be.'

'So are you ready now to help me find Alfred Korte?'

Thompson nodded.

'Good man,' said Mitchell, and placed a friendly hand on his shoulder, glancing across at a stern-faced Ginny who raised her eyebrows. She obviously thought the Englishman calling himself Ferrand was feeble. 'But next time don't risk it. You could have been killed.'

'I was a long way from the air raid and my papers are good.'

'I meant by Thérèse,' said Mitchell.

*

Mitchell and Thompson travelled west from the ninth to the eighth district of the city. The American Library on Rue de Téhéran had stayed open during the German Occupation. French subscribers depended on the library for its periodicals. But the library also supplied books to those Americans whose luck had run out, who were no longer allowed to reside in the city and who had been interned.

Thompson was told to stay on the street and keep watch for any German patrols who might visit the library while Ginny enquired about opening a subscription. If anything untoward happened while Mitchell was questioning the contact Burton had given him then Thompson and Ginny were to stage a domestic argument to distract the Germans.

Mitchell was led into the office and made his enquiry about the closed bookshop to the woman who ran the library.

'I don't care for speaking to strangers no matter who sent you. What did you say your name was again?' said the refined-looking woman behind her ornate desk. She was in her fifties, Mitchell guessed, but could pass for a woman ten years younger. By the look of her clothing and jewellery, Eva de Gerlier was from the upper echelons of Paris society, though Mitchell could not place her American accent. He didn't have the ear for the nuances of American inflection but he guessed she was East Coast and had married an upper-class Frenchman.

'Garon, Pascal Garon,' said Mitchell.

Her hand moved effortlessly across a piece of writing paper, the pen accustomed to being caressed. She laid aside the pen and glanced up at Mitchell. 'Is your name of any interest to the Germans? Would they be pleased if I handed them this sheet of paper? I ask because I have no truck with the Resistance. We obey the rules here and that is why we are still open.'

Mitchell glanced around the office, which was at the rear of the library. Hundreds of books were stacked on the floor against the wall beside French windows that looked out on to a small garden. When he had climbed the elaborate staircase to the woman's office more books had been stacked neatly on every step.

'I hadn't realized you had so many books here.'

'More than a hundred thousand, and why would you?'

'I used to live in Paris.'

'Oh? No longer?

'I taught at the university.'

'And I moved back here soon after the Occupation. But I know Dr Burton socially and he has never mentioned your name.'

'How exactly has the library managed to stay open?'

She studied him for a moment. 'You think we collaborate?'

Mitchell shrugged. 'Your clothes are expensive; so's your jewellery. As far as I can see not much has changed in Paris since the Germans arrived. The fashion houses around the Place Vendôme and the Ritz still cater for richly dressed women. People still make enough money from looking after industrialist's wives, actresses, German officers' women and those who collaborate with the enemy.'

'Very well, M'sieu Garon... if that is indeed your name. Your accent is not that of a Parisian. I suspect you are an Englishman. Your manner is... too polite.' She raised an eyebrow as if to say, *Not so?* 'We are protected by the Germans. You speak German?'

'A little.'

'Did you teach languages?'

'Mathematics.'

'Ah, then your vocabulary might be limited. *Bibliotheksschutz.*'

'Library protection?' said Mitchell.

She nodded. 'Quite so. Dr Hermann Fuchs guarantees the safety of all the libraries in occupied Europe. I met him at a conference before the war. We are not allowed to admit Jews, which is a great pity because they are some of our most loyal subscribers, and there are certain authors that are banned. If we do this then we are allowed to function without any problems.'

'And yet they destroyed the libraries in Poland when they invaded.'

'And arrested and murdered the teachers. It seems we have both been spared.'

'And lucky. One of the men who work for you is Jewish. You shelter him. Frank Burton told me he hid him in the hospital for a while and he also told me you could be trusted. And yes, I dare say the Germans would be interested in my name, sooner or later.'

She appraised him again and her icy demeanour softened. She smiled. For the second time that day a name on a piece of paper of interest to the police and Gestapo was burnt in an ashtray.

'The woman who closed her bookshop... I know where she is.'

37

Mitchell arrived at Madame Belvoir's rooms above a clothing-repair shop with Peter Thompson. They explained who had sent them and the urgency of finding Alfred Korte. The seventy-three-year-old bookshop owner leant her elbows on a small cloth-covered table, stained with food and wine spillage, where a dozen novels were stacked open. A chipped saucer served as an ashtray, almost full with burnt-down stubs, and she tipped what was left of a half-bottle of red wine without a label into her glass as she listened to the men's explanation. The small apartment had a curtained-off bed and smelt of cat urine. The windows were closed, the April sun beaming through one small pane in a shaft of stifling warmth that cut through the haze of cigarette smoke.

'Why would I know where he is?' she said finally.

'Madame,' said Thompson, 'I was supposed to help him escape from your bookshop. But when I got there the place was crawling with Germans. The streets had been cordoned off and the situation appeared impossible.'

She succumbed for a moment to a chesty, rattling cough. She drank more wine. 'I remember being told that someone was coming. *Résistants* made no mention of an Englishman.' She shrugged. 'So what. It was too late. The Germans and the police raided my bookshop and the next-door milliner's. I doubt they were looking for the old man. Just a random nuisance call.' She glared at Thompson. 'And no one ever came back. Got scared, did you?'

'Yes,' Thompson admitted.

Madame grunted. 'You young people don't know what fear is. I hid him for weeks despite their searches. Then it became too much. I had nothing but damned German customers. Officers mostly, but they scared off my French regulars. Not that anyone could afford books any more.' She sighed. 'Sooner or later they'd have found him. Anyway, I didn't want to make money from the Boche.'

'And then?' Mitchell said.

'And then what was I supposed to do? Kick him on to the street? He was an educated man. He read widely. We discussed literature.'

'Here?' said Mitchell.

'Of course here. Where do you think? He slept on the couch.' She inhaled smoke and then glared at them. 'There was no impropriety.'

'Of course not, Madame Belvoir,' said Thompson, dismissing the image such a liaison suggested.

'Then where is he now?' asked Mitchell.

'Dead most likely. He got sick a few weeks back. I got him to hospital.'

'Not the American Hospital?' Mitchell said. If so, the irony would be almost too much to bear.

She looked at Mitchell as if he were an idiot. 'No, of course not. Their wards are full.'

Mitchell hid his disappointment.

Madame stubbed out what was left of her cigarette. 'The Hôtel-Dieu took him.'

*

Mitchell phoned Frank Burton from a kiosk and asked him to send Jean Bernard across to the Hôtel-Dieu. Madame Belvoir had given the German her late husband's identity card and his name, Yves Belvoir. One elderly man staring back at anyone checking a photograph in an identity document would not look so different from another. What else could I do? she had proclaimed. She did not have access to forgers. She did the best she could. The rest was in God's hands.

'All right,' Mitchell told Thompson. 'We're going to get him and then we'll take him to the American Hospital until I can arrange a plane for him.'

'The Hôtel-Dieu is opposite the Préfecture de Police. It's a hot spot for Gestapo and police snap inspections. It's too dangerous. We must find another way.'

'Hold your nerve,' said Mitchell. 'I have a contact at both hospitals. Once we're in we will find a way out.'

'I can't. I'm sorry. It's a bloody death trap. Right opposite the Préfecture,' he said again for emphasis.

Mitchell's heightened sense of anxiety was being sorely tested. If he could get Alfred Korte out of France then he would have accomplished what his masters in London wanted and he would then be free to concentrate on harassing the enemy and finding his daughter. 'A few more hours, Peter. That's all. And then you can go home.'

Tears welled in Thompson's eyes. 'All right,' he whispered.

Mitchell, Ginny and Thompson made their way towards the hospital along side streets, avoiding the main thoroughfares. They had just turned a corner when Mitchell saw a Traction Avant angled across the street blocking access to the hospital. A half-dozen gendarmes were on the opposite pavement, their batons held in extended arms as they herded pedestrians towards the opposite wall where plainclothes Gestapo were conducting an identity-card search. A German lorry had spilt its cargo of soldiers and they spread along the length of the nearside pavement.

Mitchell's throat tightened as his heartbeat quickened. Thompson looked paralysed, his stricken face gaunt with fear. 'Keep walking,' Mitchell insisted. He grabbed Thompson's arm, forcing him to keep pace. Mitchell could feel the resistance in his body and he feared Thompson's panic would make him run and then he and Ginny would be immediately suspect.

'Don't say anything,' insisted Mitchell. 'We are taking you to the hospital because you're sick. If they search us they'll find our weapons. Be ready to use them.'

Before Thompson could object gendarmes ushered them forward into the shuffling line being processed by the plainclothes Gestapo officer. The number of people snared in the round-up meant the inspection was being processed with quick efficiency. The man who was creating so much fear looked to Mitchell's eyes to be young enough to be studying at the Sorbonne instead of inflicting terror simply by his presence on the streets of Paris.

Leitmann never broke the rhythm of checking those shuffling past him. The card inspected, the face checked, the card returned and the individual moved along. Mitchell felt the perspiration tickle his spine. Thompson was shaking uncontrollably, his hairline damp with sweat. Mitchell removed his hat without being told so that his face could be checked against the photograph on the identity card. Ginny was a couple of paces behind him.

Leitmann looked at Mitchell's companion. Thompson's hand trembled as he offered his identity card. Mitchell tensed.

Leitmann plucked the card from Thompson's hand. 'What's wrong with you?'

Thompson stuttered badly as if trying to form words.

'He's been ill for a week,' said Mitchell. 'He works in the abattoir. We think he's caught something off diseased meat. We're hoping it's not contagious.'

As Leitmann took an involuntary step back one of the approaching soldiers interrupted the search. 'Herr Leitmann, there is a radio message for you to return to headquarters immediately.'

Irritated, Leitmann turned on the soldier. 'I'll decide when I leave. Tell them another hour,' he said, distracted, tossing the identity card into Thompson's hand. 'Get him inside. You people are stupid. He shouldn't even be on the street. Move!'

Mitchell's identity had miraculously been missed. He half carried Thompson through the barrier of soldiers and was soon clear of the inspection. The soldier who had borne the message to the Gestapo officer must have said something further because Mitchell heard the Gestapo man raise his voice. 'Be quiet! I've told you – I'll go when I'm good and ready. I will determine what has priority here.'

Mitchell steadied Thompson as Ginny joined them. 'Wait across the street at the café. Once I have what we came for we'll have to play it by ear.' Ginny turned at once: she knew not to question Mitchell at such a critical time. As she went across the street Mitchell gave Thompson an encouraging smile. 'It's almost over. Well done. Come on now, couple of deep breaths and we're home and dry.'

Thompson put a brave face on it and returned Mitchell's smile. 'Sorry, old man, I flunk it when I think of what those bastards would do to me. I'm a dreadful coward, you know.'

'No, you're not,' Mitchell told him, his voice genuinely warm. 'A coward would not be able to do what you have done.'

38

When they stepped inside Jean Bernard was waiting. The long corridor appeared to stretch the full length of the building. It was strangely hushed as their shoes clattered along the marble floor. Mitchell quickly introduced Jean Bernard to Thompson and explained to the French doctor that it had been Thompson who had tried to help the fugitive German scientist in the past. Mitchell's voice was barely louder than a whisper in the vastness of the corridor.

'We must exercise caution, Pascal. Not all the nurses here are anti-German.'

'How ill is the old man?' said Thompson.

'He had pneumonia and he was malnourished but from what I've seen on his chart he has made a good recovery. He will still be weak but I believe he will be strong enough to travel,' Jean Bernard said as he ushered them through two large wooden swing doors into a five-bed ward. 'We must be careful. There's a ward nurse I've been warned about. The hospital thinks she's in the pay of the police or Gestapo and her shift is going to start soon. And a man was murdered here recently, shot in his bed. No one will talk about it but everyone is looking over their shoulder. There doesn't seem to be much doubt that it was the SS or the Gestapo.' He pointed to a man in the nearest bed and quickly pulled a privacy screen around him. 'This is the man you're looking for.'

Peter Thompson stepped forward and sat in the chair next to where Alfred Korte lay half raised. He smiled when he saw the tall Englishman and reached out his hands to clasp Thompson's.

'You came back,' he said, his accent unmistakably German. 'I knew you would.'

'I'm sorry it took me so long, but when I came to get you at the bookshop the place was swarming with soldiers and Gestapo.'

Korte patted Thompson's hand. 'Yes, it would have been impossible for you to get me out then but I was looked after. Now that you are here what is going to happen?'

Thompson nodded towards Mitchell. 'This man will get you to England. It will take a few more days yet, but you must trust him.'

'Very well. If you say that I must, then I will.' He gave a nod of acknowledgement to Mitchell.

'We should not spend too much time here right now,' said Jean Bernard. 'These are not official visiting hours. Pascal, do we know whether this Yves Belvoir is on the Gestapo or police wanted list?'

It had not occurred to Mitchell that this might be the case. He knew nothing about Madame Belvoir's late husband. Had he ever been arrested for any petty crime? Or questioned for any reason by the authorities? If he had then Alfred Korte could no longer risk using Belvoir's documents. It would take only a random identity check and the old man would be arrested.

'I don't know.' Mitchell felt the uncertainty squirm in his stomach. They were minutes away from getting Korte out on to the street.

Jean Bernard nodded. 'I thought it unlikely you would have had time to check. A man of similar age died last night. Every day the police collect the papers of anyone who's passed away. They haven't been here yet, but to give you a chance on the streets I have swapped his identity documents with the dead man's.' Jean Bernard smiled. 'Just in case. As far as I know the dead man is not on any police list.'

'How do we get Korte out?' said Mitchell.

'A mortuary van will be waiting at the front for the body. They are bound to stop the driver and check the van. That's the best diversion we can hope for.' He handed Mitchell a folded sheet of official-looking paper. 'This is a duplicate death certificate I signed for Alfred Korte. If you are discovered and they find this on you then at least it gives him a chance.'

Jean Bernard and Peter Thompson soon had the elderly Korte dressed in his suit and overcoat. He was unsteady on his feet but Mitchell supported him as they eased him out of the ward and down the long corridor towards the entrance.

'I must get back and make sure all the paperwork is in order,' said Jean Bernard. He shook hands with the three men. 'Pascal, I will speak to you again soon, no doubt. And you, sir,' he said to Korte, 'I will see you sooner than you think.' He turned back towards the ward.

'What did he mean?' asked Korte.

'You'll know soon enough,' said Mitchell. 'Peter, say your goodbyes to Herr Korte. You've done everything I have asked of you. Go home with my blessings.'

'You have family?' said Korte.

'Yes. They are waiting for me,' said Thompson.

'Ah, good. Then hurry back to your wife and children. I am grateful that you returned and brought this gentleman with you. I will soon be in England thanks to your courage.'

'Thank you, sir. You're very kind,' said Thompson and with a final nod of farewell turned down the steps towards the street.

'Now, what is your name?' said Korte, turning to Mitchell.

'Pascal Garon,' said Mitchell.

'Then where are we going now, M'sieu Garon?'

'Out the back door,' said Mitchell.

*

It was unclear to Ginny Lindhurst what happened in the minutes following Mitchell and the elderly man reaching the street. She watched from the café opposite as the mortuary van's doors were closed and its driver eased it out of the rear entrance. No sooner had the van reached the street than the police and German cordon shifted. Perhaps it was sheer bad luck or maybe someone in the hospital suspected something was wrong. Whatever the reason, the Gestapo and police stopped the mortuary van and hauled out the driver. They checked the man's papers and then the plainclothes Gestapo agent had him open the rear doors. Voices were raised and then a body was removed on a stretcher and the Gestapo agent instructed a German *Feldgendarme* to check the dead man against a pocketbook of photographs. She heard him answer that it was no one they were looking for and that the name on the death certificate was someone called Yves Belvoir. By the time the soldiers eased the body back into the mortuary van Mitchell and the man with him were fifty metres past the cordon moving away from the snap inspection. Leaving her table, Ginny moved further away into the side street. Behind her a baker was unloading his van at the back door of the café. Across the street the soldiers and gendarmes began to spread out again. She saw that Thompson was clear of the cordon. He glanced her way and gave a quick smile. He was out of danger. She looked to her right and saw two gendarmes looking down the street to where Mitchell and his slow-moving charge had stopped; the elderly man, weakened by the exertion, had slumped against the wall. Mitchell looked back as the gendarmes called for him to stay where he was.

Their command for the two men to stop caught the attention of the other soldiers and the Gestapo agent. The soldiers started shouting and the two gendarmes walked briskly to where Mitchell was trying to half carry the weak man down the street. The German and French police had their backs to Ginny and Thompson; pedestrians, sensing something was wrong, hurried past. Now the Germans cried out for Mitchell to halt. Ginny reached into her pocket for the pistol but before she could pull it free she heard Thompson shout: 'Pascal!' The Germans turned. Thompson, standing in the middle of the street, arm extended, began to shoot. Everyone scattered. Café patrons dived to the floor. Thompson kept firing, his shots missing wildly. Soldiers knelt, rifles in their shoulders. One soldier was hit, and a French gendarme. Then a volley of ragged shots tore into Thompson. He spun, arms flung wide, and fell, one leg bent beneath the other, his gun lying feet away. Blood seeped from underneath him. Cautiously the soldiers advanced on him. Ginny saw Mitchell and Korte making their escape. She turned towards the baker's van – the driver was nowhere in sight. Slamming the doors she climbed into the driver's seat and drove towards Mitchell. Soldiers shouted commands and waved her away. She slowed as she passed Thompson. His eyes were open and blood trickled from his mouth as he tried to reach the fallen pistol. In that moment their eyes met. Ginny gripped the steering wheel as she drove past the mayhem. Tears stung her eyes; her breath caught as she forced herself to concentrate. Her ears still rang from the gunfire. She had been seconds away from doing exactly what Thompson had done. An instinctive act to save another. Bile rose in her throat; she swallowed the acid liquid back, gulped air, dragged a hand across her eyes and wiped away the tears from her blurred vision, then eased the van around the corner to where Mitchell waited with the half-slumped man.

39

On the morning of the shooting outside the hospital, Stolz
had slipped from his bed leaving Dominique Lesaux with a
kiss and a reminder that they were to going to hear Edith
Piaf sing at the Casino de Paris that evening. By the time
Parisians were awake and making their way to work Stolz
had met with his staff and learnt that the man Hauptmann
Koenig had seen being dragged up the stairs and then
tortured had died from a heart attack. The only information
his interrogators had gleaned from him was that an agent
was due in the city and that his name was Pascal, which
confirmed Stolz's source, and that an apartment had been
arranged as a place of safety for the agent. It was this
information that had resulted in the sweeping cordons near
the hospital.

After the shooting Stolz had visited the scene and inspected
the body of the man who had called out the name Pascal
before being shot.

'Is this Pascal?' said Stolz as Leitmann lifted the groundsheet
that covered Peter Thompson's body. The blood was already

congealing and despite the coolness of the day flies had started to gather on the body.

Leitmann drew on a cigarette and studied the crumpled body. He shrugged as he looked at the surrounding streets. 'I don't know, colonel. Why would he make such a grandstanding gesture? He must have known he would be shot. He just stood there and fired at us. He didn't even try and take cover.'

'Perhaps he wanted to become a martyr,' said Stolz.

'Unless he was calling out to someone in the crowd and warning them.'

'Any identification on him?'

'A Charles Ferrand. Registered in a small village south of here.'

'Then it could be him. We know Pascal travelled from the south,' said Stolz. 'There was no one by that name in the immediate vicinity when you secured the area and checked identity cards?'

'No one. We had more than a hundred held outside the hospital and down that street. We bottled up the whole area, four different teams in the district around the address we got from the man we interrogated.'

'And?'

'Just an empty apartment with a couple of mattresses on the floor. It's been empty for years. There was nothing there, sir. When this man was shot I thought I recognized him as someone I had checked. He was with another man who said this one was sick. He was in a bad way and he wasn't acting. One thing that might be worth following up was the theft of a baker's delivery van from that café moments after the shooting stopped.'

'So what are we to make of this? Let us presume this man was not a fanatic and that he is not Pascal, and the place of safety the Resistance had set up has not been used. Let us further suppose that the bakery van was not taken for its contents but used as an escape vehicle. I would say Pascal has made his own decisions and that this man's' – he pointed at Thompson's corpse – 'companion is the one we need to find. Can you remember him?'

'No, colonel. We were checking too many of them for any one face to stand out.'

'There's a Milice inspector coming from a small town who interviewed a Pascal Garon. Keep this man's body in the mortuary for identification. No burial until I say so. Hand his death over to the French to investigate. And have them find that van.'

Stolz gave the dead man at his feet a final glance. The half-closed eyes were sleepily opaque and the slightly parted lips gave the impression that he was smiling.

*

The baker's van was discovered the following day south of the river, far from the American Hospital where Mitchell and Ginny had smuggled Alfred Korte through the back entrance. Burton secured a bed for him in an isolation ward for patients with an infectious disease. Only Frank Burton and Jean Bernard, along with a couple of nurses, were allowed access to him. It was hoped that two or three days in the American's care would strengthen him for his journey back to England when the moon was right for a Lysander to be flown in. Mitchell and Ginny returned to the apartment and slept for twelve hours, exhausted by the tension of escaping the Germans' net and watching helplessly as Peter Thompson sacrificed himself.

Having slept and washed, they felt refreshed and shared a breakfast until it was time for Ginny to make her scheduled transmission. She sent the message to London that their long-lost friend had been found and that transport would be needed. Mitchell sat listening to the steady, rhythmic tap of her Morse key. He admired the young woman's courage and quick thinking. Her presence of mind had probably saved Mitchell and Alfred Korte. Had she not stolen the baker's van it was likely he would have been taken – he wouldn't have managed to drag Korte much further. She had taken a big risk – she could have been stopped in the immediate aftermath of the shooting.

Thompson's death was a shock that they knew they had to recover from. If the Gideon network was to be established then plans had to be made and their action implemented. His sacrifice had been an act of incredible courage but there was no time to explore their feelings of loss. Their work had to continue. Ginny handed Mitchell a slip of paper with a decoded message.

'Alain Ory is alive. He's contacted London. They want you to meet him. He's moving around the city, scared that the Germans are on to him.'

Mitchell scanned the message. If he could meet with Ory he could find out more about the death of his wife and perhaps verify that his daughter was in La Santé prison. 'Confirm,' he said. 'Tell us where and when.'

She returned to her Morse key. Waited, listened for a response. Checked her code sheets and without the need to commit London's answer to paper quickly took down her aerial from the curtain rail. 'Every day. Café Claire, it's down a side street off Rue des Francs-Bourgeois. Five o'clock.' She switched off the set and hid the suitcase out of sight beneath the bed.

Mitchell checked his watch and unfolded a street map of Paris, his finger tracing a route from the apartment to the meeting place. 'I can't remember it. Here it is... all right, we'll go separately. You take a trolleybus here at this corner and get off a block away. The café is on the opposite side of the crossroads. If you leave now you'll get there before me. Find somewhere to keep an eye on it. Remember, don't stay in any one place too long. If he's there and he follows his training he won't stay longer than fifteen or twenty minutes. We'll watch who comes and goes.'

Ginny nodded, pulled on her coat and put her arm through her shoulder bag. 'See you back here afterwards.'

He listened as her heels tapped down the stairs. He heard the apartment door below open and close as if its occupant had watched Ginny leave. He waited a moment longer and then, satisfied that there was no one else on the stairs, grabbed his coat and hat. He wished he had time to contact Gaétan and ask him to describe Alain Ory. When Colonel Beaumont and Major Knight had first approached him they had shown him a photograph of the wireless operator, but that day in the room in his lodging seemed so long ago he had no recollection of what the man looked like.

*

Leutnant Hesler ran from the wireless room and breathlessly presented himself to Hauptmann Koenig.

'Sir, I have confirmation from London that Pascal will go to the arranged meeting place.'

'Today?'

'Yes, major.'

Koenig took the message pad slip from Hesler and glanced at it as if doubting the veracity of the wireless officer's information. 'Come with me.'

Hesler followed Koenig down the corridor to Stolz's office. Hesler could barely contain his excitement as Koenig knocked on the colonel's door. Beckoned inside, the two men snapped to attention. Stolz raised his eyes from a report he had been studying.

'Colonel, Leutnant Hesler has finally received confirmation that the English agent has agreed to go to the rendezvous.' He stepped forward and handed Stolz the sheet of paper.

'There can be no doubt?' said Stolz.

'None, sir.'

'And they did not request confirmation that their operator here was not under duress?'

Hesler smiled. 'Their security is amateurish, colonel. I believe they are relying completely on recognizing their operator's sending style.'

'And we owe that to your skills, Leutnant Hesler. I will tell Berlin so in my report. Congratulations. Stay attentive and keep monitoring the wireless operator they have in the city. Gentlemen, you must play this game with skill and patience. The longer the British believe that Alain Ory is alive, the stronger our position here in capturing their agents. Collaborators can only be relied upon to a certain extent. If Pascal is the Englishman Mitchell as I suspect then we will uncover many of the names of those who assist the terrorists. Leutnant Hesler, I will see that you are given more resources and radio detection vans to track down their operator here.'

Hesler dipped his head in acknowledgement, braced his shoulders and returned to the wireless room.

Stolz nodded towards the retreating wireless officer. 'What did I tell you, Koenig? That man is a genius. I know how to pick the best people. You included. Have Leitmann sent for immediately. After the shooting at the hospital, he might recognize this Pascal when he gets to the café. I want every precaution taken. We must box in the street and be ready to move as soon as he is identified.'

40

The urgency Mitchell felt as he elbowed his way through the crowds in the Métro was a mixture of trepidation and hope. His instincts told him that the meeting with Alain Ory was risky, but he could not stop himself hoping that the fugitive wireless operator might shed more light on what happened to his wife and daughter. The crammed Métro carriage rocked noisily as the wheels screeched on every bend in the track. Cigarette smoke clung to the air and passengers' clothing; the stifling air was rank with the sickly-sweet aroma of cheap perfume. Men and women's bodies pressed close together in an unconsummated act except, perhaps, in the imagination. Mitchell watched his fellow passengers. Most looked exhausted, faces drawn from having little food and sleep. No one appeared to pay him any attention, but the incessant worry of being followed kept his senses sharpened.

As he made his way to the street level the surge of the crowd slowed, and when they filtered through the gates on the platform Mitchell saw five or six gendarmes checking identity cards. There was no sign of plainclothes Gestapo or detectives, so he reasoned it was just a normal snap inspection. A Métro station was always a good hunting ground, but this time the inspection seemed almost cursory, the gendarmes more interested in getting the crowd through their hands as quickly as possible. One of them checked his watch, said something to another, and waved two or three people through at once. Men due to come off their shift and in a hurry to complete the random check, Mitchell guessed. As each person was stopped they were obliged to say their name, which was checked against their identity card. It was a simple ploy. A moment of tension fuelled by fear could make someone with a false identity admit their real name instead of the one on their forged papers. A man and a woman were pulled aside and questioned but released, and then another man was plucked from the crowd and taken to a sergeant who had a briefcase on a strap worn like a satchel across his chest. The restrained man's papers were checked again and the sergeant took an identity book out of the briefcase and flipped through the photographs. Satisfied, the sergeant instructed his men to return the identity card and release the suspect. It might be something as innocent as having the same name as someone the police wanted, Mitchell thought as he averted his eyes and shuffled along the line to present his identity card.

'Hat,' said the gendarme. 'You know the drill.'

Mitchell complied, staring away into the distance. Eye contact with those who controlled the law could be seen as a challenge. The gendarme studied Mitchell's face.

'Name?'

'Pascal Garon,' Mitchell replied.

The identity document was snapped closed, handed back and Mitchell told to move on. He strode towards the street.

The delay had already made him late. He was almost in the street when 'You!' an authoritative voice called after him.

Mitchell's heart beat faster. He controlled the urge to escape further questioning by taking his chances on the busy street. He turned to face the sergeant with the briefcase. He was alone, the others filtering away from the Métro stairs having checked the last of the passengers.

'I know you,' said the officer. 'It's you isn't it? Henri. Henri Mitchell. I didn't recognize you at first, not without the beard.'

Mitchell's hand sat deep in his pocket ready to pull free the automatic.

'Henri, don't look so concerned. It's me? Jules Vanves. Remember? I taught history. How are you, my friend?'

Mitchell barely contained the sigh of relief and withdrew his hand from the pistol butt to shake the man's extended hand. 'Fine, Jules. Thank you. And I did not recognize you either. It was the… er…' He dabbed a finger beneath his own nose. The gendarme had a caterpillar moustache that crawled across his lip.

'It's a new thing. It itches. I suppose that's why you got rid of the whiskers eh?'

'Exactly.'

'Come with me, let's have a drink. It's been too long.'

'Well, I was supposed to meet someone.'

'Where?'

'Near here. The Café Claire.'

'Perfect. I'm off duty. I know it well. This arrondissement is my patch.' He put a friendly arm across Mitchell's shoulder and guided him on to the street as Mitchell racked his brain to remember what he could about the man.

'I don't blame you for not recognizing me,' said Vanves. 'Me, in the police. Who'd have thought, eh?' Mitchell's memory of him began to return. He'd been a junior lecturer in the history department at the university, a good teacher who was dedicated to his students.

'Jules, I never would have thought you'd quit teaching.'

'Ah, me too. But let me tell you, you got out at the right time. I became so sick and tired of the education system. The Church, the State and the socialists, they were all interfering at the end. And they sacked more than a thousand teachers for being Freemasons. I was one of them.'

'I didn't know that,' said Mitchell. Perhaps the chance meeting with Vanves might be a gift from the gods of war. He would have contacts that could be tapped into and he might be useful in finding out about Danielle at La Santé prison – the prison guards there were all Frenchmen.

Vanves always did like the sound of his own voice and he continued with barely a breath. 'So, I had enough contacts who got me into the Préfecture as a clerk. Most of these men are pig-shit stupid so it didn't take much for me to get out on the streets from behind a desk. And that's when they made me a sergeant.'

As they approached the side street where the café was located, Mitchell felt more assured. If the arranged meeting were a trap, arriving with a uniformed policeman would deflect any attention.

*

Ginny Lindhurst had been watching from the inside of a dress shop. She had fussed and examined clothing, chatting to the sales assistant who confided that the seamstress working at the back was only part-time because she also worked at one of the city's well-known fashion houses, which meant the quality of the clothes was guaranteed and, the girl had whispered, they were able to copy the latest fashions at a fraction of the cost. Everyone knew that the Germans had strict quotas on production from the city's famous couturiers. It was idle chatter but the assistant was happy to engage because she had seen few customers that day. Ginny kept an eye on the time and on the man who sat alone and who appeared to be more nervous than anyone else sitting at the outside tables. Mitchell was late and the man she suspected of being Alain Ory had waited longer than she had expected. It had been almost an hour. Nothing would make an agent stay that long in one place unless he was so careless that it posed a threat to others who worked with him. Finally, he left the table and crossed the street. She watched. No one approached him and he quickly disappeared from view. She waited a few moments and, promising the shop assistant that she would return another day, went out on to the street, undecided whether to wait for Mitchell or follow the man. She decided to stay, concerned as she was about Mitchell's late arrival, and went along to the next shop window whose reflection allowed her to watch the café across the street.

Fifteen minutes later, long after the agreed meeting time, she saw Mitchell accompanied by a gendarme and turned so that he could see her. Mitchell caught her eye and smiled, and gave a brief shake of his head. He was showing her that he was under no threat and placed a companionable hand on the man's back as they entered the café and disappeared inside.

She knew she had been on the street too long and could be in danger if the café were being watched. She needed to be certain of what to do next and quickly crossed the street to follow Mitchell. She found him and the gendarme at a table tucked away from view of the street. She asked for change at the counter, caught Mitchell's eye and acknowledged the nod of his head that all was well. The gendarme was hunched over a drink talking effusively. There was nothing more she could do except return to the apartment and wait for him.

*

'Drink up, Henri. One of the perks of being a policeman is that I don't pay. So, where are you staying these days?' said Vanves.

Mitchell feigned embarrassment. 'Look, Jules, I'm not doing so well these days. I'm renting a room. I am searching for Suzanne and Danielle.'

'They're not in Paris?'

'They went missing when we got out,' said Mitchell, not wishing to tell the affable man about the death of his wife. If Vanves heard that she had been executed by the Germans then a line of questioning could develop that might stop any chance of Mitchell using him to get information.

Vanves lowered his glass, 'I'm sorry to hear that, Henri.' He looked at Mitchell, the tone of his voice less conversational. 'Or should I call you Pascal? I'm not stupid and I'm not deaf. I heard you tell my officer your name. Why are you using false papers?'

Mitchell knew it was the moment when Jules Vanves could either be the policeman he was or become the old acquaintance who might reach out a helping hand.

'I didn't expect you to forget, Jules. You always had a good memory for names and faces. I'm an Englishman in occupied France searching for his family. I had friends help me with the documents.' Mitchell swallowed the drink and played his last card. He placed a hand on the gendarme's arm and reached for his hat. 'I have no wish to cause you embarrassment or to put you in a difficult situation. My thanks for the drink. It was good to see you again.' Mitchell stood to leave but Vanves held his arm. His face had lost any sign of friendliness.

'How do I know you are not an English agent?'

Mitchell laughed. 'Me?'

The moment held and then Vanves's face broke into a grin. 'I'm teasing you, Henri, you are hardly the type to get involved in anything dangerous or stupid. You were always the cautious one. Come on, sit down. Let's see what I can do to help you. You were always good to me. I will never forget that.'

Mitchell eased back down into the chair. 'Thank you, Jules,' he said, careful to display enough humility to flatter a weak man who had been given authority over others.

Vanves patted his arm. 'I was always the clumsy one, was I not? Always the butt of everyone's cruel remarks. And if there was a practical joke to be played it was on me. Oh, yes, I remember the humiliation of those days. Only you defended me. Only you treated me with any respect. Well, those bastards are treating me with respect now, aren't they? You are a decent man, Henri. And now you need some help. We are both family men and these times are difficult.' He finished his drink and tugged on his képi. 'You're coming home with me for a hot meal. And I'm sure I can find a place for you to stay. I told you – I have some influence these days.'

Mitchell stood and smiled at Vanves. He was genuinely gratefully that the man had turned a blind eye to him breaking the law, and he could be a means to an end. As they stepped out into the spring sunshine, he hoped that when he had got what he needed he would not have to kill him.

41

Stolz gazed along the Avenue Foch from his office window to where the swastika banner stirred over the Arc de Triomphe. He blew cigarette smoke skyward to the heavy drifting clouds. 'What do we think?' he said without turning around to Leitmann and Koenig, who waited obediently behind him.

'There was no reason he shouldn't have shown up,' said Koenig. 'Hesler's radio message was acknowledged. And he's sent another request to London.'

'Could they be suspicious?' said Leitmann.

'Not according to Hesler,' said Koenig.

'Then why didn't this Pascal turn up at the meeting?' said Stolz, turning and grinding out the cigarette. 'You waited long enough, did you?'

'Yes, colonel. Our man at the café stayed late as well. Who knows why he didn't show? He fell ill, he had an accident, he was caught up in a swoop,' Leitmann said and shrugged. 'We will have to wait and see if London comes back to Hesler. He's trying to keep his transmission times limited. Do too much and we might raise their suspicions.'

'I agree,' said Stolz. 'Koenig, check the area to see whether we had any patrols doing spot checks. Gendarmes as well. See if they arrested anyone named Pascal.' Stolz nodded the two men away. He was convinced there had been no warning given that had alerted the suspected British agent and stopped him going to the café. Perhaps it was simply human frailty? These men and women who risked torture and death were under enormous pressure. Drink could dull the fear but the risk was that sooner or later an agent became dependent on it, and therefore ineffective. It would be understandable if he were lying in a drunken stupor somewhere. Where was he, this elusive man? Stolz's informant had passed on enough information to snare him at the safe house set up by the Resistance, but that had produced nothing except a wild gun battle that amounted to little more than a man committing suicide. The round-up of suspects was yielding little in the way of results. The Milice and Brigades Spéciales were useful in punishment beatings but they had their own crimes to solve and the cat-and-mouse game between himself and Pascal was personal. Not only would Himmler reward him if he caught the agent sent to rescue the German traitor and delivered Korte for trial and execution, but there were routes out of the city that smuggled downed airmen, and every one of those who escaped would soon be back in the skies over Berlin. Mitchell knew those routes. Had been instrumental in setting them up. Had established well-placed people in the city and beyond. Mitchell was a prize to be seized.

He adjusted the two photographs on his desk. One showed an angular-faced woman with dreamy eyes smiling at the camera; the other the same woman embracing a seven-year-old boy. Both were flaxen-haired and their laughter reached him from their unwavering gaze. The thought repeated itself. The more airmen the Resistance helped escape the more would return over the skies of Berlin. Men who had destroyed vast swathes of his home city and whose bombs had erased all traces of his beloved wife and son.

*

Dominique Lesaux waited patiently. There was no need to be nervous, she always told herself. Being Heinrich Stolz's lover was her protection. No one would harm her. Her calmness was an act of will every time she entered the Sicherheitsdienst headquarters. The fear the imposing building generated seeped downward from the fifth floor, from all the violence and pain that was inflicted on those unfortunates caught and interrogated there. Once, when she was waiting for her lover to emerge from a conference, she had heard the bellowing agony of a man being tortured. A door slammed and the agony became muted, but the terror it inflicted on her made her hands tremble as she lit a cigarette. Her access to the fourth floor was never challenged and Hauptmann Koenig always allowed her to wait in his colonel's office. The young man was pleasant enough and was grateful for her introducing him to Béatrice Claudel, with whom he had obviously fallen deeply in love. They had agreed that he would never mention that it had been she who made the introductions. It would be unseemly for her to be seen arranging girlfriends for his commanding officer's staff. Every time Dominique arrived at Stolz's office when he was in a meeting, she spent time with the mild-mannered Koenig. It gave her an insight into what was going on even though the captain was discreet and would never divulge operational matters. She sensed his disdain for violence and warmed to his passion for literature and art, which she always found slightly surprising in an accountant. They were interests he would explore fully with Béatrice once the war was won. Don't say anything, he had once begged Dominique, but he was determined to marry Béatrice as soon as hostilities ended between their two great nations. She promised faithfully she would not mention a word and then promptly told Béatrice how smitten the young German officer was and how that was no bad thing.

Koenig had left the office door open and attended to phone calls as she waited for her lover's footfall along the corridor. His desk was clear, adorned only by family photographs, along with a large blotter and a Mont Blanc fountain pen laid neatly alongside. A flourish of that pen and lives would be changed and many ended. Koenig's voice droned on an on, discussing and correcting procedural issues. How Béatrice put up with the well-intentioned but ultimately boring young officer, she had no idea. Béatrice did what was necessary to survive, she reminded herself. The fact that she herself slept with the most dangerous man in Paris was a necessity that brought its own dangers. How she would be treated when the Germans lost the war – and of that inevitability, she was convinced – she did not know, but that uncertain future would not deter her from what she, and the likes of Béatrice Claudel, did now.

She heard Stolz's voice in the corridor and the scrape of Koenig pushing back his chair to stand to attention. She sat quickly, crossed one leg over the other and straightened her dress. She heard Koenig tell Stolz of her arrival and he strode into the room.

'Dominique, what are you doing here?' he said, bending to kiss her cheek.

She sighed with feigned boredom. 'I was shopping but couldn't decide on anything so I thought I would come and persuade you to take me out to dinner.'

He settled behind his desk, hands flat, eyes checking that nothing had been touched. Satisfied, he smiled. 'And I told you that today was a busy one, that I am in and out of meetings all day and that I would not be home until late.' He studied her for a moment. 'Did you forget?'

'Oh, yes, I suppose I did. How stupid of me. Heinrich, I am so bored, you can understand that, can't you? I have seen so little of you these past few days.' She pouted. 'Please?'

'I will have my driver take you home. Have a bath and then I'll get him to pick you up at about nine and we'll eat.'

'You are an angel. Am I being difficult?'

'No. You are being beautiful. But now I really must get on with my work.'

'Of course.'

He ushered her to the door.

'Oh,' she said. 'I forgot. I have lost my lighter. That was another reason I came to your office. I thought I might have left it here last time.'

'No, you couldn't have. Think about it, Dominique. You haven't been here for a week, and I saw you use it not two days ago.'

'At home?'

'Yes.'

'The gold one you gave me?'

'Yes.'

'Oh. Well, then, I don't know where it could be.'

'It will turn up. Now, please, darling, I must get on.'

Her smile soothed his impatience, then her lips brushed his. She stepped into the outer office where a sallow-faced man sat waiting with a folded overcoat and hat on the seat next to him.

'Goodbye, captain,' she said.

'Mademoiselle,' Koenig acknowledged; then once she had stepped past him he stood in the doorway of Stolz's office. 'Colonel, Inspector Berthold from the Préfecture at Saint-Audière is here.'

'About time. Send him in,' Dominique heard Stolz answer.

42

It was a modest house that Vanves let them into, calling out
that he had brought a guest home for supper. It was a step
up from the small apartment that Mitchell remembered him
living in. Mitchell was greeted by Vanves's wife. There had also
been a change in the plain-looking woman he remembered.
She had always seemed nervous and shy, owing no doubt to
her husband's lack of status within the academic community,
but now her hair was permed, she wore a blush of rouge on
her cheeks and the apron she quickly removed on his arrival
revealed a well-cut dress of good material. At a time when
most Parisiennes had to make do, it was a sign that Vanves
was doing well for himself and his family. Denise Vanves was
more confident now and was delighted that someone she had
not seen for a couple of years was back in Paris. Vanves had
stripped off his tunic and put on a sports jacket, warning her,
in front of Mitchell, that their old friend – acquaintances were
how Mitchell would have classified Jules and Denise Vanves
from his teaching days – needed help to find his wife and
child, but that his presence should not be revealed to anyone.

With a sympathetic expression at Mitchell's dilemma, she assured her husband and the Englishman that she would be careful not to.

The evening passed amicably and Mitchell found himself relaxing in the warmth of the family home. Vanves's son had been no more than seven years old when Mitchell had last seen him, a child withdrawn from a father who bickered and bemoaned his lot; now the laughter that father and son shared was an expression of love that was hard to deny. Collaboration had proven itself to be beneficial in more ways than a full larder and a spacious apartment. The evening meal finished, the boy was sent off to do his homework and, once Denise refused Mitchell's offer to clear the table, Jules Vanves settled his guest in the living room and poured them both a brandy. 'Relax a moment. I must see to the boy. He has exams coming up.'

Mitchell waited until the boy's bedroom door closed behind Vanves. The clatter of dishes in the kitchen told him Denise was occupied. He moved quickly to the hall and opened Vanves's satchel. It was full of envelopes, slit open. Mitchell quickly pulled free the notepaper from one. He could hear Vanves explaining a point of history with his son. The rice-thin paper in his fingers revealed a scrawled hand. *My neighbour has an apartment full of quality furniture and paintings and they never go to church on Sunday, they're obviously wealthy Jews.* Mitchell teased free another letter. *I work with a man who is a communist...* They were letters of denunciation. The bedroom-door handle turned; the door opened. Vanves's back was turned, telling his son he had another hour before the light was to be switched off and he must go to bed. Vanves stepped back into the hall and glanced towards the living room where Mitchell sat waiting, appreciatively sniffing the brandy in his glass. He looked up as Vanves walked in from the hall.

'It's been a long time since I tasted such good brandy, Jules,' Mitchell said calmly, despite his racing pulse.

Vanves, suspecting nothing, sat opposite him. 'I am aware, Henri, that you must think poorly of me. Being a policeman in these times.'

Mitchell kept his thoughts to himself. 'You have provided safety and security for your family, Jules. It is understandable. Look how desperate my own life has become. We must do what we must.'

'You're right. I nearly got it badly wrong. During the round-ups of the Jews last year some of my fellow officers warned the families, which gave them time to escape. Those officers were betrayed by some of the very people they tried to help. Some who were caught tried to save their own lives by telling the Germans the names of these officers. It made no difference, they were shipped off anyway, but the policemen were shot by the Germans. I learnt my lesson: to keep my mouth shut and to do what was necessary.'

'Then, as I said before, Jules, I do not wish to put you or your family in danger by helping me.'

Vanves dismissed his comment with a wave of his hand. 'No, no. All I'm going to do is check the files on you. The Germans keep excellent records of everyone they suspect, arrest, torture, execute or send to the camps. That creates a great deal of paperwork. For several months now they have been storing old files in police stations. The fact that I am going to be looking through them will draw no suspicion at all. And once I am back at work tomorrow I will see if I can find you some better accommodation.' He savoured the brandy and extended a cigarette box to Mitchell.

'I quit,' he said.

'Take some anyway. They are always good to trade. And, dare I say it, Henri, you don't look flush with money. Am I right? Eh?'

Mitchell looked sufficiently sheepish and nodded.

'I thought not. Help yourself.'

Mitchell reached out, gathered the cigarettes into his hand and carefully tucked them into his breast pocket.

Vanves lit a cigarette and exhaled. 'I hope you will understand that I cannot offer to accommodate you here. I might have some influence but everyone is watched. All it would take is a letter of denunciation from any of my neighbours and I could be investigated for harbouring someone who is not a member of my family. I apologize, but I will see what I can do over the next couple of days to find you somewhere.' He raised the glass to his lips and peered across at Mitchell. 'But these friends who help you with your papers, I hope they are not dangerous people.'

It was a clumsy attempt to gain information, Mitchell decided. 'They are not. In fact, they are not even in Paris. They're way out in Fontainebleau,' he lied. 'So no connection here at all. I have a room in the Twelfth Arrondissement. There is nothing untoward, Jules.'

'That's off my patch. All right, leave it to me. I will do everything I can to help.' He swallowed the last of the brandy. 'Now, I still have work to do tonight so let's meet at the Préfecture day after tomorrow. Say, ten in the morning? Come to the desk and ask for me. I'll see what I can find out.' He extended his hand. Mitchell shook it.

'I appreciate it, Jules, I really do.'

'Nonsense. Now, get back to your room before curfew. That's one thing I wouldn't be able to help you with.' He smiled and helped Mitchell into his coat. Goodbyes were said. Denise embraced him, told him not to worry about anything because her husband always helped those who had shown kindness to them both. As the door closed behind him, Mitchell felt the warmth of the evening's hospitality slip away. Going to the Préfecture would be a big risk. Vanves was a collaborator, corrupted by fear. A decent man turned and used by the invader. His weakness served him well.

*

Mitchell waited an hour in a darkened side street opposite Vanves's house until he saw the policeman come out wearing his képi and tunic with an overcoat against the night's chill. The satchel across his chest. Mitchell followed him, the dull street lights keeping track of the figure who moved at a brisk pace. It was not long before he entered an apartment block. Mitchell stood on the street opposite looking up at the darkened building, hoping to see a sign of light behind the blackout curtains. There was nothing, but then a small chink of light appeared and was quickly concealed as someone checked the street below. After a few minutes, Vanves reappeared, tucking something into his breast pocket. Once again Mitchell followed him. Over the course of the next three hours, Vanves made several house calls. By the time he turned for home Mitchell knew he was going to have a long and dangerous walk back to Ginny at the apartment. The silent streets echoed only occasionally with the sound of nailed boots as routine foot patrols went on their way. The night air grew colder but Mitchell was warm from his exertion as he walked rapidly through the side streets, trusting his instinct in the darkness that he was travelling in the right direction. It took almost two hours for him to reach the apartment, step quietly up the stairs and gently ease himself inside. It was pitch black and then a bedside lamp clicked on and he saw Ginny sitting on the edge of the bed with her pistol at the ready. She exhaled with relief and lowered the weapon.

'You must have the hearing of a bat,' Mitchell said, smiling. 'Sorry. Too late to knock to let you know it was me.'

'I was watching the street from the window. I saw someone coming into the building. And after you walked off with that policeman at the café I didn't want to take any chances.'

Mitchell stripped off his coat and slumped on the couch, pulling off his shoes. Without undressing he collapsed back and yawned. 'He's someone I once knew. He could be helpful. He's a collaborator.'

'Pascal, it's getting more dangerous every day. Is using him a good idea? He could turn.'

'I have information on him. He's up to no good.' He tugged free his tie and pulled the blanket over him. 'Put the light out, won't you?'

Darkness engulfed him. His memory showed him images of a decent, put-upon man. A man who now held others' lives in his hands. He didn't know whether to pity or revile him. Moments later, still undecided, he was asleep.

43

Ginny listened to the steady rhythm of the Morse tapping through her headphones. Mitchell watched at the window for any sign of the radio detection vans. It was against the rules of survival for an agent to stay so close to his wireless operator. They were always the weak link. He had intended to bunk at the room tucked at the back of the Corsican's bar but having considered his chances of being noticed going in and out of the bar decided that staying in his old apartment offered the best chance of escape, and with the Corsican's warning he and Ginny would have time to get across the rooftops.

'They want you to go back to the café. Ory has made another request to meet you,' she said, pulling free her headphones.

'Tell them a couple of days.'

'Pascal, isn't this police officer a distraction? Shouldn't we do as they ask?'

The temptation was obvious. Alain Ory had been with Suzanne and Danielle the night they were captured. Yet the more Mitchell thought about it the less important he felt the missing wireless operator to be, whereas a contact at the

Préfecture could prove far more valuable. Weighing the risk he had decided to stay in touch with Jules Vanves.

'Tell them… tell them I'm sick.'

She looked quizzically at him.

He nodded. 'Advise we'll be in touch when I'm ready.'

Ginny tapped rapidly. Pausing in the middle of a transmission created a greater chance of her signal being pinpointed by the Germans. She wasted no time and then switched off.

'Why is Ory so keen to meet me?' Mitchell asked, still watching the street as she packed the radio away.

'They were your instructions from London, weren't they? To find him?'

Mitchell sat on the windowsill. Pedestrian traffic was building up as the day lengthened, but vehicle traffic as usual was slight. The fear of a Gestapo raid never left his thoughts. If they were discovered it would either be a rapid arrival of cars blocking the street and then the pounding of shoe leather up the stairs, or a far quieter approach – men slipping unnoticed into the building and then the sudden rush at the door catching them unprepared. He had not yet gone across to the bar on the opposite side of the street to reacquaint himself with its Corsican owner. There would be time enough for that if the man displayed the signal in the window that someone was trying to get in touch with Mitchell. So far, so good.

'Yes, but we've told London that we have found Korte. All I need now is for him to be well enough to travel and a clear night to get a Lysander in for him. Why the insistence?'

'Ory is alone, he's being hunted. Perhaps he needs you to help get him out?'

Mitchell moved away from the window, satisfied that nothing untoward was happening in the street below. 'Why?

Is he important enough to be flown back to London? He could ask London to arrange a boat from the coast. He could make his own way there himself. He's not injured, he's moving around the city. They've told us that already.'

'You think he's compromised and the Germans are using him?'

'Perhaps.'

'He would send them his duress code.'

'Yes, you would think so.' Mitchell pulled on his coat. 'And then there's the theory of probability. Mathematically we can't predict the outcome of random events but they could offer several different outcomes if they're influenced by other factors. He's bait, he's desperate, he's frightened, he has information, or... he is not who he says he is.'

The sudden realization that the enemy might be trying to entrap them showed on Ginny's face.

Mitchell pulled on his hat. 'Let's get to the hospital. See how Alfred Korte is doing.'

Ginny edged the calico curtains across the window to half obscure their coming and going. 'There's a problem,' she said.

Mitchell glanced across the street to where the bar window showed a broken slatted venetian blind.

*

Mitchell stepped out of the apartment building after instructing Ginny to stay inside until he signalled her to come down and join him. It was important that she watch his back and see that the warning signal was not a trap. Her instructions were simple: if he was compromised she would run and then signal London immediately, even if it meant sending in plain text. He stood for a few minutes looking up and down the street but saw no sign of anyone watching. He crossed the street and with one hand in his overcoat pocket gripping the pistol, opened the half-curtained door and stepped inside. 'Hello, Roccu,' he said.

A burly, dark-haired man in a collarless shirt creased by braces, his stomach held by a broad leather belt on his trousers, looked up from where he stood cleaning glasses. His unshaven face broke into a grin and he quickly stepped around the bar counter. The Corsican hugged Mitchell and kissed him on both cheeks. His voice was little more than a rasping whisper from years of drinking bootleg liquor and smoking. He stank of rancid sweat and dark stubble clouded his features.

'My friend, forgive me, I haven't shaved or washed in days. There's a problem with the plumbing. The damned Germans, they fuck up everything with their wars. Genevieve says my stubble scratches like a hedgehog's arse.'

'Genevieve?'

'My latest. One of the girls.' He put a protective arm around Mitchell and lowered his voice. 'Since you telephoned I have watched your building. I saw you coming and going and the young woman also. Hello, I say to myself. I am sure that is Henri and he's shaved off his beard. Must be a good reason, I tell myself, so I stay quiet and watch. Henri is back and he has a woman. I will say nothing. Better that way? Eh?'

'Roccu, Henri is not in Paris. Pascal Garon lives in the apartment opposite.'

'Ah. Of course. Henri? Henri who? I know no one by that name.' He beamed with genuine pleasure at seeing the man who had helped his brother, wife and family escape Paris soon after the Occupation.

'The signal in the window. What is it?' Mitchell asked quietly.

The Corsican gently guided Mitchell through the darkened bar. It was empty except for two patrons, older working men between shifts, weary perhaps of trudging home to a woman and children who had little enough food in the house and who would complain that he wasted money on a drink.

'A man came here. A big man. Rough-looking. Not a Parisian. I could tell by his accent. I liked him the moment I saw him. Hands like a bunch of bananas. There is something of the earth about him. Said he needed to speak to you and that you had given him the name of my bar and its telephone number. In there. By the cubicles.'

The Corsican stepped away allowing Mitchell to pull back a curtain into a room where a row of curtained cots were lined up for the girls the Corsican offered. The room's bare bulb showed the room was empty except for Chaval, who quickly stood from a rough wooden table and a half-carafe of red wine and a torn piece of bread.

'Chaval. What's wrong?'

'Gaétan keeps asking about you and I did not wish him to know about this place.'

'What kind of things?'

'It's as if he doesn't trust you. Asking what kind of people you had as contacts here. That kind of thing. Picking away at who you are and how much you know about the city. What could I tell him? I don't know anything about your time here.'

'The less anyone knows the better, Chaval. That goes for you too.'

'He heard about the shooting. He's getting agitated. Wants to know whether you were involved.'

Mitchell nodded. He knew he couldn't cut Gaétan out completely. 'You did the right thing coming to me, Chaval.

Don't worry about Gaétan; I'll deal with him in good time. Are the men safe?'

'Yes. We're a couple of miles from Vincennes in those barns you dropped us at. We've hidden the petrol cans, so we're just sitting on our backsides waiting for you.'

'The men mustn't become complacent, Chaval. Split them up, send them out to reconnoitre the area, make them observant of their surroundings. If you are compromised then you need to know how to get out. Remember, any problem you contact Roccu or come here yourself. Gaétan can wonder all he likes about the shooting. It's none of his business.'

'Were you involved?'

'Yes.'

'And the other Englishman?'

'Dead. Tell no one. Keep it to yourself otherwise they might panic.'

'Understood.'

He patted Chaval's shoulder. 'Get yourself back now, and keep our men on a tight rein. I'll be in touch.'

Mitchell waited until Chaval was clear of the bar before standing at the window and watching him cross the street.

'One of your friends?' said Roccu.

'Yes. A good man. If it wasn't for him and others like him I wouldn't be standing here talking to you.'

'Then the next time I see him I'll buy him a drink,' said the Corsican, raising the venetian blind.

Mitchell shook Roccu's hand and was about to leave when he saw Gaétan's man Edmond walking on the opposite pavement in the same direction that Chaval had taken. There was enough distance between the two men for the poacher not to notice the gamekeeper was following him. If Gaétan had sent him to see whether Chaval had made contact with Mitchell then that bore out what Chaval had told him. If not, then Edmond was acting under his own volition. The question Mitchell asked himself was why.

44

Ginny was introduced to Frank Burton and then she and Mitchell were ushered into the isolation ward where Alfred Korte sat in a chair by the window. Burton closed the door behind them, leaving them alone with the man who held such vital information for the British. Korte appeared less gaunt than when Mitchell had rescued him from the other hospital. He stood, extending his hand to Mitchell.

'I am pleased to see you again, Pascal. I cannot thank you enough for bringing me here. I suffer from a great sadness that your colleague gave his life for me.'

'He was a very brave man, Herr Korte.'

'One day, when circumstances permit, I would like to write to his family and express my deepest condolences at his loss and to acknowledge the act of self-sacrifice.'

'I will do everything I can to facilitate that,' said Mitchell. 'Herr Korte, this is Thérèse Fernay. She is here to help me get you to England.'

Korte bowed his head. 'Mademoiselle. You are so young to be in such danger.'

'We are all in danger, Herr Korte.'

'Are you well enough to travel?' said Mitchell.

'Today? Yes, of course.'

'No, in a few days. We will wait until the moon gives us a clear night.'

'I am ready.'

Mitchell turned to Ginny. 'Thérèse, would you give me a moment with Herr Korte?'

'Of course.' She smiled at the elderly German and left the room.

'Herr Korte, the information that you have, is it written down anywhere?' said Mitchell.

'No. That would prove too dangerous were it discovered.'

'I understand. So you have memorized all the names of those who wish to rise up against Hitler?'

'Every one.'

'And if you were captured and interrogated you would be able to feed the Gestapo different names?'

'It was something I considered carefully, M'sieu Garon. Everyone breaks sooner or later under torture and there is no doubt I would have given them the location of where I would hide such a document. Now, if captured I will no doubt be dead by the time they have checked all the false names I would have given them. And I do not suggest we transmit them by wireless to London because we Germans are clever and intercept a lot of radio traffic.'

'Very well, then we will ensure we get you to England as soon as possible.'

Mitchell went back to the corridor where Ginny sat waiting. The young woman stood, greeting him with a plucky smile. Since he had first met her at the landing zone he had recognized that she was young enough to be his daughter, so he could not help a twinge of guilt when he lied to her.

'He hid the list of names inside a book by Victor Hugo when he was in hiding at the bookshop. *Les Misérables.*'

'Well, that's appropriate,' she said and smiled again.

He agreed and pushed away the regret of the untruth. Were she the one captured and tortured then her misinformation would buy time should it be needed. It was not difficult for him to realize what this mission had done to him.

'Pascal?' a voice said softly.

Mitchell turned to see the white-coated figure of Jean Bernard walking towards them from the ward. As he reached Mitchell and Ginny he hesitated as he glanced at the young woman.

'It's all right: she is working with me. Jean Bernard, this is Thérèse Fernay. How are you? Is everything all right with Juliet and Simone?'

'I'm not sure. I am very pleased that you came to the hospital today because I think it is important that you know what we have discovered.' Jean Bernard explained quickly that Simone had discovered that his sister's young son was getting a steady supply of Swiss chocolate from somewhere. Both he and Juliet had followed the child to and from school for a couple of days but there had been no sign of anything untoward. The uncertainty had driven them to question the child's mother who insisted she had no idea where the chocolate could have come from. But Jean Bernard could tell something was wrong. And then Simone saw the child in the park with a man who bought him ice cream.

'I think my sister is under some kind of pressure,' said Jean Bernard finally. 'But if the lad's being questioned on a regular basis, I wouldn't know why. You think it's us? Because we're there?'

'You and Juliet?' said Mitchell. 'There's no connection and your papers are in order.'

'We need to know. This afternoon is the same day as last week when Simone saw him at the park.'

'All right. Is Juliet at home with your sister?'

'Yes.'

'Then leave her there. Let's not alarm your sister or alert anyone watching the apartment. It might all be innocent.'

⋆

The trees were still weeks away from blossoming. By the time May arrived many would already be spreading their canopies to offer shade to the Parisians desperate to escape the suffocating midsummer heat of their apartments. First the trees, then the heat. Then would come romance. Now, late spring sunshine warmed those who strolled in the park; some mothers pushed prams as others called after schoolchildren, laughing and running. The harsh winter that had recently passed still lingered in the bones and there were those who put down their coats on the grass beneath them and lay basking gratefully in the sunshine. Beyond the park, low buildings from another age reminded the city's inhabitants that the beauty that was once Paris would not be marred by bombs and the huge swastikas that defaced the buildings' beauty would one day be torn down. Spring brought hope.

Mitchell sat on a park bench two hundred metres from where Marcel Tatier shared a bench with a young-looking man in sports jacket and slacks. Mitchell could not make out the man's features but the child smiled affably as he licked an ice cream and spoke to the man, who, one leg crossed over the other, folded his newspaper and took out a notebook. There was no indication of any threat being made. The man reached into his folded overcoat pocket and handed whatever it was to the boy. From where Mitchell sat it looked like a slab of chocolate. The child took it, sniffed it, and laughed when the stranger spoke to him. The man ruffled the boy's hair.

Mitchell tugged his hat further down on his face, folded his overcoat over his arm and walked down the path that would take him within fifty paces of the man and boy. Beyond them, where the women watched their children playing, Ginny sat facing the sun wearing a pair of sunglasses as she gossiped with one of the mothers, even though her attention was on the other park bench. As Mitchell drew closer he almost faltered. The man next to the boy pushed a strand of hair back from his face, lifting it briefly towards the sun's rays. It was the same man who had questioned him and Thompson before they had gone into the hospital to rescue Alfred Korte. The Gestapo agent bent his head and wrote in a black notebook with a gold pen.

Mitchell's mouth grew dry. He lengthened his stride, part of him fearful that Ginny might also recognize the Gestapo officer and that her reaction might be too obvious should the man look her way. Mitchell made a surreptitious gesture for her to follow him and when they got to the park gates they sought out Jean Bernard who had remained out of sight of his nephew.

'How far to your sister's apartment?' Mitchell asked.

'Twenty minutes. What's happened?'

'Your nephew is meeting a Gestapo agent and we need to find out why.'

Jean Bernard looked stunned. He nodded. 'Follow me.'

Madame Tatier was in the bedroom folding young Marcel's clothes when she heard the front door open and close. Juliet was ushering in Jean Bernard and two strangers. The plainclothes man looked at her and she felt the pit of her stomach lurch. French police? Gestapo? She involuntarily put a hand on the base of her throat. It was only when Juliet smiled and embraced the stranger that she released her caught breath.

Bernard ushered her through to the sitting room. 'Marie, this man is a friend who helped us reach Paris. He and the young woman with him can be trusted completely. It's best that I don't tell you their names. Come along and sit down – we need to talk before Marcel comes home.' He glanced at Juliet. 'Is Simone back from school yet?'

'No, she has extra lessons today. What's happened?'

Mitchell and Ginny sat opposite as Jean Bernard took his sister's hand in his own.

'We have to know what's going on. You must be absolutely honest with us because we believe that you and Marcel are in danger.'

His sister looked from one to the other, suddenly feeling as if she were on trial. If there was any suspicion that she had been collaborating she knew things could turn unpleasant for her. She blustered. 'Why would we be in danger? Don't be foolish, Jean. You bring your friends into my house uninvited and they sit there looking sternly at me as if I am a thief in the night. Do you have no respect for me?' She went to stand up, but Jean Bernard gripped her arm.

'Marie, listen to me. Marcel has been getting contraband chocolate from someone. We have just seen him in the park eating an ice cream and talking to a Gestapo agent.'

Marie Tatier recoiled in shock. She struggled to find words for a moment but then the tears came. She lifted her apron to her face. 'May God forgive me, may God forgive me, Blessed Mary, Mother of God, forgive me,' she whispered.

'Madame Tatier, you must tell us everything,' said Mitchell. She wiped her tears and nodded. She held her brother's arm tightly. 'I was told not to say anything otherwise they would send me to the camps and Marcel to an orphanage. I had helped someone in the Resistance. I could not risk telling you, Jean, or you, Juliet – I thought the less you knew the better. Had I told you that in the past I had stored food here for *résistants* then you might have thought poorly of me. You being a doctor, and you, Juliet, how could I tell a stranger in my home of my past involvement? I thought it all over. No one had asked for my help in months. But then this man came. Said he knew I could be trusted. The next thing there was a raid. I tried to help him escape. He was caught. After that the police and Gestapo said I was to report anyone suspicious. Or else.' The flood of explanation seemed to drain her. She sighed. 'I had no idea they were using Marcel to spy on me. On us.'

Bernard embraced his sister. 'You had nothing to fear from me.'

Juliet bent and lifted Marie's hand and kissed it. 'Marie. We had a Resistance group in our village. Both Jean and I were involved.' She laughed. 'We all kept our secrets safe fearing we might endanger you and Marcel. And likewise, you sought to protect us.'

'We must get away from here,' said Jean Bernard.

'No. Not yet,' Mitchell told them. 'You must carry on as normal until I can find a better place. Say nothing to Marcel when he comes home, or Simone.' He looked at each of them.

'It is vitally important that nothing is seen to be different.' He checked his watch. 'And we must be gone before the children come home. Marcel would be obliged to tell the Gestapo that there were people here. And then it will be too late to try and cover up. Is everyone clear?'

Marie Tatier, Bernard and Juliet all nodded their agreement.

'Good. Now, Madame Tatier, I emphasize again that you have nothing to fear providing you carry on as normal. I'll be in touch through Jean. Did you know the résistant you helped?'

'No. He was a wireless operator. Said he was on the run. They shot him but he was still alive when they took him away.'

Mitchell recalled the Gestapo agent using a gold pen. 'Do you know his name?'

'Yes. Alain Ory.'

45

Mitchell and Ginny left Jean Bernard with his sister and Juliet so that Marie might be comforted and to ensure that she did not panic and do anything foolish. It was vital now that she didn't arouse Gestapo suspicion. They caught a trolleybus that took them a few streets from the apartment. Neither said anything about the discovery that Alain Ory had been captured, perhaps killed, and that the Germans had been masquerading as him. They knew that the Germans' insistence on meeting the man known as Pascal meant that the Germans were aware that another British agent had been sent to Paris. The question was how they had known. Neither Mitchell or Ginny could know whether London had inadvertently told the wireless operator masquerading as Alain Ory, or the traitor in the Resistance had betrayed him.

'Whoever the operator is, he's good if he's fooling London,' said Ginny when they were back in the apartment.

'And London is being bloody stupid because they have not asked for a duress code. Damned idiots will get a lot of people killed.'

'I can warn them,' said Ginny.

'No. We daren't risk it in case they're picking up your transmissions or intercepting London's. We might be able to use this to our advantage and feed the Germans some false information. Turn it back on them. I want to get Korte out as soon as possible when there's enough moon.'

Ginny handed him a cup. 'Not quite the real thing but it's the best I can do.'

Mitchell took the cup. It made little difference that it was toasted barley mixed with chicory; he would have preferred a cup of tea. 'This will be perfect,' he told her.

'I've been thinking,' she said.

He sipped the ersatz coffee and looked over the rim of the cup. 'That's always helpful at times like these,' he told her, smiling.

'Let's go back a few steps. Before you were sent here.' She pulled her legs beneath her on the sofa and cradled the cup. 'Alain Ory worked with the man we knew as Ferrand and he was trying to find Alfred Korte and get him back to England.'

'So the Nazis still think Korte is in hiding.'

'I suppose. We can't know that. Perhaps them knowing about you means they are hoping to entrap you in order to get to him.'

'Or it's a random act to shut down another British agent,' said Mitchell, trying to guess where the girl's logic was taking her.

'Colonel Beaumont told me about your wife.' She paused, waiting to see if she were going too far by pulling back any veil that Mitchell might have drawn over his wife's death. Mitchell remained silent, watching her, letting his own thoughts follow hers.

'Your wife and daughter were with Alain Ory the same night that one of the résistants was shot and Ory escaped.

That was when your wife and daughter were taken. So, doesn't it follow that your wife might have been part of the operation to get Korte out?'

'Yes. That might be the case. All I know is she was helping Ory. There was no mention of her being involved with any other agent. Don't forget there are résistants working in their own small groups, or as individuals.'

'But she was using her maiden name. The Germans made the connection before they... sorry.'

'They made the connection and someone sent London the photographs of her being executed,' said Mitchell.

Ginny drained the cup. 'Alfred Korte is important to them. But if they put two and two together after they caught your wife and it wasn't the Resistance who got the photos out, then what if it was the Gestapo or the SD who sent the pictures? Perhaps it's you they are after and everyone you know, or knew, in the city who were involved in getting people out. Those feeder lines across France that you helped set up with people here are still being used to help escapees.'

She reached forward and took his empty cup and saucer. 'You'd be a feather in their cap if they snared you. And a lot of people would die.'

*

Mitchell waited until early evening and then made his way towards Jules Vanves's house. Once again he concealed himself at his vantage point and as darkness fell observed the police sergeant make his way down the street in uniform with his satchel. It took three hours for Vanves to do his rounds and, by curfew, he had the streets to himself. Mitchell followed him home and as he turned the corner Mitchell stepped out and blocked his path.

'Henri!' Vanves stepped back. Mitchell grabbed him and bundled him into the half-lit passageway next to the house. Vanves was a glorified clerk and no combatant and Mitchell's training had become second nature. Vanves's shock at being so roughly handled allowed only a few stuttering protests.

'Be quiet, Jules. I cannot trust you with my life if I don't know what you're up to.'

'You accuse me? You're here with false identity papers.'

'And that is why I have to be sure about you,' said Mitchell. 'You're blackmailing those who have been denounced.'

Vanves's mouth gaped but then realization dawned. 'You looked inside my case.'

'Yes. I had no choice. I have placed my life in your hands. Did you think I would just walk into the Préfecture?'

'I've promised that I will help you,' said Vanves in a conciliatory manner. 'I can explain everything. I steal these letters from the station when they come in. There are hundreds every day. I take only a handful relating to my district before they are processed. Then I warn the families. By the time I return the letters and they are passed on for investigation the families have fled. I save lives. Who better than a gendarme walking the streets after curfew? I do it for others. And no one has any money. You can see that, can't you?'

'Open the satchel, Jules.'

Even in the dark there was just enough light to see the fear on Vanves's face. 'Henri…'

'Open it or I'll take it from you.'

Vanves undid the straps and pulled open the flap. 'It's nothing, Henri. Nothing at all. Donations from grateful families.'

Mitchell pulled out items of jewellery. The street light's dull glow caught their sparkle. 'And then you sell these to black marketeers. I saw how much food you had at home, and your wife dresses well these days.'

Vanves crumpled. 'I have to look after my family. We all do what we must. I don't hurt these people.'

'You're a collaborator, Jules, there's no hiding that. The day's coming when you'll have to face your fellow citizens.'

'And with the money I get, I'll be far away with a new identity.'

'Which you can procure easily, of course.'

Vanves did up the satchel's straps. 'What are you going to do? What is it you want from me?'

'I want to help you, Jules. I want to protect you. I know there are men who might take the risk and start killing collaborators. I want identification documents for a family. You can get them from people who have died in hospital.'

'Who in God's name are you working for?' said Vanves. 'Are you Resistance? Was I wrong about you?'

'I'm nobody. I just need your help. But I know people of violence and I will turn to them if you refuse to help me. I need an apartment big enough for four or five.'

'I can do that. But I can't do much else. It is dangerous.'

'You'll do what I ask, Jules. The alternative places you, along with your son and wife, in extreme danger.'

'My God. Don't hurt my family. I beg you. They are every-thing to me.'

'I promise you I will protect them. No harm will come to you or your family from the people I know. I need documents. Two women, two children and a man. I'll give you their ages and description and get photographs and you will find suitable identity cards and ration tickets. Agreed?'

Vanves knew he had no choice. There was no way of knowing whether the man who threatened him was bluffing.

To refuse was too great a gamble. 'Very well,' he said in barely a whisper.

'And if I am picked up or found shot on a street corner, then the people I know will come for you and your family because they will think I've been betrayed by you.'

'I can't be held responsible if you are picked up! How could I know if that happened?'

'You check the daily arrest log. And then you get me out.'

'You were my friend, Henri. Why are you doing this to me?'

'Because you have gone across to the other side, and I am the only one who can protect you. You work for me now, Jules.'

46

Mitchell finished shaving in the kitchen sink. He heard the communal toilet at the end of the landing flush with protesting pipes and listened as the footsteps approached, then another door opened and closed. Everything needed to be normal. Any change in the day-to-day routine of those in the building could herald danger.

'Madame Pivain in number seven. As regular as clockwork,' he said, wiping away the last of the shaving cream. 'Anything?' he asked, turning to where Ginny sat hunched, decoding a message from her transmission. She tore off the sheet and handed it to him.

'This is going to kill a lot of people if they go through with it. They're asking if we can do anything.'

Mitchell scanned the message. Intercepted German wireless traffic showed that the Germans were going to move some machinery from a factory in Paris by rail at night to an unknown destination in Germany. Expatriate French scientists had identified the factory as one whose retooling machines manufactured rifled barrels for self-propelled guns. The RAF intended to bomb the factory and La Chapelle marshalling yards before the essential equipment was relocated.

Ginny waited as Mitchell absorbed the message. 'They'll kill hundreds of civilians,' she said.

He nodded. He imagined his friends at Bletchley Park decoding the German wireless traffic and the information being passed along the line. They would have thought nothing more of it and gone on to the next intercept. How different it was when you were under the bombs. His thoughts raced. Trying to sabotage the train as it passed with a full head of steam across the multiple tracks at La Chapelle would be difficult. If the train could be halted beyond the city limits that would give the RAF a clearer target. And if that could be achieved then any attempt by the Germans to send out cranes and salvage engines from their sheds at La Chapelle had to be stopped.

The freight yards were thirty feet below street level and patrolled by the Railway Police, who would spot any saboteurs clambering down the wall ladders carrying explosives. He checked his watch. 'We need to make an unscheduled transmission,' he said.

They both knew the danger longer unscheduled transmissions presented with the German RDF vans sweeping the city. 'All right,' she said without hesitation.

As she set up her wireless and aerial again, Mitchell wrote out a message. 'We can find a place to stop the train once it's on the outskirts and then the RAF can catch it in the open.'

'At night?'

'Dawn if we can; if not we'll light the damned thing somehow. I'll make the message vague enough for any Germans doing a wireless sweep but London will know exactly what I mean.' He wrote a final sentence, tore off the sheet from the pad and handed it to her. She encoded it, settled the headphones and began to transmit. Mitchell pulled on his coat. 'I'm going to phone Gaétan and organize the men. Get off that key as soon as you can; the message is already too long.' He closed the door behind him and left Ginny tapping.

*

Mitchell spent the afternoon east of the city. He had to decide urgently where exactly to halt the train. Having lived in Paris and and reconnoitred escape routes for those fleeing the Occupation, he knew where he could blow the tracks and isolate the train carrying the retooling machines. The risk was that the German war machine was sufficiently well organized to send out lifting cranes and track-laying locomotives should the explosives cause only temporary damage. To stop that from happening he needed to cripple the marshalling yards that harboured the heavy-duty equipment. He followed the perimeter wire of the yards. There were only a few Railway Police patrolling because the area was so vast and lacked cover, so that anyone working in the yards would easily identify an intruder. A small, run-down café, weathered beyond its years by the coal smoke and soot from the shunting engines, backed on to the wire. The side door looked easy enough to pick and clambering on to the roof would give a way over the wire. It would be at night but that did not lessen the risk. For all he knew there might be searchlights that swept across the marshalling yards. Would the Germans risk breaking the blackout? It was a gamble and he knew he had to have a plan. A few hundred yards from the perimeter wire a huge building loomed; from where he stood it looked as big as an aircraft hangar. Its doors were open and he could see soldiers and French railway workers inside attending to several large steam locomotives, one of which was attached to a lifting-crane tender. In front of the railway sheds a turntable, big enough to accommodate any of those locomotives, swung its tracked bridge to line up with an engine in the shed. Mitchell bought a cup of ersatz coffee and watched as the turntable slowly spun the engine around so that it could roll off on to its chosen track. The engine spun its wheels and moved slowly across the yard as the signalman threw a lever, changing its direction. A French railway worker stood far beyond its intended line of travel swinging a red glass lantern, guiding the train towards some freight carriages. By the time Mitchell had drunk the bitter liquid and the locomotive had been coupled to its cargo, he knew what he had to do.

'Who is it?' said the voice behind the door after Mitchell had rapped on the door with his knuckles.

'Pascal Garon,' he answered, his face close to the door so that no one else in the apartment block would hear.

'I don't know anybody by that name,' came the reply.

'I shared a cell with you in Saint-Audière. You needed a cigarette, remember?'

The door opened a crack and the unshaven face of Gerard Vincent checked his uninvited visitor as he pulled his trouser braces up over his dirty collarless shirt. It took only a moment for the black marketeer to grin broadly and open the door to usher Mitchell in. 'It's you. Who'd have believed it? I never thought you would ever come to Paris, much less visit me.' His brow furrowed. 'Did I tell you where I lived?'

'You were grateful for me lighting that cigarette and said that if ever I needed anything to look you up.'

'So I did, so I did.'

Mitchell stepped into the spacious apartment. Cans of food were stacked in one corner; men' and women's clothing lay in heaps across the various pieces of furniture. A pan of food bubbled on a small stove in the corner and beyond Mitchell saw there was a second room: a bedroom where women's silk lingerie hung from a rail.

Gerard Vincent looked as grubby in his own apartment as he had in the wretched cell back in Saint-Audière. He moved quickly to the stove, gave whatever was in the pan a stir and switched off the gas beneath it. He shrugged apologetically. 'I don't have enough to offer you.'

Mitchell glanced at the stacked cans of food.

'They're not for eating, they're for selling. Can't eat into my profits.'

'I'm not hungry.'

Vincent took a cigarette from a silver cigarette case, tapped it and scorched its end with an expensive-looking lighter. He smiled, making a show of it. 'No need for a light socket now.'

'I can see that,' said Mitchell.

'All right, I said I would help, but I didn't say it would be free.'

Mitchell fingered some of the men's clothing. 'I can pay.'

Vincent spat a piece of loose tobacco. 'What is it you need? You got a woman? I can get you silk stockings for three hundred francs.' He gestured to where half a dozen crates were stacked. 'Cognac, Armagnac. Champagne even. I should be living in a goddamned palace instead of a shithole like this, but it serves me well. No one notices. No one suspects. And if they did...' He let the sentence hang, its intention plain enough.

'Business is good, then.'

'Good? The Occupation is the best thing that ever happened to us.'

'Black-market food for your own people, that's what you think is the best thing?'

'Ah, for fuck's sake, Pascal, are you a priest or something? This isn't for the scum like me on the streets, this is for the brothels. My God, where have you been, country bumpkin?' He laughed and picked up a silk négligée and let it run through his fingers. 'The Nazis love our brothels. These SS types speak the language, treat the whores with respect – top-class whores, that is. Christ, the women even dye their hair black so they look different to their blond masters of the universe. That champagne over there, that's for Le Chabanais, the silk and the brandy for Le Sphinx.'

'One-Two-Two club on Rue de Provence,' Mitchell said and saw his knowledge impressed the black marketeer.

'All right, so you're no bumpkin. You know your way around, eh?'

'I've no interest in you, Vincent, other than what you can give me. I don't talk about you; you don't talk about me. This is business. I want three lots of French railway workers' overalls and jackets. The grubbier the better.'

'Uh-huh. I won't ask why. Sizes?'

'For me, and one man ten centimetres shorter and skinnier. The other a man near enough the same height as me, strong arms and chest.'

'This isn't a tailor's shop, Pascal. I'll give you what I have. What else? Papers? You need railway workers' passes?'

'No.'

'All right.' He gave Pascal a knowing look. 'I know you're not from around here. Knew it the first time I laid eyes on you, so if you need a foreign worker's permit I've got a contact that can give me a *Fremdenpass*. You know they're impossible to forge. The damned bright red cover with the German eagle on it is difficult enough but the paper, impossible, and it has cross screening and watermarks. Expensive, but worth every centime.'

'No. I need a place to park a car. It has German Army plates on it.'

'Christ, who are you? Look, if you're thinking of thieving and butchering their cars for spare parts I might know someone but that's too dangerous for me.'

'The car's not stolen. It's a friend's.'

'Oh yeah. I bet. Clothes, passes, identity cards, all good. Cars with German Army plates.' He winced.

'I need somewhere out of sight for three days. No more. I'll pay whatever you want.'

Vincent's cigarette had become soggy from his wet lips. His eyes were half closed, not from the smoke but the calculation of how much he could squeeze from his old cellmate. 'I have a lock-up. Near here. It's in a back alley.' Mitchell could almost hear him calculating what he might get out of Mitchell. 'Fifty thousand francs.'

Part of Mitchell's brain saw the value in English currency: 250 pounds was going to make a big dent in the cache of bank-notes that Ginny Lindhurst had arrived with for his Gideon circuit. 'No. Twenty-five.'

'I'll do it for forty.'

'You'll do it for thirty.'

Vincent spat in his hand and extended it. Mitchell sealed the deal. 'Where do I meet you?' he asked.

'Bring it tonight,' said Vincent. 'Meet me on the corner two hours before curfew. And the money.'

'Half now, half when I pick it up.'

'All right.'

'And I want the clothes today.'

'Take them now. I have them. Shall we say eight thousand?'

'Shall we say five?'

'We shall.' Vincent grinned knowing that he was still making a decent profit.

Mitchell pulled out a wad of cash and began counting it on to the table. 'One more thing. I need a German Army uniform.'

47

Mitchell and Ginny reached the train station at Vincennes. A short walk brought them to Gaétan's house, which sat nestled down a country lane. The patrician had already summoned Chaval, Drossier, Laforge and Maillé. The gamekeeper Edmond ushered Mitchell and Ginny through the ornate iron gates of the modest manoir and as their feet crunched across the gravel Madame Gaétan opened the front door and beckoned them in. She hugged Ginny.

'My dear child, I did not expect to see you so soon. How pleased I am. Come in, Thérèse, come in,' she fussed. Mitchell was given a welcoming smile. Madame Gaétan looked more sophisticated in this edge-of-city house than she did playing the role of the country wife. Gone was the apron and the odour of cooking, now she wore well-cut clothes, jewellery and make-up.

She led them through to an orangery at the rear of the house which, Mitchell noted, was in as much need of upkeep and repair as the house in Norvé.

'Darling, Colonel Garon and Mademoiselle Thérèse are here.' She closed the door leaving the gathered men.

Gaétan stood up and greeted Mitchell; then Chaval gripped his hand, a broad grin breaking surface behind his beard. 'Pascal, good to see you again.'

'At last,' said Laforge. 'We thought you'd forgotten us.'

'He only wants us when he needs us,' moaned Maillé. 'Hello, colonel. Living well in the city?'

'Getting by, Maillé. Good to hear you're as cheerful as ever.'

The men laughed, their spirits clearly lifted by seeing Mitchell again.

'He's been even worse since we were holed up waiting for some action,' said Drossier. 'Good to see you again, Pascal. You too, mademoiselle.'

'Thank you,' said Ginny.

'Come and sit next to me,' said Chaval. 'I bathed this morning.' He grinned. 'Unlike these,' he said, nodding towards the men.

She returned his smile and joined him on the faded couch.

'Very well,' said Gaétan, 'tell us what is happening, colonel.'

Mitchell quickly outlined the news from London and what was required.

'And for this, you need my help?' said the patrician. 'The Norvé circuit is not active here, as you well know, so I'm assuming that you will be in charge of the operation.'

'I need whatever knowledge you can give me and I also need to move the men quickly across the city without raising suspicion. My proposal is twofold. We split into two teams. One will destroy the railway lines beyond the city suburbs, the other the rail-yard turntable. There must be more than sixty big locomotives in those sheds and they need to be turned to run into Germany. Once we have blown the tracks the Germans would send out their heavy-lifting locomotives to repair them, but they can't if the turntable is out of action. The operation will effectively isolate the train and the retooling machinery for the bombing run and wreak havoc with the German supply trains trying to leave Paris for months to come.'

'Then this is going to be credited to your Gideon circuit,' said Gaétan.

'Setting up the circuit here in Paris was one of my main objectives,' he answered, adding diplomatically, 'but I turn to you for assistance in these matters.' No civilian could be coerced to do as Mitchell wished, they had to be persuaded, and now that he was finally setting up the circuit in Paris he had no desire to cause affront to the patrician.

'It seems, colonel, that you have been given a great deal of authority here. You are to find and rescue a German traitor, set up a new resistance cell bypassing our own efforts in Norvé, and yet you still seek our help. My circuit has few enough men. I cannot bring them into the city away from their families. If any of them are apprehended then the Norvé circuit would cease to exist.'

It was obvious Gaétan felt he was being excluded from direct involvement in the operation.

'If you have any local men here that you can trust I will use them, if not then I would ask you to let me use Edmond on one of the teams. That will ensure that you are included in the attack and that London will know we have worked together to help save innocent lives.' Mitchell wanted the man who had followed Chaval into the city to be in on the attack. Mitchell was uncertain whether he was the source of the leak but reasoned that if he were, he wouldn't risk being killed.

'And where is the other Englishman? Is he a part of this operation?'

'Regrettably, he is not. He died during the operation to find the man we were looking for.'

Gaétan showed no sign of being affected by Peter Thompson's death. 'Then have you found the German scientist?'

'No,' Mitchell lied. There was no need for anyone else to know that within days Alfred Korte would be on a plane for England.

'It seems to me, colonel, that you are behaving in a reckless manner and gambling with men's lives.'

'It's a gamble whether any of us will survive but I would not place my men's lives in jeopardy unless it was essential.' He glanced at the men around him. 'And if anyone who has come this far with me wishes to go no further than so be it.'

Chaval grunted. 'No one else would have them, Pascal,' he said, looking at the grinning men. 'Besides, now that you've told us about the mission I'd have to kill anyone who said they wanted to walk.'

Gaétan tapped a cigarette on the table and lit it. He plumed the smoke, pausing in thought. 'There is a fundamental flaw in your plan. You say we are to help save hundreds of people when the bombs fall; well, when the Germans discover sabotage there will be massive reprisals and they will increase their round-ups and deportations. Perhaps it is better to die quickly under British bombs.'

'Chaval, do we still have those rats we packed with explosives at Norvé?'

'Yes, but they will be nowhere near enough to do what you're asking.'

'Rats?' said Gaétan.

'Yes,' said Mitchell. 'Gutted and packed with plastique. They're used for diversionary tactics but they can blow a train track apart. We'll plant some where the Germans will find them. And we'll use the plastic explosive that came in on the Lysander. It's easily identified as British and we'll ensure some of it fails to go off. That will hopefully convince the Germans that there's a British sabotage team at work.' He looked at the group. 'It's the best we can do.'

Gaétan relented. 'Very well. I can be of some help. Edmond is at your disposal. I have a contact with a senior official at Gaz de Paris. Their vans are allowed free access across the city and surrounding suburbs. I will arrange the use of two vans. They will be brought and left near here. When do we do this?'

'Tomorrow night. Vincennes is our jump-off point. I would prefer that my men stay here until we are ready to go. Is that possible?'

Gaétan nodded. 'There are outhouses, but they must stay out of sight.'

'Of course. All right, let me explain where we will stop the train to give the bombers a clear run at it,' said Mitchell, pulling out a folded map. He spread it across the tabletop as the men and Ginny gathered around. 'We can blow the tracks, here,' he said, his finger tracing the map. 'Twenty-odd kilometres east of the city. Forest on the left of the track, River Marne on the right. We isolate the train before it gets to these suburbs, Saint-Thibault-des-Vignes and Lagny. That gives the bombers clear sight and we avoid civilian casualties. Explosives here, and here. Then the train can't go forward or back. It'll be a stationary target or the engine will derail. Either way, it's an easy target for the RAF.'

'There'll be anti-aircraft guns on flatbeds. Do we try and attack those?' said Laforge.

'No. Lay the charges, set the timers and then run. We're too exposed. We're not there for a gunfight.'

'We should kill as many of the bastards as we can,' said Maillé.

'Enough of them will die in the raid,' Mitchell said. 'We can't afford to take on superior numbers. Chaval, you go with Edmond and Laforge and blow the tracks. Drossier and Maillé, you will be with me in the rail yard.'

'And where will I be?' said Ginny.

The men looked at her in surprise. They had not considered her as a combatant.

'We need you to be at your radio in case we fail,' said Mitchell.

'And if you are all killed or captured then I wouldn't know till the Gestapo break down my door. I won't need to be sending any signals at all because we will have to stop the train by a given time, a time given to London before tomorrow. That's the only transmission of any importance.'

'Mademoiselle Thérèse is correct,' said Gaétan. 'If this is to be successful it has to be executed with precision.'

She looked from Chaval to Laforge. 'And while Victor and Reynard are with Edmond planting the explosives I can be a useful lookout. An extra pair of eyes.'

'She has a point,' said Chaval.

Mitchell took a moment to decide. If everything went wrong on the operation then Ginny Lindhurst would most likely be abandoned to her own resources in the city. The young woman had proved her worth already. He reasoned she had a better chance of survival in the countryside rather than accompanying him to the railway yards.

'You travel with Victor,' he said with a nod towards Chaval, praying he would not regret his decision.

48

Time codes, which would mean nothing should any German wireless intercepts be in place using captured ciphers, were sent through to MI6 in London. Bomber Command would strike at the co-ordinate sent by Mitchell while he disabled the locomotive turntable at the marshalling yards. Gaétan arranged two Gaz de Paris vans and by late the following night the two groups formed up in the courtyard at Vincennes. Mitchell had changed from his city clothes into the railway worker's overalls, jacket and cap. Ginny and the men gathered in one of the outhouses and once Maillé and Drossier had tried on and fitted their overalls they squatted around a tarpaulin with the others where half a dozen dead rats were laid out. Next to them lay thirty 1½-lb charges of plastique. Mitchell had given Chaval's group ten blocks of it with pencil detonators. He would need twice that amount of plastique to destroy the heavy-duty turntable. He gathered four of the blocks as the others watched and packed them neatly together to make one large charge. He looked at Maillé and Drossier. 'Watch and then do as I do.' Pressing the malleable explosive rectangles together exactly as he had been taught on his training course, he made a long and perfect cube of explosive. 'We need to disguise these main charges so I had Thérèse cut up an old kit bag and sew it into four small satchels.' He pushed the block he had made into one of the sewed pockets. He held up a handful of brass pencil timers. 'Colour coded. These are for a half-hour detonation. They're accurate up to a few minutes each side of that. Crush the copper end – this releases a chemical that burns through a wire inside. When you've done that pull out this safety strip, all right?'

Everyone's attention was riveted on his instructions.

'When the wire dissolves it releases a striker that hits the detonator. Put two of these timers into each block of explosives in case one fails to work.' He checked their faces again. 'All right, now you.'

He waited patiently as Maillé and Drossier followed his example. Ginny reached across and made up the fourth. She did it quicker and more confidently than the two men, but there were soon four hefty blocks of explosives and their pencil timers laid out. Four single blocks remained. Mitchell tucked them into his haversack. 'We use these for the tracks.' He stood and checked his watch as everyone loaded their haversacks with their explosives. Those who had Stens broke them down into three pieces and eased them into the haversacks.

'The train will leave Paris at 0400. Time the charges for 0430,' Mitchell told them. 'I'll time mine for ten minutes after that.'

'And if the train leaves late?' said Laforge?

'They're Germans,' said Gaétan's man, Edmond. 'They'll be on time. Colonel, I have looked at the road next to the tracks. Once we have laid the charges we will drive south across the river, through the suburbs and then get back here.'

'Good,' said Mitchell. 'We'll plant dud explosives and the rats where they'll find them afterwards. The air strike is at 0500.' He looked at everyone. 'Timing is everything. Questions?'

No one answered.

Chaval slung his Schmeisser across his shoulder. 'We should go.'

'We meet back here, see that everyone is all right. Then Thérèse and I will get back to the city,' said Mitchell. They bade each other good luck and separated.

Olivier Gaétan and his wife watched as the gas service vans drove out of the gates.

'Perhaps we should return to Norvé and leave this Colonel Garon to his own plans. It could be getting too dangerous for us to stay so close to the city if he is planning more sabotage,' said Gaétan. 'If he is successful he will be given priority for more arms and ammunition while our circuit at home will be starved. The British do not realize how ordinary Frenchmen and -women risk their lives every day. They will always look after their own before us.' He looked at the smouldering tip of his cigar and blew on it to make the slow-burning tobacco flare. 'Perhaps it is time we plan our own operation. Then we can go back.'

'I have my charity work, *chéri*. There are senior people in the police and army who might start asking questions if I was suddenly not a part of their social gatherings. People know us.'

Gaétan sighed. 'You will be seen once too often with them and then you are vulnerable.'

'More vulnerable than this Pascal Garon? You had him followed in the city?'

'Yes. He was picked up by a gendarme. I've learnt it was a sergeant from the Préfecture. I have made enquiries; he is a collaborator.'

'Then you cannot give him your trust.' She switched off the light and began climbing the stairs to their bedroom leaving her husband in the half-light of the fire.

*

Mitchell sat in the passenger seat as Maillé eased the van along the marshalling yards' perimeter wire.

'There's a café further along that wire fence. It's where the rail workers get a coffee before they start their shift. We're going to get inside and use its rooflight to get over the wire.'

They had driven slowly past the main entrance gates where the rail workers would report each morning. A row of buildings ran along one side of the yards and the overhead floodlights would cast deep shadows should they be turned on if the alarm was raised. That would give them a chance to escape, he told the others, pointing out quickly where the night became even darker along the edge of the buildings. However, Mitchell hoped the floodlights would *not* come on should anything go wrong: the Germans might think the explosions were little more than markers for a night bombing raid and therefore be afraid of illuminating such a vast area. Here and there across the vast expanse of the rail yards, single lamps glowed dully, giving a narrow cone of blurred light. Maillé followed Mitchell's instruction and parked the van in a nearby street.

'All right, listen. There was no sign of any sentries, so they're going to be inside the locomotive sheds. If any Resistance group was going to attack and try to disable the engines they would cross the tracks easily enough but never breach those sheds. The Germans have little to fear outside of them.'

'Why?' asked Maillé.

'Because there are so many railway tracks it would be impossible to destroy them in any significant number. The treasure is inside. When we get into the yard and reach the turntable we have to place the charges inside the steel lattice, tight up against the turntable's pivot. Make sure it's wedged. Then we crimp the pencil timers. When that's done walk, not run, to the main gate. Go individually. I'll cut the lock, that way the Germans won't suspect the café owner.' The two men nodded their understanding. They looked nervous. Maillé wiped a hand across his mouth and then caught Mitchell watching him.

'My mouth is dry.' He smiled guiltily.

'That's a good sign,' Mitchell told him. 'Once we're laying the charges you'll soon forget about being afraid.'

'I never said I was scared,' Maillé said quickly.

'You'd be stupid not to be.' Mitchell wondered if the men could see his own hands trembling in the darkness of the cab. He turned to look at Drossier in the back of the van. 'Now we need to get into the café. How are your lock-picking skills?'

He saw a flash of a smile in the darkness.

*

The darkness almost overwhelmed Chaval and the others as they scurried along the railway lines. His poacher's night vision helped him discern shapes, which made him more surefooted than Laforge behind him. He had tied a strip of torn white shirt around his neck to help guide the *résistant*, whispering urgently for him to keep up. Laforge stumbled once or twice, sprawling across the gravel beneath the rails, cursing under his breath. Edmond, however, was as used to night work as the man who led them and needed no help.

And then the hulking figure in front of Laforge stopped and half turned, putting out a restraining hand to stop his companion bumping into him in the darkness. 'Edmond, put yours here.' There was no reason the gamekeeper would argue but Chaval didn't wait and whispered quickly to a sweating Laforge, 'Reynard, come on, another twenty metres and you lay your charges.' He strode away along the tracks, which now glimmered with the occasional reflection as the moon's light filtered through the passing clouds. Chaval cast a weather eye towards the sky, reckoning that in less than an hour the clouds would blow clear. He and the others needed to be far away by then. 'Here. Charges both sides of the track just like Pascal told us.'

He saw Laforge go down on one knee and sling free his haversack. By the time he had taken out the first of his explosives Chaval was further along the track. He looked back and saw the men's movement in the darkness. On the other side of the narrow strip of road that ran parallel two metres below the rail embankment the solid block of forest shielded them from sight. The river was not that far away on the other side and would reflect any light that the night sky yielded. He knew that if he were a pilot he would follow the silver ribbon to his target like a night owl gliding towards its kill. He eased the haversack from his shoulder and lay down the Schmeisser against the track; then he moulded the slightly tacky surface of the plastique into the track's recess above the bolts that secured it to the sleeper. All being well they would be finished in half an hour.

They had parked the van up a dirt track into the forest, invisible to anyone who might pass by. The curfew was long in place but there was always the chance of a German patrol passing along the narrow road between forest and railway line. Ginny tightened her raincoat belt as she hid in the ditch by the roadside. Clouds scuttled past overhead and for a few seconds she clearly saw the three men crouching against the skyline. She had worn the black woollen beret for warmth but had kept its rim above her ears, ignoring the bite of cold, wanting to make sure that she heard any approaching vehicle or the boot scrapes of a foot patrol.

Thankfully the moon was soon obscured again and she stood up from her cramped position. The night was never completely silent; she had learnt that. Wind through the forest rubbed branches together in a dull persistent groan. It also deadened any sound and she failed to hear the downwind approach of a small car until its rough engine caught her attention. She spun around and saw the gamekeeper and Chaval gesture wildly to her because their keen hearing had already heard the car's approach. Then the men lay flat as a small two-seater sports car came around a bend fifty metres away, its headlights sweeping the road ahead, catching her full in its beams. She froze like a rabbit caught in their glare. Somewhere behind her she heard weapons being cocked as the car slowed and stopped ten paces from where she stood. It would have been foolish to run and create immediate suspicion. She raised her hand to stop the headlights blinding her and made out two men in an open-top sports car. They wore shaped caps and there was sufficient light for her to see the Luftwaffe wings on their brims and pinned on their leather jackets. One of the men called out. His voice didn't sound distrustful, more concerned as he asked her in French if everything was all right.

She walked towards them smiling, greeting them and thanking them for stopping because she had fallen off her bicycle and it was broken in the ditch. By the time she reached the two young flying officers she could see that they had been drinking and were probably returning to base. The driver turned to his passenger, suggesting they help. The second man seemed less intoxicated than his friend. Had he seen movement up on the railway line? His hand reached for the small leather holster at his belt. As they raised their eyes to her they saw the young woman had levelled a pistol at them. The shock held them motionless and she fired two shots into each man at close range. The Luftwaffe pilots' bodies bucked and lay contorted, caps askew. For a moment she stayed rigid, arm extended, uncertain whether to shoot again, but clearly the men were dead. She released the breath held tight in her chest and turned to face the saboteurs on the railway track who had half raised themselves with weapons at the ready.

'Hurry,' she called.

49

Mitchell led the way across the multiple rail tracks, silver curves snaking this way and that in the flitting moonlight. A dozen railway lines fed out from the closed sheds into the vast turntable that was capable of turning engines on to any chosen track in the yard. Locomotives were always taken into their stalls front first, then backed out on to the turntable and spun around to roll off on the desired track. In the distance the fireboxes in the cabs of a couple of small locomotives glowed. Hissing steam eased from valves. The men could smell heated oil and coal smoke but neither of the little steam engines was moving. Mitchell guessed they were used for shunting wagons around the yard. He peered into the gloom, stooped beneath the weight of his haversack and the desire to appear as small as possible. The armoured train leaving Paris carrying the retooling machines would pass by these marshalling yards. Mitchell was anxious about setting the timers to detonate at the correct time. Too soon and the vital train would be alerted and return to the city yards. Too late and the heavy locomotives and their lifting gear would be able to get down the tracks and make the repairs. How timely would the bombing run be? Doubts clouded his mind but he consoled himself that if the bombers never came – were cancelled for any reason – then at least he would have stranded the vital tooling machines in the French countryside and that would give the Allies the luxury of destroying it when they wished. And there was the satisfaction of knowing he would have stopped hundreds of French civilians being killed.

'Here,' he hissed, hunching down outside the vast sheds. The scale and depth of the turntable brought him up short. The men would have to clamber a couple of metres down into the concrete pit. Drossier would plant his explosives on the lower track, the circle of rail that lined the circumference of the turntable pit allowing the turntable to be spun on bogey wheels. While Drossier did that Mitchell and Maillé would plant their heavyweight plastique in the turntable's base, close to the central pivot.

The others crouched. Mitchell held up a finger. 'One,' he whispered and pointed to Maillé. 'Two.' He gestured to Drossier, who nodded and followed Maillé as they eased off their haversacks, lay belly down and lowered their cargo into the turntable's well. Mitchell ran to the far side of the bridge that carried the turning track straddling the middle of the sunken turntable. With two heavy charges on either side of the pivot's mechanism, the turntable would be rendered useless. Mitchell was sweating, his shirt stuck to his back, but he steadied his breathing, eased the haversack down and then lowered himself into the pit. Banishing any doubt about the scale of the mechanism he quickly unpacked the explosives and bent beneath the steel latticework. Laying the charges seemed to take much longer than he planned. Time crawled agonizingly slowly. Panic began to grip him. He swore to himself. Shook it free from his mind. The charges were well concealed. He had arranged with Maillé, unseen on the other side of the turning base, to acknowledge Mitchell's tap on the steel structure so they could co-ordinate the timer charges. He tapped twice. He waited, crimping pliers in hand. There was no return signal. Doubts about Maillé's reliability taunted him. There was nothing he could do. And then he heard the dull double tap in response. He crimped the copper end of the timer. Grabbing his rucksack he made for the wall, jumped up for the top of the rim and tried to haul himself over the lip but he didn't have the strength to pull his body up the turntable wall. He leapt again, found a better purchase, scraping his shins as he struggled to heave himself up. Suddenly two hands reached down and grabbed his haversack straps and hauled him upwards. Fear lurched in his stomach. Thoughts of German soldiers lying in ambush flashed through his mind. Once he was over the wall he rolled on his back ready to fight and kick his way clear until he saw Drossier's grinning face leering down at him.

'No time to hang about, Pascal. Reckoned you'd need a helping hand. Maillé and I helped each other out.'

Mitchell wasted no time thanking him. A curt nod was enough. 'Timer's set?'

Drossier nodded. 'Yeah. Me and Maillé crimped them at the same time. Doubt there's little more than a few seconds between you and us. Had no idea it was going to be so huge.'

Mitchell didn't admit to having the same impression. 'They always are,' he said. He saw Maillé walking towards the distant gate and then bending down to place something under a track.

'The rats,' said Mitchell. 'Have you planted yours?'

'Yeah. On the tracks away from the turntable. They'll spot them because I left the timer in plain sight sticking out of the rat's arse.'

Mitchell raised his luminescent watch face. They had done well in planting the explosives but time was tight. He reckoned that they had less than ten minutes to clear the yard before the explosions. They followed Maillé. Mitchell stopped, quickly eased the haversack down and emptied out the two smaller blocks of plastique. He handed one to Drossier and together they pushed in a pencil timer without crimping the copper end. When found it would look as though the saboteurs had been disturbed or careless but would also hopefully identify them as being British agents. They placed the explosives several yards apart, spanning either side of what looked to be the main track leading out the yards from the direction of the turntable. Once done they followed Maillé, who was nearing the gate. One of the heavy metal doors of the locomotive shed began to grind open. Dull outside lights flickered into life. They heard steam hiss and the chug of pressure as smoke puffed from the smokestack. A sudden screech of metal against metal echoed from the cavernous shed as the driving wheels found purchase. The doors widened; all three men crouched as dimmed lights in the shed bathed the massive locomotive. A French railwayman emerged and walked ahead of the engine swinging a lantern, guiding the way forward.

'They're on the move,' hissed Drossier.

It was obvious the engine was scheduled to be coupled up to one of the many lines of boxcars across the yard. A coal tender sat several tracks away. Mitchell saw the direction the locomotive would take. Once on the turntable it would swing around, link up with the intended track and then back on to the coal tender. Soldiers appeared behind the locomotive as it eased out of the shed. A few feet away from where Mitchell and Drossier stood railway lines clanged as points were changed. Mitchell spun around. In the distance he could make out a signal box's light showing men heaving on levers.

'Walk,' said Mitchell. 'Slowly. Don't look back. There'll be men coming out on to the tracks anytime soon if they're preparing this train.' He prayed Maillé would not open fire on the distant soldiers. They were out of range from where he had stopped and at the moment posed no threat. Drossier's nerve held and he walked towards where Maillé had pressed himself against the perimeter wire. Mitchell waited a moment longer, peered at his watch face and strained to hear the sound of the train carrying the machine tools, which would pass by the marshalling yards. He looked back to where the locomotive edged towards the turntable. It would be an added bonus if the engine was on the turntable when the explosives went off. There was no time to wait and see. He angled his approach some distance from Drossier's so it would not appear that the two men were together. Every step made his back crawl. If they were challenged they were caught in the open. He heard the sound of a train beyond the yards. It was travelling fast, heading in the direction of Chaval and the others. Mitchell prayed his mathematical skills had not let him down because he had estimated the speed of the train and the distance it needed to travel to reach Chaval's position. In the stillness of the night the train's bellowing engine threw sparks into the night sky, where the clouds scuttered across the face of the moon. He quickened his pace, taking longer strides, urging himself not to break into a run. He was close to Maillé now. Drossier reached the gate and then Mitchell was with them. He had forgotten to retrieve the bolt cutters from his haversack.

'Get the cutters,' he said, jabbing a thumb over his shoulder. Maillé caught on, undid the straps on Mitchell's haversack and pulled out the bolt cutters.

'Now?' asked Maillé.

Mitchell turned and saw that the turntable was being cranked to face the waiting engine.

'Hear that?' said Drossier. 'The freight train's gone past. A few minutes more and there's going to be the sweetest sound.'

'We stand here gossiping like women in a damned bread queue and the last sound you'll hear is German bullets ripping your head off,' said Maillé.

'Cut the lock,' said Mitchell, turning back to watch the agonizingly slow-moving turntable. If any of the railway workers were studying the bogey wheels they might spot Drossier's charges and then the mission would fail. There was still time for an alert soldier to pull the timers out of the plastique. The turntable stopped. Had they seen something? He sucked in his breath, and then the turntable began its torturous grinding journey again as the pivot turned to line up on the locomotive.

The gate was open.

Mitchell ushered the men through, closed the gate behind him, tugged the thick chain back through the bars and with a final glance at the locomotive, which had now edged on to the revolving track, prayed that the explosives packed against the central pivot under the steel framework had not been dislodged. He followed Drossier and Maillé across the dark streets towards the van. They climbed in but Mitchell stood outside, head tilted slightly towards the sky. He checked his watch.

'Pascal!' Maillé hissed. 'For God's sake. Come on.'

Mitchell half turned, raised a hand to quieten him, and then walked away from the van to where the street broadened into another. Once again he checked his watch. And then he heard the dull thunder of explosions in the distance. He grinned and stepped back towards the van. He thought he heard shouts from the yards, distant cries of warning. And then the air reverberated with the shockwave from their charges going off.

'The gate! Drive past the gate!' he urged Maillé.

The van's gears complained as Maillé swung it across the street. Drossier braced himself in the back and readied his sub-machine gun in case they were pursued but the mayhem and flames in the marshalling yards had caused widespread panic. Maillé slowed; Mitchell leant out of the window and caught a glimpse of the locomotive stuck firmly on the turntable being engulfed by flames.

Drossier slapped him on the back. 'We did it. We did it.'

Maillé grinned. 'We're getting good at this, Pascal. Let's find more targets, eh? Let's hit the bastards again.'

'We will,' said Mitchell. 'When the time is right, we'll hurt them again. But right now don't drive too fast. All right, Maillé?

'All right, Pascal. You're the boss.'

50

As the train had derailed Chaval and the others stood shocked at the scale of destruction. The tracks had curled like putty and the locomotive, which was by then travelling at speed, lurched from the rails and ploughed into the low embankment. The anti-aircraft crews on the front flatbed wagons were hurled to their death, their guns careering into the narrow road and crushing them. The first four boxcars followed the engine off the tracks but the remainder of the train was intact with all the machinery secured on flatbed wagons. Soldiers thrown from the sudden impact rallied quickly. Many were injured but an officer or a sergeant – Chaval and the others couldn't make out which – started bellowing commands. Steam hissed into the sudden stillness accompanied by groaning metal as the engine's weight shifted. The small road was effectively blocked but there were enough soldiers remaining to quickly fan out to secure the area. Edmond had led Chaval and the others into the forest where they retrieved the van and then made a dash for the bridge. It was their good fortune that the bombing run was a few minutes later than expected because when the aircraft came they came in low and fast. The sky shattered with a roar. RAF Mosquitoes, with the distinctive sound of their twin Rolls-Royce Merlin engines, swept in and raked the stranded train with cannon fire, dropping their bombs along the length of the train. Men were vaporized. The ground erupted, throwing wagons and machines high in the air, shrapnel tearing into the edge of the forest. Flames soared. Shockwaves from the blasts bent the trees and flung anyone beyond the train to the ground. Within seconds the destruction was complete and the Mosquitoes powered away without loss. Chaval had stopped the van on the bridge and the awestruck team watched the dawn light turn to flames. The degree of devastation and the swiftness of it left them stunned. With senses numbed by the sound and fury of the attack, they drove away slowly towards the rendezvous with Mitchell and the others.

*

There was jubilation back at Gaétan's house. Chaval and Edmond, with Ginny and Laforge, were already waiting for Mitchell and his men when they arrived. Brandy and cider were brought up from Gaétan's cellar and Madame Gaétan beamed with pleasure as she proudly laid plates of food down for them in the barn. Their voices, raised in excitement at their success, were muted by the thick windowless walls. They shouted over each other, the men backslapping and then eagerly embracing Ginny.

'You have struck a blow tonight, colonel,' said Gaétan, raising a glass to toast Mitchell. 'One that will give hope to many.'

Mitchell felt more exhaustion than elation. The intensity of the operation had drained him. 'Everyone played their part. You too. We could not establish ourselves here without your help. I just pray that the Germans do not take reprisals.'

Gaétan shrugged. 'Blame for a bombing raid cannot be laid at anyone's door except the RAF.'

'The Germans are not stupid. They'll see the connection between the destruction of the turntable and the raid.'

'Let them. Once they identify the explosives they will concentrate on tracking you down. British agents in Paris will inflame them.' Gaétan swallowed the drink in his glass and placed a hand on Mitchell's shoulder. 'Everyone must sleep here for a few hours then go back before curfew.'

Mitchell suddenly felt hungrier than he had in days. He scooped spoonfuls of food into his mouth and listened to the others, bolstered by their daring, telling stories, embellished no doubt with every glass of alcohol. Ginny and Madame Gaétan laughed along with the men.

Chaval edged towards him and clinked his glass. 'Pascal. This is the start of great things for us.'

'And more dangerous times, my friend,' said Mitchell. He looked to where Edmond and Gaétan hunched together in conversation. 'Edmond?'

Chaval glanced at the gamekeeper. 'He did well. I still don't like him but he did what was needed. He knows more about Paris than we think. He knows clubs and brothels. Knows where to find black marketeers. He might be a gamekeeper down in Norvé but he's streetwise here.'

'Then the old man must use him to get food and drink. We can't suspect him of more than that, can we?' Mitchell made no mention of having spotted Edmond the day he and Chaval met. Clearly, Edmond had been following Chaval to either determine that he was trustworthy or in an attempt to find where Mitchell and Ginny were in hiding. The question that Mitchell could not answer was whether Edmond had trailed Mitchell without him knowing it. If he had, was the apartment compromised?

Chaval gave Mitchell a thoughtful look. 'I don't know, Pascal. What do you think? Might he have contact with the Germans and have betrayed that wireless operator? Was your plane shot down by chance? In these times we cannot give our full trust to anyone.' He downed his drink. 'He's a gamekeeper, my natural enemy. Don't listen to me.'

'You're the one man I do listen to, Chaval. Keep this to yourself for now but I am going to get Juliet, Simone and Jean Bernard's family another place to stay. The Gestapo have been watching them.'

The threat registered in Chaval's eyes. 'Do they know what Madame Bonnier and the doctor were doing in Saint-Just? If they have learnt that she was running a Resistance group down there then she will be on their wanted list.'

'Too far away, Chaval; they won't know anything. There's no link. No, this has to do with the missing wireless operator in Paris.' He paused, uncertain how much to explain. 'It might just be coincidence. He's dead.'

Chaval frowned and looked at Ginny. 'If they track either of you down she'll also be in grave danger.'

'Yes.'

'Pascal, I haven't told you what happened out there. She was keeping watch when a car came by just as we were laying the charges. A couple of Luftwaffe pilots. I don't know what happened but she shot them dead. Bang bang. Just like that. Cool as you like. She might not look much but I reckon she'll handle herself well no matter what. She's a very brave girl.'

'And the car?'

'Obliterated in the bombing raid along with them in it.' Chaval stood and clasped a hand on Mitchell's shoulder. 'I hope to God I never get in her way,' he said and grinned.

51

Oberst Ulrich Bauer of the Abwehr watched the civilians drafted in by the army to help in trying to clear the damaged turntable. It was stuck fast with its central pivot completely destroyed. The lifting cranes required to raise the locomotive from the track on the revolving bridge were trapped inside the sheds. The attack on the turntable and the destruction of the train a few kilometres away had been a complete success. More than a hundred soldiers had been drafted in to search the yards and do what they could to assist in clearing the torn steel from the turntable. Even more had been sent to the site of the destroyed train. These men were not the army's combat engineers who fought on the front line but from a pioneer battalion used for labouring tasks. The few engineer corps officers in Paris had been hastily roused from their beds soon after the bombing raid and despatched to each area. In the marshalling yards two of the smaller locomotives had been moved across the complex track system and were now stationed either side of the trapped train engine on the turntable. It was hoped that by pushing and pulling it could be shunted clear to allow the available engineers to assess whether any movement of the turntable was possible. Bauer allowed a beat of approval for the saboteurs' daring and skill. The trapped locomotive was caught between two sets of tracks so why, he wondered, were the engineers even attempting to move it? To be seen to be doing something was the answer, he decided. Men's raised voices joined the clamour of metal being struck by sledgehammers and the hissing cut of oxyacetylene torches. Bauer saw the SS car arrive and Stolz and Koenig step out. Bauer ground out his cigarette, watching Stolz stride across the tracks. For a moment he wished the Nazi would trip and go headlong into the gravel and iron. With any luck he'd break his neck.

'Well?' Stolz said. 'How bad?'

'It will take weeks to repair.'

'A co-ordinated attack. I've had my ear burnt on the phone this morning by Himmler. The Führer is enraged.'

Bauer lit another cigarette. It would help calm his resentment towards Stolz and his masters. The Nazi Party was run by a failed chicken farmer and a lance corporal paper hanger.

'I want reprisals,' demanded Stolz.

Bauer raised a hand. 'Just a moment.'

An engineering officer approached and saluted, then gestured for the soldier with him to lay out the dummy rats and blocks of plastique with their timers. 'Oberst Bauer, these were discovered in various different places. It looks as though the saboteurs didn't have time to set their charges. I have men spread out across the tracks searching for any more explosives but it's a slow process.'

'Thank you, captain.' Bauer picked up one of the rats. He extended it to Stolz who pulled back. 'A neat idea,' said Bauer. 'I've seen them before. Have you?'

'What are you talking about?'

'Dead rats packed with explosives and a timer shoved up their rear end. A bit like us. Primed and ready to explode.' He tossed it to Stolz who caught it in a reflex action and then flung it from him in fear.

'Damn you, Bauer. This isn't a game.'

'Don't worry, Stolz, it won't explode unless the timer is crimped. It's a British game. These were obviously British saboteurs. The rats, the timers, the explosives. British.'

'There's nothing obvious about it. It's the Resistance using their explosives. I want reprisals. One in three railway workers and fifty locals.'

'That would be stupid,' said Bauer.

'It would be effective,' snapped Stolz.

'No, it would not. The railway personnel were in as much danger as our men in the sheds. And shooting locals will make this clean-up even more difficult. We've sent so many to forced labour in Germany we won't have the manpower. We need every man we can get, though most of them are so malnourished we'll be lucky if they can wield a broom. I've already dragged a hundred civilians here. And there's a shortage of railway workers. You'd make matters worse for us all. We…' Bauer paused. 'The *Third Reich*' – he emphasised the words – 'needs them. For once, colonel, you'll have to forgo your bloodlust.'

'Sir, may I speak?' said Koenig. 'The bombing raid spared civilians and that plays well into British hands. The colonel is correct about the number of men we need, but I would suggest also that in this instance, if we take reprisals, it is likely shooting hostages will inflame resentment towards us. The population here will never give us information, should they have any. The French railway workers shared the same risk as our men. If anything that act alone might convince others to speak out against the saboteurs if they know anything.'

Stolz glared at the younger man. 'There are times, Koenig, when you can be insufferable.' He stared across the marshalling yards as Koenig lowered his eyes. 'But your logic is sound enough.' He turned to Bauer. 'The Gestapo will arrest thirty men and interrogate them.' He raised a hand quickly to stop Koenig's interjection. 'I know, I know, Koenig. Torture will doubtlessly give us nothing in this instance. But I must be seen to do something.'

'Then let my men and French police round them up and question them and when little is forthcoming you can blame me. Wouldn't that serve you better?' suggested Bauer. 'Another feather in the cap of the Sicherheitsdienst in the tussle between the security service and military intelligence. And our methods do not cause such hatred towards the Reich but turn it instead towards their own countrymen who arrest them.'

Stolz recognized that the proposal had merit. 'I want a copy of the list of those arrested and your report.' He turned away with Koenig at his heels. Bauer watched them leave. Sooner or later his men would find something he could use against the Nazi and then the power would shift back his way.

In the background the sound of metal being wrenched apart put his teeth on edge.

52

When Milice Inspector Paul Berthold had been ushered into the Head of Sicherheitsdienst's office, a beautiful, well-dressed young Frenchwoman had come out. It seemed to Berthold that Standartenführer Heinrich Stolz might be a man who enjoyed the good things in life in this haven of a posting, and might introduce him to some of those good things. He was soon disabused of any such notion by the lash of the ruthless SD officer's displeasure. According to Stolz's information, it seemed possible that Berthold had interrogated a suspected British agent who went by the name of Pascal. The Nazi wanted a full description. How in God's name was he supposed to remember one face among the many he had interrogated? he asked. He was told in no uncertain terms that he had better start remembering or his time as an inspector would soon be over. Berthold had suffered the humiliation and gone back to the police barracks where a bed had been arranged for him. Paris. The great open city, virtually unharmed from the Occupation, beckoned him with its nightclubs and restaurants and willing women for those in authority. And now any anticipation of such pleasures had to be put on hold while he tried to satisfy the requirements of the Aryan bastard who lorded it over the city. There was only one hope for Berthold and that was to find Gerard Vincent. He thought the man the Nazis were so interested in had shared a cell with the black marketeer. He telephoned the Préfecture at Saint-Audière and had the desk sergeant check the arrest log: when had Vincent been detained and what was the name of the man who had been brought in after the boy, whose name he could not remember, had been shot? The dates tallied. The man he had questioned was Pascal Garon. If Gerard Vincent was known to the authorities in Paris then Berthold would bring enough pressure to bear on him to get a description of the other man in his cell that day. What Berthold could not recall was Gerard Vincent's Paris address. Their dealings had been off the record and the war profiteer's location in the city had barely been mentioned. It lurked somewhere in Berthold's memory but refused to yield to his probing.

He approached the Brigades Spéciales and then the local Milice but neither were willing to help him. Their resentment surprised him. Back home he carried authority; here he was an outsider, a country bumpkin brought to the city by their German masters, someone who might usurp any success they achieved themselves. Any sense of... he searched for the word and then settled on 'brotherhood'... brotherhood was sorely lacking in Paris. Milice officers jealously guarded their own patch and influence and Brigades Spéciales thought themselves the right hand of God. He was on his own.

He had roamed the streets, barely able to find his way back to the barracks, as lost in the city as any counterpart would be in the countryside, but then the city yielded the nudge his memory needed. He was sitting in a pavement café looking across to the opposite side of the street and the long queue at a bus stop. A trolleybus went past with its destination showing in the panel above the driver's cab. Rue Bertier. He tossed a few coins on the table, ran across the street and held his identity card for the huddled crowd to see. Ignoring the murmured resentment he pushed his way on to the crowded bus. Twenty minutes later the bus turned to make its way back and Inspector Paul Berthold's memory finally gave up the number 29.

*

Leutnant Hesler studied the triangulation information that he had worked on so diligently for the past weeks. His RDF vans had quartered the city, closing in, district by district until now, finally, Hesler had got his lucky break. He knew it was pointless reporting to Stolz unless he had key information. And the chart he held in his hands was key. It was a game between the British wireless operators and himself and they were always the weak link when any enemy agent was sent. He thought of those he knew who had been caught, tortured and executed. Brave people, he admitted to himself. It was a courage he did not have. As he immersed himself in the challenge he occasionally thought of the operator he was hunting. A sense of compassion lurked dangerously within him, but it was always put to one side, and when his prey made a mistake, as he predicted she would, then that was when he, Leutnant Karl Hesler, would find her.

Stolz looked at the markers that Hesler had drawn on the graph paper. 'Explain.'

'Sir, this is the operating frequency that she often uses and this is where we compared signal strengths in different locations. This operator increased her wireless traffic before and after the bombing raid and the destruction of the turntable at the marshalling yards. Normally she does not transmit for more than ten minutes at a time, but this time she did. It might have been a long message or there could have been a break in her signal, or London did not understand the message and she had to repeat it. I did not have her codes for this transmission, she must have different ones, but she took a risk. I suspect, sir, that she must have been sending co-ordinates and timings for the bombers. I sent the vans in an ever-tighter circuit and we did not lose the signal. I cannot yet pinpoint the street or the building but I will. She is definitely in the Ninth Arrondissement and I believe' – Hesler laid a map on the desk next to his graph – 'that she is within this area here. It's only a matter of time, colonel.'

'Hesler, when we capture a radio operator we hold the key to a door. It opens their whole circuit to us.'

'I will have her, sir, and when I do, you will have the English agent Pascal.'

'And you are certain there is only one enemy wireless operator transmitting in the city? And that it is a woman?'

'Yes, sir. As we can imagine a clandestine operator's life is a fearful one. They are alone in enemy territory. They often need a sense of not being… abandoned. She always signs off the same way.'

'Which is?'

'"Love to everyone."'

53

Mitchell nursed a drink as he sat in a café. The intensity of the journey from the night of the aircraft crash to the demands of setting up in Paris had tired him more than he thought possible. The loss of the men who had helped him, who had sacrificed themselves, weighed heavily, as did that of the men he had killed. But the fear that Juliet and her daughter were under surveillance by the Gestapo because of Jean Bernard's sister caused even greater anxiety. Luck had been on his side so far, but he knew that sooner or later it would run out. It was time to get Alfred Korte away from Paris and that would at least mean he had achieved a major part of his mission here. It was still impossible to know who the traitor might be. There were too many people involved who had sufficient knowledge to betray an agent. It might also be the case that London was wrong. The city was riddled with informers and corrupt officials. For a moment he reflected on how clever it was of the Germans to use the French to betray their fellow citizens. Only another Frenchman would pick up indiscreet comments that could lead to arrests, torture and further information. The hatred the French felt now was directed less towards the brutality of the German occupiers and more towards their fellow countrymen who betrayed them. There was no doubt that a day of reckoning would come. Despite Mitchell achieving as much as he had there was still one essential piece of information that he had not yet discovered and that was where his daughter was being held – if she was still alive. He waited patiently for Vanves to show himself. The sergeant would have documents for Juliet and Simone and Jean Bernard's family and they would be relocated that night. What gnawed at him was that he had instructed the corrupt gendarme to discover the fate of his daughter, Danielle. It was news he dreaded but hope rose above such fear.

Mitchell drained the glass when he saw Jules Vanves leave the Préfecture and set off home, where he had agreed to meet him with the new identity cards for the family. Watching the gendarme leave work was an added precaution to ensure the man was not being followed – Mitchell did not know if Vanves had dared to betray him or had been clumsy enough to arouse suspicion. By the time Vanves was out of sight Mitchell was satisfied that he was not being tailed. He made his way towards Vanves's house, criss-crossing the streets and making sure that he was not being followed either. He was still uncertain about Gaétan's man, Edmond. By the time he reached Vanves's house the policeman had already been home for an hour and was nervously waiting for him.

'You're late,' he said, tilting the window blinds in case anybody was watching.

'I had to check neither of us was followed. It's all right, Jules. No one knows about us.'

Madame Vanves stepped out of the kitchen, wiping her hands on her apron. She looked as concerned as her husband;

the confidence she had exuded when he last saw her was gone. 'Henri, is Jules in trouble? Please tell us. I know that he has been so worried since you came back to the city.'

'Denise, please. This is private business between Henri and myself,' said her husband.

Mitchell stepped towards her and took her cold, damp hands in his own. 'It's nothing to worry about. Jules is a good friend who is helping me find my daughter. That's all. You mustn't worry. I would not put your family in danger.'

She looked up into his face and nodded. 'Please,' she whispered. 'Do not let any harm come to us. I beg you.'

'I won't,' said Mitchell.

She walked back to the kitchen, and then turned. 'Are you staying for supper, Henri?'

'No, thank you, Denise,' he said gently and smiled.

The two men waited until the kitchen door closed behind her. Vanves opened his satchel and took out the ration cards 'This is the best I could do. I will have the identity cards in the next couple of days.'

'Good. Well done, Jules.'

Vanves's hands trembled as he gave Mitchell a set of keys. 'This apartment has been empty for a year. The furniture is still there. The family were not deported; they escaped to Sweden. He was a businessman. No one will ask any questions. Here's the address.' He handed Mitchell a slip of paper. 'I have arranged everything, Henri. Exactly as you instructed. But there is also bad news for you. I have checked the records.'

Mitchell's throat tightened.

'Your wife, Suzanne Colbert, was executed. I am so very sorry, Henri. Denise and I liked her very much.'

Although Mitchell had not admitted he knew of his wife's death, the image of her being shot loomed into his thoughts.

His grief-stricken look was genuine and Vanves reached out a comforting hand and gripped his shoulder. 'Take heart. Your daughter is alive. She is imprisoned in La Santé. Now I know that is bad,' he said quickly, 'but I have a contact there. The conditions are terrible, certainly, but she is with other women and has not been molested or harmed in any way. That is a comfort I can offer you. That and... this.' He handed Mitchell a grubby identity card. It was stained, and some of the dark stains Mitchell thought to be blood. He thumbed open the card and saw the innocent face of his daughter. For a moment he almost choked. He swallowed hard.

'Thank you, Jules. You have done well,' he said, the rush of relief making him light-headed for a moment.

'But I must ask you something. Once I deliver the identity cards, will that be enough for you to leave us in peace?'

'I won't bother you again unless I have no choice.' Vanves's face crumpled in despair, and now it was Mitchell who gripped his arm. 'I am going to make sure that you and Denise and your son remain safe. You have my word on that.'

He left the frightened man and paced the back streets, routes familiar from his past. The confirmation of his daughter's place of incarceration had caused a pressure in his chest. At every step, he thought through different plans of getting her released. And at every turn, his logic defeated such ideas. Somehow he had to use Vanves to find the answer but a lowly gendarme sergeant would have no influence with the German Army Command. When he eventually lifted his head he realized that he had made his way to Montparnasse and thoughts of his daughter had guided him to Rue de La Santé. Mitchell stopped and gazed up at the high grey-green walls of the imposing prison. Somewhere in the darkness within those walls his child was confined in a hell hole of filth and violence, a place where prisoners were guillotined in front of other inmates. He turned his back on the grim edifice and pushed his despair from his mind. There would be a way to get her out. He just hadn't found it yet.

*

Mitchell went to the address that Vanves had given him for the apartment. It was in the Fifth Arrondissement. It would take at least three hours for Jean Bernard to gather everyone; they would leave his sister's apartment with little more than the clothes they wore and a small case for each adult and child. Their leaving should not cause any suspicion as many Parisians carried suitcases these days: a few possessions bartered or sold on the black market kept many alive. After twenty minutes of observing the street and pedestrian traffic he was confident no one was watching the building. He found a telephone booth and telephoned Frank Burton at the hospital and explained that he wanted an escape plan for Juliet and the others in place within the next twenty-four hours. Train tickets for the family were to be delivered to the new apartment by someone Burton trusted. The conversation was brief and to the point. After he hung up Mitchell crossed the road and let himself into the building. If there was a concierge there was no sign of them. He climbed the stairs to the third floor. The apartment smelled musty but was bright and spacious, and it was obvious that the family who had escaped the city were comfortably well off. A large oriental rug spread across the wooden herringbone floor in the living room. There were three bedrooms, a bathroom and an alcove kitchen. Mitchell ran the taps and turned on the gas. Heavy curtains hung each side of the window that gave on to a park and a good line of sight up and down the street. He settled into one of the overstuffed chairs and felt a wave of tiredness engulf him. His head dropped to his chest.

The steady, slow tapping on the apartment door startled him awake. His heartbeat settled as he peered through the peephole and then opened the door to Jean Bernard, his sister and Marcel with Juliet and Simone. The two women had shopping bags and a small suitcase barely big enough to hold a change of clothes. The children had their school satchels and carried a small suitcase.

'If anyone asked I was going to tell them the family were going to visit relatives in the country,' said Jean Bernard as they were ushered inside.

The size of the apartment clearly impressed everyone. Madame Tatier threw off her coat and delved into her shopping bag, pulling out two loaves of bread and other pieces of food wrapped in brown paper. Juliet did the same.

'We didn't know how long we would be staying so just in case we couldn't get any food we brought what we could,' said Juliet.

'Cheese and some meat that I bartered,' said Madame Tatier.

Simone hugged Mitchell. 'Uncle Pascal. I haven't seen you for ages. I missed you.'

Now he'd had news of his daughter and seen her picture again, Mitchell felt able to admit to himself that he had enormous affection for this child. He kissed the top of her head. 'Come with me. I'm going to show you a nice room for you and your mother.' She took his hand as he led her through to one of the bedrooms. It held two single beds. 'I thought you might like to have the one nearest the wall, away from the window. What you think?'

Simone tested the bed and smiled. 'This is a wonderful place. Are we going to live here forever?'

Mitchell held back from telling her his plans. A child's joy and sense of safety should be protected. 'We'll see.'

He joined the others in the main room where the two women quickly arranged food and prepared the dining table with place settings. There was already water boiling on the stove. 'You have found everything then?' said Mitchell.

Juliet held up some cutlery she was laying on the table. 'Everything is here. You have wealthy friends by the look of it.' She smiled as if this was a dinner party for friends and there was no lurking danger. Her smile held him and without thinking he touched her arm as he stepped past. The tender gesture was unconscious and he saw the flush of warmth creep up her neck.

Marcel had run around the apartment in and out of every room. Jean Bernard settled him down to read a book and stood close to Mitchell so he would not be overheard. 'There has been no contact with the boy from the Gestapo agent but if he's not in the park then they'll know something is wrong and raid my sister's apartment.'

'They won't find you here. We're on the other side of the city.'

'They'll go to the hospital looking for me though. They know where I work.'

'I've spoken to Frank. We have people who will get you all to Spain. I'll explain later. In the meantime, he'll tell anyone who asks that you just didn't turn up for your shift. He tried phoning your apartment but got no reply. It's Paris. People go missing all the time.' He glanced at Marcel. 'I will have new identity cards for you all. Will your sister be able to convince the boy that he has to play along with a new name?'

'He's a good kid. He'll be fine.'

Mitchell nodded. 'All right, everyone. I have to leave so I need to explain what's happening.'

He gathered them around the table. Marie Tatier brought Marcel to sit with her. 'You had to leave your apartment, Madame Tatier, because sooner or later the Germans would have arrested you, and then Jean Bernard and Juliet along with Simone would all have been in danger. I have food tickets. You won't need them all; you won't be here long enough. I suggest Madame Tatier and Juliet do the shopping. Simone, you are going to be Marcel's teacher for a couple of days. This will be your classroom.'

'No school?' said Marcel happily.

'No. You and Simone will stay in the apartment. Your mothers can take you out to the park across the road. Jean Bernard will pick up identity cards that are being arranged for you in the next day or so. For your own safety I'm not going to tell you where you're going. Not yet. But you have to trust me. No harm will come to you here. No one will ask questions because they won't want to take the risk. For all they know you could be friends of people with influence.'

Juliet saw him to the door, embraced him and kissed his cheek. 'Thank you for everything.'

'You're going to Spain, Juliet,' he told her quietly. 'Jean Bernard knows already. I didn't want to say anything in front of the children. We have a feeder line with people we trust. You and Simone will see out the war there. I thought you might have been safe here in Paris but that's not the case any longer.'

She studied his face. 'Are they after you?'

'I think so. Probably. And I'm running out of time to finish what still has to be done.'

She pressed herself gently against him. 'Come with us, Pascal. I fear for you.'

The moment caught him by surprise as he felt an urgent desire for her. A sense of loss swept over him as he realized he did not want to lose her. He heard himself say, 'Get your coat. There's a small hotel nearby.'

54

They undressed slowly, smiling with anticipation yet still slightly uncertain and embarrassed. He was already aroused when she gave a playful, teasing striptease, loosening her bra, hiding her breasts and then letting her arms drop. Her arms and legs were tanned; she had a lithe body with thighs strong enough to walk miles across rugged ground and their tautness extended to her bottom. She didn't look old enough to have a thirteen-year-old daughter. It was she who took the initiative and pulled his head down to her lips. They shared a sexual urgency that released tension and relinquished grief from the loss both had endured. After they made love for the first time she laughed with joy, and insisted he stay on top of her, still inside, his weight suffocating the hidden pain and distress the months had inflicted on her. In whispers she told him how frightened she had been, and how as their journey north had unfolded she had watched him and felt her attraction towards him grow, and how she had recognized the gentleness that was disguised by the actions he had been obliged to take and his burden of responsibility for their lives.

And finally she told him how she had determined to seek the safety of his protection.

Afterwards, they lay entwined in the sheets, the thin blankets crumpled, the warmth of their bodies defeating the chill of the unheated room. They drifted into sleep, awakening in darkness and reaching for each other again. This time their movements were slowed by their desire to make the pleasure last. The chink of light through the curtains lit her upturned face as he caressed and kissed it. Mitchell thought of his wife, and searched within himself for any sense of regret or guilt, whatever the elusive emotion was, but could not find it. Recently, the intensity of his work at Bletchley Park had subjugated any wish for sexual encounters, and the women at Bletchley were segregated in their own work huts and liaisons were forbidden on grounds of security anyway. Besides, he had not been attracted to anyone. That, and the love he felt for his wife, had extinguished desire. Now that love for Suzanne had been eased aside. Perhaps, he thought, this had been a cathartic act. And yet the image of her death refused to leave him. Fear would continue to drive him until he found his daughter and then he would turn his back on what he had been compelled to do and pursue a different life.

In the darkness of the hotel room doubt taunted him as he listened to Juliet's contented breathing as she slept. Juliet and Simone were an even greater responsibility now. What if his feelings threatened to get in the way of everything that still needed to be done? He could not afford to lose focus. Lives depended on him seeing the operation through and being sufficiently detached to make quick decisions. He began to regret his feelings. They imposed an additional burden. His mind was taking a grip on his heart. He would need to dedicate all his time and energy to what still needed to be done.

Choose, insisted the provocateur in his mind.

*

Mitchell returned Juliet to the apartment as soon as curfew was lifted with the promise that he would arrange everyone's safe departure from the city. They kissed before the apartment door was opened and exchanged a whispered desire that the other would stay safe. He was due to get the new identity cards but his blackmail against Vanves would not last for long. Sooner or later the corrupt gendarme would be compromised and the moment that happened Vanves would tell the authorities everything. Mitchell had a plan to stop him panicking, but first he had to arrange for Alfred Korte to be flown out. He had left instructions with Ginny to arrange a night flight from the north-east of Paris where there was flat farmland and no industrial complexes. There was a good moon for the next few nights and if the cloud base lifted then Korte would soon be in England. Mitchell had alerted Chaval to ready the men without telling Gaétan. The patrician's involvement was going to be limited from now on. To establish the Gideon circuit in Paris meant Mitchell had to exercise complete control. Gaétan and his men controlled the south at Norvé and they would filter supplies and any other personnel from their area into Paris. It would strengthen the British and French agents' infiltration when the time came to seize back France.

It was an hour's walk from the Fifth to the Ninth Arrondissement and by the time he reached the Pont Neuf across the Seine he felt more confident. He was within touching distance of achieving everything that had been asked of him. He even harboured an irrational notion that he would find a way to get Danielle out of La Santé. He knew it defied logic and although he acknowledged the improbability of it something, a gut instinct, told him it could be done. With such uncritical hope in his heart he climbed the stairs, knocked gently on his apartment door and let himself in. Ginny greeted him with a generous smile as she tapped out her morning transmission. Her pistol lay next to her Morse key. He peeled off his coat.

'I'm starving,' he said, but she ignored him – she was concentrating on receiving a message – so he rummaged in the kitchen cupboard and found bread and cheese. By the time he had boiled some water she had pulled down the aerial from beneath the open skylight and packed the wireless away.

'Not tonight. The next couple of nights are possible. They have identified a field near Messy. It will take us about an hour and a bit to get there by car. If we pick up Chaval and the others, then what? Two hours all in all? Anyway, they'll confirm on the next transmission.'

He poured hot water on to what passed as coffee grounds as she looked out of the window. 'Something's wrong,' she said. 'Harry!'

Two Citroën Traction Avants had swung across the road blocking each end of the building. It happened so fast that by the time four plainclothes men had piled out of the cars, slamming the doors behind them, the street had been cordoned off by gendarmes wielding sub-machine guns.

'Gestapo!' she said, scrambling for her pistol. Mitchell jammed a chair beneath the front-door handle but by then there were already footsteps pounding up the stairs. There was no escape. Mitchell and Ginny stood ready, arms extended, automatic pistols levelled. Capture was not an option. Voices bellowed, echoing up the stairwell. The sound of wood splintering and then the crashing of the door below. Shouts, cries of alarm. The noise of a struggle. The fight moved further beneath them and then a gunshot shattered the air. Ginny flinched, a vivid image of the man in the apartment below being accosted and then arrested filling her mind. The voices diminished as they dragged the man downstairs. Mitchell edged to the window, saw their neighbour being pushed into one of the cars, blood streaming from a leg wound. The car doors slammed, the cars sped off and the gendarmes dispersed. It had happened so fast that they were dumbstruck. Mitchell's hand trembled. He clenched his fist and calmed his breathing. He tucked the .45 into his waistband and pulled on his coat.

'I'm going to try and find out what happened.'

She nodded and pulled the chair away from the door, but as he stepped into the corridor he heard the lock being turned and the chair being scraped back beneath the handle.

Mitchell went quickly down the stairs past a carpenter, who had obviously been despatched by the police, hammering wooden slats across the broken door. By the time the Englishman reached the street everything had returned to normal. People were going about their business as he pushed through the bar door. The place was empty except for the Corsican who stood behind the bar pouring himself a cognac. When Mitchell stepped inside he took down another glass.

'Every time those bastards mount a raid or make an arrest it's bad for business. I had a dozen customers in here before they roared up.' He handed Mitchell the glass.

'I thought they were coming for me,' said Mitchell.

'Me too. I couldn't have warned you.' He clinked their glasses. 'Health.'

They drank and Roccu recharged their drinks.

'Enough for me, I haven't eaten for hours,' said Mitchell.

Roccu reached below the counter and pulled out a plate of half-eaten eggs and sausage. 'Mine was interrupted. Finish it. It's real sausage. I know a butcher who likes his drink too much.'

Mitchell didn't argue and savoured the taste of real meat, shovelling in the eggs as soon as he'd chewed and swallowed the sausage.

'Slow down. You'll give yourself a heart attack,' Roccu said. 'I spoke to one of the gendarmes I know. He said the bloke they went for was pimping over in the Eleventh. He also did a bit of burglary on the side. Stupid bastard stepped on someone's toes, someone who was probably getting a kickback. That's him cooked.'

'Not the Gestapo, then?'

Roccu shook his head. 'As good as. Brigades Spéciales. If he lives he'll be in a lot of pain pretty soon. They'll find his stash and maybe then treat his wound.'

Mitchell ran a finger around the rim of the plate, scooping up the last of the egg yolk. He sat back on the bar stool and belched. 'Thanks, Roccu.'

'Shall we close the bar and get pissed?'

'I'd like nothing more. But I have things to do.'

'You going to stay up there in the apartment?'

'Probably a damned sight safer now.' He pulled out some banknotes, but the Corsican's fist closed over his hand.

'Don't insult me, my friend. Anything I have is yours.'

'You're not in my debt, Roccu. You have taken enough risks.'

'Let me be the judge of that. Now, go on, get out of here and watch yourself. And keep an eye on my window. If I need you I'll make the signal.'

Mitchell shook his hand and turned away. Simple acts of kindness and gratitude softened the ever-present danger. Paris felt more like the home he remembered.

55

It was that strange kind of half-light between day and evening when Mitchell made his way across the city and stood in plain sight of the German Army headquarters. Barely anyone gave him a second look; those that did ignored him, for his clothing meant he could easily be mistaken for a plainclothes Gestapo or SD officer. Who else would be climbing into a Peugeot with army registration plates? Mitchell turned the ignition, let the engine idle for a while and then eased the car across the near-deserted street. The petrol tank showed it was nearly full – they had filled it from the stolen and now hidden petrol. It was time to visit Gerard Vincent and park the car closer to home so they could get Alfred Korte from the hospital to the landing zone.

Twenty minutes later he turned into Rue Martel and then soon after Rue Bertier. The tight corner that led to the workshops behind Gerard Vincent's apartment block was a narrow fit for the Peugeot. He identified the garage doors, climbed out, leaving the engine running but the car's lights off, swung open the doors, was relieved to see the cavernous space and then reversed the car inside. The narrow entrance would either be a blessing or a curse. If suspicions were raised, or he was betrayed, then the narrow side-street opening would be blocked as easily as a cork in a bottle. On the other hand, he reasoned as he made his way to Vincent's apartment, if there was to be a gunfight he could easily jam the car in the street and make a run for it over the rooftops.

Gerard Vincent's apartment was lit by candles. 'You've got the money?' he said, stepping aside from the door to let Mitchell inside.

'Yes,' said Mitchell. 'No electricity?'

'It comes and goes.' He gestured Mitchell to the table in the centre of the room. 'You found the garage?'

'Yes.'

'I told you, didn't I? Plenty of room to store contraband. I have other places like it. All right, let's conclude our business.'

Mitchell noticed Vincent held a pistol at his side. 'Are you planning to use that?'

Vincent seemed to have forgotten it was even in his hand. 'Oh, no.' He placed it on the table. 'Can't be too careful. Hey, you need a gun? I can sell you this one. I have others.'

'I have my own,' said Mitchell looking him in the eyes, making sure that the black marketeer got his meaning. 'You can't be too careful.'

Vincent's shadowed face split into a grin. 'I like you, Pascal Garon.' He reached for a parcel wrapped in brown paper and bound with string. 'Don't get stopped with this. German Army, your size, as close as I could get, forage cap as well but you didn't ask for boots.'

'I don't need them.'

Vincent shrugged. 'As you like.'

Mitchell handed over a roll of banknotes. 'You can count it but I'm not going to cheat you when you have my car in your lock-up, am I?'

Vincent curled his fist around the wad of money. He smelt it and pretended to be weighing it in his hand. 'Seems to be all there.' He grinned, shoved the roll into a briefcase on a nearby chair and then quickly poured a measure of Armagnac into two shot glasses and toasted Mitchell. 'I'm not the only one who likes you,' he said, watching Mitchell's reaction. 'I had a visitor.'

'Oh?' said Mitchell, keeping the sudden alarm from his voice.

'You remember Berthold? The Milice inspector from Saint-Audière? He knocked on my door. Gave me a right turn, I can tell you. Thought he was here for business, but he wasn't. I shoved a bottle of cognac his way and some caviar but he damned near threw them back at me. He's looking for you.'

'Why would he come all the way to Paris and knock on your door to look for me?'

Vincent lit another cigarette from the stub. 'You tell me. You must be someone important, Pascal. I must have underestimated you.'

'That's always a dangerous thing to do in your line of business, I'd have thought.'

There was a hint of menace in Mitchell's tone and Vincent was sharp enough to pick it up. 'He wanted a description of you. He couldn't remember what you looked like.'

'And you told him.'

'Of course I did. He threatened to report me to the authorities and then some other bastard would benefit from all my hard work. Yes, I told him, right down to your shoe size.' He shrugged and grinned. 'I guessed that part.'

Mitchell's thoughts quickly focused on the information. If Berthold was in Paris he would have been sent for and that order would have come from the SD. Stolz. Standartenführer Heinrich Stolz, the man who had to be responsible for controlling – among everything else – the wireless operation now that Alain Ory was most likely dead.

'Did he say anything else?'

'No.'

'All right, thank you for telling me.'

'Hey, Pascal, I'm a low life, I sell to the bastards, but I'm not on their side. I have a healthy sense of self-preservation. I couldn't lie to him because he would have realized I'd given him a false description. I made no mention of you coming here. None. I swear on that.' Vincent poured another drink and pushed it towards Mitchell who took it, glad of the warmth the alcohol gave him. 'Watch yourself, Pascal.'

'I will. Thanks.'

'I don't give a shit about you, my friend. If you get lifted they'll hurt you and you'll tell them I helped you.' He grinned to soften the reality of his pragmatism.

*

When Mitchell left, Vincent blew out some of the candles so that there was only a dull glow in the room. He eased aside the blackout curtains and watched the street below. It seemed to him that Pascal Garon's sense of self-preservation was as healthy as his own, but also that Inspector Paul Berthold was intent on capturing him – so intent, Vincent had reasoned that the *milicien* scum would stake out his apartment and do it himself. He couldn't bring in gendarmes, *miliciens* or anyone else; they'd stick out like rats scurrying across a wall. Berthold was trying to impress someone above – why else would a provincial cop dig him out and put the screws on him? The blue-painted glass on the street lamps of Paris cast the dimmest of lights on to the streets, casting virtually no shadow. Intended to aid the blackout, they let those who needed the night to keep their secrets move more freely. He watched Mitchell crossing the deserted street, stepping between each cone of light, and then waiting, watching, listening. Christ, Vincent thought to himself, who was this man? He was damned near as feral as himself. Then, when Mitchell moved off, another form in a darkened alley shifted. Vincent grunted with satisfaction. He had been correct. Berthold was following Mitchell.

*

Paul Berthold had stood uncomplaining opposite the building these past nights. A policeman's instinct was his stock-in-trade and he had dealt with enough criminals to know when they were burying the truth. Gerard Vincent had caved in quickly when questioned; he wanted Berthold out of his door and his life. Saving his own skin was one thing but what else wasn't he telling? He'd been too rushed, too confident and willing to describe Pascal Garon in such detail that Berthold had remembered him clearly. If Vincent was in the business of illicit trade then it seemed a strong possibility that a relationship had been sparked back in that cell in Saint-Audière. If the SD and Gestapo were interested in Garon and they believed he was in Paris then that told him Garon might well turn to someone who could supply anything he needed. And what benefit would there be for Berthold in going back to Stolz and giving him a description? he had asked himself. None. He would be back on a slow train to deal with petty criminals and poachers. But if he found the elusive man and brought him to the SD, then he would have done something the security service had not. He would find promotion and status in the city. Standing outside for hours during these chilled damp nights was a small price to pay. And then his reward stepped across the street.

He followed at a distance. The man in front of him used street corners and shop doorways to check he wasn't being followed. Who was he? Berthold wondered. He certainly wasn't the insurance salesman he had pretended to be when questioned in Saint-Audière and he doubted now whether Juliet Bonnier was his lover. Could he be a rogue policeman? A *résistant* perhaps? No, he decided, a *résistant* did not have these skills. Garon knew what he was doing. Patience was on Berthold's side, that and a greater ability at following than the man in front could know. Berthold focused on every step that Garon took and anticipated where and when he would backtrack or cross the street. The sudden scrape of nailed boots striking the cobbles in unison came from a side street. A six-man German foot patrol turned a corner, marching in step, the steady rhythm almost hypnotic, the soldiers staring dully ahead, thinking whatever thoughts a foot soldier thinks when tasked with such monotonous duty. Their appearance was brief and they turned away into another street but it was enough for Berthold to gain ground on the unsuspecting man who stepped out of the shadows, his back to him. Berthold approached so quickly and silently that when he pushed his service pistol next to Garon's face the shock was so immediate that he heard his victim inhale. Garon's hands raised immediately, the parcel dropping at his feet. Berthold kicked it away.

'Do not turn around. Keep your hands high. Lean against the wall. Lean!' He pushed Mitchell against the wall, kicked his ankles apart and quickly and expertly searched him with his free hand. He tugged out the automatic and shoved into his own coat pocket.

'Insurance salesman, eh? Well, Monsieur Garon, I doubt you have a policy to cover you for arrest and interrogation.'

Mitchell recognized the rasping voice. 'Inspector. You're a long way from home,' he said, muscles tense, waiting for an opportunity to risk fighting the *milicien*.

Berthold was tugging out his identity card and going through his pockets carefully.

'I have money, inspector. It's hidden. I can get it.'

Berthold punched him in the kidneys. His knees gave way but Berthold had the strength to grab the scruff of his collar and keep him upright. 'You go down and I'll put a bullet in your leg. You stay where you are. You're valuable, Garon. The Germans wanted a description of you so you must be on their wanted list. Well, I'm going one better, I'm taking you in personally. What are you, an agent? Is that it?'

Mitchell heard the clank of handcuffs.

'Keep one hand on the wall, the other behind your back. Now.'

Mitchell tentatively did as he was told, finding the balance with only one hand to support him. And then Berthold made the mistake that Mitchell had hoped for. The policeman rammed the pistol's nuzzle into the nape of Mitchell's neck. Second nature from those long arduous days of training kicked in. There was an advantage in knowing exactly where the gun was. The moment the metal made contact with his neck he twisted his body to the left, inside of Berthold's right arm that held the weapon. Mitchell's shoulder and left arm slammed down across Berthold's body, catching his gun arm, forcing the pistol away. A shot ricocheted off the wall. He head-butted the bridge of Berthold's nose. The man staggered but didn't go down. In that instant, Mitchell knew that Berthold was the stronger man. The sickening reality was that Mitchell might not beat him. Berthold used his free hand to block Mitchell's rapid follow-up blow as he tried to ram the heel of his hand under the policeman's chin to snap his neck. As Berthold deflected the blow he swung the pistol across Mitchell's head. Mitchell saw stars; flashes of pain cut behind his eyes. His legs gave way and he fell.

Berthold bent over him, blood spilling from his nose; he spat it free and pressed the gun into Mitchell's knee. One quick shot and Mitchell would be completely incapacitated. A movement behind Berthold suddenly caused a dull crunching sound that resulted in him dropping his head and his weapon as he fell almost on top of Mitchell, who rolled clear. Gerard Vincent stood, legs braced, both hands gripping a metal pipe. His breath came short and fast, his eyes glared down at the fallen *milicien*. He seemed momentarily stunned by the action of striking down Berthold.

'You all right?' Vincent gasped.

Mitchell clambered to his feet, but Vincent still stood over the fallen man, iron bar ready to strike again. Even in the dim light Mitchell could see that the back of Berthold's head had been crushed. He felt for a pulse.

'Did I kill him?'

'Yes.'

Vincent dropped the pipe and wiped his mouth with the back of his hand. 'Good. The bastard.' He spat on the corpse.

Mitchell quickly retrieved his pistol, wallet and identity card. He tucked Berthold's gun into his pocket. 'There was a German patrol. They'll have heard the shot. Help me.' He grabbed one of Berthold's arms, Vincent took hold of the other and they dragged him a few feet into the alley. While

Mitchell quickly searched the body Vincent went back and grabbed the man's fallen hat. Mitchell took the dead man's wallet and identity card and found a knife with a folding blade in his jacket pocket. 'Get the pipe,' he told Vincent, who brought it into the alleyway. 'A shot echoes. We don't know how long we have until it's traced here.'

Mitchell forced the knife's blade beneath a drain cover as Vincent knelt next to him ready to push the metal bar beneath its rim. The two men rolled the heavy iron cover aside. The stench from the sewers below assaulted their nostrils. Vincent gagged. Mitchell grabbed Berthold's arm and dragged him towards the exposed sewer. Vincent spat the stench from his throat, grabbed Berthold's legs and helped tip him down into the flowing sewage. Mitchell heaved the cover back over the hole. Sweat trickled into his eyes. He leant against the wall, aching from the struggle. But there was no time to linger.

'I owe you,' said Mitchell, retrieving the parcel.

Vincent grinned. 'I'll collect one day.'

'You took a big risk. You didn't have to.'

'He was blackmailing me. He would have shut me down. He got less than he deserved. Besides' – Vincent grinned – 'I look after my paying customers. ' He extended his hand. 'Use the garage and keep me out of it.'

56

Hauptmann Martin Koenig had stayed late at the office. Stolz had gone to the opera with Mademoiselle Lesaux and he had been instructed to finalize the deportation list for the train due to leave for Ravensbrück and other *Konzentrationslager*. Both men and women were to be deported, which served the purpose of emptying the prisons of undesirables. More space in the prisons was required on a daily basis and Stolz was ready to order another sweep rounding up suspects across the city and suburbs. So far Koenig had listed 2,465 prisoners to be deported from the overcrowded La Santé prison. It required efficient organization to get them from prison to train yard and he prided himself on his skills in ensuring the smooth running of a complex operation around the city. He had correlated the names of the inmates from each prison – Fresnes, La Roquette, La Santé and Romainville – and had already liaised with the French authorities to supply the many buses needed at each prison and the gendarmes to accompany them. Once on the train the SS would take over guard duties. The buses would transport their human cargo to the Gare de Pantin, the small suburban station on the eastern outskirts of the city. It was the preferred station for everything the occupying army sent back to Germany, be it food, art or prisoners, and the tracks bypassed the terrorist attack on the turntable at the marshalling yards east of the station. Three days and four nights later the male and female prisoners would be separated and the women marched to Ravensbrück. Now he unfurled the last sheet of paper from the typewriter having double-checked the names again. Simple errors on the page could confuse those checking prisoners' names against the list. Laying his hand on the folder containing the typed sheets he remembered Leitmann once remarking that when the prisoners entered these camps God stayed outside.

The memory prompted him to consider going to mass, but no. Tonight he would ignore prayers of contrition and let pleasure offer him succour. Sleeping with Béatrice had made it easier to turn his back on the human misery in which he was complicit. Shrugging off the burden of the day's work, he left the office. When he reached her apartment building he walked slowly up the stairs, savouring the thought of her supple body. Months ago he had secured extra ration cards and knew that she would have a meal ready for him. He put the key in the lock and eased open the door. The smell of tobacco reached him rather than the expected odour of a cooked meal. Perhaps, he thought as he called her name, she had already opened the wine and the meal would wait.

'Béatrice,' he called again and stepped from the entrance lobby into the main room. He saw a *Feldgendarme* standing at the far end of the room. The leather-coated military policeman looked incongruous against the softness of the apartment's furnishings. The metal regimental gorget at his throat reflected the gentle lighting that Beatrice loved so much. A room had to be sensuous, she had always told him. Koenig's stomach clenched and in a reflex action he fumbled for his sidearm but the helmeted soldier quickly levelled his sub-machine gun. The surreal moment passed as Koenig quickly moved his hand away. He found his voice.

'Who are you and what are you...' His trembling words trailed away as Oberst Ulrich Bauer stepped out of the bedroom. The top of his tunic was undone; smoke curled from the cigarette between his fingers.

'Captain, we have been waiting for you. It's late. Standarten-führer Stolz must be working you very hard.'

Colonel... I... I...' The immediate threat strangled him. He tried to find the logic in his swirling thoughts. 'Where is Béatrice?' he finally managed to ask.

Bauer stepped aside, allowing Koenig to go past him into the bedroom. The first thing that was apparent was that Béatrice was not alone in the room. A stern-faced Wehrmacht woman stood next to the wardrobe watching the young woman who sat hunched on the bedroom chair, her face tear-streaked from the mascara Koenig had bought for her only a few days before. There was no sign of physical hurt; her clothes were not torn. He went quickly to her and embraced her. She looked at him, holding his face in her hands.

'My darling,' she whispered. 'Help me, Martin, please. I beg you.'

'That's enough,' said Bauer without menace. 'She has not been harmed, Koenig, but she quickly confessed when I presented her with the evidence. She stays under guard. I don't want her jumping out of the window.'

Koenig failed to grasp anything. 'Confessed to what? Sir –?'

Bauer raised a hand to stop any questioning. 'Come back out here,' he said and closed the bedroom door behind the nervous captain. He turned to the *Feldgendarme*. 'Wait outside.'

The burly military policeman strode across the room leaving the Abwehr colonel and Koenig alone. 'Sit down, captain,' said Bauer sociably. He took a brandy bottle from the sideboard and poured two drinks, offering one to Koenig. 'You looked after her very well, captain. Drink. There are things you need to know. They are not pleasant.'

Koenig mutely took the drink and brought it to his lips, clasping the glass with trembling hands.

'You are a churchgoer, aren't you, Koenig?'

'Yes, sir.'

'And do you consider yourself a good Catholic?'

'We are all sinners, colonel. I attend mass and confession.'

'And I wonder if you have a deep affection for this girl?'

Koenig felt an immediate reluctance to disclose his feelings for Béatrice. Bauer studied the young man for a moment and then reached inside his tunic and pulled out a sheaf of folded papers. 'Make no mistake, captain, you are in serious trouble and will likely be arrested for treason against the Reich and the Führer.'

Koenig jumped to his feet. 'I am loyal!'

'Sit down,' Bauer commanded.

Panic gripped Koenig but he meekly obeyed.

Bauer raised his hand with the folded documents. 'These are letters of free passage that come from the SD office. They declare that the bearer be given all assistance by the authorities as they are a friend of the Third Reich. They bear the official stamp of the SD and they were found in this apartment.'

The shock on Koenig's face was as if he had been slapped. The glass fell from his hand.

'You have been used, Koenig. Like so many foolish officers here in Paris who take Frenchwomen as their lovers. Did you supply these documents?'

Koenig finally managed to find his voice. 'I did not. I swear it. And there is no possible explanation why Béatrice could have had them. I believe they must have been planted by someone who wishes me, or her, ill.'

'Are you accusing me or my agents in the Abwehr?'

'I am not, sir. But this girl did not have access to the SD office and I did not supply them.'

Bauer paused. It paid to allow a dramatic silence to drive home what he said next. 'I believe you, captain.'

Koenig gasped. 'Thank you, sir. Thank you.'

Bauer shrugged. 'But you will still be arrested and charged. Someone has to be blamed. Don't look so shocked. Do you think Standartenführer Stolz is going to accept responsibility?'

'Stolz?'

'If you did not supply them who do you think did?'

'I... I don't know...'

'You are naïve, Koenig. You have no place being anywhere but in an accountancy office. You were brought into a place of violence, you rub shoulders with the SS, the Gestapo, men who inflict great pain on fellow human beings,' said Bauer casually. 'How does that fit in with your religious beliefs?'

'I abhor it. It goes against everything I believe in.'

'You delude yourself, my boy. And then you are tempted by a voluptuous young woman. Did you know she was an abortionist?'

An unseen force crushed Koenig's chest, threatening to squeeze the breath out of him. He felt dizzy. The image of Bauer sitting opposite him blurred momentarily. Anger displaced shock and Koenig defiantly rallied to his lover's defence. 'She would never do such a thing. Never!'

'Like I said. You're naïve. There's sufficient evidence and witness statements. She will be arrested. You know the penalty for abortionists. She will be sentenced to death by guillotine at La Santé and you will have the additional charge of being her accomplice added to that of treason. Do not be in any doubt that you will both be executed, captain, for one reason or another.'

A sob caught in Koenig's throat.

Bauer's tone softened like a father concerned for a troubled son. 'Let me help you. I know how these documents came to be in Mademoiselle's possession. I need a little more time to close my case.'

'I don't see what I can do,' said Koenig plaintively, ignoring the admission from Bauer and concentrating on the lifeline he had been thrown.

'What I want from you is everything you know about trapping the English agent and his wireless operator.'

'Betray Standartenführer Stolz?'

'I seek only Alfred Korte. If I find the agent I find the man I want. Stolz, I will deal with later.'

'And Béatrice?'

'You cannot save her. Save yourself. Abandon her. '

Koenig was stunned into silence. He wiped away the tear edging down his cheek.

And then he nodded.

57

The Corsican threw a bucket of water across the pavement in front of his bar. With one eye on the apartment building opposite he bent to scour the pavement with a broom. He was agitated because Mitchell had not yet responded to the signal in the window and he had seen more of the fake bakery vans circling the streets. It didn't take a genius to know they were RDFs. He kept the closed sign on the door and checked his watch; anytime soon and the first of the customers would want food and drink. Night-shift workers from one of the factories or those starting their shift would come and trade ration tickets and after some bartering Roccu would serve them drinks at a fraction of their cost or charge them extra for food. It was a give-and-take economy but Roccu always made certain the benefits were in his favour. He saw Mitchell across the street about to enter his building. He must have been out all night, Roccu decided. Probably got a woman somewhere. He threw down the bucket and its clanging attracted the attention of those pedestrians on both sides of the streets, including Mitchell, who visibly flinched. The

Corsican caught his eye, the intention obvious. Mitchell strode across the street and as Roccu opened the door for him he saw that there was dried blood on the side of his scalp just below the rim of his hat.

'What happened to you? You look like shit,' he said as he closed the door behind them. 'You need a drink.'

'No, I have to get back to the apartment. Is there a problem?'

'Your man has been here since before the curfew last night. I gave him a cot in the back and a woman for the night.' Roccu shrugged. 'No charge this time. But I've also seen radio vans around. They might be closing in on you.'

Mitchell clapped a hand of appreciation on the Corsican's shoulder and pushed through the curtain to where Chaval was finishing getting dressed.

'I thought I heard your voice,' said the poacher. There was no sign of the prostitute. Chaval tucked in his shirt. 'I came here last night but the train broke down so it was late. Roccu gave me a bed and a meal.'

'And some company,' said Mitchell, looking at the rumpled bedding.

'It's been a while since I've had a woman and a man can't turn down an offer like that.'

'Of course not. What's happened?

Roccu put his head around the curtain and walked in with a tray of coffee and bread. 'Excuse me, but I thought you would need this.' He placed the tray down and went back to the bar. Mitchell and Chaval yielded to their hunger.

'It's Gaétan,' said Chaval through a mouthful of bread. 'He said he was expecting you to contact him, to tell him what London wants us to do next. He thinks we should keep hitting the Germans. He's getting impatient. Look, Pascal, he's planning a raid and he wants to use us. Laforge, Drossier,

Maillé and me. Says he can't bring his men up from his operating base in Norvé.'

'What is he after?'

'He won't say but Maillé is listening more to the old man than he is to me. I can only restrain him for so long without tying him up or punching him.'

'Don't blame yourself, Chaval. Maillé was always going to be the one who caused us trouble.'

'Me and Gaétan, we don't get along,' said Chaval. 'I've tried to keep my mouth shut but he keeps promising the men a share of the spoils. His man Edmond is leading the raid. Says he can get them through any patrols. He's a good man but you know how a poacher feels about a gamekeeper... Anyway, Gaétan's already convinced Maillé and the others that it's worth the risk. I'm sorry, Pascal, but Maillé is easily swayed and he still thinks that killing Germans is a game worth playing.'

Conflicting thoughts crossed Mitchell's mind. Gaétan might well have a legitimate target in mind and did not have any men other than Edmond with him, so using Mitchell's men made some sense. But he couldn't dismiss the notion that Gaétan was throwing Mitchell's men to the wolves. If Mitchell were to set up the Gideon circuit he needed those men to fight and help recruit others. 'Perhaps Gaétan thinks we're stepping on his toes and he's securing his own fiefdom.'

'And if he takes our men as his own he's already achieved that,' said Chaval. 'There aren't many around left to fight, Pascal. Anyone who served in the army is in a prison camp or has been sent away as forced labour. All I know is that Drossier has stolen a lorry and Maillé has his tail up. What are we going to do?'

'Try and stop it before it's too late.'

★

It was a complication that Mitchell did not need. Frank Burton was arranging tickets for Jean Bernard's family, Juliet and Simone to travel. Contacts had been made with the feeder lines and the members of the Resistance in the south to get them across the Pyrenees and into Spain. Now he had the added worry of the RDF vans that Roccu had noticed. How much longer could Ginny's luck hold? He needed to move her out of the apartment and he planned to take over where Jean Bernard and the others were staying. In the meantime, they were hours away from her making her scheduled transmission so that silent time meant the vans would have nothing to detect. Briefly leaving Chaval he went and fetched her, feeling more confident about her safety if she were with him, and the three of them set off for Vincennes.

They waited two hours for a train. Electricity was intermittent and the crowds jostled to get aboard the overcrowded carriages. Twice the train ground to a halt and the suffocating press of bodies in the carriages caused ill temper among the passengers. He cursed himself for not using the Peugeot to get to Gaétan's house but the car's value lay more in getting Alfred Korte to the landing zone. Once the train finally reached the route along the Seine random security checks of those disembarking at the stations choked the platforms and slowed the train's departure. Finally, as it rolled eastwards there were delays due to problems on the line. Ironically, thought Mitchell, it might have been because of the damage he and his men had caused to the yards and railway lines.

By the time they reached the gates of Gaétan's house a journey that should have taken an hour on a good day had taken four times as long. Laforge stepped out of one of the outbuildings.

'Pascal, they've gone already. There was no way I was getting involved. Maybe I should have but the whole thing is crazy.'

'You were right not to, Reynard. Where's Gaétan?'

'In the house. His wife's just parked the car. She was in town.'

Mitchell saw the car at the side of the house. Edmond was not in sight but the Citroën's engine was clicking as it cooled. 'Wait outside. Keep watch. Chaval? You too. God knows how dangerous this situation is.'

Madame Gaétan looked distressed when they knocked on the door.

'My husband is in the drawing room,' she said, but she showed scant pleasure in seeing Mitchell and his companions. 'I have had a disagreement with him and he has told me he does not wish to be disturbed.'

'Madame, I don't give a damn. Your husband has placed my men in danger. Show me where he is.'

She fought the conflict she obviously felt, and then relented. 'I wish we were not involved,' she said, ushering them further into the house. 'I am sorry, colonel, but there are times I wish the English had never sent you. It was enough that we helped the previous agent and accommodated supply drops in Norvé, but for us, being here in Paris at the same time as you trying to establish a circuit is too dangerous for us all. It is causing great strain for my husband.'

'But you go into the city, madame. You get permits for petrol, you secure food for the orphanages. You are respected,' said Ginny. 'There are members of Parisian society who still have enough money and contacts to help you in your charity work. Isn't that dangerous?'

'Everyone knows what I do and if the Germans think for one moment that I am involved with the Resistance not only will I be sent to Ravensbrück but hundreds of children will suffer. Everything will be closed down, and perhaps my husband will be shot.'

Ginny placed a comforting arm on Madame Gaétan's arm. 'Madame, we are not here to cause you harm. Everyone who wishes to see the Nazis defeated runs the risk you fear.'

'In here?' said Mitchell as they stood outside tall double-panel doors. He did not wait for an answer but pushed through into a bright room with ancestral pictures on the walls and classical-style furnishings showing years of wear. The patrician was standing over the fireplace, one hand leaning on the marble mantel, the other placing a log on to the fire in the grate. He turned to face them defiantly.

'You do not command me, Colonel Garon. Do not force your way into my home and start making demands. I am tired of it. I know what is necessary and what needs to be done. Louise, I told you I did not wish to be disturbed. For God's sake, woman, do as I say.'

Mitchell stood close to him. 'My men. Where are they? Where is Maillé? Where is Drossier?'

Gaétan seemed unperturbed by Mitchell's strident questions. 'Colonel, you bring peasants to fight in a city. Maillé is an oaf, but he will fight if the rewards are great enough. Forget patriotism; people like him only understand profit and what benefits them personally. He is good for one thing and one thing only and that is killing Germans.'

'These men under my command,' said Mitchell.

Gaétan raised a hand to silence him. 'And you were not here. We succeeded in destroying the train and I determined it was time to strike again. Vigour is what is needed and the courage to undertake acts that hurt the enemy.'

The old man paced back and forth, his resentment rising to the surface. Mitchell blocked him.

'I was sent here on a mission and I am close to succeeding in it. I am then to establish an operational unit in the city and co-ordinate operations with all the smaller groups who lie scattered across the countryside, and that includes you and your men at Norvé. If you do not wish to be part of this then I shall tell London to exclude you. Where have you sent Maillé and Drossier?'

Gaétan slammed his palm against the table. 'Why should I tell you? You have been seen with Jules Vanves, a known collaborator. A Frenchman prepared to help arrest his fellow countrymen.'

'I know who he is. He is little more than a clerk, and yes, he's part of the mass collaboration, but right now he is serving a purpose. He has information I want. There was no need to have me followed.'

Flecks of spittle formed in the corner of Gaétan's lips. 'I remind you that the Norvé circuit has lost men over the years since we started helping the British. It is we who have carried the burden. Maillé is little more than a resource that I needed. And he and the other petty thief that you brought here, they serve my purpose. I was and still am a confidant and compatriot of de Gaulle himself, so do not presume to come to my country and dictate terms and conditions of how I conduct myself. My man Edmond leads them.'

The argument was unlikely to be resolved in a civil manner now Gaétan's resentment towards the British had been made so nakedly apparent.

'You have allowed your own sense of importance to distort your judgement,' said Mitchell. 'If Maillé or Drossier are caught the Gestapo will torture them until they can fit the pieces together of the journey from the south, of the stolen fuel, of your involvement.'

Gaétan seemed to have calmed but his barbed words were clearly meant to inflict whatever damage he could. 'At any time, day or night, we can all be arrested and we will all yield under pain. This is a French war. Go home, colonel. Send us the guns and the ammunition we need. That is all we require.'

Ginny Lindhurst stepped forward before Mitchell could answer. 'You are wrong, Monsieur Gaétan. This is not only a French war. Churchill offered the French nation a "Grand Union" to share all of our resources and create one government to help defeat the Nazis. But your Marshall Pétain distrusted us so much that he said this would make France a British dominion and that he would rather be in a Nazi province. Well, you've got that now!'

Ginny's outburst stunned everyone in the room into silence.

After a moment, Madame Gaétan spoke up. 'Tell them where you have sent the men.'

'Be quiet, Louise,' ordered Gaétan.

'It makes no difference,' she said gently, imploring him. 'Tell him or I will.'

Gaétan looked at her. Finally, he nodded. 'Very well. There are several warehouses near the Rue Daguerre. It's where the Germans store food supplies before shipping them to their troops at the front. Seizing at least some of it would keep many families from starvation. We wish not only to hurt the enemy but to aid our people.'

'Call it off!' said Mitchell. 'That food is too precious a commodity. The place will be heavily guarded.'

'No, it is a soft target guarded only by gendarmes.' Gaétan looked from one to the other. He shook his head. 'Anyway, it is too late.'

58

Mitchell had racked his brains trying to place Rue Daguerre's location. It was in the Fourteenth Arrondissement, a few streets south of the Fifth. To get there from Vincennes by train would take too long. They would have to travel back into the city, change trains and then go south of the river, and with the slow progress on the rail system it would be impossible to reach the men before the attack took place. They were already going to need a miracle to get past German checkpoints in the city and reach the warehouses in time. If they were lucky it would take at least an hour and a half. Probably even longer. Gaétan told Mitchell that if the raid was successful then Edmond would take the stolen lorry and the food to an abandoned school a few blocks south of the warehouses.

'Give me your car keys,' said Mitchell to Madame Gaétan.

'You get stopped you compromise us,' insisted Gaétan.

'Then you say it's stolen,' said Mitchell. 'If things have gone badly for the men then we might need it to bring them back here. Whatever the outcome, one of us will bring the car back.'

Madame Gaétan barely hesitated in handing over the car keys despite her husband's protestations.

*

Ginny sat in front with Mitchell driving. Chaval and Laforge hid their weapons beneath their feet. Mitchell had determined that if the worst came to the worst then they would fight their way clear of any German patrol. They wended their way through the mostly empty streets, aware how conspicuous the car was. It was dark when Mitchell pulled into the schoolyard. There was no sign of the lorry or the men.

'Check the buildings,' Mitchell told the others.

A quick search confirmed that Maillé, Drossier and Edmond had not reached the lay-up. Mitchell reversed the car into a space between two buildings. It was out of sight of the road. 'We'll take a roundabout route towards the warehouses,' he told them. He pointed at Chaval and Laforge. 'You have the sub-machine guns. Stay behind Thérèse and me. If we're challenged we'll run for it. Cover us if any shooting starts.' Chaval and Laforge looked nervous at the prospect of taking on army patrols on foot, but they nodded their assent and followed Mitchell as he led them towards the warehouses. They travelled individually, staggering their approach on both sides of the street as Mitchell skirted right and then left to try and avoid crossing any main thoroughfares. As they approached the crossroads that gave access to the warehouses they saw that there was a substantial army presence.

'If there are soldiers here with those gendarmes then the alarm has been raised,' said Ginny as she joined Mitchell at the corner and peered around at the activity on the street. Mobile lights had been brought in and a generator kicked into life. Vehicle headlights were on and arc lamps swung in criss-cross patterns down the broad boulevard ahead. A German dog unit tumbled out of a van. Further down the street NCOs barked orders to waiting search parties. Two German officers studied a street map spread across the bonnet of their car. A stationary German ambulance was parked behind the staggered line of soldiers. Stretchers bore dead or wounded men.

'Those are gendarmes on the stretchers,' said Mitchell. 'The fight's already over.' He thought for a moment. 'Ginny, we have to find out what's happened. Take Laforge, go left, see if there's a way around these blocked roads. If Maillé and Drossier are still with Edmond then he will have got them into the back streets. Let's see if we can get them out. Give it thirty minutes and then make your way back to the car.' As Ginny went back to Laforge on the other side of the street, Mitchell beckoned Chaval to him and pointed to where he was going. The party split up and tried to encircle the Germans, using the dim glow of the street lights to ease them into nearby darkness.

'Those alleyways ahead are so narrow they wouldn't get a vehicle down them. That's where I'd head if I needed to escape,' said Chaval.

'Me too,' said Mitchell and ran forward, crouching. As the alley crossed another, shadows flickered and danced in the distance where the lane met a bigger street. A lorry burnt. Had the flaming lorry not caught their attention they would have run into the German dog patrol that emerged from one of the passageways ahead. Mitchell and Chaval pressed back against the wall and then followed the sniffer dogs and their handlers at a safe distance. The dogs suddenly barked and pawed at a door but their handlers cursed them and yanked them away. By the time Mitchell and Chaval reached the doorway they had moved on. The door was firmly closed but even Mitchell could taste the smell of offal – it was a butcher's. As they stepped past the door opened a crack.

'Here,' whispered a voice.

It halted the two men mid-stride. The crack in the door showed a woman's beckoning hand. They stepped inside behind the blacked-out windows and when the door closed behind them the wick on an oil lamp was raised. The light revealed an older woman wearing a grubby apron and bloodstained sawdust on the floor. Without another word the woman stepped through a plastic curtain that separated the shop from a stone-flagged cold room. Parts of a horse carcass hung on meat hooks. She pointed down at a badly wounded Drossier, who lay half propped against the wall. A bedsheet had been ripped and its pieces used to try and staunch the blood, but they were all soaked and Drossier's trousers and jacket were dark with gore. Mitchell went down on one knee, and laid a gentle hand on the badly wounded man. He gestured for the woman to bring the lamp closer. When she did so Mitchell could see how profusely Drossier's wounds bled. It seemed incredible that he was still alive. Drossier's eyes opened at Mitchell's touch. Blood trickled through his teeth.

'Pascal. Thank God. Thank God… We fucked up.'

'Don't talk, Camille. We'll get you out of here.' Chaval bent on one knee and eased another piece of the sheet into what looked to be one of Drossier's worst wounds.

Drossier smiled weakly and managed to place his bloodied hand on Chaval's. 'Hey… Chaval… you were right… should've listened…'

'Where's Maillé and Edmond?' Mitchell asked gently.

Drossier's head went from side to side. 'Maillé… stupid bastard. He opened fire… There were too many. Christ, they were everywhere... We killed some... The police... took Maillé... He was wounded... Gendarmes took him...'

'To the Préfecture?' said Chaval quietly to Drossier, who nodded agreement.

'And Edmond?' Mitchell asked.

Drossier looked puzzled for a moment. He blinked a few times. 'Dunno... He was firing but... he must have got away.'

Doubts about Gaétan's trusted gamekeeper crept into Mitchell's mind. Whatever had gone wrong with this attack the lone survivor – if he had indeed survived – would have the answers. But those questions would need to wait. Drossier was trying to reach for something from his inside pocket but he had little strength left. Mitchell eased his hand across the man's chest wounds and felt something firm in the pocket between his fingers. Drossier nodded as Mitchell withdrew a cigarette case.

'Stole it when we were at Norvé,' he said in barely a whisper. He looked at Chaval. 'Remember? When I was in Gaétan's car... lifted it then...' It took some effort but he gripped Mitchell's hand. 'Clean it up... give it back to the old man... Sorry, Pascal...' He smiled. 'Once a thief always a...'

His voice trailed away.

Mitchell checked his pulse. There was none. His bloodied hand closed Drossier's eyes.

'He's dead?' asked the woman.

Mitchell and Chaval got to their feet. 'Yes,' said Mitchell. 'Thank you for helping him.'

She nodded. 'You have to take his body. I can do nothing more.'

Mitchell turned to Chaval. 'Take his identity card. We'll leave him in one of the alleys.'

Mitchell helped to lift the dead man on to the poacher's shoulders.

The woman took a sack of sawdust and began to sprinkle handfuls on to the thick bloodstains. 'There's a back door,' she said.

59

Once they had left Drossier's body in a nearby alley, Mitchell and Chaval retreated to the schoolyard and the concealed car. Mitchell worked the lever on the school's water pump and washed the blood from his hands.

'Drossier's dead. Maillé's been taken to the Préfecture.'

'The police have him? Not the Germans?' said Ginny.

Mitchell shook his head. 'This could ruin everything if he talks.'

'And he will,' said Laforge. 'He's a hard-nosed bastard but sooner or later…'

'I know,' said Mitchell, desperately trying to think through the odds of getting to him before the interrogation began. 'But if everything gets blown so too does the safety of Jean Bernard and the Bonniers. My police contact knows where they are and is getting new identity cards for them.'

'Then we're all fucked,' spat Laforge. 'Would've been better if he'd died.'

'I'm going to the Préfecture,' said Mitchell.

'What?' said Chaval. 'You'll walk into a hornet's nest.'

'I have to get to Maillé and see how badly hurt he is. I can't lose those documents. If he talks, then my man will go to ground and turn me in.'

They fell silent.

Ginny looked Mitchell straight in the eye. 'If you get into the cells, kill him.'

★

Mitchell parked the car a couple of streets away from the Pont Saint-Michel with instructions that once he was across the bridge Chaval was to drive the car north across the river. Mitchell's plan was simple but, he hoped, would prove effective. He had surrendered his weapon to Chaval. If he got into the building he would certainly be searched, particularly after the thwarted raid. He walked alone across to the Île de la Cité and the Préfecture. The twin towers of Notre-Dame loomed into the evening sky as he quickened his pace, aware that it was barely a couple of hours before curfew. Armed gendarmes stood at the entrance to the police station; one of them pulled him over. 'Sergent Jules Vanves is expecting me,' Mitchell said confidently. The officer frisked him and curtly nodded him through. Despite the hour and because of what had happened at the warehouses there was sufficient activity in the main entrance hall to make Mitchell feel overwhelmed. And trapped. A couple of dozen people sat huddled on the side benches. They didn't look as though they were criminals or suspects. Just ordinary people trying to live their lives. The Préfecture's various departments handled the bureaucracy that drove the ordinary citizen mad with frustration. Some slept; probably, Mitchell thought, because they had been kept waiting for hours. At least he would not stand out among all the huddled men and women. He removed his hat and approached the desk sergeant, who was writing in a ledger.

'What?' said the burly sergeant, lifting his eyes.

'Jules Vanves,' said Mitchell without further explanation. The less said in a police station the better. A stranger walking in through the main door and asking for a police officer by name might be an informer, but the desk sergeant didn't seem to care. He turned to a gendarme at a desk. 'Get Sergent Vanves.' He glared down at Mitchell and flicked his pen towards a bench. 'Wait over there.'

Mitchell squeezed next to the others who were waiting and watched as the hall echoed with police footfalls and occasional calls for a patrol. It was barely a couple of minutes before Vanves appeared. Worry flashed across his face when he saw Mitchell.

'Merciful God, what are you doing here? There's a panic on,' he said as he pulled Mitchell into a quiet corner.

'I need to see the man called Maillé,' said Mitchell. He knew he'd have to trade something to get what he wanted.

Vanves's voice dropped to a hoarse whisper. 'You're part of this?'

'No. But I know his family. I need to see him and I need those identity cards I asked for.'

'You are mad. To come here. To place me in such danger.'

'Do you have the documents?' said Mitchell in an even voice.

'Yes.'

'Get them. Where is Maillé?'

'The cells. Where the hell do you think he is?'

'Is he hurt?'

'Yes. Wounded. Listen to me: you cannot see him. At first we thought it was a police matter, black-market gangsters raiding a food warehouse, but then we found a British weapon – a Sten gun – on this man so the Gestapo are coming for him. He's a résistant.'

'Were you warned?' said Mitchell.

'About the raid? I don't know.'

There had been no mention of Edmond so Mitchell assumed he had got away. But how, in what appeared to have been a furious gun battle?

'How can I get into the cells? A couple of minutes is all I need.'

'Impossible.'

'I have a gold coin.'

Vanves shook his head, glancing over his shoulder, seeing that the desk sergeant was looking his way.

'Listen to me, Jules. This man you have in the cells. He has information about you and your family.'

'What?'

'I told you I would protect you. I have influence with these people. I knew something was supposed to happen tonight, though I didn't know exactly what. But if he can tell me anything about their plans then I can help you. Do you understand me, Jules? I risked everything coming here to try and help you and your family. Now get me in there,' said Mitchell, hoping that the flood of lies would be sufficiently convincing.

Vanves bit his lip and then nodded. 'Give me the coin.'

Mitchell pressed it into Vanves's palm. He approached the desk sergeant and had a whispered conversation. Mitchell watched as the coin changed hands and the desk sergeant nodded. Vanves beckoned Mitchell. He led Mitchell down corridors that became ever bleaker until the curved plastered walls bore only wire-caged lamps in the ceiling and walls. The air in the dimly lit passage felt damp and chill. At the end of the corridor another bisected it and Vanves slid open a bolt on a heavy iron door. Beyond the door it was virtually dark, the dull glow from a solitary ceiling bulb barely reaching the end of the narrow passage. To his left was a series of cages. Vanves stopped at the metal door.

'Third on the left. Be quick, Henri. The Gestapo are coming for him. I'll get those identity cards and then you must get out of here.' Vanves bolted the door behind him. As the heavy door thudded closed the sense of finality made Mitchell shudder. Each of the first cells had two or three men huddled together on what looked like a stained straw mattress. At the third set of bars, Mitchell could just see Maillé manacled to the wall by one wrist as he sat slumped against the cold stone wall, his chin resting on his chest. Dried blood clung to the shirtsleeve on his wounded arm and stained his trousers. They had already stripped his trouser belt and boots from him and his feet were caked in filth. Within reach of the manacle was a latrine bucket.

Mitchell squatted next to the bars and whispered the man's name with increasing urgency until he raised his head. Mitchell saw the bruising on his face and his closed left eye. Maillé's lips were flecked with dried blood. He turned his head and good eye towards Mitchell.

'Pascal, is that you?'

'Yes, it's me, Nicolas.'

Maillé sighed. 'Sorry, boss. It all went wrong. Drossier?'

Mitchell shook his head.

'Oh, shit,' Maillé groaned. 'Thought he had a chance. He made a run for it. What about Edmond?'

'We don't know. Was he with you at the warehouse?'

Maillé nodded. 'He covered our backs when Drossier and I drove the truck to the loading bay. There were only two gendarmes on duty. We thought it would be easy, but there was a dozen of them inside. They were waiting for us. We walked right into it. We killed a few of them.' He tried to moisten his lips with his tongue but Mitchell could see there was no spittle in his mouth. Maillé shrugged. 'If I hadn't shot first instead of using my knife we might have had a chance.'

'We do things on instinct, like I did when I shot those soldiers. Look what happened. A whole village wiped out. What's done is done. Nicolas.'

'Still... you got us this far... but I ended it. Sorry, Pascal. Tell Chaval and the others. I should have listened.'

'I can't help you, you know that.'

The condemned man nodded. 'The gendarmes beat me because I killed some of their own, but they said the Gestapo are coming for me.'

'Hold on as long as you can. I need time to secure Jean Bernard and Madame Bonnier and her child. Give them information. Drip-feed it to them. Tell them we were responsible for stealing the petrol. Then tell them where we stashed it. They will check and when they see that you have told the truth it will go in your favour. Tell them about me. It doesn't matter any more.'

'It does matter. I know that. I won't die a coward's death, I promise you that. I'm sorry for what I did, for getting Drossier killed and for putting you and the others at risk.' He grinned. 'I threw my identity card away when they closed in on me. I'll tell them I'm Pascal, which'll throw them – for a while at least. That'll help, won't it?'

Mitchell nodded. 'Yes, it will.'

A tear welled in Maillé's eye. He reached out his free arm towards the bars. Mitchell stretched and held his hand.

The heavy bolt slid free. Vanves stood in the doorway. 'Quickly,' he hissed.

With a gentle squeeze of Maillé's hand, Mitchell pulled free from his grip and turned for the door.

60

Mitchell followed Vanves's rapid strides. As they got close to the main entrance and the desk sergeant Vanves turned and shoved a handful of identity cards into Mitchell's hand. 'Two women, two children and the man. These identities are old. They were filed for two years so no one will know these people were deported.'

Mitchell quickly flipped through the documents. His friends' faces stared back at him. The official stamps edging across the photographs would halt any suspicion that they were forgeries. 'Good. Well done, Jules.' Mitchell knew it was the moment that posed the most danger for himself and the others. Once he was out of the police station Vanves was free to save his own skin by betraying Mitchell, and he would not blame him. He had to secure Vanves's silence. He pulled out an envelope full of cash.

'What is this? Are you trying to buy my silence?'

'It's as I thought, Jules. You have to get home. They're coming for you. Get home and pack and get your wife and son out.'

Vanves's features sagged. 'What?'

'Can you leave here now?'

Confusion danced behind his eyes. 'Now? Yes, yes. If I must.'

'Is there somewhere you can go outside of Paris?'

'I have family in Lyon.'

'Good. Take the money. You've earned it. I said I would look after you, so help me to do so. I'll wait for you outside your house. Be as quick as you can. I'll stop them if I can before they get there. It's tonight, Jules.'

Vanves grasped Mitchell's arm with both hands. 'Thank you, Henri. God bless you.'

Mitchell tucked the identity cards in his overcoat pocket. The cells, the narrow, dim passage and the overarching stench of fear clawed at him and he was desperate to get into the night air. As Vanves took him to the main entrance a squad of German soldiers pushed their way in and began to close off any escape. Two plainclothes Gestapo agents strode in behind them. 'Security here leaves a lot to be desired!' one of them bellowed. 'Identity check!' Soldiers began herding any civilians in the hall to one side. Mitchell felt panic grip him. If he was caught with the identity documents he would end up at Avenue Foch with Maillé. The burly desk sergeant must have realized that if Mitchell was taken then he too could be named as having helped him. Reacting quickly he took a few quick strides towards Mitchell, grabbed him roughly and bellowing curses marched him unceremoniously past the Gestapo towards the main door.

'You bastard reporters! You come here when we have had men killed! Four gendarmes dead and all you do is sniff around for a story?' He cuffed Mitchell, who was genuinely stunned, and then shoved him with sufficient force so that he fell headlong through the main doors. The desk sergeant spat in Mitchell's direction and bent down and tossed his hat after him. Then he turned and swore at a cowering civilian who had not moved quickly enough across the hall to join the others waiting to have their identity cards checked. 'Stinking press.' He glared at the frightened civilian. 'You heard what the officer said! Get your arse over there!' The man quickly complied as the soldiers and the two Gestapo men grinned.

Jules Vanves swallowed the bitter vomit that had stung the back of his throat. He quickly nodded his thanks to the desk sergeant.

'Check them,' ordered the senior Gestapo agent to his subordinate. 'Where is the terrorist?'

Vanves hurriedly made his way to his office. It was time to find Mitchell again and pray it was not too late to get his family out of Paris.

*

Jules Vanves walked as quickly as he could to his house. His police overcoat became a burden but he thought it unseemly for a gendarme to take it off, so he suffered the sweat that clung to his undervest and shirt. He'd spent a lifetime trying to sustain a sense of dignity, and even in such times of imminent danger, he couldn't abandon it. As he turned the corner to his street he was relieved to see that his house was intact. Mitchell stepped out the shadows and joined him at the front door.

'Denise,' Vanves called, stripping off the heavy overcoat and tossing his cap on to the hall stand. No reply. 'Denise?' A note of concern crept into his voice as he walked into the drawing room. Madame Vanves appeared from the bathroom with curlers in her hair.

'Jules? What is it? What's wrong?' She looked alarmed when she saw Mitchell.

'We have to leave immediately,' her husband told her.

She opened her mouth to speak but Vanves cut her off. 'Immediately. Do as I say. Henri is helping us. Get Jean-Louis dressed and pack one suitcase. Take anything of value. Your jewellery, anything.'

Denise Vanves seemed to shrink with fear, freezing like a tiny bird in the face of a predator. Mitchell thought Vanves was about to castigate her but he embraced her tenderly and, ignoring Mitchell's presence, spoke lovingly to her. 'My darling Denise. We will be safe. We have enough money and we will soon be on the morning train to Lyon. Now, pack quickly and rouse our son from his bed. Yes?' He kissed her forehead and she seemed to perk up.

Mitchell eased aside the blackout curtain allowing a crack of light into the darkness. There was no sign of any movement in the street. Vanves glanced questioningly at him.

'Nothing,' said Mitchell, closing the curtain.

The lack of danger gave Madame Vanves confidence. 'Could we not stay in our home, Jules? You are an important man and I am certain the police would protect their own. And besides, perhaps Henri is wrong about the information he has.' She faced Mitchell. 'Is that not possible, Henri?'

'It is possible, Denise, but the man I questioned this evening was adamant that –'

The sound of a car engine revving and tyres squealing outside interrupted Mitchell. 'Down!' he yelled. Vanves smothered his wife on to the sofa as a burst of machine-gun fire tore into the front of the building, narrowly missing the window. Denise Vanves screamed and shook uncontrollably as the sound of the car roaring away diminished.

'Denise!' Vanves said harshly, needing to shock her into action. She found the strength to push herself free of him. Spurred on by terror she ran into the bedroom.

'I'll keep watch,' said Mitchell. 'Hurry, Jules.'

It took only a few minutes for Vanves to dress his son and to throw on a civilian jacket. Madame Vanves hauled a suitcase from the bedroom as Vanves loosened a floorboard and took a bag that he pushed into his pocket. Obviously, thought Mitchell, it was contraband: a nest egg for an emergency such as this. Their son looked bewildered but once again Vanves managed to control his voice and offer calm reassurance to his family.

'It's clear,' said Mitchell. 'Good luck.'

Vanves's wife embraced and kissed Mitchell. 'Thank you,' she whispered and took her son's hand. Mitchell stood at the front door. The street was empty. Vanves looked nervously left and right and then shook Mitchell's hand.

'I am grateful.' He checked the street once more and hurried his family into the night.

Mitchell made his way down the street and as he passed an unlit alley a car's headlights flashed. He climbed in.

'Did it work?' said Chaval.

'Yes.' But Mitchell felt a sense of regret at deceiving Vanves, and threatening such a vulnerable personality.

'So we won't have to worry about him talking?' said Ginny.

'No. He's on the run now. He won't come back to Paris.'

'He was screwing his own kind. You should have let us kill him when we had the chance. Shooting up his house would have been as good a time as ever to get rid of him,' said Laforge.

'No, his wife and son need him. He blackmailed people. He didn't cause their deaths,' said Mitchell. 'Fear made him as frail as the rest of us.'

Laforge eased the car forward. 'Maillé?' he asked.

In the car's darkness, Mitchell shook his head. 'He's wounded. The Gestapo came for him. He was brave.'

'Then he's still alive?' said Chaval.

'Yes. But they'll break him sooner or later. I told him to tell them where we hid the petrol. We have a couple of hours to move half of it.'

No one spoke until Ginny broke the silence. 'Time is short now, Pascal. We have to get the Lysander flight ready. I need to contact London.'

'It can wait until the next scheduled transmission. I have to get Jean Bernard and the family out. I've got their documents. The Gestapo agents will expect to question Madame Tatier's son and when he's not in the park after school they'll raid her apartment. If we're lucky Maillé's arrest will delay that meeting.'

'Where to?' said Laforge.

'Go back across the river. I'll show you where to drop Thérèse and me off.' He squinted at his watch in the dim light. 'Pick up half the petrol cans and find another place for them, but don't tell Gaétan where. We need to keep the information we have to ourselves now. When you've done that take the car back to Gaétan and find out about Edmond. Tell Gaétan what happened at the warehouse if Edmond's not there; if he is, get his version of events.'

'Shit, you think he ran out on Maillé and Drossier?' said Laforge.

'I don't know. We'll find out the truth – and if he betrayed them, then he will be punished. But make no threats, either of you. We have to see how this plays out. Understand?'

Everyone fell silent. The shock of the failed attack, of Drossier's death and Maillé's capture, compounded the suspicion that someone associated with the Norvé circuit leader might be an informer.

'Pascal, I need to make an unscheduled transmission or we won't get the plane in time,' Ginny insisted quietly.

'The apartment is getting too dangerous. Roccu said he saw a lot of RDF vans in the area. I need to get you out of there.'

'It's a necessary risk,' she insisted.

'I'll decide when,' he told her curtly. 'For Christ's sake, they're going to torture Maillé. You think I wanted any of this to happen? Damn the plane: I don't want you getting caught – or anyone else for that matter. Tomorrow we'll meet up and decide on our next move. Chaval, bring Laforge to Roccu's bar for noon. Hide the weapons where we can reach them and then I'll use the Peugeot when we need it. Don't mention anything to Gaétan about Vanves or that I went to see Maillé.'

61

It was obvious to Ginny when they stepped inside the apartment in the Fifth Arrondissement that Juliet Bonnier's feelings for Mitchell were deeper than when she and the Frenchwoman had previously met. Between then and now something had changed. Her eyes shone with an intensity that Ginny had only witnessed between her own mother and father. She felt a pang but could not determine what it meant. Was it jealousy? Had she spent so much time with Mitchell living on the edge that she felt a proprietorial claim on him? She dismissed the irritation and greeted everyone in the apartment. Their relief at seeing Mitchell again told her how much he had achieved in the short time he had been in France. He had led a group of survivors across hostile territory, saved two families, re-established his contacts in Paris and destroyed a vital train shipment. He had also inspired loyalty in the men he commanded, two of whom might have been led astray by another's foolish attack but they had taken the risk because of the courage and confidence instilled in them by his leadership. They could not be condemned for their actions and if, as Mitchell intimated, they had been betrayed, then their deaths might help reveal a traitor.

Madame Tatier playfully castigated Juliet who was embracing Mitchell. 'Don't leave the poor man standing in the hall. Jean, stand aside and show Mademoiselle Thérèse to a chair. Juliet, you can let him go; he won't fall down.' She urged everyone into the apartment. 'Juliet, let's get Pascal and Thérèse something hot to eat and drink.'

Ginny watched Mitchell as Juliet, beaming with pleasure at seeing him again, pecked his cheek and turned for the kitchenette. Ginny noticed that Mitchell seemed uncertain how to respond. Was that barely noticeable reticence a sign of guilt? Mitchell must still feel the keenness of his wife's death. Perhaps this Frenchwoman had eased herself into his heart. She dismissed the thought as Mitchell laid out the new identity cards. Jean Bernard opened and closed each one.

'They are perfect. I don't know how you got them.'

'Never mind. Did you get the tickets from Dr Burton?'

'Yes, they're here,' said Jean Bernard, reaching for them on a side table. 'But there was a problem.'

'Tell me.'

'We were supposed to leave from Gare d'Austerlitz for Irún,' said Jean Bernard.

Mitchell felt the uncertainty of a plan going wrong and looked quickly at the tickets in his hand. 'Gare de Lyon?' he said quietly.

'Dr Burton said the Gestapo and plainclothes police were swarming all over Austerlitz. They seized several members of the Resistance.'

'Did he say who was taken?' said Mitchell.

'He only mentioned one name: Pierre Dupin. Do you know him?

Mitchell shook his head.

'Anyway, he said he was sending us a different way, and that you would know the people down in Perpignan.'

Mitchell studied the tickets carefully. Everything had to be correct because any errors meant questioning by the authorities, especially if the Germans were doing a swoop on the main railway stations. 'Gare de Lyon for Perpignan tomorrow morning. Nevers, Moulins, then a delay at Vichy on to Clermont-Ferrand. You won't get to Langeac until the following night. You will need to make the connection but...' He studied the tickets. 'It's awkward, but you won't get out of there for another twelve hours. Make sure you keep everyone together. Don't let the children run off – no doubt they'll be bored – but you must not let them be questioned away from you.'

'Is anyone going to meet us before we get to Perpignan?' said Juliet.

'No. Make certain that if any of the trains are delayed or you have to change that you stay on the same route as on the tickets. Nîmes, Montpellier, Béziers and Narbonne where you will be contacted and escorted to Perpignan and from there across the border.' He looked at the two women in the kitchenette. 'It's not as quick a journey as I had hoped. I'm sorry, but Frank Burton knows what he is doing and if this longer route is safer then so be it. Four or five days on the train means you must use the food tickets tomorrow and buy enough food for the week.'

'Monsieur Pascal, no one in this room has ever lived on the left bank. We do not know how to get to Gare de Lyon from here,' said Marie Tatier.

Mitchell realized that had been the one thing he had not considered. Marie Tatier was the only Parisian among the others and like many Parisians knew her own arrondissement but little elsewhere.

'The park leads to the river but you can't go through because the gates will be locked. I'll draw you a map. It's easy but you must allow an hour or more. Better to get to the station early. Split up. Juliet and Simone and then Jean Bernard, Madame Tatier and Marcel. There's a German anti-aircraft battery on the Quai Saint-Bernard. Stay to the right of the park and you'll avoid it once you reach the river. When you are on the other side the station is on your right. You won't miss it.'

'We'll be fine,' said Jean Bernard. 'Don't worry about us.'

'You will have to be firm with the children. They must learn their new names.'

Ginny noticed Mitchell's brief look of concern. 'Why don't you stay and take them? I'll go back to the apartment. I have to make my schedule and then I'll move in here with the radio tomorrow night as you planned.'

'We have too much to do tomorrow,' said Mitchell.

'There's time,' said Ginny and smiled to try and give Mitchell the assurance she felt he needed. 'You were right, it doesn't matter about the transmission today, tomorrow will still be all right.'

'We will be fine,' added Juliet. 'You have done more for us than we could have hoped. You're a wanted man, Pascal. No need to risk being picked up in a random sweep. Please, don't even consider it.'

Mitchell was torn. The moon was good for another couple of nights and he had to get Alfred Korte out of Paris as soon as possible, but a part of him wanted to ensure that those who had saved him when his aircraft crashed were given their final chance of freedom. The family or the mission? He glanced at Juliet. No matter how close they had become he still had unfinished business in Paris. He could not allow his emotions to dictate his actions. Yet it was bad enough that as soon as they left this apartment the two families would be on their own.

'We've missed curfew. We'll sleep here and leave early tomorrow. Thérèse and I will walk to the river with Jean and Madame Tatier with Marcel, and then fifty metres behind Juliet and Simone. There will be others going to work so we won't bunch together. If I'm stopped then everyone should cross the street and keep walking.'

Mitchell saw the look of relief on Marie's face. Juliet smiled. 'Thank you,' she said, touching his face. The gesture made him feel closer to her than he could have imagined only weeks before. He picked up the tickets and identity cards to check them again. He knew it was a distraction to let his feelings settle. For a moment he was shocked to realize that what he felt for her was something more than desire.

62

Early next morning, as Mitchell guided the two families along Rue Buffon towards the river, Standartenführer Heinrich Stolz's irritation at being drawn from his bed and Dominique's sensuous embrace turned to a surge of elation when the voice at the end of the telephone told him that a failed terrorist attack had resulted in the capture of one survivor, a man who claimed to be Pascal Garon. That man was now held on the fifth floor at Avenue Foch. Stolz's desire to return to bed and spend an extra half-hour entwined with Dominique was quashed by a greater need to confront the terrorist. He washed, shaved and dressed with renewed urgency.

At Avenue Foch, he bounded up the stairs to his office. Koenig wasn't there.

'Where is Hauptmann Koenig?' he said to one of his aides.

'I don't know, sir,' came the reply.

'Find him and bring me my coffee,' said Stolz, stripping off his belt and sidearm. He picked up the telephone receiver: 'Interrogation,' he demanded of the operator. As the ringtone sounded, the aide returned with a small black coffee and sugar. Stolz swallowed it in one as he looked out of the window at the clearing blue sky. 'Leitmann. You have Garon?'

'He claims to be, sir,' said the voice from the fifth floor.

Stolz laughed. 'Well, if he knows the name, he knows the man. It's a start, yes? I'm on my way up. Have you seen Koenig this morning?'

'No, he's probably still got his leg over his whore.'

'I'll forgive him this once,' said Stolz.

All was quiet as Stolz reached the fifth floor; there was no sound of punishment being inflicted. When he stepped into the room he saw a broad-shouldered man whose manacled arms stretched across a small table. One side of his face was badly bruised, his eye swollen closed. Dried blood on his shirtsleeve mingled with fresh blood seeping from a wound in his shoulder. Clearly, the burly jacketless interrogator in the room had been working on the wound. He stepped back as Stolz entered the room.

Stolz wrinkled his nose at the stench. 'For God's sake, get him to a wet cell and hose him down.'

'I'm sorry, sir,' said Leitmann. 'His bowels went when we opened his wound. His legs have gone and if we drag him it'll go everywhere.'

'Then get some air in here,' Stolz snarled.

Stolz circled the wounded Maillé as the thug opened the window a crack, barely enough to allow the stench to escape, but it was better than nothing. No one would dare open a window unless a senior officer ordered it. No matter what vile smell stifled the room, victim and interrogator usually endured it together. Stolz picked up one of the batons that the torturers used to pulverize muscle and bone and pushed it beneath Maillé's chin.

'You have nothing to smile about,' said Stolz as Maillé bared his teeth.

'A man doesn't mind the smell of his own shit. And it's better than the stench of you bastards,' said Maillé.

Stolz replaced the baton on the table, among a host of other implements used for causing pain. 'Has he told you anything at all?'

'Slowly,' said Leitmann. 'It took some time, but he explained how he survived the plane crash and made his way here into the city with others in his group.'

'You have names?'

'A couple. One died in a raid on a petrol depot. He's confessed to destroying the turntable and organizing the airstrike on the train. I sent men out before dawn and we found where he had hidden the petrol. His accomplice died last night in the warehouse attack. We're checking the rest of the information.'

'What about his identity card?'

Leitmann shook his head, opened his cigarette case and offered it to Stolz, who eased out a cigarette and lit it, glad to inhale the pungent smoke rather than the odour in the room. 'He had no card.'

'Perhaps that is too convenient,' said Stolz. 'Where's Inspector Berthold? He can identify Garon.'

'I'll send word to where he's billeted,' said Leitmann, lifting the phone receiver.

Maillé peered at them with his good eye. 'I am Pascal Garon.'

'No, I suspect you're a French peasant with an accent as strong as the stench of your own excrement,' said Stolz. 'But you clearly know enough about him and his activities here.'

'Shit is shit in anybody's language. I'm no educated man like you, colonel. But I know my own name.'

'Then who and where is Henry Mitchell, the Englishman. His code name is Pascal.'

'The Englishman? Come on, give me a cigarette, eh? The Englishman is dead. You killed him at the swoop at the hospital. I run the Maquis de Pascal. Mitchell was sent to organize us.'

Doubt creased Stolz's face. He looked at Leitmann. 'Could it be?'

'You're going to kill me anyway, I know that. There's nothing left of my circuit now, so give me a pad and pencil and a cigarette before you finish me off and I'll spill the beans.' He snorted congealed blood and phlegm and spat on to the floor. Stolz stepped back. 'Besides, I can't take much more of this,' he said. 'Water and a cigarette and I'll tell you where the radio operator is hiding.'

'We know that already,' bluffed Leitmann.

'Oh, yeah, sure. Then why are we still transmitting, eh? Give me the paper and pen and I'll tell you everything. I can't sit in my own mess any more. Better to be dead than to be like this.'

Stolz looked at the interrogator. 'Fetch a bucket of water and disinfectant.' The interrogator left the room. Stolz blew out a plume of smoke as he continued to study Maillé. 'The wireless operator the British sent. It's a woman.'

'Asking or telling?' said Maillé. 'If you're not going to give me a cigarette then I'm not talking.'

Leitmann pressed his thumb into Maillé's shoulder wound. The mechanic bellowed, eyes wide, and sucked in air. 'Fuck you! All right! Do your worst. I made you an offer. For a lousy cigarette. Well, fuck you. And your mother. And your sister!' He groaned again and slumped on to the table.

Leitmann raised his hand to strike him again, but Stolz's gesture stopped him.

'He's too tough and he's too weak. Take the manacles off him. Give him a cigarette. And water.'

'Sir?' Leitmann queried.

'Just do it. He's not going anywhere. Let's get this information.' He picked up a pad and pen from the interrogator's table as Leitmann pulled back Maillé's head and placed his cigarette between the man's cracked lips. Then he stretched across the half-conscious man and released the manacles. As he gathered the chains in his hands Maillé lunged with unexpected force. His supposedly lifeless legs braced as he grabbed Leitmann, forcing him on to his heels, powering him backwards, knocking aside the table. Taken by complete surprise at the man's animal strength, Stolz stumbled clear as Maillé hurled Leitmann at the window. The force of the assault shattered the glass and frame and Leitmann's back caught the window ledge. Such was Maillé's strength that Leitmann lost his balance and tipped backwards through the window, arms flailing, a strangled shout as his body plummeted down the floors. It took only seconds for Stolz to react, the cry still ringing in his ears. He snatched at Maillé, who punched him, but the SD man had known combat and pain and he head-butted his prisoner with enough force to loosen the injured man's grip. Maillé was pressed against the opening and with furious determination he snatched at Stolz's collar in an attempt to pull him to his death too, but his wounded arm betrayed him. His fingers curled around Stolz's Knight's Cross and tunic ribbons. Then Maillé wrenched himself free and deliberately threw himself backwards into the void.

Stolz gasped for air as he peered down into the street below. Two shattered bodies lay sprawled in pools of blood. The impossibility of the moment shook him like a man emerging from an artillery bombardment. He stumbled to the door and flung it open.

'Koenig! Where are you? Come here, man!' he bellowed as he clung to the bannister, his voice echoing down to the main entrance where startled members of staff gazed up at him.

From the floor below a familiar face peered up.

'Koenig is under arrest,' said Bauer.

63

Stolz peered down from his office window as he wiped the blood from his face. German medical staff were gathering up the bodies of Leitmann and Maillé, putting them into an ambulance as soldiers cordoned off the pavement and street. He flung aside the wet towel and buttoned his tunic, fingering the frayed threads where his campaign ribbons had been ripped away. The adrenaline from the struggle had ebbed and he faced Bauer with renewed hostility.

'You have arrested a member of my staff. That goes beyond your remit, Bauer. Whatever charge you have concocted to try and hurt this department and my staff will not go unpunished. The Abwehr has no jurisdiction over the SS, the SD or the Gestapo. Confine yourself to military intelligence. Get out of my office and release Hauptmann Koenig. Do it now and I will take the matter no further.'

Bauer showed no signs of being intimidated. 'You have not asked on what charge?'

'I know the man. He's a damned harmless accountant. You've used your agents to entrap him somehow.'

'No, I did not use my people. I used the French.'

Stolz opened a desk drawer, took out a bottle of cognac and poured himself a stiff drink. He lit a cigarette. 'What? Don't be stupid. I would know about it. There is no one. Brigades Spéciales? Milice? They are in my pocket. They would not dare conduct an unauthorized operation against any member of my staff.'

'And of course I knew that, so I approached contacts I had in the Sûreté.'

'You are an old fool, Bauer. We closed French Intelligence down when we occupied France. I wager your so-called contacts are bitter men, cast aside and, like you, full of enough animosity to help you create false charges.'

Bauer smiled. 'You forget that they were re-organized as the Bureau of Anti-national Activities and that we gave them certain duties to act on our behalf against their own kind, specifically the communists and members of the Resistance.'

'And not against the German security service.'

'I agree. But, fortunately, they are both dedicated to their cause and assiduous in their duties – and, as I said, they are, if you like, brothers-in-arms to us in the Abwehr. You, the SS and the Gestapo have little to do with them, whereas we have always maintained cordial relations.' Bauer lit a cigarette. 'And what they discovered was that Hauptmann Koenig's lover, one Béatrice Claudel, was not only an active member of the communist Resistance but also an abortionist. Two for the price of one, if you get my gist.'

Stolz barely hesitated at the revelation of Koenig's involvement with a woman whose background was suspect. There was no evidence being offered. It was an accusation easily rebutted. 'And you suspect Koenig of aiding and abetting abortions? He's a dyed-in-the-wool Catholic. And he loathes the atheists. You'll have to do better than that.'

'Oh I can,' said Bauer and placed the bundle of documents he had found in the girl's apartment in front of Stolz.

Stolz opened one of the folded pages, and then another. The seriousness of the charges became apparent. He could no longer sustain his aggressive attitude. 'Koenig gave the girl these? With my forged signature?' Stolz tossed the document away as if it were contaminated. 'Impossible. I don't believe it.'

'Neither do I,' said Bauer.

'What do you mean?'

'Your loyalty to your men is admirable, and I believe to be well founded. He is a good man.' Bauer let the inconclusive response sow its uncertainty in Stolz's mind.

'You're not making sense.' And then Stolz's face clouded. 'My God. You're accusing me. You're trying to bring me down.'

'That does depend on how you respond to the additional evidence that I have.'

Stolz was an experienced SS officer. He knew how an accusation like this could mean you found yourself against a wall in front of a firing squad. 'Evidence?' he said quietly, resisting the urge to loosen his tunic collar.

'Yes,' Bauer continued at a languid pace, inflicting as damaging a wound as he could. 'Koenig's lover was introduced to him by Mademoiselle Dominique Lesaux, the lady with whom you have an ongoing relationship.' He reached into his pocket and placed a gold cigarette lighter on the desk.

Stolz stared at it.

'As you will know the inscription reads: "To Dominique, with affection, Heinrich." We found the lighter during our search of Béatrice Claudel's apartment where Mademoiselle Lesaux had obviously lost it.'

Bauer watched as Stolz swallowed hard. Perspiration beaded his brow. He did not reach for the cigarette lighter. He knew he was a heartbeat away from the firing squad.

Bauer unbuttoned his tunic breast pocket and took out a folded piece of paper. He opened it carefully and slid it across the desk to rest next to the gold lighter. 'The French have more access to these matters than we give them credit for. She worked for an aristocratic family in Bordeaux who escaped to Switzerland at the outbreak of war. That is how she came up with the cover story which gave her access to Parisian society. The family abandoned her. That is a copy of a birth certificate; I have the original with all the supporting documents that show Dominique Lesaux was born of Jewish parents in Marseille. She changed her name and had secured false documents by the time she got to Paris.'

The death blow.

Stolz pushed his chair back, a feeble attempt to distance himself from the evidence. Bauer watched his victim squirm.

But the SS man's survival instincts pulled him back from the inevitable. 'What do you want?'

Bauer shrugged. 'Everything.'

Stolz stared at the intelligence officer, who showed no sign of emotion, no hint of his triumph. 'What is everything?'

'Hauptmann Koenig said that you were close to trapping the wireless operator. The woman. *Everything* is your complete co-operation in giving her to me. Everything is the Abwehr interrogating her. I want Alfred Korte. If your people find him, I want him. Anything to do with the English agent comes under my control. You can pursue your war against the Resistance but *everything* else comes to me. And if you withhold any information then my evidence will be used against you.'

Stolz knew his career and life could be crushed as surely as his stubbed-out cigarette. 'And what of Hauptman Koenig?'

Bauer's code of conduct had been instilled in him long ago by Admiral Canaris, who decreed that his intelligence officers should always work with good conscience. His staff were never asked to act against their principles. There was never to be any accusation that the Abwehr were murderers. That sobriquet would lie with the SS, the SD and the Gestapo, not the Abwehr.

'He is innocent,' said Bauer. He reflected for a moment on Stolz's question, realizing that for this once he was going against his and Canaris's doctrine. The ends justified the means. 'Someone has to be held responsible,' he said regretfully. 'He will be sacrificed.'

64

Mitchell had embraced Juliet before he had taken them within sight of the Gare de Lyon across the river. Three-quarters of the way across they stopped and gazed down at the Seine. She held Simone close under one arm as if they were looking at the progress of a barge passing below.

'I can't run and hide, Pascal. I'm only going as far as Clermont-Ferrand, then Simone and I are going back to Norvé. I want to help my country. France needs us all. Too many good people have died trying to save her.'

He had barely hidden his despair. 'Too many people have risked everything to get you those travel documents. You cannot go back there. It's too dangerous.'

'Madame Gaétan and I warmed to each other. She'll find me work. I have discussed it with Simone. There's a village school for her. That's our decision.' She took a step closer to him. 'And you will be close, here in Paris. It's what I want.' She had smiled, kissed her fingers and placed them on his lips, giving him no time to argue before she turned and walked away from him. He had lingered on the bridge watching them make their way towards freedom.

Now, as he stared out of his apartment's window watching for anything unusual in the street below, he imagined how far the train would have already travelled. A part of him travelled with them. With Juliet. He could not deny that he missed her, yet he could not deny either that this sense of loss conflicted with the guilt he felt when he thought of his wife. He pushed the conflict aside. All that was important now was to complete his mission and find a means of rescuing Danielle. His instinct as a father insisted she was still alive.

Ginny transmitted to London and then waited as a response came through. She worked quickly and diligently, copying down the groups of letters to be decoded. Mitchell felt some assurance that there had been no suspicious activity in the street. He knew the Germans used foot patrols of plainclothes men. They were usually easily identifiable as they looked fatter than anyone else, not because they were better fed than the starving Parisians, but rather because underneath their raincoats they wore a radio detection device strapped to their chest that allowed them to pinpoint transmissions from a radio within a shorter radius than the detection vans. Gestapo and German security services lay across Paris like a vast net and it was no wonder that they had succeeded in arresting so many of the people that Mitchell had once known working in the Resistance. It was likely that the *résistants* arrested at the Gare d'Austerlitz had been taken because of idle gossip or an unguarded comment. This suffocating atmosphere increased the pressure on those trying to aid the Allied cause. He looked at the stained cloth he was using to clean Drossier's blood from the stolen cigarette case and immediately saw the dying man in his mind's eye. He opened the case. Blood had seeped between the clasp and tainted some of the cigarettes but there were still enough worth saving. He laid them out carefully on the window seat and renewed his attempt to remove the last of the marks from the case before returning it to Gaétan.

'Tonight,' said Ginny as she deciphered the message. 'Moon's good and the Lysander will be on the ground at 2100.'

Mitchell's attention switched between the street and cigarette case. 'Good, that gives us a couple of hours before curfew. I need to get the car and fetch Korte out of the hospital.' He checked his watch. 'We'll finish what food we have, snatch a couple of hours' sleep and then we'll get the others ready for the landing zone. When I leave to collect Korte, make your way to the other apartment. Use a bus rather than the Métro – safer that way. I'll come back here and double-check we have left nothing incriminating and then close the place up.' He gave the brave girl an encouraging smile. 'I'll be glad to get him out of here.'

'Yes, me too.'

The tip of his finger caught a rough edge of metal inside the cigarette case, behind the elastic band that held the cigarettes in place. He probed with his fingernail, feeling it catch, and then pulling more firmly he found himself prising open the back of the cigarette case. A false back, with a thin piece of paper folded inside it. He opened it out. A half-dozen names were written out in tiny letters. His stomach tightened as he looked up wide-eyed at Ginny, who faltered as she tucked away her code pads.

'What is it?' she said.

'I know who the traitor is.'

*

By late afternoon Mitchell had picked up the Peugeot and driven around the back of Roccu's bar where Chaval and Laforge were waiting. He gave Laforge the German uniform to wear, to act as the driver. That, together with the false army plates, might see them through any casual observation by German patrols.

'Fuck it,' Laforge cursed. 'If I'm going to die I don't want to die wearing my enemy's uniform.'

Chaval placed a hand on his shoulder. 'Don't be a prick. You're the only one it fits. I'll make you a deal. You get killed, I'll strip it off you.' The big man grinned. Laforge shook his head in despair and surrender and pulled on the hated grey uniform as Chaval relayed to Mitchell what Edmond had told him when he had returned to Gaétan's house at Vincennes following the failed attack on the warehouse.

'The gamekeeper wasn't wounded but he said he'd tried to cover Maillé and Drossier. He said Maillé shot a gendarme and then all hell broke loose and they were quickly overwhelmed.'

Mitchell listened closely. The story tallied with what the dying Drossier had told him and had been confirmed by Maillé. 'A traitor could easily keep himself out of danger once the shooting started,' he said.

'That's what I thought as well,' said Chaval. 'Gaétan was pissed off. He blamed Maillé for the failed mission. I think you have a big problem with Gaétan. He still feels left out. We refused to tell him where we were going with you.'

'You weren't followed?' said Mitchell.

Chaval shook his head. 'He'd have used Edmond but I made sure we were in the clear. Gamekeepers don't always keep up with poachers.'

Mitchell sat in the passenger seat and directed Laforge to take them out to the hospital at Neuilly using as many side streets as he could remember. Had it been blindingly obvious that Gaétan had been the traitor or could it still be the secretive Edmond, a man who seemed to be able to move at night with such ease? Gaétan had secured many a supply drop and brought in Peter Thompson safely. He had got Thompson into Paris to find Korte before the weight of German secret police agents and French collaboration forces made the nervous man's mission untenable. Gaétan spent months in the city every year and it had been proven that Edmond, despite being a countryman, knew his way around the city. Mitchell became more uncertain. By the time he pulled up close to the hospital he was still undecided. Was it Gaétan or Edmond who had been passing on the information?

They waited as arranged several streets away from the hospital. An ambulance arrived and Alfred Korte was quickly transferred into the car. With five hours left to get to the landing zone, Mitchell had Laforge drive slowly using back streets again to escape the city. It was a tortuous route but one that gave him options should trouble arise. He carried a Sten gun beneath his overcoat and Chaval sat with Korte in the back, ready to shoot their way clear should they be challenged. The sun set behind them in a haze as they drove north-east and found the derelict barn that would give them shelter until the Lysander arrived. The weathered boarding had once been creosoted but winter winds, blowing unhindered across the sparse open land, had cracked and twisted the timbers. On the far horizon, a splintered line of bare trees stood as a skeletal guard of honour for the men who had died in long-forgotten battles centuries before, spilling their blood on to this ancient landscape.

Laforge stripped off the German uniform and stood guard with Chaval in the ruined outbuilding that gave a clear view of the surrounding featureless countryside. Korte still looked unwell but his spirit was undiminished.

He sat quietly in the front passenger seat and then finally spoke. 'I am frail, colonel, and I might die before I am of any use to British Intelligence. Your War Office have been waiting some months to hear what I know.'

'I am certain you will be fine, professor. And I'm no colonel. I'm a teacher.'

'You are a lecturer. Dr Burton told me. Your modesty is only exceeded by your courage. But let us not delude ourselves. Is it not a fact that sometimes these brave pilots who come from England are shot down by German fighter planes?'

'Yes, it can happen. They are excellent pilots who fly low and sometimes their luck runs out. There are no guarantees for any of us, but you have come this far and within a couple of hours you will have hot food and a decent bed.'

'You are correct, I have come a long way and so far I have been fortunate. Some of those who have helped me have been less so, and that I regret. That others have died to protect me grieves me.'

Mitchell kept his eyes scanning the far fields, seeing where to place the car and use its headlights to help guide in the Lysander. 'We all have our duty to do and you have taken more risks than most.'

'Perhaps. There are others like me who deplore what has happened to my country, the evil that has befallen it. I have many friends – churchmen, scientists and ordinary citizens – who spoke out and who died for their indiscretion and beliefs. It would be a tragedy if I did not reach England.' The elderly scientist took out a small brass tube capped with a rubber stopper. He thumbed the stopper and unfurled a piece of paper, rolling it out between finger and thumb. 'Can you see this?'

Mitchell took it from him and used what light there was to gaze at a horizontal lines of letters that would make no sense to a casual observer.

'It's code,' said Mitchell.

'I had many hours lying in the safety of the hospital and I thought that if I did not survive then the information that I have must.'

'So you changed your mind and committed it to paper.'

Korte nodded. 'If you hear that we did not land in England and that I am dead then you must send this by courier to London through the people you know in Spain. That is the last resort.'

Mitchell gazed at the jumbled letters. 'It will take time to decipher.'

'Your friend Dr Burton said you were a mathematician. It will not be difficult once you know the key and if by chance the list falls into German hands I have also included some high-ranking Nazi party members to cause some excitement and to prove that it is fake in their eyes. Although it would be a wonderful irony if they thought Hermann Goering was against Hitler.' Mitchell saw the old man smile. 'The day will come when those names that are genuine will rise up and seize power. All they will need is the word from your Allied command.'

Mitchell kept his eyes on the jumbled letters. He could not yet see how the code had been set.

'It will come to you,' said Korte. He passed Mitchell the rubber stopper. 'Keep it safe, my friend. Remember, the truth will set us free. Now, forgive me if I close my eyes for an hour or so before I undertake the journey.'

★

As the veiled moon's glow bathed the land Mitchell rolled the piece of paper back into its container and tucked it away in the bottom of his inside pocket, feeling the assurance of its hard shell against his ribs. He nudged the scientist awake.

'It's time.'

With Chaval leading the way across the field using a dimmed torchlight, Mitchell eased the car forward. Once in position, he reversed the car and pointed it towards the landing zone. The torchlight showed the green illuminated dial on his watch. The breeze touching their faces would herald the noise of an approaching engine but there was still no sound of a low-flying aircraft. It would be risky to illuminate the LZ too soon. Then Chaval turned and called quietly.

'I hear something.'

'All right. Take up your positions.' He helped Korte from the car and walked him twenty paces into the field. 'When I put the headlights on, point this upwards,' he said, handing him a torch.

'I understand,' said Korte.

The low growl in the sky became more distinct but was still some distance away. It was time to guide the pilot down. Mitchell flashed the headlights and then left them on. Korte pointed his torch as did Laforge and Chaval further downfield. There was no sign of the aircraft despite the heavens being clear other than a gossamer sheen of very high cloud. It diffused the moonlight but was still bright enough to show the ground to the pilot. The men strained their eyes but the pilot was already below the line of the distant trees and the welcome party were almost caught unawares as he expertly throttled back the aircraft's engines. It was down and taxiing, spinning around, its backdraught ripping Korte's hat from his head. The pilot gave a thumbs-up as Mitchell escorted Korte to the side ladder and helped him up. Laforge ran forward with the old man's hat and handed it to Mitchell, who shoved it down into the cockpit. The old man smiled and said something. Mitchell bent closer and Korte cupped his mouth to Mitchell's ear. Giving thanks. The cockpit Perspex closed; Mitchell clambered down and waved the pilot away, returning the thumbs up.

The dark-painted aircraft waggled its tail like a strutting cock pheasant and loomed off into the night.

Moments later silence settled.

The lights were dimmed. The men gazed across the landscape. There was no sign of danger. The remote field had not drawn any attention.

'It's done,' said Laforge.

'Not yet,' said Mitchell. 'We have to unmask the traitor.'

65

Mitchell cut the Peugeot's lights and killed the engine, letting the car freewheel silently into Gaétan's yard. There was only a sliver of dull light barely visible through the join in the downstairs curtains, but there was still sufficient moonlight to see the shape of the building and the shadows it cast. Mitchell and the two men stepped out into the yard, leaving the car doors open. Mitchell quietly instructed Chaval and Laforge to seek out Edmond in his sleeping quarters and to bring him into the house when he called. Mitchell tugged the lever set in the doorframe and heard the gentle ring of the bell. He stepped back from the front door and glanced towards the downstairs room. The curtain twitched and he knew whoever was in the room had checked to see who was calling so close to curfew. Moments later the door opened into a near-dark entrance porch. Madame Gaétan shielded a candle and beckoned him inside. As she turned to pull aside the blackout curtain in the porch Mitchell closed the door but did not turn the key in the lock.

'Why are you here this late, Pascal? Is everything all right?'

'Where is your husband? It's important that I see him.'

'Of course, this way, the drawing room.' She blew out the candle and opened the door into the warmth of the room. 'You were right, it was Pascal's car,' she told her husband who waited, drink in hand, his back to the open fireplace. 'Let me take your coat,' she said. 'Have you eaten? Shall I make up a tray?'

Mitchell shrugged off his overcoat, forgetting for an instant that his automatic pistol nestled in its pocket. It made no difference, he told himself; he would be able to summon help should Gaétan or Edmond – once he had been brought into the room – resist. 'No food thank you, madame. But I would appreciate a drink.'

'Of course. Olivier?' she said, looking to her husband to do the honours.

'He can pour it himself. He's not here on a social visit. Not at this time of night.'

Madame Gaétan was about to protest. 'It's all right, I'll help myself,' said Mitchell and poured a decent amount from the decanter into a glass. He pulled free his tie and loosened his collar. Gaétan and his wife waited. Mitchell let the cognac warm him.

Madame Gaétan smiled apologetically. ' I'll go and prepare that tray for you. I'm sure you're hungry really,' she said and left the room.

Gaétan scowled. 'What do you want? I am beginning to tire of your involvement in my circuit. You bring me inferior men and they fail at every turn. They could have brought the Gestapo down on us.'

'My men are the ones who died. Where is Edmond?'

'Sleeping. He barely escaped with his life after your damned fool idiot opened fire too soon. I told your man Chaval as much. Is that why you are here? To argue?'

'I'm here because I suspect the attack on the warehouse failed because my men were betrayed. It's convenient that Edmond escaped unharmed, wouldn't you say? There were extra gendarmes inside, just as if they had been waiting for an attack.'

'Don't you damned well come into my house and accuse me,' said Gaétan, his temper barely controlled. 'Edmond is loyal. He risked his life along with the others. We had an opportunity to do some good and now we are at risk because one of your men was taken alive.'

'Maillé won't talk about you or your circuit at Norvé. I suspect he is already dead. He was a brave man.'

'He was a hot-headed fool. There was no betrayal. It's war, and bad luck and stupidity are travelling companions.'

'Perhaps you're right. I might have misunderstood everything. It's been a hard journey to try and find Alfred Korte,' said Mitchell, as if giving way to the more experienced man.

Mitchell's tone softened the patrician's response. 'And we have to see that as a priority. Is there news?'

'He's critically ill. It's doubtful he'll survive much longer,' Mitchell lied.

'He's in a hospital?'

'Yes.'

'Which one? My wife and I both have contacts in some of them. You should have come to us sooner and explained. We could have helped. You need to trust us more, Pascal.'

'He's safe now.'

'Then you have moved him?'

'Yes.'

Gaétan seemed about to press Mitchell further but paused, and then changed tack. 'I understand, colonel, that he has great value but our task is to also harass the enemy as best we can with the limited resources we have.'

Mitchell nursed the drink, wary lest too much of it might go to his head after the long day and night without food, but he needed to at least numb his senses for what was to come. 'I agree,' he said, 'but the Gestapo and security service have informants everywhere and unless we can consolidate with the other groups –'

'You mean the communists?' said Gaétan. 'No, not them. Everything they do they do for political control.'

'Perhaps you're right,' said Mitchell congenially. 'Oh, I almost forgot...' He dipped a hand into his trouser pocket. 'We got to Drossier before he died. You know he was always a petty thief and when we were in Norvé he stole this.' Mitchell placed the cigarette case on the table. 'He begged forgiveness before he died and I promised to return it to you.'

Gaétan picked it up and grunted, 'So that's where it went.' He turned as his wife came in carrying a tray with bread, cheese and cold cuts. 'Louise, here's your cigarette case. Drossier stole it back in Norvé.'

Mitchell barely managed to disguise his shock as Madame Gaétan put down the tray and took the cigarette case. 'Thank you,' she said. She smiled at Mitchell but held his gaze a moment too long, her eyes asking whether her secret had been revealed. She calmly placed it on the table. Mitchell stepped forward, 'Allow me,' he said, opening the case, leaving it ajar in front of her with the false back flapped down and the piece of folded paper still visible.

Gaétan stepped forward and snatched it from him but for once there were no words of condemnation or accusation. Instead, he glanced at his wife's distraught look and said quietly, 'Enough, Pascal. This matter ends here.'

Mitchell stepped to the chair where his overcoat had been draped and took out the .45, holding it loosely at his side. 'It does not end here,' he said and tapped on the window.

'Only the communists,' said Madame Gaétan. 'We betrayed only them.'

Chaval and Laforge came into the room with Edmond under their guns.

'Sir? What's going on?' asked the gamekeeper.

'Be quiet,' said Mitchell to Gaétan, who had opened his mouth to answer and warn his trusted man. 'Edmond, what were your instructions the night of the warehouse raid?'

'To take Maillé and Drossier there, to let them seize the warehouse while I stayed back to cover them.'

'And you did that, didn't you?'

'Yes, colonel, I tried to protect them but they were overwhelmed and I was told that if we were suddenly outnumbered then I had to escape and get word back to Monsieur Gaétan.'

Mitchell had not taken his gaze off Gaétan. 'But you were not given any instructions to kill Maillé or Drossier if they were caught? Before they could be tortured and reveal the Norvé circuit's involvement with Monsieur Gaétan here at Vincennes?'

'Kill our own men? No! Of course not.'

'Of course not, Edmond, because what you did not know was that it made no difference whether they talked because the Germans already knew about Monsieur and Madame Gaétan's involvement.'

Edmond's face creased in puzzlement. 'Colonel, I don't understand.'

'Every time an operation was planned, an airdrop discovered, an attack failed, people you were supposed to guide in didn't make it, you were kept safe, Edmond, because Monsieur Gaétan and his wife were informants for the Germans.'

'No. Impossible.' He looked from Gaétan to his wife but they averted their eyes.

Mitchell handed him the cigarette case. 'Take out that piece of paper. Read it.'

Edmond looked at the list of names.

'Do you know those people? Pierre Dupin and the others?' said Mitchell.

'Yes. They helped us a few months ago. They were going to set up a new escape line from Belgium.'

Mitchell took back the cigarette case from him. 'I believe that when Madame Gaétan attended social events and mingled with the Germans she passed on their names so they could be arrested. Those *résistants* were arrested at Gare d'Austerlitz.'

It was obvious to Mitchell than Edmond had no idea of his employer's treachery. The loyal gamekeeper shook his head and sank into a chair.

'They were communists,' said Madame Gaétan with quiet defiance. 'I served with honour in the Great War, I saw what the Bolsheviks began even then. More than anyone else they had to be stopped. The British have armed communist groups across France but they must never be allowed to control France when this war ends.'

'And my men?' said Mitchell.

'They were expendable,' said Gaétan, who stood next to his wife and held her hand. 'They were a necessary price to pay to convince the Germans that we were still well placed to deal with them.'

Mitchell had held back the question that most needed to be asked. 'And what of the wireless operator, Alain Ory? Why did you betray him?' he asked, not knowing whether it had in fact been the Gaétans who were responsible.

Gaétan and his wife looked genuinely surprised. 'We did not,' said Gaétan. 'He worked with Peter Thompson and as you know we protected the Englishman.'

'Because you could keep him hidden and use him as a bargaining chip should you have to?' said Mitchell.

The two accused remained silent, which was answer enough for Mitchell, but he felt a sense of relief that the people standing before him had not been the instigators of his wife's death.

Edmond pointed accusingly. 'You sent one of our best men from Norvé to secure a safe house for Colonel Garon. He was taken by the Gestapo. Did you betray him as well?'

'He was sacrificed because I was trying to give the Germans Garon. It was unfortunate, Edmond, but sometimes distasteful decisions need to be made.'

Edmond leapt suddenly towards Gaétan, but Mitchell stepped between them and levelled the automatic at him. 'No! They deserve to be punished, but not by you.'

Chaval stepped behind him and tugged the shocked Edmond back into his seat. 'You bastards,' said Edmond to the two people he had steadfastly served for so many years. He spat on the floor at their feet.

Olivier Gaétan ignored his gamekeeper and poured himself and his wife a drink. He had regained his composure and faced his accuser calmly. 'We are loyal to de Gaulle and when he formed the exiled government in England I was his confidant. You will not cause us any harm, colonel. Do you believe for one moment that he does not understand what it means for a commander in the field to make difficult and unpleasant decisions? Général de Gaulle is the man we follow and to whom we owe our allegiance. It is not to anyone else.

It is we French who will save France's honour. We will not hand her over to Stalin and his disciples. We have de Gaulle's protection. He will determine our fate.'

Mitchell tucked the pistol into his waistband. 'Yes, he will. When I discovered what was in the cigarette case I contacted London asking them what they wished me to do. They told me de Gaulle wants you in England. There's a Lysander coming in for you tonight. Pack a small case.' He turned to Chaval and Laforge. 'Take them to their rooms. Do not speak to them. Make sure they do not hide any weapons, and then we'll take them to the landing zone.'

Olivier and Louise Gaétan exchanged glances; each appeared comforted that their fate would be determined by the man they served. Gaétan embraced his wife and kissed her cheek. Neither showed any sign of remorse. As they were escorted from the room Mitchell poured Edmond a drink, who nodded his appreciation.

'I wish I had known. The man he sent to Paris and betrayed was a good friend of mine.'

Mitchell had found a sheet of writing paper in a bureau drawer and was writing something. 'Edmond, you have to return to Norvé and run the circuit. Can you do that?' he asked as he folded the paper into his pocket.

The gamekeeper looked surprised and then understood that the suggestion made sense. 'Yes. I can do that.'

'Madame Bonnier and her daughter, Simone. They have gone back there. To help the Resistance. They're expecting Gaétan and his wife. I would take it as a personal favour if you would help them. Do what you can for them. She's a brave and capable woman.'

'It will be an honour to do that, colonel. I have good men down there and we'll help the British however we can.'

Mitchell placed a hand on his shoulder. 'Go first thing tomorrow. Take their car.' He extended his hand to Edmond, who stood and shook it. 'If anything happens to me I am going to instruct Chaval and Laforge to return to Norvé and work with you. Treat them well and treat them as equals. Goodbye, Edmond. And good luck.'

*

They drove Gaétan and his wife to where the Lysander had picked up Alfred Korte a few hours earlier. They were ushered from the car on to the field without haste, each with their small suitcase.

'Will there be room for the two of us in the plane?' said Madame Gaétan, turning up the fur collar on her coat, perhaps, thought Mitchell, because of the pre-dawn chill or a shiver of fear at what might await them in England. The moon was low in the sky surrounded by a tinged ring of light.

'Yes, there's room,' said Mitchell. 'You'll have to put your suitcases under your feet.'

Louise Gaétan lifted her husband's hand to her lips as they stared at the moon. 'Do you know, darling, I shall be glad to be out of this. I think that we shall be exonerated because what we did, we did for the love of France and the hope of –'

Mitchell shot her in the back of the head and then, as Gaétan turned in shock, shot her husband in the temple.

He gazed down at the sprawled bodies and took out the folded paper from his pocket. He placed it on their bodies and secured it with a palm-sized stone. The moon's glow was bright enough to see what had been written in a bold hand: *Traitors to France.*

66

When Rudi Leitmann and Maillé had died at SD headquarters and Standartenführer Heinrich Stolz had agreed to Bauer's demands, Stolz had immediately ordered the Gestapo to arrest Dominique.

She was sitting at her dressing table when she heard tyres crunching on the gravel approach. She saw the car pull up and three plainclothes agents spill out, and the pulse in her neck quickened. No one on Stolz's staff would arrive in such a manner were he at home, so they must have come for her. She had time to pull on a skirt and sweater before the house servant answered their insistent banging on the front door and let them in. Their raised voices and pounding footfalls gave her little chance of escape. She swung open the glass doors on to the small balcony and was halfway out of the room when the first of the men grabbed her. He hauled her back inside and slapped her hard.

'Jew bitch!' he snarled. The blow flung her across the room; her head spun and she tasted blood. The second man strode towards her without a word and kicked her in the stomach. She doubled up and vomited. The Gestapo agent who had slapped her grabbed a handful of hair and yanked her to her feet. Her blurred vision showed her the third man, who seemed to know exactly where to go in Stolz's wardrobe to find a fresh tunic. She could make no connection between that action and what was happening to her, and her mind swirled in terror. A part of her wished they would kill her there and then but she knew a more terrifying fate awaited. Somehow her charade had been discovered and Stolz, betrayed, would inflict the worst punishment on her. They dragged her outside and with a final vicious punch to her neck threw her half-conscious on to the back seat of the car. As she slipped into the comfort of darkness she heard one of the men instruct the other to drive to La Santé Prison.

By the time the man that Stolz and the Abwehr colonel sought was being driven across Paris to be flown to freedom, Dominique Lesaux, bloodied and still barely conscious, had been thrown on to the floor of a rat-infested cell that held half a dozen other women. As the guard slammed closed the door one of the prisoners bent down to help her rest her back against the wall. She filled a metal cup from the water bucket and eased the stale liquid between Dominique's swollen lips, and then gently patted the cool water on to her face. Dominique's eyes focused on the tear-stained face of her friend Béatrice Claudel.

'My God, Béatrice, you as well?'

Béatrice nodded, fighting back her emotions. 'They're putting us on the train for the camps. Dominique... they took Martin... they shot him.'

Dominique kissed her friend's hand as they clung to each other.

As Standartenführer Stolz's agent returned to Avenue Foch and stepped across the dark stains on the pavement where Leitmann and Maillé had fallen, Leutnant Hesler had been waiting impatiently in the corridor outside Stolz's office for some time. Staff of various ranks came and went and it was obvious that since the killing of Leitmann and the terrorist's suicide something was happening beyond the narrow confines of the radio officer's work. Rumours ebbed and flowed through the building as typists and clerks exchanged gossip but one thing was certain: Leutnant Hesler's friend Hauptmann Koenig had been involved and the one rumour that had the ring of truth was that he had been executed. Hesler wanted to speak to Stolz but he was afraid. Would his friendship with Koenig now reflect badly on him? Two Gestapo men pushed past him, one carrying a fresh tunic for the colonel. When Stolz emerged with an Abwehr colonel Hesler took the risk and stepped out boldly in front of the two serious-faced men.

'Sir, apologies. I have information.'

'This is Leutnant Hesler, our radio genius. He's tracking down our... your agent,' said Stolz, correcting himself. 'Go on, Hesler.'

'Well, sir, I have been narrowing the area where I believe this woman is operating. She made a scheduled transmission as expected. It was longer than usual. I have narrowed it down to one block on Rue de Loret, Ninth Arrondissement.'

'I told you, Hesler, you report to me when you have pinpointed her, not when you know the general locale. If there's nothing more, I will brief you later as from now on you will also be passing information to Oberst Bauer.'

Hesler's uncertainty at the change in command caused him to hesitate and continue blocking Stolz and Bauer's passage.

'Lieutenant!' spat an irritated Stolz.

Hesler stepped aside but had the temerity to raise a hand. 'Sir, that is exactly what I wish to report. She made another longer unscheduled message. I have her. I have pinpointed her.'

*

Ginny Lindhurst had painstakingly gathered the sixty feet of wire aerial for her radio. She secured it tidily and then packed the radio and its battery away. She had transmitted using the mains terminal for half of the message and battery for the remainder. It was a habit she had used since being in Paris in case the wireless-hunting Germans switched off electricity to individual blocks of apartments; that way they could see where in the city and then more specifically in what building she was transmitting from. This break in transmission as she crossed from mains to battery could be problematic or slow, and meant London sometimes asked her to retransmit. In this instance, by the time she had decoded their message she had spent longer than she would have liked sending her message.

After Mitchell had left the apartment on his way to collect Alfred Korte, she had reconnected and made an unscheduled transmission. She had failed to tell London that she might be going quiet for a few days. If she missed her usual schedule they might think she had been compromised. Better to tell them. But the signal had weakened. Perhaps the Germans were jamming. She had tried another frequency. It took some time but she got through and received confirmation. Now she was packed and ready to go to the new apartment. Being familiar with the bus timetable she decided to wait as long as possible until the bus was almost due rather than stand in a queue with the suspiciously heavy suitcase. She had scoured the room to make sure there were no tell-tale signs that could lead anyone to her or Mitchell. She had deliberately taken her time and not rushed her search, which had yielded nothing until she had bent down to look beneath the bed and found two pieces of stripped wire from when she had been obliged to make a fresh connection into the radio's key socket. Those tiny slivers could be identified. She went down the corridor to the communal bathroom and flushed them away. Finally, satisfied that Mitchell would not be obliged to spend too long checking what would be his abandoned apartment, she sat with hat and coat on and waited.

Wireless operators were most vulnerable to their own fears. So many hours every day spent alone in their location gave them no outside contact and only occasional time with the agent they supported. She was grateful that Mitchell had included her as much as he had operationally. Facing danger sharpened the senses but sitting alone, waiting for a suspicious footfall outside the door or seeing a car suddenly arrive outside the building, gnawed at the nerves. She lit a cigarette and forced her mind to remain calm. Time could be suffocating; she glanced at her watch – barely three minutes had passed. It was not difficult to understand why a wireless operator's life in the field was so nerve-racking. One mistake: one wrong turn in the street carrying the suitcase and walking into a patrol; too many minutes on the transmission key and being raided; too long alone without emotional comfort and leaving the safe house only to be discovered. Every time she transmitted she imagined an unknown operator in England receiving her coded message. Perhaps it was a young woman her own age. Safe in a bunker. Did she, in turn, think of the woman in France who was reaching out? Are you there? Are you thinking of me? I am frightened but I cannot tell you. *Love to everyone.*

In the street below car doors slammed.

67

Mitchell, Chaval and Laforge drove back to the city, no one speaking about the execution. Mitchell considered what he had done and felt less shame than he would have imagined. He felt a grim satisfaction that his shooting would not be interpreted as a revenge killing. Had Gaétan betrayed Alain Ory then the patrician would also have been responsible for what happened to Mitchell's wife and daughter. He had killed them because they were traitors. He had promised Major Knight that he would do what was necessary in the field and he had laid to rest the ghost of his refusal to kill. He had crossed that line before and the bile no longer rose in his throat. Perhaps, he reasoned, a callus had formed over his heart.

With the car safely hidden in Vincent's lock-up, Mitchell and Chaval stripped down their weapons and hid them in the rafters. They each carried a pistol in their jacket pocket that was quick to reach to either use or discard, whatever the situation dictated. They bought breakfast a few streets away and then made their way to Roccu's bar. London would need to be informed about the execution and once Mitchell had double-checked his apartment he would then make his way to the Fifth Arrondissement and have Ginny advise London that the Norvé circuit was still operational under new leadership. The three men walked separately at varying distances from each other so that they might observe anyone behaving suspiciously. Mitchell sent Chaval and Laforge to the rear of the Corsican's bar while he crossed the street towards his apartment building, looking back at the bar's window to see that all was clear. The broken slatted blind hung down in warning.

With mounting tension he recrossed the street and entered the bar. Roccu looked up and walked immediately through the curtain to the back room where Laforge and Chaval sat on the cots.

'What's happened?' said Mitchell.

Roccu stood at the curtain door keeping a wary eye on the front of the café and a couple of people drinking at the counter. 'I don't know, but all hell broke loose here. They had one of those radio vans at each end of the street and then the place was suddenly crawling with police and soldiers. When they saw me standing watching they pushed me inside and had a couple of gendarmes in here with me to make sure I didn't get to see anything. But I did see plainclothes *flics* running inside with guns in their hands.'

'Gestapo?'

'Don't think so. Some of them were French but they weren't those murdering bastards from the Spéciales. Just cops, I think. I thought you might have been in there and that you had been rumbled.'

'Were there any shots?' said Mitchell.

'No. Not one.'

'Who did they take away?' Mitchell said, suspecting he already knew the answer. 'Roccu, did they take my girl?'

The Corsican shook his head. 'I don't know, and those gendarmes wouldn't tell me anything.'

'I have to go and check inside,' said Mitchell.

'Are you crazy?' said Laforge.

'If they have taken Thérèse then I have to know one way or the other – and quickly because her radio and code books will be in German hands.' He thought it through. If Ginny had been boxed in and the street secure she would have had no choice but to go through the skylight and across the roof and he knew how difficult that would have been lugging the weight of the radio suitcase. He turned to his two companions. 'There's a bus stop down the street. Wait and watch from there. Can you get them a room for a few nights if I'm taken?' he said, turning to Roccu.

The Corsican nodded. 'I can't keep them back here because I'll have customers for my girls but one of them was taken to hospital with appendicitis. They can stay in her room. It's not far from here.' He looked at Chaval and Laforge. 'I'll feed you here.'

'Good,' said Mitchell. 'All right, let me think…' Whatever happened he could not abandon the men who had come this far with him. He gave Laforge the keys to the car. 'Keep these. Worst comes to the worst, I'll be unable to contact you.'

'We should go across the street with you,' said Chaval. 'Three armed men are better than one.'

'No, shooting our way clear in the confines of a building will get us all killed. You know how this works; we've been through enough together. If I run into trouble outside and there's shooting, cover me from the street. We'll meet back at the car and make a run for it. If I'm taken then wait twenty-four hours and make your way back to Norvé. Work with Edmond. He's experienced and he's been told to expect you. All right, get down to that bus stop.'

Laforge shook Mitchell's hand. 'Good luck, Pascal. We'll cover your back, be sure of it.'

Chaval murmured a low growl. 'You're a brave man, my friend. I take it as a privilege that I found you in the field that night. You know, it's not my place to say this, but after all this is over you should go and find Madame Bonnier. She's the right woman for you.'

'She's going to Norvé,' Mitchell told him.

'Then that is where we should all be. Maquis de Pascal and the Gideon circuit, we could form an army behind you.' He grinned and embraced Mitchell, kissing each cheek.

Mitchell watched as Chaval and Laforge made their separate ways towards the bus stop. He regretted leaving the German uniform in the hidden car as it would have allowed him to cross the street and enter the building without the initial risk of being questioned should any plainclothes police be hiding there. He pressed the tube containing the coded information into the Corsican's paw. 'This, my friend, is vital. Keep it well hidden.'

'It will be here when you return,' said the bar owner as Mitchell checked the clip in the automatic.

68

Mitchell made his way across the street, letting cyclists pass him, watching for any sign of a Citroën which might indicate the presence of the police or the Gestapo. He glanced up at the apartment's window, wishing he could discern some movement to either reassure or warn him, but the angle was too steep to see anything. He went into the entrance lobby. The tiled floor picked up the sound of his footsteps, which seemed as loud as a fanfare announcing his arrival. He went up the stairs. On the third floor he thought he heard the sound of doors being gently opened and closed below, but when he peered down the stairwell there was no sign of anyone. As he passed the raided apartment underneath his own, he saw that it was still boarded up. And then as he ascended to his own floor he heard the reassuring sound of the communal toilet being flushed. He tentatively turned the door handle to his apartment and felt it give. For a moment he tried to reason it out. If Ginny had left before the raid would she not have locked the door behind her? But if she had been forced to escape through the skylight perhaps she would not have had time to lock it. His hand tightened on the automatic and he eased it out of his pocket. As the door swung open a man's voice beckoned him inside.

'Come inside, please, Colonel Garon. And do not be foolish.'

Mitchell turned on his heel. Two plainclothes men stood on the half-turn on the stairs below levelling their pistols at him, and behind him another appeared from where he had heard the toilet flush, gun raised, pointing directly at him. Inside the apartment a grey-haired German officer stepped into view and lit a cigarette.

'Please,' he said again.

Mitchell raised his hands and as the two men below kept him covered the plainclothes man behind him relieved him of his pistol. Mitchell did not resist as he was frisked for more weapons. The man nudged him into the apartment. The German officer looked past Mitchell. 'Very well, wait outside.' The door closed and Mitchell lowered his arms as the man who stood in front of him had nothing more lethal than a burning cigarette in his hand. He glanced down at the table where a thermos flask sat, its small cup already unscrewed. Next to that was the German's cap and his sidearm. There was no sign of the Death's Head SS insignia. The small Walther pistol was within the German's easy reach. Bauer saw Mitchell take note.

'As you have observed I am not SS or security service. I am Oberst Ulrich Bauer of the Abwehr. Those men outside are mine. Please, colonel, you look tired and I have some real coffee and a decent cigarette to offer you.' Bauer stepped a pace back and made a small gesture towards the flask. 'I'm relieved you finally arrived, I have been wanting a cigarette for some time, but did not dare light one in case you smelt it.'

Mitchell remained silent and quickly cast his eyes towards the skylight.

'Yes, your wireless operator went across the roofs. She must be a remarkable woman.' He noticed Mitchell's flicker of response. 'We know it's a woman. Now, let us be civilized about this. You cannot escape. I evacuated the building and put my men in every apartment. I had no desire to cause innocent casualties should you have started shooting but I needed to ensure that you were outnumbered and trapped.'

Bauer poured from the flask and Mitchell's mouth watered at the aroma of real coffee. He accepted the drink but declined the cigarette that Bauer offered. As Bauer sat in the chair Mitchell took the sofa.

'I reasoned that you would return here sooner rather than later. Though it's common practice for an agent to keep his distance from the weak link that is his wireless operator, I thought it worth a few hours of my time.'

Mitchell savoured the coffee and for once wished he had not given up smoking. Cigarettes went some way to calm the nerves and at that moment his badly needed calming. Imprisonment was now unavoidable. 'Have you harmed her?'

'No. She escaped.'

Relief gave Mitchell hope. With luck, Ginny would be in the other apartment by now.

'You should count yourself fortunate that you have not fallen into the hands of the Sicherheitsdienst and Gestapo. It was they who tracked down your operator.' He watched as Mitchell sipped the comforting brew. 'It seems there are those who use your name and rank to honour you. With some effort we recovered the identity card of a man who was captured after a raid on a food warehouse. A man called Nicolas Maillé who claimed to be you. Was he one of your men?'

'Yes.'

'I thought as much. During his interrogation he killed a Gestapo agent and nearly killed the SS officer who has led the hunt for you. Your man died well. He committed suicide by jumping out of a window without giving them any information.'

So, Maillé had kept his word and gone down fighting. Mitchell blessed the man's courage. 'Then why are you here? The SS or Gestapo wouldn't let a prize like a British wireless operator slip through their fingers.'

'I brought some influence to bear,' Bauer said, blowing out a long plume of smoke. To all intents and purposes, it was almost a congenial scene, two men having a conversation in an officer's mess or private club. 'The coffee, it's good?'

'Yes, thank you.'

'Where is Alfred Korte?'

'Who?'

Bauer smiled. 'Come now. The British have been trying to get him out of Paris for some considerable time and have already paid a high price for their attempts. Men and women have died, colonel, and they would not send a British agent here were it not to exfiltrate him. There are plenty of independent Resistance cells; most commit small acts of sabotage or at worst kill a soldier or two. They are amateurs. You, like others before you, have not been sent to work with those cells but to find Korte and the information he holds.' Bauer studied Mitchell for a moment. 'He is your bargaining chip, colonel. He will buy you your life.'

Mitchell finished the coffee. 'He is dead.'

Bauer remained expressionless, but he was clearly considering the information. 'Of course, you would say that, but then why would you still be in Paris, hunted every step of the way? Why would you risk a young woman's life keeping her transmitting? No, he is not dead. You have him somewhere safe.'

'Safe in God's arms,' said Mitchell. 'If you believe in God.'

'You don't?'

'Mathematically He doesn't add up. And I stayed because I have other business to attend to.'

'Sabotage? Like the turntable and train?'

'Yes.'

'Then without your help in this matter, I would have no choice but to hand you over. Saboteurs are summarily executed by the SS. Really, there must be something more important for a British agent to do than blow up a few tracks. Your life must have more meaning than that.'

Mitchell reached for the flask. 'May I?'

'Of course.'

He poured the coffee, buying time to think. This intelligence colonel was sharper than the thugs in the SS. An old hand like Colonel Beaumont. Mitchell knew that it was unlikely he could stall much longer before being handed over to those who would inflict pain and misery on him.

Before Mitchell could decide what to say next Bauer delivered a striking comment.

'Herr Mitchell...'

Mitchell's throat tightened. They knew who he was.

'I apologize for explaining myself in this manner... but I saw Madame Colbert when she was captured and taken to the Gestapo cells. Your wife was a very brave woman. I did what I could to stop her... maltreatment.'

Mitchell could not disguise his reaction. His expression confirmed that Suzanne Colbert was his wife.

'Quite so,' said Bauer compassionately. 'She said nothing under torture but there was a paper trail that explained the connection between you. She could not be saved, and I am sorry for her death.'

Mitchell knew that if the Germans had so much information on him he would be too much of a liability to continue working in Paris even if he managed to escape, which seemed an impossibility, other than leaping out of the window as Maillé had done. He dipped a hand into his coat pocket and took out a folded sheet of paper that he handed to Bauer. He hoped Jean Bernard's signature was sufficiently legible to be traced back to him as a doctor working at the hospital. 'Alfred Korte's death certificate. He died in Hôtel-Dieu.'

'Did you get to him?'

'Yes. Too late.'

Bauer thought for a moment as he studied the death certificate. 'This was signed the day of the shooting outside the hospital. When a man proclaiming himself to be you, or at least shouting out your name, was shot dead. So, colonel, that man was not you, obviously, but he might well have been warning you, and if that was the case then he wanted you to escape the Gestapo swoop or to draw attention from you as you did so. Escaped with Alfred Korte perhaps. I am intrigued. And my instincts tell me that you are lying, that this document is false and that you have Korte.'

'I swear to you, colonel, I do not.'

'Very well. Then his secrets died with him.'

'Do you know what it was he had?'

Bauer nodded. 'Yes. Did he write anything down? Is that what you have in his stead?'

Mitchell saw a glimmer of hope. If he admitted to knowing the information had been committed to paper then he might still have something to bargain. It was time to let the military intelligence officer know that he was aware of what Korte knew. 'Tell me, colonel, would you have had the old man beaten until he told you? And when he had revealed those names you would have purged many more.'

'Those names?' Bauer smiled. 'Then you do know. In answer to your question, I would not have harmed him unless exposure of that information to the wrong people demanded I do so. I would have kept him hidden for as long as possible.'

Mitchell's surprise was obvious.

'You see, my name is on that list.'

Mitchell was stunned. Oberst Ulrich Bauer of the Abwehr was part of a plot to overthrow Hitler.

'And now you know too much, Herr Mitchell, and I am afraid it will end badly for you. Shall we have one last throw of the dice?' He reached for his overcoat that lay across a chair and took out a sheaf of papers. 'If you have those names written down then I will offer you an exchange.' He handed to Mitchell the typed list that Hauptmann Martin Koenig had so diligently prepared. 'Look for yourself,' he said. 'It's a deportation list.'

Mitchell's eyes locked on his daughter's name halfway down the page. La Santé was a fortress. His desire to find his daughter and organize her release had been little more than a wild hope. And here was her way out. They were opening the prison gates. He raised his eyes from the page. As long as Alfred Korte's escape was kept from Bauer so that he continued to believe his secret was still secure, then London held the trump card. They could decide how best to use the list of potential allies within the hierarchy of the scientific community and German Officer Corps when the time came. It made no difference whether Bauer was given the list; what was important was that he believed the information could still fall into the hands of the Nazis.

'It's in code,' he said.

'Have you deciphered it?' said Bauer eagerly.

'I had no time. Alfred Korte gave it to me and said that if he died I should send it by courier to London.'

Bauer studied him. 'You swear that is the truth.' He paused. 'On your daughter's life.'

'On my daughter's life,' Mitchell said without hesitation because it was the truth.

Bauer seemed satisfied. He stood and pulled on his overcoat. 'I pray it is not too late to get her off that train.'

'I am not going to tell you where it is hidden, colonel. My men have instructions to get it out of Paris if I do not return safely. The risk to you is that they will be caught and the list exposed before you get your hands on it.'

'Then we must hurry. Get to Gare de Pantin before five. Bring the list before misadventure befalls us both.'

'You expect me to show myself? If the SS or Gestapo are tipped off by any of your people then I am a dead man.'

'I control this operation. Your wellbeing is now my guarantee. If you fear betrayal then you will make a copy for your people to be used should you and your daughter not return to them; that way we have a mutual interest in the success of this arrangement.'

'And if there's a copy then it can still be used against you,' said Mitchell.

'You must surely see that at this moment in time we are virtually allies. Your daughter for my own life.' Bauer smiled. 'The vagaries of war, Herr Mitchell. Let us behave well in this matter. Once my cipher officer has satisfied himself that it can be decoded and it is genuine then your daughter will be handed over to you. I will accept your word that any copy would be destroyed. Are we agreed?'

'We are agreed.'

69

Mitchell had quickly put together a plan of escape for them all should the Abwehr colonel keep his word. Mitchell trusted no one but he had to risk doing what Bauer had suggested. His eyes burnt with tiredness as he studied the coded roll of paper in the airtight tube. All he needed was one line to make some sense and then he would know that whatever was written on the small scroll was genuine. Frank Burton had been contacted and told how a small miracle might have delivered Danielle into Mitchell's hands but that he needed Burton's help. Chaval and Laforge had been given instructions to travel to the American Hospital and to do exactly as Burton instructed. Roccu had closed his bar to give Mitchell peace and quiet to concentrate on his work and whenever he put his head around the door and saw Mitchell asleep, head on the bar, he shook him hard and poured more ersatz coffee laced with cognac into him. Time was short. Bauer would not be able to delay the train from leaving for the camps. Quotas had to be met in a timely fashion as all shipments of prisoners for the camps were monitored by Berlin.

The rows of letters stared back at Mitchell. They blurred. He concentrated. Alfred Korte had been no cryptographer, so there had to be a reasonably simple explanation. Mitchell scratched out his efforts so far. He stopped glaring at the paper and leant back and closed his eyes. He did his best to rid his thoughts of his daughter, of the horror that awaited her should he fail to determine that the code was genuine and not a smokescreen. He drifted into a half-sleep. Eyes closed, he knew where he was, knew he was not fully asleep but hovering somewhere between slumber and wakefulness. Korte's words came to him. *The truth will set us free.* They were the words of a devout man quoting a biblical passage, giving Mitchell the key. Numbers and letters blurred in his mind's eye until he saw a pattern across three different columns. Mitchell was suddenly alert. He pushed letters and numbers across the block of garbled text until a name began to emerge. The name of an army general. Mitchell had no need to go any further. The code was genuine.

*

La Santé's prison guards' bellowing voices echoed across the upper and lower levels, ricocheting off the cells' steel doors, calling for their charges to move out into the yard. The divisional officers herded their prisoners along as they murmured to each other, wondering whether there was to be an execution today. There had been no official announcement, but in the prison yard, the guillotine stood always ready for use to further terrorize those incarcerated in the fortress-like prison. Dominique Lesaux squinted in the daylight as she and hundreds of other prisoners reached the yard. Dirty and wretched and weakened from the appalling conditions and lack of nourishment, they stood in wavering rows as prison guards barked roll call for their respective wings. Satisfied that everyone was accounted for, the guards separated the men from the women and shepherded them towards La Santé's imposing gate where they were loaded fifty at a time on to one of the sixty French city buses waiting in line.

Dominique and Béatrice Claudel clasped hands for comfort. Béatrice had been sentenced to be guillotined at La Santé, but now, it seemed, this exodus had saved her. Dominique noticed one guard who seemed less aggressive than the others and she implored him to tell her where they were going. As he hurried them along he told them that the prisons were being emptied across the city and that she and the others were being sent to a concentration camp in the south run by the French. The glimmer of hope flared briefly but was soon extinguished when the guard told them that it would only be a stopover and that they were then being taken to Auschwitz or Ravensbrück. Dominique had kept her own dim candle of hope burning. Self-delusion was better than facing the harshness of what lay ahead.

As they shuffled through the looming gates on to Rue de la Santé she peered up and down the street for a German staff car like the one she had travelled in so often with Stolz. Surely there was a grain of feeling in him? He had professed his affection over the years and she had not stopped hoping that he would relent and put her in a less vicious prison than La Santé. She had not had the opportunity to beg his forgiveness or deny the charges against her; she knew in her heart that she could have convinced him of her innocence, despite any evidence to the contrary. She searched in vain. There were no Germans in sight. The French police had been ordered to carry out the deportation of their own citizens. Gendarmes armed with sub-machine guns lined the street as guards counted off blocks of prisoners clambering aboard the buses. As each bus filled, the doors closed and it rolled slowly forward and waited in the queue while another took its place. Only when the convoy was complete would the sixty buses bearing 3,000 inmates be driven through the city under the gaze of Parisians to Gare de Pantin where the death train awaited them.

At the rail yard, the buses disgorged their human cargo and peeled away. German soldiers joined the gendarmes as boxcar doors slid open and the prisoners were forced aboard. There were no steps and barked shins and splintered hands had to be ignored as those who had the strength bent down to help the elderly, sick or injured to climb inside. Soldiers jabbed rifle butts, yelling at the deportees to be quicker. The engine had a head of steam and was hissing impatiently, waiting to haul its human shipment away from the City of Light and into a place of darkness. A cacophony of voices rose from the thousands being loaded, interspersed with the harsh shouts of the soldiers. Gendarmes lined the loading bays in case anyone broke free from the trackside. Despite the huge number of prisoners, the garrison troops forced the men and women inside the boxcars and then slid the doors closed. Dominique and Béatrice were in a final group being pushed and cajoled towards the suffocating wagons when she saw a German staff car arrive at the end of the track. Her hopes soared as she raised her arm and cried out. 'Heinrich! I'm here! Heinrich!'

A soldier struck her with his open hand across the back of her head, tumbling her forward on to the gravel. Her hands and knees were cut open, but she squirmed forward, trying to catch a glimpse through the prisoners' legs of the German officer who had stepped out of the car.

'Dominique!' Béatrice shouted. Her friend had regained her feet, pushed her way into the open with failing strength and was running towards him. Tears blurred her eyes, veiling his identity. Another guard stepped out of the mêlée and swung his rifle butt, catching her on the side of her head. Pain shot through her; her face struck the gravel. In her final moments of consciousness, she clung to the dimming thought that when she woke Stolz would have saved her.

The soldiers ordered the unconscious woman to be hauled on to the train. 'Dominique! Dominique!' Béatrice called out her name in desperation as she was pushed inside a boxcar two carriages away.

Soldiers took a pace backwards as Oberst Ulrich Bauer walked down the line with an undisguised scowl of disgust. He found the army major in charge of the operation, who sat at a table collating the numbers. A brief exchange established that all the prisoners from La Santé had been accounted for but that it could not be established in which boxcar any single prisoner might have been placed. Bauer looked down the long line of boxcars just as the final doors were being closed.

'Hold the train,' said Bauer.

The major hesitated. He was solely responsible for ensuring the train left on time but a colonel from military intelligence carried authority.

'Yes, colonel.'

'Find a woman called Danielle Mitchell.'

'How, sir? In these thousands?'

'Do it,' ordered Bauer.

The train commander ran down to his subordinates and shouted his orders and they, in turn, called out to the soldiers, who went along the boxcars hitting the closed doors with their rifle butts, yelling Danielle's name. Bauer watched impatiently. He looked towards the end of the platform where an ambulance was reversing into the loading area.

Mitchell stepped out and stood looking down the length of the train. He turned his back, watching the soldiers, seeing the panic-stricken look on the train commander's face as vital minutes ticked away. If the girl had not survived the abysmal conditions of La Santé before the prison was emptied there might not have been time to take her name off the list, but she might now be lying unconscious in one of the boxcars, already overcome by the overcrowded carriage. The major ran back towards Bauer.

'She's not here, colonel.'

Bauer's agitation was plain to see. 'Wait here,' he ordered. 'The train does not leave until I give my permission.' He strode towards Mitchell, who had stood back from the soldiers and gendarmes. The ambulance's engine ticked over.

Mitchell turned to Chaval and Laforge who sat in the cab dressed in medics' uniforms. 'Something's wrong. If they take me, get out of here.'

Bauer reached him. 'You have it?'

'Yes. Where's my daughter?'

'On that train, but we can't find her and if I delay it much longer I will have the general – Karl Oberg himself – wanting to know why. I think she might be afraid of identifying herself. Us calling out using your name might be making her think that she is to be delivered for interrogation. Walk with me and let her hear your voice. Speak in French, Mitchell.'

Mitchell nodded, shrugging off the trepidation of walking through the lines of soldiers. Bauer walked a couple of paces behind, his presence ensuring that no soldier barred their way.

As he stood beside each boxcar Mitchell raised his voice. 'Danielle, it's your father. Answer me.' Time and again he called her name until they were two-thirds of the way down the train. A faint voice answered.

'Papa? It's me. I am here.'

Bauer gestured for the soldiers to open the door. Mitchell stepped back as the press of bodies nearly fell on to the tracks from the tightly packed wagon.

'Danielle! Where are you?'

Feet shuffled as prisoners tried to squeeze aside and the frail girl finally emerged, wary but with hopeful tear-filled eyes. Mitchell reached up for her and lifted her down into his arms. He buried his face into her matted hair and kissed her face, ignoring the stench of months of imprisonment. He gently hushed her sobbing and turned towards the waiting ambulance as Bauer ordered the boxcar to be closed again, then turned and gestured for his driver to follow him.

When Chaval and Laforge saw Mitchell approaching they jumped down from the cab and pulled out the stretcher from the ambulance. Mitchell laid his daughter down gently. She clung to him, weeping with joy at seeing him, almost incoherent. Mitchell swallowed back his own emotions and, clasping her hands in his own, urged her to listen.

'These are my friends and they are going to take you to hospital.'

'Don't leave me, Papa, please don't leave me.'

'I am going to be right behind you. I promise. Be strong for a while longer. Yes? Can you do that for me?'

Danielle nodded through her tears but she clung to his hands. He eased her fingers aside and gently kissed them. 'Be brave. It is over now.'

She nodded and whispered, 'Papa... you came for me...'

Tears stung Mitchell's eyes. 'Yes,' he said tenderly, 'I came for you.'

EPILOGUE

Mitchell showed the codebreaker from Bauer's own Abwehr unit Alfred Korte's cipher, and once it was established that the code – and the list – was genuine both men were as good as their word. The exchange was complete. The locomotive gathered power, wheels spinning from the weight of its burden, and pulled away, leaving behind the stench of soot and despair clinging to the warm Parisian air. The soldiers and gendarmes dispersed, and now the two men looked about the desolate rail yard. The surge of human misery that had taken place there would always haunt their memories.

'Get out of Paris, Herr Mitchell. I can give you forty-eight hours. After that, you and I are enemies once again and the SS and Gestapo will be on your tail. I cannot deliver to you the man who caused your family so much pain and grief. And if you took your revenge and killed him then the retribution against the civilian population would be savage. He is still powerful and has friends who could destroy me, given the opportunity. But I have information on him and one day, in months to come, when his arrogance makes him feel invulnerable, I will be the one to destroy him. His life will be forfeit. That is the only consolation I can offer you.'

'Thank you, colonel,' said Mitchell. 'Could I ask you one last favour?'

'If it is within my power, yes.'

'I'd like one of your cigarettes.'

Bauer smiled and extended his cigarette case. Mitchell took one and held it to his nose, sniffing the quality tobacco. Bauer extended his lighter and the flame scorched the cigarette tip. Mitchell inhaled, coughed, and then inhaled again. 'I might get used to these again,' he said. 'Thank you.'

Bauer nodded. 'You and your wireless operator are brave adversaries. Let us hope that in the future those of us who survive this war may find a common ground and regain that part of ourselves that we have had to sacrifice.' He climbed into his staff car, tapped the driver's shoulder and the car sped away from the empty rail yard.

*

The isolation ward for infectious diseases in the American Hospital was strictly out of bounds to everyone except for the courageous Dr Frank Burton and his few chosen, trusted staff. They cared for Danielle Mitchell there in secret. Nurses bathed her and gave her fresh clothes, and she spent the next thirty-six hours being treated for malnutrition and the skin diseases resulting from the squalid conditions in the lice- and rat-infested cells. Mitchell sat at her bedside for hours, patiently explaining everything that had happened since they had been parted. He had a plan, he told her, for when they left Paris, but he wanted her to be part of his decision.

Chaval and Laforge made use of the hidden German uniform and stolen Peugeot and brought Ginny Lindhurst to the hospital. Within hours of Danielle being taken from the train what remained of the Maquis de Pascal was gathered in the isolation wing of the hospital while Frank Burton arranged new identity cards and the various papers needed for Mitchell and the others to escape the city. Ginny set up her radio and made brief transmissions to London with Mitchell's plan for the future of operations in his region of France. Beaumont and Knight agreed with everything he suggested and began to prepare the escalation of covert warfare. Now that Korte had been safely delivered, British Intelligence had an insight into the dissatisfaction within the Nazi régime. Perhaps the day might come when they would rise up and strike from within.

*

'This place is quiet,' Mitchell told Danielle as the local bus met the Norvé train after an uneventful journey from Paris down into what was once Vichy France. The bus trundled through the narrow tree-lined roads. 'Chickens and pigs and cows. Not much happens unless we make it happen.'

Danielle, still weak from her ordeal, drew strength from being close to her father. His protection and love eased the scarred memory of her mother's death. 'I'm happy to be with you and your friends, Papa, and I'm looking forward to meeting Madame Bonnier and Simone.' The girl hesitated, a look of uncertainty. 'I can tell by the way you speak of her that she is someone special to you.'

Mitchell put his arm around her. 'She saved my life. She's a brave woman who stood by my side when I was alone and frightened. But your mother... Danielle, I cannot abandon her so soon.'

Danielle kissed his cheek. 'We will never forget Mama, I know that, but... I am alive because you saved me, Papa,

483

and you did that because Madame Bonnier helped you. I am grateful to her.' She smiled with an understanding wiser than her years. 'Don't be alone and frightened again.'

She turned her gaze to the sun-speckled branches, the flickering light causing her eyelids to grow heavy. The rolling gentleness of the countryside smoothed away the sharp-edged memories of the city. She could smell the sweet cut grass. As she closed her eyes she let the low rumble of the bus lull her asleep with the promise of awakening to a new beginning.

In his mind's eye, Mitchell saw Gaétan's old house, the chickens and the lazy cat in the yard and the ghosts of the traitors that would haunt the place for some time to come. But Juliet would have made her own warm mark on the house by now and Edmond would have prepared the way for Mitchell to take control of the Norvé group with Ginny Lindhurst as his radio operator. It would be renamed the Gideon circuit. His new identity as the mathematics teacher at the local school meant that from this quiet backwater he would ensure that the enemy knew what it meant for terror to come in the night. There was still much to be done to defeat the enemy.

He wondered if there would ever be a time for them to return to England. He eased a strand of hair from the face of the frail child who slept in his arms. Until that time came he was content knowing that France and Juliet Bonnier held his heart captive.

ACKNOWLEDGEMENTS

I am indebted to my publisher Nic Cheetham at Head of Zeus, who extends unconditional encouragement when I write a standalone novel in between my ongoing *Master of War* series. In 2017 he published my one-off novel *The Last Horseman*, which became a finalist in the Wilbur Smith Adventure Writing Prize. That he has once again extended me leeway to write *Night Flight to Paris* indicates, yet again, his wonderful support. I would like to express my thanks to the fabulous team at Head of Zeus who work so diligently on my behalf.

I cannot sufficiently thank my editor, Richenda Todd, who painstakingly edits my work with such consummate skill and immense patience. Her dogged questioning of anything that is not written clearly enough makes an enormous difference.

My thanks to my tenacious agent Isobel Dixon and the team at Blake Friedmann Literary Agency, a great bunch of people. James Pusey and Emanuela Anechoum continue to sell my books to other countries. Samuel Hodder and Daisy Way keep tabs on all the things that I cannot in the complex world of foreign tax forms and payments. Resham Naqvi deals with contracts and always gets me to sign in the correct place while Juliet Pickering has widened my ever-increasing audience by handling the audio rights for my books both here and abroad. There are numerous people in various foreign markets who work with my sub-agents, and I am grateful for the degree of enthusiasm from them and my overseas publishers who translate, publish and arrange audio recordings of my books.

Finally, I am always encouraged by my readers and Facebook friends when they contact me via my website or on social media; their generous comments are very welcome and appreciated, as are those from readers who post reviews on sites such as Amazon and Goodreads and other social media. Sharing their enthusiasm has widened the readership for my various books. I thank you all.

David Gilman
Devonshire
2018

A letter from the publisher

We hope you enjoyed this book. We are an independent publisher dedicated to discovering brilliant books, new authors and great storytelling. If you want to hear more, why not join our community of book-lovers at:

www.headofzeus.com

We'll keep you up-to-date with our latest books, author blogs, tempting offers, chances to win signed editions, events across the UK and much more.

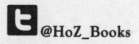 @HoZ_Books

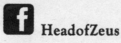 HeadofZeus

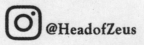 @HeadofZeus

HEAD of ZEUS